Don't Die Before You're Dead

DON'T DIE
BEFORE YOU'RE DEAD

Yevgeny Yevtushenko
Translated by Antonina W. Bouis

KEY PORTER BOOKS

Canadian Cataloguing in Publication Data

Yevtushenko, Yevgeny Alexandrovich, 1933–
Don't die before you're dead

Translation of: Ne umiral prezhde smerti.
ISBN 1-55013-658-5

I. Title.

PG3476.E96N413   1995   891.73'44   C95-930145-3

The publisher gratefully acknowledges the assistance of the Canada Council, the Ontario Publishing Centre and the Government of Ontario.

Key Porter Books Limited
70 The Esplanade
Toronto, Ontario
Canada M5E 1R2

Printed and bound in Canada

95 96 97 98 99 5 4 3 2 1

I am deeply grateful to my wife Masha
For her ironic and inventive editing. Without her help
my novel would be even worse, which is
hard to imagine.

Author's Note

========================

THIS NOVEL IS MY CONFESSION, both intimate and political. I am an old hand in poetry, but still quite young as a prose writer and, perhaps to everyone's surprise, I might still be able to leap high. After reading my rather hastily written *Precocious Autobiography*, liking in particular the chapter about Stalin's funeral, John Steinbeck said, "You know, perhaps in some future encyclopedia they will write about you as a prose writer who began as a celebrated poet. . . ." Only time will tell whether this classic American writer was right.

I always loved Thomas Wolfe for his "disheveledness," for his "over-loadedness." If I were a horse I would not eat hay pressed into squares. My life, like my poetry and now my prose, is rather "disheveled" and "over-loaded." Thomas Wolfe had a remarkable editor, Maxwell Perkins, who, though he did not comb him out too much, nevertheless kept him from being too disorderly, too "shaggy." Barbara Berson has been such an editor for me. I don't regret that some things that are dear to me were lost. I am a movie director and I respect the opinions of the film editor — of course, as long as it is not censorship or tasteless diktat. Ms. Berson has done everything possible so that this novel will be accessible to every reader in the English world. Whether it is a good or bad book is not for me to decide. But in opening it, you open the soul of today's Russia.

Yevgeny Yevtushenko
8 Oct. 1994
Frankfurt

Contents

───────────

The Second Day

The Third Day

Afterward

The oak was green and now is rotten,
But the skies are blue above.
Love is doomed to be forgotten,
But there is no forgotten love.
— Siberian song

The past is never dead.
It's not even past.
— William Faulkner

THREE MONTHS BEFORE THE COUP

The Handcuffs

———————

THE REMARKABLE THING ABOUT the personal life of Stepan Palchikov, Special Investigator, was that he had no personal life. At least, that's what his wife, Alevtina, head of the Invertebrate Department at the Moscow Zoo, insisted when he was God-knows-where on their tenth anniversary and didn't even send her a telegram from God-knows-where for the occasion.

When he did appear finally, a few weeks later, stinking of trains and cheap hotels, he tried to worm his way into her good graces by handing her a flimsy bouquet of wilted carnations, which he had pulled out of his scuffed, overstuffed briefcase. He hugged her clumsily and kissed the still tenderly curling tendrils on her nape. Softening, she had almost fallen for it, until she brought the bouquet to her nose rather sentimentally.

Right in the middle of the bouquet, like a particularly aromatic flower, was her husband's sock, soiled and sticky, long wear having eradicated its elasticity and color.

Realizing that his family life was over, Palchikov mumbled something in justification about organized crime, but Alevtina was inexorable.

Palchikov's belongings, along with Palchikov himself, and the sock inside the anniversary bouquet, were left outside the door.

Palchikov was forced to move into his office at the Ministry of Internal Affairs. He slept on the vinyl-covered couch, using files of criminal cases as a pillow, and washed his socks, underwear and shirts in the hall toilet at night, when everyone was gone.

Once, as he was interrogating an enterprising and grown-up grandson, who had managed, before his own move abroad, to fill his deceased granny's skull with diamonds from Yakutia and send the galvanized coffin on the Sheremetyevo Airport–Brighton Beach route, allegedly so that she could rest in peace with her other relatives, Palchikov noticed that the suspect began laughing, totally inappropriately considering his shaky legal position, while looking up over Palchikov's head.

Palchikov turned, looked up, and to his horror saw his socks, which he had hung to dry the night before, dangling from atop the administrative map of the Soviet Union. One of the pair had been the culprit in the demise of his family life.

Despite all of Palchikov's attempts to hide his drama from his colleagues, they caught on, thanks to the professional acuity of their observation and to their solidarity before those who underestimated the daily heroism of the knights of public law and order.

His co-workers, out of their professional habit of fabricating and exaggerating, created a beautiful, tormented story about Palchikov, in which he had been forced to leave his wife out of principle because, perversely, she preferred not just someone else to him and his meager salary, but a computer-cooperative owner whose pride and joy was a home terrarium full of mini-invertebrates.

People in our country, and that includes the police, vastly prefer the modest and miserable to the immodest and fortunate, and that's why Palchikov's reputation, supported by a cover story which elicited compassion and respect, grew stronger, and each case he was given was more important than the last.

Once, he was sent to a local capital to investigate an incident codenamed "Steam Engine."

The regional capital city had a hospital for children with polio. It was outside town, on the former estate of the prerevolutionary chairman of the local nobility who, on a romantic impulse, in the early days of the Revolution had donated his white marble property for a people's hospital. He was thanked with a bullet between the eyes during the Civil War, allegedly for corresponding with the last tsar to plot his escape from the Ipatyev house when he was imprisoned in Ekaterinburg.

The hospital housed almost two hundred children with polio. Despite the poor equipment and shortage of medicine, the heroic Russian country doctors saved all the children they could—if not all, then many.

Then, suddenly, in the middle of a harsh winter, the huge rusted boiler burst, a boiler cast at the Putilov Factory before the Revolution. The walls of the hospital grew hoary with frost, and the recovery rooms were filled with children it was mortally dangerous to move. The experience of Russian history suggested setting up *burzhuiki*—pot-bellied stoves—but this was a temporary measure at best. A new boiler was urgently needed to save the children.

The closest boiler factory, in Leningrad, would need two months. The city fathers got together. In a burst of genius, one had the brilliantly simple idea of putting a steam engine in the yard and piping the steam heat into the hospital.

They found an old steam engine with a working boiler. But the closest railroad spur was about five kilometers away. The military came to the rescue. They would haul the steam engine to the hospital.

This was to be an unprecedented event in the city's history, and in anticipation, all the offices in town closed. Crowds waving red flags and paper flowers lined the street, as if it were the first state visit of the head of some hard-currency country. Three men on motorcycles, in camouflage jackets and with automatic rifles over their shoulders, led off the procession. Behind them marched squads of Pioneers, or Red Scouts, banging on drums which resounded in the frosty air. Then came a military band, with brass boa constrictors encircling their snow-dusted uniforms. Bringing up the rear were four military tractors, tearing up the asphalt with their treads and resisting iron wheels, and dragging the steam engine, which bore on its sooty, laboring chest, a sign reading "Communism Is the Destination."

Along the sidewalk, parallel to the procession, drove a small truck, quite unpresentable, shabby and coughing, but on its running board were brilliantly polished boots, pleated like an accordion that could play any jig at all. The boots' owner, a ruddy and slightly tipsy major, brimming with front-line energy and resembling a *matryoshka* wooden doll in army costume, commanded the operation. When the steam engine got stuck, the major shouted into a megaphone with no less inspiration than General Suvorov in the Alps.

"Well, come on now, boys, pull. Let's not shame Russia, my eagles! Let's help those kids. Forward, pull!"

With the moral support of the people and the brass band, they managed to haul the steam engine into the hospital yard. They found piping and soldered up a system. Coal was delivered. But then came the rub — who was going to tend the boiler?

They needed professionals for that, railroad boilermen, and where do you find them? Here was a profession that had vanished along with the ghost of the steam engine that had never made it to Communism.

They found two old men who had retired from the trade, but they turned out to be greedy creeps, albeit elderly ones. They made so much on their field strawberries that they demanded 5,000 rubles each for two months' work as stokers. And where could a regional polio hospital find so much money?

The lumber mill director, whose generous Russian merchant heart unfortunately was cramped by the criminal code, took a risk for the sake of the children. He paid the money, faking papers so that the pensioners and their wives were put on the payroll as lumberjacks. From sparks burst flames, and the pensioners went about heating the hospital.

For two winter months the veteran steam engine sent saving smoke into the clouds, and the city's inhabitants, beholding the miracle, praised their Russian ability to make do. "We really figured that one out, didn't we?"

But in those two months, the Leningrad company made a new boiler, and the steam engine boiler was turned off, to the disappointment of the children, who had grown accustomed to its friendly warmth. Now the city fathers had new problems. Where would they get money to repair the asphalt churned up by the tractors and engine? And where were they going to put the huge steam engine? They couldn't drag it back along the street!

At last, the chairman of the city council, considered an intellectual because he played the flute in the amateur orchestra, slapped himself on the forehead and exclaimed the magic Soviet words with glee: "Scrap metal!"

They carved up the steam engine with acetylene torches, sold the pieces by weight and used the money to repair the streets.

But suddenly this merry, inventive and very human Operation Steam Engine installed to save children with polio from freezing was turned into a criminal case against its authors.

The mess was brewed up by the local deputy prosecutor, who in his phone calls to Moscow hinted at political underpinnings to the effect that the steam engine had been used to sabotage democratic change in the country.

Palchikov was sent to investigate and found that, according to the lumber mill's payments, the team consisting of two old men and two old women, average age seventy-five, had broken the world record in logging by cubic meters, which was rather amazing when you consider that one of the old women, who was listed as the driver of the skidding tractor, had been paralyzed for the last five years and could skid logs only from a wheelchair.

The deputy prosecutor, with the long shaggy arms of a Pithecanthropus and the short legs of a Napoleon, drilled his gaze into the eyes of the big-city investigator, gummy with insomnia caused by his family problems, and reported without beating around the bush, democrat to democrat:

"This fake team, Comrade Palchikov, is merely one thread, which I pulled out in time, from a ball of crime.

"Here are the following criminal facts: squandering state property in the form of a steam engine by the local railroad authorities; malicious destruction of three kilometers of asphalt by our local militarists' use of tractors with the aim of undermining perestroika; and finally, stealing, dismembering and illegally selling the steam engine for the profit of the corrupt hospital administration." The Party *apparat* and its protégés never sleep.

Oho, thought Palchikov with a grimace. What an instinct for survival. Just seven years ago this great foe of the Party *apparat* sent the local music teacher to the camps in Mordova for anti-Soviet agitation simply because they found Solzhenitsyn's *Live Without Lies*, a photograph of Sakharov and cassettes of Galich's dissident songs in her apartment.

The deputy prosecutor leaned over the table and breathed conspiratorially, "Perestroika is in danger, Comrade Palchikov. I managed to uncover this case only because my direct superior, our regional prosecutor, is on vacation—in the Crimea, naturally, in Oreanda, that warm nest of the *nomenklatura*, of course. I, for one, have applied five years in a row for a vacation at Oreanda, but they always stick me in the pitiful Truskovets. And as long as that Brezhnev brownnose is on the job, my hands are tied."

So that's your game, thought Palchikov. You're worried about perks, not about perestroika. You want to ride that steam engine into the prosecutor's office. . . . It's all so boring and disgusting—I can't stand any more.

But the deputy prosecutor kept on breathing his progressive intentions at him. "We have to use that steam engine to strike against the old guard. We have to turn this into a national case."

You want to go all the way to the top, thought Palchikov wryly, adopting his most sympathetic expression and nodding encouragingly.

The deputy prosecutor leaned over the table so far that it looked as if he were planning to give him a juicy kiss. "I'd like you to bring our conversation to the attention of your boss. He is a real worker for perestroika. Actually, I'd like to meet with him . . . tête-à-tête. I have a few ideas. . . ."

"I'll be glad to do that. But haven't you heard that as of yesterday we have a new boss? The newspapers will have the story tomorrow." And here Palchikov did not deny himself the pleasure of watching that great progressive's face change. "Yes, yes. You're right. Him. As they say, he's a Crystal-Clear Communist."

The deputy prosecutor half rose from his seat, his Napoleonic legs straining from the need for reorientation. But he collected himself and bloomed judiciously with joy.

"At last!" he exclaimed. "What we need at the helm are Crystal-Clear Communists, and not those who, under the guise of perestroika, are actually destroying our great superpower. . . . We've had enough democratic debauchery!"

And he returned to his conspiratorial breathing, which was now more superpower-oriented. "All the more reason for a meeting with your new boss, all the more. I have to open his eyes to the situation in our region, which is approaching a conspiracy against socialism. Our regional prosecutor, for all his showcase Party membership, has long been a puppet of anti-Soviet extremists.

"The case with the steam engine is an example of the discrediting of our people's socialist ideals. Cutting up that bullet-riddled steel hero of the Civil and Patriotic Wars for scrap metal, selling off that honored veteran of the early Five-Year Plans by weight — it smacks of political vivisection. It's time to save our superpower."

"Want some advice?" Palchikov asked, imbuing his voice with all the warmth that had emanated from the now-dismembered steam engine.

"That's why I asked you here," replied the deputy prosecutor.

"Drop the steam-engine case," said Palchikov, with the slightly ominous, exaggerated concern of a kindly grandfather lecturing his ignorant grandson.

"And why is that?" asked the stunned deputy prosecutor.

"It could be misunderstood," Palchikov said, staring hypnotically.

"In what sense?"

"They might think that you want to build your career on railroad scrap. They'll accuse you of anti-Semitism since the chief surgeon at the hospital is a Jew. Don't waste your enormous prospects on this small change. You have a great future with the state," Palchikov predicted, while thinking grimly: The terrible thing is that it's true. The victors won't be the superpower pythons or the liberal rabbits. The chameleons will win.

"I care about the country's future, not my own," sighed the deputy prosecutor, with an altruism begging to be noticed. "Like the song—'Let my country be.' And I appreciate your advice. So, will you set up an appointment for me with your boss?"

That evening, before leaving town, Palchikov paid another visit to the polio hospital, had a drink of straight spirit alcohol with the chief surgeon, and told him that they need not worry, the case was dropped.

In the hospital's nocturnal courtyard, squares of golden light from surrounding windows lay upon the ground. In one square was the silhouette of a teenaged boy, seated on the sill and reading a book. The silhouette was not quite right, somehow bent, as if evil hands had mauled the child's body, had tried to break it but had not succeeded.

Palchikov avoided stepping in the window's light so as not to step on the boy's silhouette, and then quietly, in the darkness, he approached the window.

The boy was reading aloud to the other patients lying in the post-op room.

> "Tell me, beauty," I asked, "what were you doing today on the roof?"
> "I was looking to see which way the wind was blowing."
> "What is it to you?"
> "Whichever way the winds blows, happiness comes."
> "Well then, were you calling happiness with your song?"
> "Wherever you feel like singing, there you feel happiness."

"And what if you sing yourself some misfortune instead?"

"And what of it? Where it is not better, there it will be worse, and it's not far back again from bad to good."

Where does that come from? wondered Palchikov. It's something so familiar, something near and dear, but what is it?

He had no more time to listen because he was taking the night train to Moscow. But before leaving in the dilapidated ambulance driven by the chief surgeon, Palchikov stood a bit by the only remaining part of the steam engine — the black, well-oiled chimney standing in the hospital yard like a monument to the warmth that the engine had given to the children.

Palchikov entered the office of the stationmaster, who was phlegmatically drinking pallid tea under a ficus, fading in an unwatered pot, while beating out a melancholy tune with his teaspoon on the keyboard.

Palchikov flashed his red badge at him.

"Could I immorally use an official phone for a personal call?" Palchikov asked.

"It's more immoral in these perestroika times to breathe vodka fumes on people who would like a drink, too," the stationmaster said unhappily, barely hiding his hope for a drink.

"It's spirit alcohol," Palchikov said. "Alcohol barbarously stolen from hospitalized children." And he offered the little cough-medicine bottle that the surgeon had given him for the trip.

The stationmaster's eyes sparkled at the sight of the bottle and he dialed the number for Palchikov, who heard Alevtina's voice in Moscow.

"Hello," Palchikov said.

"Well?" she replied archly.

"What do you mean?"

"Well, say something."

"Listen, do you remember where this is from: 'Tell me, beauty, what you were doing on the roof today?'"

"Palchikov, are you crazy?"

"There's more: 'Whichever way the wind blows, happiness comes.' Do you know what book that's from?"

"Palchikov, don't call me anymore. Forget that anyone ever invented the telephone."

At that moment the stationmaster took a sip from the bottle and gagged on the undiluted spirits. He felt around for a crust of bread, anything solid to chew, or for some water to chase the alcohol, and accidentally brushed his elbow against a key that broadcast Alevtina's voice over the loudspeaker in the waiting room, waking up passengers who had been resting on their bags and suitcases and who jumped up with wild eyes, expecting a fire. The angry peals of a woman's rant shook the bronze statues of Marx, Engels and Lenin, huddled together in a hostile railroad station, looking like transit passengers who never managed to get tickets. The fourth pedestal in their group was empty, and instead of the absent Stalin a grisly bum in a general's cap lay sleeping, gently clutching a naked, one-legged doll to his chest. Alevtina's screeches couldn't wake him.

"Never call me again, Palchikov! Call Maigret and Simenon! Sherlock Holmes and Doctor Watson! But leave me alone! Leave me alone with my anacondas, boa constrictors, pythons and vipers! They make me happier than you do, Palchikov! Much happier! That's it!"

And as a final chord, deafening everyone in the crowded station, came the dial tone as loud as a train whistle.

The stationmaster turned off the loudspeaker, belatedly. "I'm sorry. I didn't mean to make your personal conversation known to the public. It's the glasnost syndrome." He shrugged and returned the bottle, of which in fairness he had drunk only half. "By the way, that line you asked about is familiar. I think I heard it in school. Isn't there something else about, 'Where it isn't better, there it will be worse, and it's not far back again from bad to good'?"

"Yes, there is," said Palchikov, clutching the man's sleeve in hope. "But where does it come from?"

Unfortunately, the stationmaster couldn't remember.

On his return, Palchikov again had to sleep in his office.

His next case seemed inconsequential but was curious. The Red Toy Factory kept losing large lots of expensive electronic moonwalkers, which appeared later in the hands of street vendors near Children's World Department Store, at the Izmailovo Flea Market, and in the metro underpasses.

They had checked the fence around the factory thoroughly. They had set up a checkpoint at the door. But the moonwalkers kept vanishing.

Palchikov got caught up in the case. He started spending nights at the factory, but to no avail. One night, napping on some cases in the warehouse, he was awakened by a voice.

"Come on, sweeties, my little darlings, godspeed. Don't get lost, keep going straight ahead, straight where you're supposed to go. You'll be met, given a nice tea with raspberry jam, and put to bed. . . . "

Hiding behind a stack of crates, Palchikov crept as close to the voice as he could get, and this is what he saw.

An old man with a white beard like a spade, looking for all the world like an ancient dulcimer player, sat on the floor and seemed to be talking to himself.

He was actually talking to the toy moonwalkers, addressing them as if they were living, attentive and docile creatures.

The watchman's fingers, wrinkled but agile, put batteries into the toys and pushed the start button, and the moonwalkers, lumbering like hedgehogs, and in single file, strode into the open door of the ventilation duct under the floor, vanishing forever.

Anyway, we Russians will survive, I can see that! thought Palchikov. He was dying to embrace that charming old scoundrel, who embodied the unvanquished national know-how, and give him an invisible official medal for protecting the human rights of moonwalkers.

But the logic of his profession forced Palchikov to establish where with such determination the toys were headed, who was taking care of them and who was going to feed them their promised raspberry jam.

Palchikov was not wrong in his hunch that the duct came out on the other side of the fence. But he expected, if not a spaceship, then at least a motor vehicle ready to load the fugitives and flee from the state monopoly on children's toys. But what Palchikov saw there was more like a socialist variant of a prerevolutionary Russian folk tale.

The other end of the duct, covered in green moss, peeked out of a ravine covered with burdock and plantain. A crude but comfortable wooden bench, made of two circles and a slab, was set up right at the end of the duct. Palchikov concluded that this was not the bench's first year, since it was gray and cracked from snow, rain and sun, the nail heads were rusty and it was worm-eaten too.

The same old man with the white beard sat on the bench and again seemed to be talking to himself. "Well, my precious, long-awaited sweeties, what's taking so long? It's not nice to be so late, to make an old man worry about you. Aha, I hear your steps, I hear you. You didn't let me down, my little walkers, you didn't get lost, my little ones. . . ."

The end of the duct trembled. Then came a barely audible but growing stomping which made the duct ring. Then deep in the duct came a tiny beam, with which the moonwalker illuminated its path in the dark, and then one appeared and landed in the old man's gentle waiting hands.

Next to the bench on the grass stood an open homemade satchel, patched and with handles, into which the old man placed the moonwalkers, after quickly removing the batteries that he had put in on the other end of the duct.

But how could that old man be on both sides of the fence at the same time? Palchikov was confused. Maybe I'm hallucinating?

Then he figured it out. They were twins.

Palchikov made a decision that could have cost him his job. He told no one that he had solved this amusing crime. He liked the way the moonwalkers marched themselves to freedom.

When he was unexpectedly called in to see his new boss, the Crystal-Clear Communist, Palchikov thought that he was being called on the carpet for these two failures in a row, which could also be classified as cover-ups.

But Palchikov, quite typically, had underestimated himself.

The Crystal-Clear Communist took Palchikov much more seriously than Palchikov did. "Judging by the geography of your trips, you must know the Russian backcountry quite well," he said. His hair looked like sideburns growing around a bald spot. "What is your general conclusion about the situation?"

"They're stealing."

"Not everyone, surely?"

"Not everyone."

"And what do the ones who aren't stealing think?"

"That you can't get by without stealing."

"Cute. But that's a double negative. What are people hoping?"

"I haven't found that out," Palchikov replied dryly.

"But it's impossible to live without hope. Hope is part of order. And order in the absence of hope can be hope," said the Crystal-Clear Communist, looking interrogatively at Palchikov.

"So that's what you're thinking . . . order as hope. That kind of hope has been offered to humanity before . . . by Hitler, by Stalin." Palchikov ground his teeth, almost silently.

As if sensing his concerns, the Crystal-Clear Communist went on. "Naturally, the order I mean must be moral. Democratic, but . . ." He paused, searching for a word. "But . . . if necessary, firm and inexorable."

"What does 'if necessary' mean?" Palchikov wondered aloud. "Necessary to whom and for what? And inexorable toward what or whom?"

"By the way, I had a call from the deputy prosecutor of that region where you went recently," said the Crystal-Clear Communist, changing the subject. "He said that his Party conscience was not letting him keep silent. He asked for an appointment. Should I see him?"

"I really don't like speeches about 'I can't keep silent!' over the hot line," muttered Palchikov, realizing that the deputy prosecutor was coming to the final stretch without his help, his loyal breast about to touch the ribbon just beyond which this conversation was taking place. I have to trim this bastard's sails before it's too late, and with a straight razor if possible! Palchikov thought, justifying to himself the lie he now told. "They say he's close to the Interregional Group, those so-called liberals."

"Don't be intolerant, Palchikov," said the Crystal-Clear Communist, but with a gentle, approving smile, and Palchikov understood that the deputy prosecutor's future with the Crystal-Clear Communist was past.

"You shouldn't be surprised that we're talking so much about politics," said the Crystal-Clear Communist soothingly. "Of course, it's primarily the prerogative of the KGB, not our ministry. But even Sakharov recognized the necessity of convergence in the modern world. Just think, Comrade Palchikov. Why do our so-called liberals demand the depoliticization of the security organs so furiously? Because they want to deny you and me our elementary human rights, including political ones, and keep them only for themselves. How can you have democracy without freedom of choice?"

"You can't," Palchikov said, bowing his head and thinking bitterly,

Alevtina, Alevtina, was that your freedom of choice, throwing me out on the street and staying alone with your invertebrates?

"I'm glad to find myself shoulder-to-shoulder with someone who shares my views," said the Crystal-Clear Communist, making an effort to conjure comradely warmth in his severe eyes. "I have an important assignment for you. Take this package marked 'Top Secret' to the chief of this installation. The number and address are on the package. It contains a state order of top priority. Make sure that the order is handled urgently."

That was an order.

"Yes, sir," Palchikov said clearly, accepting the package.

The Crystal-Clear Communist came out from behind his desk, put his arm around Palchikov as charmingly as possible, even though charm clearly was not one of the new boss's specialties of the house.

"I'm a man who doesn't intrude in personal affairs. But if you need a bigger apartment, and we all know how many years everyone has to wait, don't hesitate . . ."

"What's the big secret in this package, if he's even promising me an apartment?" wondered Palchikov later, playing cards in the speeding express train all night and marking the scores on the side of his scuffed suitcase.

A bump made him break his pencil point.

"Trains didn't bounce like this under Stalin," grumbled his cards partner, a retired government official, his bald head spotted with pigmentation so that it resembled a cuckoo's egg.

"That's the truth," sighed another player, an auditor from the Ministry of Finance, with a foxlike face and a squeaky, mosquitolike voice. "This earthquake shaking on the railroads began under old Nikita."

The fourth player, a cosmetician at the Enchantress Beauty Salon, which specialized in red noses and blackheads, fanned her plump and shiny face with the cards and added angrily, "I swear people pick on Brezhnev for nothing. Things were smoother under him. But with Gorbachev, it's like Parkinson's disease."

"You said it," Palchikov agreed, out of his professional habit of listening to the opinions of the workers. "What a life! You can't even play a game of cards without them flying out of your hands."

Early in the morning, arriving at a small, sweet city closed to foreigners, Palchikov took a shower in the small, sweet, closed hotel, had a snack in the small, sweet, closed cafeteria, and decided to walk to the secret installation, or "post office box" in security code, indicated on the package. Strolling through the shady park, Palchikov shuddered at the sound of a roar quite nearby. If that was a dog, then it was gigantic. Bears were not supposed to be in the area.

First Palchikov thought that he had imagined the roar, but it was repeated, accompanied by whimpering, squeals and bird calls. Palchikov headed in the direction of the roar, and a familiar smell hit his nostrils, one that plunged him into nostalgia for Alevtina—the smell of zoo.

A lion was acting up in his cage, resembling a red-haired actor in the role of King Lear. The lion's roars caused the golden antelopes in the field to wiggle their ears, and large and small parrots, like flying pieces of a smashed rainbow, to screech in their cage. Kipling's black panther with malachite eyes paid no attention to the roar, tenderly offering its pink nipples to coal-black baby panthers. Nor did an elegant giraffe, who calmly finished chewing a bouquet of Russian daisies that someone had thrown over the fence.

Some backwoods hole this is, thought Palchikov, aching for Alevtina because, unlike the zoo in Moscow, this small one was beautifully maintained. But Palchikov's mind also worked like a computer: Where does the chief of a top-secret installation have the money for the lion, giraffe and panther?

The Chief was a huge, good-humored man, who resembled either a retired weight lifter or an elderly Pierre Bezukhov from *War and Peace*, who made a career in the military-industrial complex. He opened the proffered package and started reading.

To Palchikov's amazement, the spacious office was filled with abstract and surrealist paintings, enough for an exhibition. Palchikov thought at first that they were Western reproductions, but as he walked around the room to examine them, he was even more surprised by the signatures, which were clearly domestic—Kosykh, Nalimyuk, Cherpachkova, Svistulkin, the Zagulov brothers. A photograph, of the rebel singer Vysotsky playing Hamlet, inscribed to the Chief of the Top-Secret Installation with unexpected tenderness, hung in a birch frame.

"Why did you bring me this prison order?" the Chief asked with hostility when he had finished reading.

"I don't know what the order is," Palchikov replied. "But my boss says that the order must be expedited."

"The order is for handcuffs. We're a defense plant, not a police factory," the Chief of the Top-Secret Installation said with hurt pride.

"Don't blame the police—they can come in handy," Palchikov replied, just as hurt. "When you have criminal hands, you need handcuffs."

"But why so many? Two hundred and fifty! Why so many, and why in such a rush?" The Chief slammed his fist on the desk.

"Excuse me, but that's a tiny number compared to the amount of criminal activity in the country," Palchikov said with a shrug.

"You misunderstood me." The Chief raised his forefinger menacingly. "Two hundred and fifty *thousand!*"

Palchikov was stunned.

He thought of the deputy prosecutor's words, "It's time to save the superpower!" and those of the Crystal-Clear Communist, "And order in the absence of hope can be hope!" and of the retired official, "Trains didn't bounce like this under Stalin," which all blurred together into something slimy and colorless crawling toward him.

"I'd better call the Mindefs," said the Chief and lunged for the hot line.

"Who?"

"That's my neologism. Mindefs are the people in charge of us at the Ministry of Defense," said the Chief with a chuckle, as he covered the mouthpiece of the phone. Someone came on and he spoke into the receiver. "Good day, Comrade General. I'd like your advice. I have a strange order here—an urgent commission brought by messenger. But it's not signed by you. That's what I . . . Oh, you know about it. . . . Yes, the order is for those unpleasant objects, for two hundred and fifty thousand of them. It's not a mistake? Seems like a lot. . . . Well, if it's been approved by you, then we'll take it on. Yes, yes, urgently. By the way, thank you for the medicine you sent. My blood pressure went down immediately. I hope that you're in good shape too."

The Chief of the Top-Secret Installation hung up and exclaimed, "I don't like all this, not at all." He gave Palchikov an oblique look. Would he give him away?

"Who are these artists?" Palchikov asked, pointing at the walls.

The Handcuffs

"Locals—exclusively local Matisses and Picassos," the Chief said, transformed, as he rose from his desk. "Just don't think that this is merely dues-paying to perestroika. I started buying these paintings back under Khrushchev, when he called such painters 'fags.' They needed support, otherwise they'd have starved. We're a top-secret installation, and we don't have to explain our cultural expenses to anyone. This is only a small part of our collection. Most of it is in the plant shops. Would you like a look?"

"I would," said Palchikov, thinking: Too bad Alevtina isn't with me. She understands more about art than I do.

"What if they don't let you go abroad once they learn that you've been inside such a sensitive state secret as our factory?" the Chief asked, only half joking. "I'm not allowed to go even to Bulgaria."

"I'm in no danger of going abroad," Palchikov joked.

The shops of the supersecret military-industrial giant were turned into a huge art gallery by the paintings on every wall. This did not interfere with the electronic technology silently working for war.

These were paintings by provincial heroes, the district doctors of Russian art, who did not exhibit at Sotheby's and who worked on canvas which, along with paint, was obtained miraculously. These were paintings by artists born in peasant huts, in barracks, in communal apartments, who had spent their lives in lines for ordinary products like milk, sugar and vodka, who had never tasted oysters, kiwis or artichokes. These were paintings by artists who had never been abroad, who bought a monograph of Salvador Dali or Max Ernst by sharing the expense ten ways, and Bulgakov's novel *The Master and Margarita* three ways, like a bottle of vodka. These were paintings that elicited the interest not of the local museum but of the local KGB. These were paintings that got their painters into psychiatric wards.

"Who gave you permission to exhibit them?" Palchikov asked, not believing his own eyes.

"Top secrecy," said the Chief of the Top-Secret Installation, laughing. "No 'idiotologists' can get in here. That's another of my words—the linguistic experiments of a shark of Soviet imperialism."

"Aren't you sorry that almost no one gets to see these pictures?"
"Yes."

"Don't you want to give them to a museum?"

"I'd rather have our installation be declassified. Which artist do you like best?"

"Svistulkin. Especially his triptych *Angel in Power*, where the angel's face gradually degenerates and turns into a devil. It gives me goose bumps," Palchikov confessed. "How old is Svistulkin?"

The Chief looked grim. "He's dead. Killed. I put him on payroll as the installation's artist. We gave him a studio, but stupidly it was inside the zone. Once he was at home drinking with his friends and they finished everything in the house. He remembered he had something in the studio, and he climbed over the fence into the forbidden zone. The guards shot him. That's the flip side of secrecy. . . ."

"And where did you get your Noah's Ark? I mean — your zoo . . . ?" Palchikov had to know.

The Chief smiled. "One time we had an inspector from Moscow come and he asked cautiously, 'Tell me, what does it mean, this lion in your expenses?' And I answered with a severe government face: 'That is our code for a special military order, and I don't suggest that you dig into it.' He waved his hands — scared him, poor fellow. That's all there is to the secret of the zoo. And now tell me — but honestly — why are those two hundred and fifty thousand handcuffs needed so urgently?"

Palchikov had no answer.

He took the night train back to Moscow, tossing and turning on the top berth and thinking about the handcuffs. He had seen handcuffs many times and there were occasions when he had clicked them shut. But two hundred and fifty thousand was a figure much greater than the number of people imprisoned in the Santiago de Chile stadium during the Pinochet coup.

And Palchikov also thought about Alevtina, and how she had wanted a baby for ten years and kept having miscarriages, and how right she was to take in the little girl whose mother was killed by the zoo's polar bear, crazed by pain when some bastard slipped it a cake with needles inside. Now he and Alevtina were responsible for the girl and they must not be separated. And suddenly, just as he was falling asleep, with a jolt and tears in his eyes, he saw handcuffs closing with a snap on her small wrists (incongruous with her deep voice), her hands covered with golden freckles and violet ink stains.

Somehow, all of Alevtina's pens leaked.

THE FIRST DAY

My Dog
And Me

========

MY DOG BIM HOWLED THE whole night long at the Peredelkino dacha, gnawing at the grating and trying to batter down the fence with his head and chest. He wanted desperately to get out beyond the fence, where his beloved, just as shaggy and huge, was longing for him.

They were of the same breed, both Moscow guard dogs related to the Saint Bernard. But poor Bim's tragedy lay in the fact that he did not have papers certifying his pedigree, and the bitch's owners did not want to waste her passion on puppies fathered by a dog who was passportless, and therefore dubious in the eyes of the canine bureaucracy.

When I came outside to calm Bim down, he was so exhausted by his struggle with the fence, this barrier to his desires, that he lay in the grass under the apple tree and rubbed his hot nose against the nose of his beloved through the fence, and the two dogs whimpered pathetically, shedding tears as big as August gooseberries.

The moon was generous, and in its cold spreading light shone apples, not abundant that year, like green lamps; and the amber beads of the *oblepikha* berry; and the agate necklaces of blackberries; and the loving, tear-filled eyes of dogs; and the dew on the leaves of grass, like the tiny eyes of the earth. The red berries of wing lights on planes flying over Peredelkino seemed part of nature, too.

Bim was so saddened that he had quieted down, and a nocturnal moth dared to settle on his shaggy, passion-soaked mane. It could have been a trembling white flower thrown over the fence by his shaggy beloved, as reward for the fidelity of his unrequited love.

I went back into the house, where my younger son, year-old Mitya, slept peacefully, looking like a little turtle, and my older son, two-year-old Zhenya, even with his eyes shut, tossed from side to side, shaking his head and kicking off his blanket, full of agitation, as if he had inherited, along with his father's name, his father's total inability to sit or lie still in one spot.

"The striped one is coming, he's coming," he muttered in his sleep, meaning everything that was tigerlike, frightening, unexpected and that would bite.

"No, he won't, don't be afraid. Papa is here," I whispered, covering him up, and he quieted down. I was the only one to whom he listened.

My wife, Masha, was sleeping, and only the blue veins under the translucent skin of her northern face were awake, pulsing, trembling like tiny streams under the thinnest crust of first ice, and my breath caught with love, as it did the first time that we were alone, in a fairytale hut in Karelia five years earlier, and the white nights had filled the room with tremulous light. Masha herself had looked like a white night with lakes for eyes, and I was afraid to kiss her, as if my kisses could destroy her—a vision made of fog.

I managed to fall asleep toward dawn.

But I did not get to sleep long. Around nine the phone woke me. My sister's hoarse voice said, "They've dumped Misha."

"Misha Katz?" I asked about our mutual good spirit, an engineer from Donetsk who belonged to that dying breed of people who call and ask, "Do you need anything? Some help? Some money?" So why would he be fired, Misha, who on holidays proudly put on the small metal insignia that read "Guards," in which he had fought as a young infantryman; and who was such a sentimental internationalist that he might not have been born Jewish, or Russian, but a mix; and who was perhaps the only living example of an accidentally successful man from a dream about Communism? Why would he be fired, Misha, who like Santa Claus of a summer Christmas would send us, through the kind offices of a conductor on a train from Donetsk, a bucket of ruby cherries or a basket of torpedo-sized eggplant or pickled watermelon, the secret of which was hidden under one of the remaining black curls on the very edge of his bald spot, which glowed goodness at mankind like a small lighthouse of compassion?

"No, not Misha Katz," Lyolya interrupted my thoughts. "Gorbachev. Turn on the TV."

I love my sister, Lyolya, but God keep you from being underfoot when she's angry, especially from getting the rough side of her tongue, for Barkov, Limonov, Viktor Erofeyev, and other outstanding linguists are merely pathetic tyros once one has experienced the blinding pearls of refined obscenity that exist in the depths of my sister's mind.

Lyolya is a great underappreciated actress, even though to some degree all actresses are underappreciated. When I saw her screen test for Empress Anna Ioannovna, I had chills. Her Empress was so terribly majestic, as if she were pouring the cold water of her gaze over all of humanity in the freezing air of the ice house of her brief but cruel reign.

Lyolya was our family news agency, but of a special sort. Someone had said that a historian was a prophet forecasting the past. My sister was a historian of the future. According to her phone calls, Brezhnev had died five times before his death.

"Well, and was I wrong?" Lyolya shrugged. "He did eventually die, didn't he?"

So, when Lyolya's deep voice announced that Gorbachev was removed and told me to turn on the TV, I allowed myself not to worry too much, but I did turn on the set.

Something gray, stifling, like poison gas came from the TV, eating away my lungs.

"In connection with his poor health and the inability of Mikhail Sergeyevich Gorbachev to perform his duties as president of the USSR and the transfer of the powers of the president of the USSR, in accordance with Article 127 of the Constitution of the USSR, to Vice-President Gennady Ivanovich Yanayev . . ."

I felt fear for my two sons, playing on the floor with their buzzing cars, for my beloved wife with the lovely white scar, which embarrassed her for some reason, on the delicate inner bend of her knee, for my eighty-year-old mother, the oldest newspaper kiosk lady in the Soviet Union, who one fine morning might read in the newspapers she sells that her son was executed as an enemy of the people.

"If the President has health problems, then where, I'd like to know, is the medical report?" The scornfully prickly voice of my wife, Masha, came from behind me, as if she were covered with a pike's prickly scales. But her hands rested on my shoulders with a mermaid's tenderness, and I felt an anxious pulse in her fingertips and a light chill of fear creeping into her breath, still warm from sleep.

The television avoided an answer and went on mumbling in the voice of the woman announcer, who in shame did not raise her blue-shadowed eyes.

". . . in the goal of overcoming profound and multifaceted crisis, political, inter-ethnic, and civil confrontation, chaos and anarchy . . ."

My two-year-old, indefatigable miniature—Yevgeny Yevtushenko, Jr.—as warm and rosy as if he were fresh-baked and just taken out of a Russian stove on a wooden paddle, tugged at my trouser leg, and whining and pleading, "Zhenya wants cartoon . . . wants Chip and Dale . . ."

His younger brother, year-old Mitya, was concentrating on catching our cat, Kuzya, by the tail.

Thank God, the children didn't understand.

Their nanny from Petrozavodsk, imbued with the family *antinomen-klatura* feeling since all her relatives had become fierce democrats, sobbed, dropping her thin hands, heavy-veined and knotty from her former work as a mica shredder. "Oh, Yevgeny Alexandrovich, I hope they don't kill Gorbachev. Of course, he's an *apparatchik*, too, but I feel sorry for him . . ."

My housekeeper was reacting differently, sitting grimly silent before the television, like a sphinx made of determinedly independent thoughts. One of her constant dislikes were the rallies, congresses and demonstrations, in fact, any place where there was a lot of talk, even though she herself liked talking. She always made a scornful face, and sometimes raised her not very quiet voice to the level of our dacha alarm bell: "Well, how long can you wag your tongue? Who's going to do the work?"

She had a constant love, too—the army. When we were walking through the Peredelkino cemetery one day, her eyes filled with tears when we passed the simple graves of soldiers marked with rough iron stars, not far from Pasternak's grave. She placed a bouquet of wild flowers tenderly on one of them, not because she knew even one of the men buried there, but because they were soldiers. I imagine that she must have loved a man with a red star on his cap, either during or right after the war, and she had lost him forever, but I've never asked.

She would not tolerate a single word of criticism, even justified, of the army. We had a major argument when she announced that Sakharov had slandered the army when he said that we had killed our own soldiers by friendly fire in Afghanistan. Fiery words, distorted with civic rage, flew from her mouth like incendiary bombs.

She was never right or left, but always on the side of the army. She also loved miners, because she grew up in a mining town where the strip-mined lands sometimes bloomed with delicate bluebells, or daisies like doll-sized fried eggs, from seeds blown in along with steppe soil. She was always tormented and brooding whenever the miners struck and the generals demanded that the strikes be stopped.

And she faced the same torment today, in front of the television, when the announcer's unwilling lips, trembling with uncertainty and shame, pronounced words that were not hers and which — and this was clear — caused fear and disgust in her.

". . . responding to the demands of broad masses of the populace for the need to take the most decisive steps in preventing the decline of society to a national catastrophe, to guarantee legality and order, we introduce an emergency situation . . ."

Will there be Gulags, psycho wards and censorship again? These were my fleeting thoughts, and from the tips of my toenails to the roots of my hair a paralyzing poison spread through me, the almost forgotten, damned feeling that I hated in myself—fear.

Lyza And
His Hedgehog

ON THE MORNING OF AUGUST 19, 1991, sixty-year-old Prokhor Zalyzin, nicknamed Lyza, a former USSR All-Star soccer player, now a night watchman of an athletic-supply store and a drunkard, was sleeping soundly, in his bachelor apartment furnished with the prizes of victories of his glorious past and the empty bottles of his ignominious present.

His trousers were an index of how hard he had been drinking.

In stage one, his trousers were hung up in the closet on a plastic hanger with metal clips, even though only one of the legs might be clipped. In stage two, the trousers were folded neatly along the crease, hung not in the closet, but over the back of a chair. Three: Tossed in a shapeless mass, but on the chair. Four: On the floor next to the bed. And stage five: On the bed along with their owner, who was in no shape to remove them.

On this day, Zalyzin's trousers were in that fifth stage, actually in the sixth, which meant that they were in bed along with his shoes. In fact, only one shoe was on, which hinted at yesterday's attempted intention to remove both.

Walking sadly and hungrily around the sleeping soccer star was the only other living creature in the apartment, a hedgehog named Chunya, picked up in the woods outside Moscow a year ago and brought home in a cap, the lining of which still showed a faintly gilt Eiffel Tower.

The hedgehog's shiny black nose poked at the empty dish that had not held milk since the day before, and Chunya pattered quietly but persistently near the bed, from which hung his master's feet — one in a black sock with an eye hole for a heel, and one in the shoe. The half-untied laces moved rhythmically in time to the peaceful snoring above the tirelessly pacing Chunya, who was a bundle of needles and hunger.

Chunya wanted to be back in the forest, to rustle in the living grass, to wash his prickly body in its fresh dew, to gather berries hiding under lacy leaves, to rub his needles against another's warm needles, but he did not want to leave his master, whom he had come to love. His master was the first person ever to talk with him, and Chunya gradually came to understand and was very sorry that he couldn't speak the human language. He consoled himself with the fact that people sometimes tried to speak the language of animals, birds and fish, but failed.

His master taught Chunya not only to eat out of his hand, but also to push a soccer ball with his nose and paws, and Chunya became perhaps the world's only soccer-playing hedgehog.

The people who came to visit were mostly former ball players, and were nice to Chunya. Of course, they did drink a lot, and Chunya couldn't stand the smell of alcohol. So he hid in the corner behind the empty, not-so-smelly bottles.

He had a special affinity for a bronze statuette of a soccer player about to kick a tiny bronze ball, his bronze foot frozen in motion. Standing among cups and plaques on a shelf behind the glass door of a cupboard holding all the master's prizes, that nameless player seemed desperate to jump down to the floor and play with the bronze ball. Chunya kept thinking that the little man had something to tell him, if only the metal lips could open.

There were many photographs on the walls of very young soccer players, in jerseys with the sleeves down (they hadn't learned yet from the British to push them up) and in shorts that were long in the Soviet style. They were clumsily dressed, but they could beat those Western millionaires, breaking through to the goal despite their tripping feet and awkward blocks, hitting the ball with their wild heads in acrobatic, flying leaps and triumphantly raising the crystal cup, inscribed USSR, over their heads.

These slender, wild-eyed young men, brought up in the deserted lots of the city, whose kicks had shaken the goalposts of the world, were now the gray-haired, balding men, too fat and weary looking, who came to visit, and banged dried fish against the edge of the kitchen table spread with a copy of the evening news.

Chunya learned a lot about his master from the photographs on the walls.

In one, Zalyzin stood with the boys from his street team, eyes round for the camera's lens. Photographed for the first time, these great soccer players of the future were unused to the attention.

They were photographed on a deserted dirt field, where their feet trampled the ruins of a bombed building which had turned to brick dust. Behind them was the goal, made out of rusty pipes—a step up from their recent goals of a few bricks, or school satchels and caps tossed into a heap.

And the ball wasn't made of rags, like the ones they used to play with, but of something resembling man-made leather—*kirza*, from the scraps left over from army boots. The boys playing goalie complained that those *kirza* balls made their hands swell even when they wore gloves.

The heroes of the deserted-lot playing fields were dressed in a motley way. Some in T-shirts, some in checked shirts, some bare to the waist. They didn't have real soccer boots, of course, and they wore basketball Keds or rundown shoes, and one kid wore army boots made out of the same *kirza* as the ball.

Zalyzin was a scrawny and unkempt teenager dubbed Lyza then, and the nickname stuck like a burr. In the picture he is wearing a torn, striped sailor's jersey, a bathing suit, ski boots and striped gaiters on his bare calves to hold up his socks.

In later pictures, he was better dressed. He had real boots, a soccer shirt with a number, and even though the team name changed several times, most often his shirt said USSR.

In the photographs, wearing that shirt, he takes the ball recklessly from the Portuguese player Jioebio, as elegant as a black lizard; in that shirt he rams his back-streets pompadour against the thin hair, erect in its desire to reach the ball in midair, of the aristocratic head of Bobby Charlton; and in that shirt he is clutched desperately by the hands of the usually proper Italian Mazzola, handsome, with a narrow mustache and eyes like olives.

In one of the photographs Zalyzin is trading his wet, red USSR shirt for an equally sweaty yellow shirt that reads BRAZIL with Pele, whose blinding smile looks as if he had bitten a chunk of Russian snow.

The precious Brazilian shirt from the shoulders of the king of soccer, never washed in all those years out of respect for his sweat, hung in a hallowed corner of Zalyzin's apartment, behind glass and in a frame he made himself.

Lifting his muzzle and running his beady brown eyes over the walls, Chunya observed that his master's face in the photographs changed, grew weary, weighted by wrinkles, and approached the face that unexpectedly bent over him on the forest path a year ago.

But there was a gap between his master's face today and his faces in the photographs that was not captured by any reporter. And what happened to Zalyzin in that gap was what happens to everyone who is forgotten. He stopped being of interest to people. He seemed to cease to exist. He moved from the elite of those who are photographed and mentioned, to the state of the majority of humanity — unphotographed, unrecorded.

His wife had left him long ago, for she had married him for his celebrity. His grown children did not visit him.

In the whole year living with Zalyzin, Chunya had never seen a woman in his apartment, and there wasn't a single photograph of a woman in the place — not even of his mother.

Actually, his master did have a photograph of a woman, but he kept it in a tattered leather wallet, along with his certificate as honored Master of Sport. Sometimes he took out the picture and looked at it, and when he did, he looked at it for a long time. Once, when he was pretty drunk, he dropped the picture on the floor and Chunya got a look at it.

It was of a young woman of twenty or so, standing atop a cliff with a coil of rope over her shoulder, winding the end in order to toss it down to someone and pull him up to her. That someone was out of the shot, but his presence was felt in the eyes of the girl, who was looking at him and who loved him, because only people in love have eyes like that.

Chunya guessed that the person down below was his master, just as young as the girl.

The girl's windblown hair was like a white storm cloud settled on her head and escaping the bonds of her scarf. She looked like a merry and powerful giantess who lived in the mountains and was born of them. She was big and kind.

In a large, schoolmistress-like hand, the photo's inscription read: "From Boat, who is always expecting you."

But Chunya never saw this girl in Zalyzin's apartment.

That August morning, while Chunya pattered around his empty dish, waiting for his snoring master to awaken and give him some milk, the telephone rang. But Zalyzin's snoring drowned out the jangling telephone. It stopped, and then someone tried to get through several more times with brief, anxious rings. Zalyzin turned, without opening his eyes, took the receiver off the hook, and threw it down next to the phone.

An hour later someone was knocking, since the doorbell had been pulled out of the door by an avid and mysterious collector of electrical equipment. The knocking was delicate at first, but then turned into banging. It sounded like very big fists.

Chunya hoped that the knocking would help him get breakfast, but he hoped in vain. Zalyzin slept like the dead. The banging stopped.

About ten minutes later, Chunya heard a strange scratching sound, and being so long hedgehogless, he even thought it might be another hedgehog come to help him. But the sound wasn't coming from the floor. The noise was up higher.

Chunya looked up and saw a face in the window.

As long as Chunya could remember, there had never been a face at that window. After all, they were on the third floor.

It was a woman's face, large, not young, but with young eyes that looked like light blue lanterns shining from a cloud of white-gray hair. One heavy hand, almost a man's hand, held tight to the window ledge, while the other scratched against the glass.

Chunya recognized the girl on the cliff, but much older.

The hand wasn't scratching. It was knocking with strong, red knuckles.

But Zalyzin went on sleeping.

The hand tried to push in the window, but it was locked.

Chunya knew something was happening.

He got up on his hind feet, sank his tiny teeth into the dangling laces of Zalyzin's shoe, and pulled it once and then twice. Zalyzin had taught him all kinds of tricks.

Zalyzin's leg jerked, but the stubborn hedgehog kept at him. Zalyzin jerked away again, but the hedgehog held onto the shoelace, hissing and whistling. Zalyzin opened his eyes at last and rose slowly, trying to figure out who was pulling his leg. But he felt a presence at the window, turned his head, and froze in astonishment.

"It's me, Boat," came a voice, muffled by the glass.

Zalyzin leaped up, almost stepping on Chunya, opened the window and pulled in his visitor, who was losing her grip on the crumbling ledge.

"I've forbidden you to come here. Especially through the window," he grumbled. "We had an agreement. . . ."

"What's the matter, don't you know?"

"What am I supposed to know?"

"They could be coming back, Lyza."

"Who?"

"The ones who put people away."

"What makes you say that?"

"Turn on the TV."

"It's broken."

"Then the radio!"

"I don't have one."

"How do you live?"

"Like this."

The woman who called herself Boat pushed Zalyzin down on the chair, put his left shoe on over the holey black sock and, while she was at it, tied the shoelaces of his right shoe, which had honestly spent the night on Zalyzin's foot, formerly his long-distance kicker.

"Do you have a neighbor with a working TV?"

"You always hated TV."

"You have to watch it today. There are tanks on the street. . . . Wake up, Lyza."

Zalyzin's neighbors were awake: The exhausted, chain-smoking, hard-drinking ("sandbagged," as they say) fiery-haired plumber called Van Gogh, famous for having only one ear since his left one had been cut off when he was a POW in Afghanistan, from where he had managed to escape; Van Gogh's wife, who embroidered cross- and satin-stitch, a plump, giggly woman as quiet as a mouse this morning; Van Gogh's mother-in-law, a former sniper in World War II and now a dry cleaner, unlike her daughter a sullen monster who dreamed to aim a gun at someone, anyone; Van Gogh's half-paralyzed, wheelchair-bound father, who had returned from ten years in the Kolyma camps fully rehabilitated and fully shattered; and three red-headed children, looking like three sunflowers of various sizes. That was the audience sitting around the television with a strange intensity, watching a screen that showed not tanks, but "lyrical" landscapes accompanied by the music of *Swan Lake*.

"What did you drag me here for?" Zalyzin whispered into Boat's ear.

But Van Gogh, seeing his lack of comprehension, shook a warning finger at him to keep quiet and then pointed the finger at the TV, as if to say, just wait, you'll understand everything soon.

And it wasn't a long wait.

An obviously nervous announcer appeared on the screen, resembling none other than a confused and worried mother thinking about her children. Trying to retain her smooth delivery and calm appearance, she read an appeal to the nation from some strange committee for the salvation of everyone who had not asked to be saved.

"Right! At last!" barked Van Gogh's mother-in-law, the former sniper. "All those stinking democrats should have been shot long ago. We don't have the right chemicals at the cleaner's. We haven't been able to remove spots this whole year. And people complain about us. Not Gorbachev or Yeltsin, but me!"

"Mama, why do you want to shoot at the slightest provocation?" Van Gogh's wife bubbled. "I feel sorry for Gorbachev myself. Are they going to put him away now?"

"That Gorbachev of yours and his pushy wife should be sent COD to America like that—what's his name—Solzhenitser guy."

Suddenly Van Gogh's father spoke. He spoke with difficulty, his head back against the wheelchair, his eyes half shut, grimacing with pain at every word. "So, more shooting, arresting, expelling. . . . And that makes you happy, Klavdiya Mitrofanovna?"

"Yes, it does!" She shook her wig affirmatively, and the red rose of her plastic earring slipped into her now cold Cream-of-wheat. "Less ballast! All those democrats, thieves and alcoholics . . ." And she cast a gloating look at her one-eared son-in-law.

"But we have three grandchildren, Klavdiya Mitrofanovna. Do you really want them to live in the twenty-first century in a huge concentration camp, the way we did in our time?" he asked sadly.

"They'll survive. And at least there will be discipline. . . . You and I survived, didn't we?" And Van Gogh's mother-in-law blew her nose into a lace hankie, as if blowing away her doubts.

"But millions didn't survive. . . . It's a bad word, *survive*, Klavdiya Mitrofanovna. *Live* is the word, live like normal people, not just survive." Van Gogh's father shook his head.

Van Gogh was thinking hard, in silence. He looked at Zalyzin, seeking advice in his eyes, but he didn't find it. He got up, wandered to the refrigerator, took out a bottle of vodka and poured out the remaining contents into two teacups, one for Zalyzin and one for himself. But neither of them drank.

Drowning out *Swan Lake*, which was back on the air, a mighty roar came from the street. Everyone except Van Gogh's father rushed to the windows. Tanks were moving through Moscow, but not for a parade. There was something stealthy about their armored faces. People on the street shook their fists at them.

"There they go, the dearies, the red stars," Van Gogh's mother-in-law cooed.

"Shush!" Van Gogh shut her up. "I'm still the boss here." The sight of the tanks had sobered him up. "And shut off the TV. It's clear to me what's going on. Let's listen to what they're saying overseas."

He twirled the dial on his old shortwave and found Liberty.

"Radio Liberty is inside the Parliament building. . . . I can see the tanks approaching. . . . They're surrounding the White House. . . . An attack is possible. . . . We are waiting for the president of Russia to make a statement."

Van Gogh turned off the radio.

His lackluster, sandbagged look had vanished, and he was intense and collected, his bleary eyes focused.

"Well, guys, who can tell me what a self-respecting man should be doing at a historic moment like this?" he asked the three little Van Goghs.

Three hands shot up.

"Do your homework," said the biggest little Van Gogh.

"Ask Mama what to do," said the middle little Van Gogh.

"Feed the cat and go fight," said the littlest little Van Gogh.

"You're all correct," said the biggest big Van Gogh. "But first, a self-respecting man has to shave."

Van Gogh plugged in his electric razor and buzzed in concentration before the mirror, then splashed some cologne on his cheeks, rubbed it in and took a sip from the bottle. "Oh, Mikhail Sergeyevich, you took away our last consolation, our vodka, and now we have to go rescue you."

His fresh-shaven cheeks glistened as they absorbed his sacrificed drink. Van Gogh tried to bring some order to his fiery hair with a few swipes of the comb, then kicked off his slippers and jammed his feet into his shoes. His all-understanding wife was already behind him with a clean shirt, helping him put his hairy, tattooed arms through the starched sleeves.

"You're so handsome now!" she whispered, biting her lip to keep from crying.

"I'm always handsome. You didn't even know that all my customers break their pipes just to have me come fix them?" he teased.

"Alcoholic bum. . . . Think of your children!" his mother-in-law mumbled audibly.

Van Gogh kissed each child's head in turn and then placed his own head under his father's barely moving lips.

"Good son," said his father. "Good."

Van Gogh put on his greasy cap, adjusted it to a rakish streetwise angle, and picked up a heavy wrench. With a wink to Zalyzin, he said, "Just in case . . ."

And then he looked him straight in the eye. "What about you, neighbor?"

"I'm old," Zalyzin said, avoiding his look, as they went out to the stairway landing.

"You're not old. I've seen you playing soccer with the kids in the yard."

Van Gogh ran down the stairs, smacking his hand into the door to open it, and out onto the street smelling of tanks and coups.

"I'm old," repeated Zalyzin quietly, as he and Boat entered his apartment. He poured milk for Chunya.

"Old age doesn't exist, Lyza. There's exhaustion, and illness, and fear, but we invent our own old age," Boat said, putting her hands on his shoulders and trying to shine her eyes like blue lanterns into his.

[3 3]

He looked away.

She went on. "Do you remember how you used to like it when I would make a roof over us out of my hair, and we could hide there and whisper our secrets? May I do it now, even though my hair is gray, and we can whisper? Here we are under the roof. Now listen. I invented my own old age myself, Lyza. I got to the point where I was counting wrinkles, looking in the mirror front and profile, and telling myself that I was so old and that you couldn't love me anymore. But what can I do with myself? I still love you. And if I love you, then I'm not old. Loving means you're not old. Don't be afraid of the fact that you don't love a woman at the moment. You don't have to love someone to stay young. You can love something. You don't love me, but I know that you love people, and this hedgehog, and books, and your soccer, of course, which you still play with kids. And if you love something, you're not old."

"I'm worse than old. I'm dead."

"No way. Don't die before you're dead, Lyza. Do you know why I climbed in your window today? Do you think it was my great passion for you? Do you think that I'm a menopausal old fool who flipped out after forty years of unrequited love for you? Of course not! I just didn't want you dying before your death. And that can happen to you if you don't go where you have to be today."

"Why do I have to be there? I don't owe anyone anything."

"Because there are debts that are owed even if you didn't take anything."

"What can I do, when they're using such force?"

"You may not help the political situation, but you'll help yourself. I know you. If you don't go there with your neighbor, you'll hate yourself, you'll drink yourself to death, you'll die before your death."

"What can one extra man do, just a forgotten former soccer player?"

"No one's extra when there's danger. And even if you are a former player, that doesn't make you a former Russian. And you're not just a soccer player, Zalyzin, you're a genius, and there's no such thing as a former genius. If you can't play like a genius now, you can live like a genius."

"And what does that mean?"

"Very simple. Follow your conscience—that's all. That's a life of genius. Your neighbor Van Gogh and the other Van Gogh were geniuses in their in their own way. Your neighbor picked up his wrench with the same inspiration as the artist picked up his brush. So get ready to go, Zalyzin, get out from under my roof of hair."

"Wait, can I have a word or two, honestly?" He didn't want to get out.

"Of course, but no more than two words, or I'll throw you on the bed and rape you. I still want you every night, which I guess I should be ashamed of at my age. Talk, or I'll start kissing you, even though you've forbidden me to do that."

"I hate the ones who sent tanks to the Parliament. But I don't have that much trust for the ones inside the Parliament, either. I went to all the rallies. I voted for the democrats. But before, they were in a mousetrap. Now they're inside the cheese, fighting over how to share it. They tunneled all these new corridors of power in the cheese. They're like mice who've turned into fat cats. Their whiskers are heavy with cream. . . ."

"I once read a book about the French Revolution, and it said, 'Revolutions are thought up by Utopians, realized by fanatics, and exploited by scoundrels.' If that's true, then it's terrible, Lyza. But that aphorism doesn't leave room for plain honest people, and that's not right. We shouldn't worry too much now about the future. The main thing is to be able to say that we've done everything we could. Let's go, Lyza, let's go. You're going to go anyway. I wouldn't love you otherwise. So there, my roof of hair is gone."

But he lowered her hair over his head again, as he used to do, hiding from the world, and her blue lanterns met his eyes, and she his arms, which had grown unaccustomed to her. After so many years, he never could have imagined that she would be here, in his lonely room, and that once again he would look into her astonishing eyes.

Forty-Five Years Earlier: Soccer And Rock Climbing

THE FIRST TIME LYZA HAD seen those eyes was long, long ago, under rather unromantic circumstances when, on the day he had turned 15, he was out on the fifth-floor balcony of a building in Izmailovo, vomiting with all the awesome strength of youth into a pot with a dried ficus plant.

The plant and the balcony belonged to his unmarried aunt, head of the insignia department at the Military Store on Kalinin Prospect, who had thoughtlessly asked her nephew to keep an eye on her apartment while she vacationed in the Crimea.

Lyza was the son of a hard-drinking plumber and a hospital orderly who drank, but not that hard, and all three lived in a seven-meter cell in a communal basement flat, where the only window, set halfway up to street level, afforded a view not of the faces of passersby, but of felt boots and galoshes in winter, and canvas shoes whitened with tooth powder and sateen sandals on wooden soles in summer, and in all seasons oiled cloth boots and the wooden, rubber-tipped pegs of war veterans.

The relatives whom the Zalyzins visited lived in similar cells and were also drinkers—hard or not—and drank the same vodka with the black cap. The vodka with the white cap was for people from a different Russia, ones with individual apartments.

The aunt was Lyza's only rich relative. She had an apartment, a silver fox coat and a friend who was a general. As she left for her vacation, his aunt had wagged a plump, manicured finger, living well in the company of various rings on the other plump, manicured fingers, which no longer resembled the thin, girlish fingers of a wartime signaler who had clutched flags at bombed intersections.

She had said, "Just no bonfires on the piano."

She didn't have a grand piano, just an upright, a spoil of war from Germany that was given to her, according to envious rumors, by her lover general when he was still a major and she gave herself to him (again, by those rumors) in tanks and gun carriages, serving as his wartime "field wife."

There were no pictures of his aunt and the general together, either because of his caution or her tact, but there were two yellowed snapshots hanging over her bed, separate but inseparable, under glass in a single frame of Karelian birch. One showed a skinny signaler, with a mop of curls peeking out from beneath her jauntily angled army cap, saluting in front of a marker reading "Berlin 50 km"; and the other, a young major glowing with the joy of victory and perhaps a bit drunk, playing a soldier's accordion with unofficerlike glee before the charred Reichstag. Of course, both she and the general had aged since then. However, the rumors had it that she still occasionally slept with him. Otherwise, why did a black limo stand in front of 11 Park Street, its pedigree nose poking the bushes, the soldier driver dozing through the clamor of furious, unpedigreed games of dominoes?

Visiting his aunt, Lyza noted that she always kept a red and gold box of Red Guards cigarettes, an expensive brand, on her night table, even though she didn't smoke, and once he even found two butts with wilful masculine teeth marks in the ashtray.

His aunt loved Lyza, who had been expelled from school for his love of soccer, and who earned money hauling crates and sacks in a vegetable store and cupboards in a furniture store. He was considered a wastrel even by his drinking family, and since his aunt was also considered lost because of her vague personal life, this made the two of them close and trusting. And so, when she left for the Crimea, she gave her keys not just to anyone, but to Lyza, with three conditions—feed her cat, Kotofei, entertain no girls and light no bonfires on the piano.

Lyza fed Kotofei faithfully, didn't bring in girls because he was terrified of catching something or being caught in marriage, and he hadn't lit any bonfires on the piano yet. But his half-starved soccer mates of the deserted lots came to see his aunt's private apartment, a rarity in the female eyes looking at him with compassion from the next balcony. The face was almost invisible, blending into the whiteness of the sheets pinned to a clothesline behind her. The eyes looked like two blue lanterns hanging in the air.

"Uh-huh," muttered Lyza, and he doubled over and was turned inside out. Even the shame of being seen, and by a girl, could not stop him.

"I'll be right there," the girl said. "I'll help you."

She stepped over her balcony railing, a large sturdy girl, but light and gentle of foot, and walked along the metal-plated cornice, hugging the brick wall and searching for holds with her fingertips. The balconies were close and it took only a few steps, but each of them might have cost her her life. In an instant, the girl had jumped down over the railing to Lyza.

"Ooh, do you stink! Why are you men all so stupid? Stick two fingers down your throat. And I'll hold your head. . . . There . . . And now I'll massage the back of your head. You have nasty bumps there. That's where all the vile stuff collects. Don't worry, I'll make them go away. I know how to do that. My father often used to get this way."

"You're crazy," Lyza muttered, gradually coming to his senses. "You could have fallen."

"I'm categorically normal," said the girl. "I'm a climber. See my watch?"

"What about it?" said Lyza, barely able to focus.

"Do you know what causes those scratches on the glass? Hugging . . ."

"Hugging?"

"Not with drunks like you. . . . Hugging cliffs."

Lyza finally got a look at her face. Matching her body, it was large with high cheekbones, weathered and peeling, tanned to a copper color. But it was a farming-fishing tan, not a resort tan. Her wide nose, sprinkled with freckles, was slightly flattened, and the nostrils with peeling skin shone hotly. She was molded crudely but impressively. She was both ugly and beautiful at the same time. Her hair fell into two uncontrollable and blindingly white cascades, divided by a severe part, onto her steep shoulders, and her brows were just as white. Below them were the two blue lanterns that Lyza had seen on the neighboring balcony. Lyza noticed that her reddish and huge fists were covered with scratches. Don't mess with a girl like her, he thought. Any problem, and she'd punch you, and there'd be nothing left of you. But her voice was melodic and enveloping. It was a voice for telling fairy tales. And she talked to him as if she were his granny.

"And why'd you get so soused, you silly boy?"

"It's my birthday."

"And how old are you?"

"Fifteen."

"You're still little."

"And you're big?"

"Of course. I'm already nineteen, so you have to listen to me. Besides which, I'm a master of sport. In climbing."

"And I am in soccer," Lyza lied.

"And who's that groaning in there?" the girl asked, turning toward the sound.

"People," Lyza mumbled reluctantly.

The girl stepped boldly into the apartment and shook her head as she surveyed the damage. "How can you call them people? They're pigs!"

The whole apartment was covered in vomit, including the parquet floor, the walls and even the keyboard of the war-spoils piano. The miserable victims of the American invention crawled convulsively on the floor. Only one had the hygienically sound idea of vomiting into the laundry tub, returning the swill to its source.

They all had throbbing heads and they all groaned in chorus to the soundless accompaniment of the accordion in the hands of the young major in front of the Reichstag on the yellowed photograph.

"My eye burst," whimpered a slant-eyed defenseman called Banzai.

His left eye, filled with blood, really did look horrible.

"Let me see! Your eye didn't burst, silly. It's just a blood vessel in the eye. Don't worry, it'll heal by your wedding day."

"Oh, my head. . . . Oh, I'll never drink again. Mama, where are you, my mama?" sobbed the goalie Kolya Radchenko, rubbing his crew-cut head into the tapestry (probably also from Germany) with vomit-covered shepherdesses.

"I'm your mama, and I'm here," she soothed him, putting her hands around his head, digging her fingers deeper and taking out the pain. "You stupid little sillies. What am I supposed to do with you? Hey, all of you, into the shower."

Lyza, sobering up from the shock, watched as tirelessly she picked up his semiconscious team members, stripped them like toddlers and pushed them into the tub, fitting in three forwards and one goalie and pouring water over their heads from the rubber shower hose.

"She could work as a nanny," thought Lyza. He was beginning to like her.

Leaving the soccer talents to soak in the tub, the girl picked up a mop and started cleaning up the apartment.

Just then, Banzai, who had crawled to a corner, found a half-full bottle of vodka and decided to get the girl's attention with a bit of alcoholic sophistication. Using the piano, he pulled himself up, poured vodka into a saucer and lit it.

"Watch the hocus-pocus!" Banzai announced with a giggle.

"No tricks!" the girl waved her mop at him. "Put out that fire instantly!"

"Not to worry! At ease, Pioneer counselor!" said Banzai. "This is a death-defying trick—fireworks in the guts!"

Banzai picked up the saucer with flames floating in it and started to drink the fire from the edge.

But the hot vodka dribbled onto his chin and one of the tongues of flame, like a tiny aerialist in blue tights, somersaulted onto Kotofei's fluffy tail. Kotofei howled bloody murder and raced up the cupboard. Beating at the flames on his skin, Banzai spilled the saucer right on the piano where thrilled, purple imps danced on the keys.

Desperately Lyza spilled the contents of the swill tub onto the piano.

And then a female voice thundered, "Well, well, nephew, couldn't do without the bonfire on the piano?"

Lyza froze.

In the middle of the room, her suitcase on the hacked parquet floor, stood his aunt, like a golden bar of molten Crimean suntan. Behind her and equally tanned was the real general, with red stripes on his trousers, holding a bouquet of gray Crimean feather grass in one hand and in the other a wooden crate of ladyfinger grapes.

Hearing suspicious sounds emanating from the bathroom, the aunt looked in there, only to find four naked teenagers in the overflowing tub, like four piglets in a puddle.

"This is a Roman orgy!" the aunt exclaimed, calling on all humanity to witness it.

The general was indignant and silent.

Banzai crawled into a corner behind the piano.

"It's my birthday," Lyza said and lowered his head.

"You'd be better off if you had never been born. If I hadn't a nephew, my apartment wouldn't be a brothel. Well, just explain, why did you have to chop up the floor?"

Suddenly, the unfamiliar huge creature of the female persuasion appeared, a mop in her big red hands, wearing ski pants out of season and ridge-soled climbing boots.

"And who's this floozy? How did she get in here?"

"Over the balcony. But I'm actually from Siberia," the huge creature replied without any embarrassment. "Tell me, did anyone ever call you a floozy?"

"Me? Never!" the aunt replied proudly.

"I think that there isn't a single honest woman who's never been called a floozy by somebody," the girl replied calmly and went on washing up.

"Bull's-eye!" thought Lyza.

His aunt looked stunned, and something like unexpected respect flashed in her eyes for the tall girl who had come to her apartment and was using her mop without permission.

The embarrassed participants in the "Roman orgy" began coming out of the bathroom, buttoning their pants.

And then the general spoke.

"Now, boys, you probably think that I'm a martinet . . ."

"No, we think nothing like that," Banzai said, heartened and coming out of his corner.

"Well, if you think nothing, then you're wrong, too," the general said, smiling tightly in an attempt to look friendly. "I'll talk to you boys simply, like an old soldier. I like to have a good time, too, but there have to be limits. My comrade, Tonya, and I didn't fight in the war so that you can vomit all over our Homeland . . ."

"May I ask a question, Comrade General?" asked the girl, leaning on her mop and smiling slyly.

"Of course you may, you should. I'm all for dialogue," said the general with condescending approbation.

"Tell me, Comrade General, did you never get drunk and sick? Be honest now. Never ever?" The Siberian hussy drilled into the general's pre-general past.

The aunt suddenly burst out laughing, so hard that her earrings tinkled and her eyes, surrounded with rays of laugh lines, began to cry with laughter, and her makeup began running in black streaks. She kept sending out peals of laughter, as if the young signaler with curls under her cap had peeked out of her older and fuller body.

"I don't understand your laughter, Tonya," the general said with a shrug, finally setting down the crate of grapes, but still holding the bouquet of feather grass.

"I'm laughing because I remembered how you vomited all over me near Potsdam when you got into Goering's wine cellars. What a riot," Tonya said, still laughing. "And now you and I are lecturing young people. Look what we've turned into, Comrade Major." She stopped abruptly. "Forgive me, Comrade General."

And then she turned to Lyza, wiping her eyes. "I like your girl, nephew. She can stand up for herself. She's a bit tall, of course, but at least no one can steal her away. Marry her. You don't find girls like her lying by the roadside. Marry her. You won't find anyone better. But tell me one thing. Why did you chop the floor?"

But Lyza didn't marry her. He was afraid of her. He was afraid because she fell in love with him.

He was not used to being loved. Neither his mother nor his father had wanted him to be born, and they called him their "accident." He had been conceived drunkenly and his mother gave birth to him drunk. He was in the way at home, underfoot, and it drove his parents crazy that they had to feed and clothe him.

He had a horrible memory of childhood. His mother took him to the beach. It was a hot day and there were many people. She didn't go into the water for a long time. She bought him three ice cream bars and she drank out of a bottle wrapped in a towel so no one would see what she was drinking. Gradually the bottle emptied and so did the beach. Only then did she pick him up and go into the water. When the water was up to her bra, his mother let go of him. He was only five and didn't know how to swim. He panicked and cried "Mama!" She stood there, eyes filled with tears, but she didn't move. Desperately his legs and arms thrashed in the water, and suddenly the water that had been trying to drown him began to help him, holding him up, and he was swimming. He did not swim toward his mother, though, because even though she was weeping, there was something alien and horrible in her eyes. Crawling onto the shore, he waited, shivering, for her to come out of the water. When she did she began hitting him, throwing his underwear and shorts and sandals at him. "Can't you even dress yourself! Do I have to baby you forever?"

That night, he pretended to be asleep and, still shivering with the chill that would not go away, eavesdropped on his parents' conversation.

"But we agreed," the father wheezed. "Felt sorry for him? Got weak?"

"He's a survivor, he is. Just like you. No one could drown you, either. And there are times when I really wish I could," his mother answered angrily.

His teachers didn't like Lyza.

The principal of School 254 on Meshchanskaya Street once hit him with his keys because he thought it was Lyza who had put flypaper, which stuck to his ironed twill trousers and made the class roar with laughter, on his chair.

Once, when he was in the hallway waiting to be called in for his oral exam in physics, he sighed to a classmate, "She's going to flunk me, that dried-up old fish. She looks like death. All she needs is a rusty scythe."

At that instant the door opened. To his horror, Lyza realized that she had been just on the other side of the door and had heard everything. In the furious eyes of his physics teacher, who did look like a dried fish, Lyza read his inevitable future of repeating seventh grade. Later, it seemed that every time he ever said something nasty about someone, the person found out and took revenge. And sometimes people avenged themselves on Lyza not because he said something, but because he didn't say or think anything at all. They were offended by that, too.

The chemistry teacher angrily told Lyza that he was as primitive as H_2O, the zoology teacher called him a Pithecanthropus. The constitution teacher was afraid of him because once, when she was telling the class about the Trotskyite-Bukharinite saboteurs, Lyza raised his hand and asked, "So, were they all killed?"

The teacher grew visibly nervous. "Well, that's not the right word, Zalyzin. They were executed."

"How many?" Lyza persisted.

"As many as were necessary," the teacher said miserably, burst into tears and ran from the room.

The only teacher to defend Lyza was the literature teacher, nick-named Owl, a lame, gray-haired old woman with huge, round glasses perched on her beak-like, witch's nose. Strangely, she appreciated one of Lyza's traits, his irrepressible imagination when he wrote dictations in class, to which he added his own smart remarks. For instance, the romantic "The sea laughed with thousands of silvery smiles" got "like a jewelry store before it was robbed." The famous exclamation, "And what Russian doesn't like riding fast!" received ". . . even if he ends up in a pothole." But sometimes he added his own romantic images. Instead of the clichéd "The dew sparkled on the grass like diamonds," his notebook read, "The dew sparkled on the grass like the Earth's tiny eyes."

He wrote his own lines not to show off, but because it was boring to copy someone else's writing.

The Owl allowed him these liberties, and often took delight in them. "You should be a writer, Zalyzin," she said.

The Owl was probably the only woman who took delight in him. So, when the girl from the balcony delighted in him, he got scared. He had not tried to make her fall in love. After they met on the balcony, he had simply invited her to watch him play on the junior Stormy Petrel team, and the crazy rock climber fell in love with him when she saw how he flowered and sparkled on the playing field, and how cruelly he was kicked in the legs as he crossed that trampled soccer field, leaving behind the basement cell, with its view of cheap boots and crutches, for the huge, unknown world. Lyza controlled the game, calling out one defense player after another, easily getting around them and, at the moment when everyone expected him to try for a goal, passing the ball three times to a free player, who had nothing to do but score.

After the game, the girl was waiting for Lyza with a single dahlia, which she had picked with her sturdy hands from the stadium flower bed, as if it were the thing to do, under the eyes of the stunned militiaman. She never worried about what people thought of her.

She handed the flower to Lyza and said loudly so that all his teammates could hear as they came out of the locker room with him, "I love you."

No one had ever said that to him. He was bewildered.

And then she said, "You're a genius."

No one had ever said that either. He was embarrassed. Unfortunately, his teammates heard it too, and they were no longer smiling.

"I didn't get a single goal today," Lyza said.

"You got three, but with other people's feet," she said.

They heard that, too, and never forgot it.

"The girl is right, you know," came a creaky voice. "Using other people for victory in war is underhanded. But in soccer, using other people's legs for a goal is a special talent. Passing is three-fourths of a goal. You, young man, are more of a half-defense than a forward. Would you like to be a backup half-defense for us?"

The creaky voice belonged to a man who did not look like someone who had anything to do with soccer, if only because he wasn't wearing a cap, but a soft gray hat. Of course, it was of bouclé knit, the soccer player's favorite fabric. And he wore professorial, gold-rimmed pince-nez and looked over them at Lyza with professorial, non-soccer eyes.

Lyza was stunned. The great coach Boris Arkadyev had come to their dirty regional stadium. Lyza felt a cap from Stoleshnikov Alley on his head. And the girl with scratches on her watch crystal felt that he would never belong to her, and she loved him harder because you always love the ones you can't have.

They left Stormy Petrel Stadium and wandered past the animal theater, where they could hear the roars of animals who had not come to terms with captivity, with being turned into toys. Lyza made a clumsy pass at the girl, roughly embracing her, almost digging his hand into her ribs. She removed his hand, kissed it, breathed into his palm and said, "Don't force me. I'll be yours. Wherever you want. In your favorite place. But on one condition. You'll be mine in my favorite place. Promise?"

"I promise," he said. "But my favorite place is the stadium."

"Dynamo?"

"No, I've never played there. Stormy Petrel. And what's yours?"

"Lake Baikal. I was born in Listvyanka. I'm studying in Moscow at the Institute of Physical Culture to be a climbing coach. Of course, they don't have the most important textbooks here, the cliffs. So, you'll come to me in the Baikal?"

"I promised, didn't I?" said Lyza and squirmed. He did promise, but how was he to know that her favorite place was so damned remote?

Late that evening they came back to the tiny, dirty stadium, the treasure chest of local soccer talent, and Lyza didn't have to help her climb over the iron fence, because she was better at climbing than he was. And then they walked hand in hand, past the flower bed where she had picked the first flower he had ever received, past the plaster discus thrower who looked like cottage cheese in the twilight and who was separated by a gilt, dwarf Lenin from the lonely plaster woman embarrassed by her broken-off nose. And they crossed the cinder track, where a black cat sat on the striped barrier, its gleaming eyes fixed mysteriously on something.

They strolled, holding hands, onto the moonlit soccer field mowed to a crew cut, and reached the goalposts where the Milky Way seemed to move in the net like a school of fish caught by a trawler. The girl picked a spot behind the goalposts where the grass was not trampled by play, kicked off her climbing boots from feet in hand-knitted wool socks, and without any shame pulled off her ski pants and her narrow men's bathing suit from her full, fairy-tale hips, which could have borne not only babies but church bells, and lay down on her pants. She was wearing a checked shirt, below which showed a narrow, silvery peninsula, just as white as the waves that fell from her head to her shoulders, and when the lucky couple made love in the Stormy Petrel, which would be the most famous stadium in their future memory, the goal's fishnet shadows danced on their faces. And then, behind the fence, chipped where the ball hit it, she found a miraculously whole clover flower. She put that flower to his parched lips so that he could drink its juice hidden in the white roots of the pink petals. And then, playing like a big, innocent animal, she took a few petals from his mouth with her lips, and whispered, even though no one could hear except the plaster discus thrower, "Back on the Baikal, there is always a boat waiting for me. It will wait for you, too. Do you want me to be the boat that's always there waiting for you?"

"I do," he said, and then regretted it because he didn't have the right. Ever since then, even though her name was Masha, he called her Boat.

And then they walked through Moscow and drank sparkling water out of the heavy cut glasses that glowed like mountain crystals in the kindly belly of vending machines; and street-cleaning trucks splashed them with their gray mustachioed spray; and the prostitutes with beehive hairdos, who sat outside the Grand Hotel in taxis with green lights beckoning, watched enviously as they kissed, and the Marine on duty on the U.S. Embassy roof by the National noticed the strange couple waltzing in the middle of Manege Square after midnight, which was not a Communist threat of any kind.

And then they wanted each other again, and ducked into a green yard on the Arbat and went into a wooden shed, making the pigeons squawk and flutter, a white cloud in an iron cage, and when in the dark they held each other, standing up, Lyza felt his right leg step into something wet. He discovered that he had one foot in a bucket of sky-blue oil paint. But they were young and, laughing wildly, strode down the street arm in arm through Moscow, golden in the first rays of the sun, and early passersby stared at the fellow with his right trouser leg sky blue up to the knee and leaving sky-blue tracks on the street.

Boat overwhelmed Lyza with the avalanche of her love. She liked covering their faces with the white waves of her hair, pressing her eyes to his, isolating them under a silky roof from the rest of the world.

She liked giving him flowers. She lived on a miserable student stipend, so she stole them. She gave him gladioli from the square opposite the Bolshoi Theater, snapdragons from Gorky Park, lilies from the Botanical Gardens, and once she gave him a turquoise branch from a Kremlin fir. Boat had no problem taking flowers from statues—the ones from the flower beds, not the cut flowers laid on the pedestals. She felt that the monuments would not mind, since people needed flowers more than statues did.

"These pansies are from Gogol," she said with a smile. "And these tulips from Pushkin." And once Boat put a finger warningly to her lips and whispered to Lyza, "These carnations are from Karl Marx himself."

And she liked climbing. There were no cliffs in the city, but she climbed whatever she could.

She saw a pink balloon stuck in the crown of a poplar and climbed up to extricate the balloon from the branches, but did not keep it. She let it go and it floated up into blue freedom, bobbing gratefully. To the delight of a crowd of boys, she climbed up a water pipe to save a paper kite trapped on a "Communism Is Inevitable" sign above the homeopathic pharmacy. Once, when she and Lyza passed a fire, where it seemed the firemen had saved every living creature from the burning house, her Siberian hunter's eyes saw an aquarium on the third-floor windowsill.

"I feel sorry for the fish," she explained to Lyza.

He knew better than to try and stop her, and turned away so as not to watch her climb into the fire.

She was back quickly with a sooty face and hands covered with rust from the fire escape, holding an aquarium with strange, rainbow fish that looked like autumn leaves with eyes.

"I thought they were goldfish," she said. "But they're still pretty, aren't they?"

Once she did something incredible, especially for those days. On New Year's Eve they were coming back through Red Square from a party. The snow was so heavy that the air had turned into a curtain made of snowflakes the size of chrysanthemums. It was impossible to see three paces ahead. The mausoleum looked like an enormous snowbank, the sentries like snowmen. One could just barely make out the ruby stars on the Kremlin towers in an aureole of ruby-red snow.

"Listen, Lyza dear, I have a marvelous little idea," Boat began, cuddling up to him and kissing the snow from his lashes.

"What?" He grew tense.

When she was that sweet, it always meant that she wanted to climb something.

Longingly, Boat looked over and up at the pulsing star atop the invisible tower.

"Are you crazy? They'll arrest you, maybe even shoot you as you climb."

"They won't be able to see me, Lyza. . . . No one will ever notice. I'll be quiet. And I'll be quick."

And she dove into the snowflakes and seemed to turn to snow.

Lyza knew there was no point in trying to stop her and he stood there, kicking one foot with the other and staring into the snow until his eyes hurt, but there wasn't even a hint of a human snowy form climbing up the Kremlin tower. But he had no doubt that she was up there.

A few cars moved along Red Square. It wasn't closed to traffic in those days. He couldn't see the actual cars, only the uncertain beams of their headlights searching through the snowy mush covering up the stones that still remembered the bloody boots of young Peter the Great who liked to chop off the heads of rebellious guards — personally.

A beat-up old car with a mound of snow on its roof accelerated on the rise and apparently hit a patch of ice. The car spun out of control and headed straight for the mausoleum. The car's front wheels struck the marble steps, and a headlight fell off and rolled right to the boots of the guards. The tipsy driver jumped out of his car filled with tipsy painted dollies drinking champagne straight from the bottle, and with cowardly but quick stealth grabbed the headlight, plunked himself back down in the driver's seat, and the crazed car, hips swaying like a hooker's, vanished into the snowfall as if it had been a dream. The sentries did not stir, as though there were no people inside the snow-covered coats.

And then Lyza was embraced from behind. He saw hands in Siberian mittens, one holding a multi-ringed solid icicle with a fresh break at the base. The icicle glowed like a delicate candle.

"Take a bite," Boat said. "This is no ordinary icicle. It comes from a Kremlin tower."

But there was one time when she didn't want to climb.

They were walking up Gorky Street, past the Central Telegraph Office, which had a globe turning over the archway, showing so many countries that they didn't even dream of ever seeing. High above the globe, and surrounded with multicolored lights, was a portrait of Stalin.

"He's hanging crooked," she said.

"Well, are you going to climb and fix it?" he joked.

"No," she said firmly. "Let him hang crooked. Where I grew up, there were a lot of camps. I saw people behind the wire. They didn't look like enemies at all. One time three escaped. They were caught and pushed into

a shed with a barrel of quicklime. They all suffocated. I heard them screaming. It was scarier than wolves howling. That's why I won't fix that picture."

And then Boat pressed close to Lyza, hanging her white waves of hair
over his head, hiding there and whispering conspiratorially, "Now if they
ever hung a portrait of you crooked, I'd climb whatever I had to in order to
straighten it."

He didn't know what to do with this girl, so unlike a Muscovite.
Before her, girls had slept with him but hadn't loved him. They were less
trouble. You could just say casually, "So long," and go your separate ways.
But the two blue lanterns always asked, as they parted, "When?"

They had nowhere to make love and so they made love everywhere—
in dusty, cobwebbed attics, on stairways, in old bomb shelters, on the tables
in sleepy courtyards where people played dominoes in the daytime. He was
sometimes embarrassed by the fact that nothing embarrassed Boat. She was
always ready to take him in her mighty, insatiable body, wherever and
whenever, holding him in her bone-crunching embrace and tightening on
him inside, as if knowing that someone would take him away from her. In
her lovemaking she was more inventive and shameless than all the local
whores he had visited, when he was younger and dying of the most unbearable desire—desire for its own sake—and had feverishly stuffed fivers
into rather dirty hands with chipped manicures. Boat gave herself to him
even on her bad days, asking forgiveness for the curse of mother nature,
and choking on her own whispers, she breathed into his ear that it was even
better for her that way. She furiously tore off the rubber condom when he
tried once to use it, and punched him with her red, heavy fists.

"That's like kissing through a kitchen tablecloth, Lyza. Are you afraid
I'll get pregnant? That's my business, not yours. Are you afraid it will interfere with your soccer? You won't be pregnant, I will. Don't be afraid that I'll
push you against the wall with my belly. I won't force you to marry me. . . .
Just love me a little, Lyza, just a quarter of how much I love you. That will
be enough for me. . . . They taught us in school that man is born for happiness the way a bird is born for flight. But I think that man is born for love,
even though it's not always happiness. I'm unhappy that you will never love
me the way I love you. But I'm happy that I love you. Get it? . . . But you
still owe me Baikal, Lyza. You won't get away without it."

So, when they took Lyza on the team, and he got an advance, they flew to Baikal, where a boat really was waiting for them.

The boat lay on the shore and languorously rubbed its broad-beamed, low-slung, well-oiled body against the marvelous blue bear called the Baikal, which turned over in its den, its gray paws smacking the shoreline cliffs. The Baikal could be tender to runaway convicts when they crossed it in fish barrels, and it could be horrible to people who were innocent. "The Baikal took him," Boat said of her fisherman father, who died in a storm.

Her mother, just as tall and powerful, but whose white hair was tamed beneath a widow's black scarf, met Lyza with a low but wary bow.

"And who is he to you—a husband?" she asked her daughter in front of Lyza.

"More than a husband. A lover," Boat laughed and, without being embarrassed by her mother, cuddled up to Lyza.

"Who needs a husband who isn't a lover," her mother rumbled, but gave them separate beds for the sake of decency.

In the night Lyza was awakened by loud, repeated blows coming from the yard. Barefoot and trying to keep the floor boards from squeaking, he went out on the porch and saw Boat's mother chopping wood with a man's habitual grunt, lifting the axe high over her head, the blade looking like a piece of the moon set on an axe handle.

"May I help you?" Lyza asked uncertainly.

She squinted at him out of the corner of her eye, shook her head and went on chopping. A wood chip, like a fish, leaped out and roughly skimmed his cheek.

And then she stuck the axe in the chopping block, put her heavy hands on Lyza's shoulders and stared him in the eye.

"Don't hurt my daughter. Hurting her is a sin. She's blessed, you know."

"What do you mean?"

"Not that she's soft in the head or abnormal. She belongs to God. And God's people always seem abnormal or stupid."

After staring at Lyza, her eyes warmed and she sighed. "You're so young. But someday you'll be old, too, and you won't even notice. Don't hurt my daughter."

And she went back to chopping wood so furiously that the white chips seemed to fly from beneath her axe up to the Milky Way, becoming part of its light.

In the morning Lyza and the girl he called Boat went out to sea in the motor boat, and the oiled-bottomed vessel leaped on the Baikal waves, springing as though atop the athletic and terrible muscles of a sporting animal. They came to Sandy Bay, where the pine trees, with roots exposed like claws, crept up the sand like crabs that, through some trick of nature, had grown branches. And they skinny-dipped as if it were the day of creation in the burningly cold water as clean as the tears of recent childhood. And they set nets from which they later dumped dancing slivers of silver called *omul*, and the girl pointed to a rainbow stripe on the fish's scales.

"Do you know what that is? It's an *omul* wearing a wedding dress. When fish make love, they become more beautiful, too."

She showed him a tiny, pink, completely transparent fish, and under it she put a piece of paper on which she had drawn a tiny female with long hair, extending her arms to another, male person, who had a soccer ball with nose and eyes for a head.

She taught him how to climb, and he understood that climbing was like making love, because it was simultaneously dangerous and tender, because you could fall into an abyss at any moment, and in order to keep from falling, you had to press yourself into what you were embracing.

She led him to an old hunter's cabin where, by Siberian tradition, the previous visitors had left salt and matches, and she royally showered the plank bed with taiga flowers she had picked, and orange saranki with brown speckles, fiery hot. They made love on the bed of flowers, the petals sticking to their heated skin, and shifted from one body to the other. And then, happily sated, they lay blessedly close, and Boat moved her flashlight along the cobwebbed ceiling of the hut.

"Guess what I'm doing," Boat asked.

Lyza watched. "You're writing something on the ceiling."

"What am I writing?"

"I love you," Lyza half-read and half-guessed.

The flashlight went out, and they made love again.

But when she breathed into his ear, "Marry me, Lyza. I'll bear so many children for you, and they'll all climb up the Kremlin towers," he was afraid of her again.

They were separated by his thirst for fame.

He didn't have fame yet, but his desire was cruel to everything that might get in the way — even love.

The vision of a squealing army of his kids, pissing on the heads of humanity as they climbed up to the ruby stars of the Kremlin, stood between him and fame. He was too much of a child himself to want children.

When they returned to Moscow, he told Boat they had to stop seeing each other.

He was put on a second-string team, although not the team he had wanted.

The team's coach was an eccentric man, labyrinthine and kaleidoscopic. They say that when he was young, he hardly ever played, even though he had been a member of various famous teams and received all the medals along with the rest. He was usually brought on about fifteen minutes before the end, and only if the outcome was obvious. Nevertheless, he was taken on as a coach immediately, because he looked so impressive and charming that it was impossible not to make him a coach. Everyone knew him, and he knew everybody.

In sports, as in winemaking, there are those who do and those who only taste. He was the Great Degustator. He carried his curly gray head of hair as carefully as a silver cup won in heavy battle. Since he hadn't played enough ball *per se* in his youth, he compensated now, on the threshold of terrifying old age, by playing with those who played ball. After a training session, he said to Lyza with one of his most charming smiles, "Shall we sit a bit?"

"What do you mean?"

"Have a talk. Right here, in the grass. Sit down. Let's be Antaeuses, drawing strength from our mother, the earth, or, in this case, the soccer field churned up by boots."

The Great Degustator even pronounced his words with pleasure, tasting them on the tip of his tongue before letting them jump off.

"I believe you're in love?"

"What about it?" Lyza bristled.

"A coach has to know everything about every player," the Great

Degustator replied dryly, "the way Christ knew everything about each player on his team that met for the Last Supper. He even knew who would betray him. . . . So, is it serious?"

"Yes."

"That's good," the Great Degustator said carefully and then, changing his tone, "But not for the role that I am preparing for you."

"And what's that?"

"The role of Great Player." The Great Degustator raised a finger. "Do you know the difference between great people and ordinary ones? A great person is his own gardener. The great person cuts off his own unneeded branches. Sometimes you have to cut off even love. No, no, I'm not against love itself. But there is a law of sublimation of energy. Petrarch and Dante could not have been great soccer players. I'm suggesting you take a break from your love. For a year or so. Along the way, you'll be able to see just how serious this love is."

When Lyza, staring at the ground, told Boat that his coach advised testing their love by not seeing each other for a whole year, she turned to stone, into a Baikal cliff.

Their conversation took place on an autumn evening in Gorky Park, next to the sleeping Ferris wheel, and the red and yellow leaves picked up by the stiff gusts of wind lashed Lyza's cheeks, as if they knew he deserved it.

"And what about me?" Boat asked, barely able to squeeze out the heavy, ossified words.

"But it's only a year," Lyza muttered.

"A whole three hundred and sixty-five days without you, Lyza! Your coach is a killer. He's never loved anyone, or he wouldn't have thought of this. He's just jealous, Lyza. You mean, I won't be able to hug you, or kiss you, or caress you? Like this?" She pressed close to him, holding him tight, afraid to let go even for an instant.

"I guess not," Lyza mumbled.

"But can we walk around the streets? Just once in a while, hmm, Lyza?" She rubbed her wet eyes on his shoulder.

"No," Lyza said. "We can't."

She covered her face and moaned and wept. "But can I call you?"

"Yes," Lyza said. "The coach said once a week."

"Oh, how kind he is," she growled. "I'll kill him for this kindness. And will this Nazi allow me to come to the games to watch you play?"

"He didn't say anything about it." Lyza felt like a louse and wanted to be swallowed up by the earth.

"Oh, so if the master didn't say no, then it's okay?" she mocked. "Aren't you worried that my gaze from the stands might have a demoralizing effect? What row is my limit according to the great man? No closer than row forty? And has the soccer slave driver allowed any letters? How many a year?"

The Great Degustator had thought about epistolary danger. He allowed no more than one letter each month. But Lyza was too ashamed to admit it.

"Write as much as you want," he said, looking away.

"But today, can I love you today?" she said, piteously wrapping herself around him.

"Yes," he said, still not daring to look up.

At that moment the wind swirled the red and yellow whirlwind and Boat descended on Lyza with the leaves in a whirlwind of kisses, embraces and words: "Don't leave me, darling, don't. . . . I won't be able to stand it. I feel that something terrible will happen if we're not together. Why do we have to be separated, if we love each other?"

And then they lay in a pile of leaves and listened to the creak of the empty seats of the Ferris wheel in the black starry sky above them.

She pointed at the sky. "That's where I want to go, Lyza, to the stars!"

A moment later she was climbing up the metal construction of the Ferris wheel, over the swaying roofs of the cabins, and her voice came from somewhere in the clouds. "Lyza! Come to me! I found something here."

She's really nuts, he thought. And then he thought that he could break his leg on that damned wheel and the USSR quarter-finals were next week. But the voice from the clouds pleaded, "Lyza, I won't be asking you for anything for a whole year. It's so wonderful up here. And I'll show you something."

He had to go up. It was scary—especially standing up on the cabin roofs, which shook and were slippery with leaves. Boat's blue eyes shone down from the very top. She gave him a hand and pulled him into her cabin.

"Look who's here with me," Boat said.

A worn teddy bear with one sad glass eye sat on the seat.

"He's been forgotten, poor thing." Boat patted the bear on his ear, which dangled by a few threads. He's very lonely here, but I'll take him home and we'll wait for you together."

"You're crazy," Lyza sighed.

"Do you think that loving is crazy? Suffering because you won't see the one you love is crazy?" she whispered hotly in his ear.

"What are you doing?" Lyza jumped, as he felt her demanding hands pull at him greedily, shameless with love.

"What am I doing? I'm loving you. I want you. Now. Here. Next to the stars."

And she pressed her face so close to his that their eyelashes mingled, and they loved each other in the Ferris wheel, the cabin swaying above the spellbound carousel, the white shells of the stilled stages, the empty dance floors upon which only the autumn leaves danced now. And on the next day, the Great Experiment, set by the Great Degustator, began.

Lyza and Boat stopped seeing each other. She called him only once a week, but said almost nothing. She had so many words saved up that she couldn't decide where to start.

But he got letters from her every day. They were full of love and despair.

One letter came in a small package. The package contained the teddy bear's ear.

"Teddy's ear fell off after all," Boat wrote. "I'm sending it to you so that you can hear, at least with this ear, how hard I'm praying for our love. I pray every night that you come back to me. Remember—Teddy's sole glass eye sees everything that you're doing, and Teddy will tell me. So behave yourself."

After the letter, Lyza was upset. The Great Degustator noticed this when in the finals he brought him in during the second time out and Lyza missed a pass from his partner between two defenders.

"What's the matter with you?" the Great Degustator asked harshly. "This wasn't some game for an empty glass, this was the USSR Cup."

"A letter," Lyza muttered. "I got a letter from her. And the ear of a teddy bear. I have to see her."

"What the hell teddy bear are you talking about! Don't be trapped in childhood," the Great Degustator hissed. "We agreed that I would make a Great Player out of you. Sentimentality is not a trait of great men. When you have snot and tears in your eyes, you lose sight of your goal. Don't read the letters. Unplug your phone. All your passion goes into the ball."

The phone was unplugged. Boat's letters were placed in an unread pile. The Great Degustator would have been pleased. Apparently, Lyza had conquered an emotion as rudimentary as love.

But sometimes, during a game, he would shudder, feeling Boat's eyes on him. It was impossible to find her blue lantern eyes among the tens of thousands of eyes in the stands. But he could tell that her eyes were there.

In Tbilisi, catching the ball with his toe, Lyza cleverly threw it over the shiny pate of the Georgian defense to himself. But the ball went too far and, rolling ever more slowly in the grass, ended up between rivals running toward it wildly from two sides — Lyza and the Georgian goalie with black mustache and wasp waist, like a dancer from a folklore group. The goalie had the upper hand, because the ball was rolling in his direction and away from Lyza.

Lyza managed to reach the ball with the tip of his boot before the goalie's helplessly spread gloves could touch it.

The too-slow goalie got hold of Lyza's boot, but the ball quietly sidled somehow to the white line of the goal and seemed to stop on it, exactly with the middle of its belly. But then the ball stirred, as if an invisible finger had given it a push, and crossed the border beyond which a mere ball becomes a goal.

After this miracle, Lyza instinctively looked around, and he thought that among the glowing cigarette tips in the stands he saw the flash of two light-blue pulsing dots, which had pushed the ball into the goal with the force of their gaze.

Another time, in Kiev, Lyza fell down, caught by two Dynamo players smelling of bacon and garlic. They came for him with a stretcher, but he heard a whisper from the stands, "You're not hurt, Lyza, you're not hurt, Lyza, you're not hurt . . ." He got up, limped around the edge of the field, and a few minutes later the same hands were gripping his soaked shirt, trying to hold him back, and two blue dots flashed on and off in the stands.

He imagined that her eyes were glowing, like Siberian forget-me-nots, in stadiums all over the country, traveling with him, flying on planes.

He was right about the last.

In order to follow him, Boat got a job as a stewardess.

Aeroflot didn't know about her love for Zalyzin, who was becoming more famous, but assumed that she was just a crazy soccer fan. They teased her, but put her on flights to the cities where Lyza's team was playing.

Once, during the Moscow–Baku flight, as she walked down the aisle with a tray holding quietly hissing plastic cups of mineral water, Boat went stock still. Right before her was Lyza, sitting next to the Great Degustator. They were both reading. The Great Degustator was engrossed in Feucht-wanger's *False Nero* and Lyza in Belyaev's *Amphibious Man*. Without looking up, they each took a glass. Lyza's hand shook and drops of the Borzhomi mineral water splashed right on the desperate screams of the miserable father who lost the boy with gills in the stormy sea: "Oh, Ichtiander, my son, where are you?"

Boat had seen Lyza only from afar, and in his soccer uniform, so she couldn't tell how much he had changed.

Now, a different man sat before her.

His wild hair had turned into a small, neat pompadour with a perfect part. His face, so recently covered with nicks from dull razor blades and adolescent pimples and blotches, had taken on a manly sheen imbued with the classy scent of *Chypre*, the emerald cologne popular in those years. Lyza wore an old Bulgarian jacket, bought at an Odessa flea market, a domestic but made-to-order burgundy knit shirt with white buttons, a silvery Polish tie with brown squiggles, green corduroy trousers from Czechoslovakia and Armenian cherry-colored shoes with rubber soles. And in the pocket of the seat back in front of him, as a sign of his membership in the highest soccer caste, was a bouclé cap with a button, made for him by the famous Uncle Zhora.

But it wasn't his hair and clothes that most struck her. Boat saw in Lyza's face something that she didn't understand, but that didn't bode well. Teddy's glass eye may have seen from a distance what Lyza had been doing, but out of pity, Teddy hadn't told her.

Here's what was happening with Lyza.

The Great Degustator did not like people who could love. He did not believe that they were truly in love and thought that they were pretending. All clean people seemed like imposters, hypocrites, to him, and he took pleasure in trying to make them be like him. He felt that the basis of life was psychological, rather than physical, multiplication. Cynics feel morally secure when they create more cynics.

Otherwise the Great Degustator would have had to stop liking himself, and that wouldn't have been easy, since that was the nearest to love that he felt.

He did not need players who were in love. He considered being in love a disease that ruined careers. In those days, the word "sex" was used in the Soviet Union only as a symbol of Western decadence. But there were womanizers, of course. "Polishing the blood" without sentimentality was beneficial, the Great Degustator thought, because it gave men the self-respect they needed for their careers.

The Great Degustator had put his cards on Zalyzin and he decided to cure him of his love.

He started getting women for him.

Oh, no, these weren't the stinking whores from railroad stations or the painted taxitutes in beckoning cabs. These were practically honest lays — secretutes, who didn't necessarily want money, but accepted perfumes, not very expensive jewelry, stockings, clothes and dinners out — although they didn't mind cash, either. When needed, they arrived politely and almost sincerely, and when the need was satisfied, they left tactfully, shutting their purses with a soft click.

As the Great Degustator told Lyza, smiling sweetly, "A call girl is as convenient as masturbation — you get pleasure and you don't have to see her home."

But Lyza, who was no longer accustomed to using the services of these consolers of the flesh, had developed a fear of venereal disease.

In the last years of Stalin's regime, there were only a few permitted categories of private entrepreneurs: capmakers, shoemakers, shoeshine men and venereologists.

Terrified of the diagnosis, Lyza began making frequent visits to a shabby house on Sretenka, where on the torn vinyl padding of the door there was a white enamel sign:

Dr. Shneerson, Venereologist
Confidentiality Guaranteed

Shneerson, a small, balding old man with pince-nez over his sly raisin-like eyes, had not lost his sense of humor observing the sad and often long-lasting consequences of temporary pleasures.

"Are you going to try to tell me once again that you have VD, young man? Is it simply because you like all those lovely foreign words, like *chancre*, *trichomonad*? Why do you want to have syphilis so much? Some people live without it all their lives, and quite happily, I assure you. Or maybe you just have a lot of money and you want to support me in my old age? Since you've become my patient, I've re-roofed my house and now I'm even thinking of importing German tiles."

Seeing Lyza on the plane, Boat was not wrong in sensing that something was wrong with him, and that she might lose him forever.

Unnoticed by him, Boat left his seat and walked along the aisle with an empty tray, and she stayed in the cockpit with the pilots until the landing in Baku, holding onto the tray and staring ahead.

That evening, without changing out of her Aeroflot uniform, she was at the stadium, gasping with delight, clapping her hands amid the funereal silence of the Azerbaijani fans, as the rising star of Soviet soccer, Zalyzin, her Lyza, with his neat head sent the ball on its birdlike flight and scored a goal.

At halftime, the man next to her, generously forgiving her applause of the Moscow team, hospitably shared his aromatic and treacherously light Akhtamar cognac with her, the bottle wrapped in a copy of the *Baku Worker*. They ate a mix of nuts and raisins.

This neighbor was tact incarnate. Nature had made him tactfully delicate, giving others size and leaving grace to him. He had miniature shaggy hands, miniature feet in children's shoes, miniature doll-like whiskers, a miniature but aquiline nose, and a disproportionately large cap, beneath which were larger-than-life-size eyes, beautiful and sad. He spoke Russian almost well.

"And so you're alone like this at the game?" he asked.

"Alone like this."

"And you fly alone?"

"I fly alone," Boat sighed.

"What do they call you?"

"Masha. But one man calls me Boat."

"I have two names, too. My Armenian mother calls me Razmik, and my Azeri father calls me Mamed. I'm from Karabakh. So I'm a Little Karabakh."

When the second half began, Little Karabakh noted that the Russian girl was transported onto the field. But she wasn't like a regular fan.

Little Karabakh was observant, and he saw that she was most concerned when the ball was with the young player, Number 10, with a short pompadour and long eyes that found a suitable partner at every corner of the field.

When the game was over, the Russian girl started bawling without reason. Maybe because the players, including Number 10, were leaving, and she thought it was forever.

"Why are you crying? Moscow won, Baku lost. I should be crying," said Little Karabakh, and then joked sadly. "When Baku and Yerevan play, whoever wins, I cry. Have some more to drink—as you Russians say, the sweet dregs."

She took another swallow from the bottle, and another, and then drained it, but she went on crying, and Little Karabakh was sure that she wasn't crying over the game.

He took off his cap out of respect for her tears.

Then she understood why his cap was so big. It managed to contain a huge mound of curly black hair, which resembled an explosion, and immediately sprang out in every direction.

"You love Number 10," Little Karabakh said. "Right?"

"Right," Boat admitted, feeling her head spin from the cognac. "How did you know?"

"Because I am at the same time a pretty smart Armenian and a pretty smart Azeri," said Little Karabakh. "Does Number 10 love you?"

"He does."

"Then why are you crying?"

"He loves me, but he doesn't want to love me," Boat sobbed. And then she shouted, "HE WON'T SLEEP WITH ME!"

Fortunately, the stadium had emptied by then, and the empty stands looked like a huge, coiled, sleeping snake.

Little Karabakh was a bit embarrassed, because no Armenian or Azerbaijani woman would have answered like that.

"Why won't he sleep with you if he loves you?" Little Karabakh asked, finding the strength for this difficult question.

"Because he's stupid," Boat said, weeping.

"Let's go make the fool smart. I have a big car, but no big love. But I respect love. I'll take you to Number 10."

The gates of the stadium, covered in steel mesh, were shut. But the Russian girl, who had just been weeping and sobbing, shaped up the minute she saw the obstacle. She even seemed to cheer up. Her strong fingers were in the holes of the fence, the toes of her shoes, too, and in an instant, smiling and showing her white marble teeth, she was astride the top of the gate, throwing down the end of her long scarf.

"Don't worry, it's strong!" she called, and Little Karabakh held on to the scarf and suddenly found himself being lifted like a feather by a powerful, magical force, which caught him under the arms for a second, and then carefully and easily lowered him by the scarf to the other side of the gate.

It reminded him of the magic-carpet tale that his Armenian grandmother used to tell him, not remembering that his Azeri grandmother had told him the same story, in another language, when the two women had shared their grandson, but neither could have claimed him as hers alone.

Little Karabakh led Boat to a scruffy milk truck waiting for him in an alley. He looked even tinier next to the truck, and confessed, "I wanted to lie to you, that I was the director of a store. That would have added respect and height. But I changed my mind. Why lie, if you weren't lying to me? I drive a milk truck. This is my big car. Let's go for your big love.

But Russians are a crazy people. They sleep with the one they don't love and they don't sleep with the one they do."

The administrator of the Intourist Hotel gave the tall Aeroflot stewardess and the Little Karabakh who barely reached her shoulder a suspicious look: they were very hard to imagine as a couple.

Boat asked for the soccer player Zalyzin.

"We're not supposed to let people call them. At the coach's request — oh, and there he is," she said. The administrator had only one concern on her mind. The Boss of Azerbaijan had ordered that the suite for the revolutionary poet Nazym Hikmet be bugged. Hikmet was arriving the next day, recently released from the hell of a Turkish prison and still not knowing what heaven he was entering.

Despite his team's win, the Great Degustator was not in a very good mood as he came through the hotel lobby. He had just "polished the blood" in his room with the floor lady, who had hastily offered him her cold and pimply rear end while holding on to the toilet seat. Hypocritically, she had left the door to the hall open, because that was the rule. Someone could have burst in at any moment. The Great Degustator did not like women taking too long, but he couldn't stand it when they hurried and were afraid. Besides, she had a sour smell, perhaps of various hotel residents blended into one.

The Great Degustator did not respect himself after this unsuccessful attempt at pleasure, and not respecting himself was an unusual and painful thing.

He recognized the Aeroflot stewardess as the crazy Siberian rock climber who had been messing up the future Great Player.

How did she get here? he began calculating coldly. Has Zalyzin broken our agreement about not seeing her for a year? And that means that he's a wimp, and a wimp, even an outstanding one, cannot be the symbol of Soviet sport.

But the Great Degustator liked brief contacts, just a taste, particularly with women. Especially now that he needed to take revenge as quickly as possible, to restore his self-respect.

"It's a pleasure to see the lovely cliff tamer in Baku," he said. "Does this mean that you're planning to collect eagle feathers with your brave hands from the impassible cliffs of the Caucasus?"

"Where's my Lyza?" Boat grabbed his lapels with her brave hands. It scared him. But with relief, he realized that she was drunk. He was in his element, dealing with drunken women.

"Must be in his room," the Great Degustator said with a shrug. "You know, I don't keep tabs on him. He's a grown-up."

"I have to talk to you," Boat said, not letting go of his lapels. Behind her was a man of very small size but with a very big cap.

"We have a very important matter with Number 10," said Little Karabakh, searing the coach with his fiery eyes. "Vitally important."

"And what is this little trinket?" the Great Degustator said, mockingly measuring him with his eyes as he dialed Lyza's room. "Zalyzin? Some people to see you here. You'll find out in a minute. But, my dear boy, don't make me out to be a policeman. You're a free man and can do what you want with your time." The Great Degustator paused and then added, "And with your future."

Boat tore the receiver out of his hand. "Lyza, I'm here, in the hotel. Lyza, I love you. I can't take being apart, Lyza."

"But we have a deal," said the iron voice, a stranger's voice. "A year. Seven months and five days have passed. Let me get on my own two feet, be part of the All-Stars. . . . Don't call me anymore. Don't follow. Wait another four months and twenty-six days. That's less than half the time. That's it."

She heard the dial tone.

Boat hung up slowly, as though the receiver were very heavy.

"Do you want me to go to Number 10 and bring him down here?" Little Karabakh offered, eyes blazing with loyalty.

Boat seemed dead.

"Go away, young man, go away. We'll handle this ourselves," the Great Degustator said in a fatherly, soothing manner. He was part of a subspecies of necrophiles—he liked women who lacked resistance because of failed love. Even the most insubordinate were vulnerable at a time like this. It bothered his conscience a little, but . . .

Little Karabakh didn't want to leave. He didn't like this man with the voice as sweet as Turkish delight and eyes like those of a rotting fish that had lain for too long on a counter at the bazaar on a hot day.

"Let's go to the restaurant for a bit. Have some coffee—they do it very well here, almost like in Turkey. And then we'll try calling your Lyza again. Maybe he's just tired after the game," the Great Degustator said, consoling Boat. And in irritation, he repeated to her escort, "And you go away, young man, don't let me keep you."

Little Karabakh was a proud man. He had been asked to leave twice and not asked to stay even once. So he left. Driving the milk truck home, where no one was waiting for him, he almost ran over a cat. To save it, he drove up onto the sidewalk and knocked over a garbage can. And he thought that he shouldn't have left the Russian girl in the hands of that coach, who would make a much better store director than Little Karabakh.

Boat was drinking more cognac, glass after glass, and not eating.

"Call Lyza again," she told the Great Degustator. "Tell him that I want to see him. Make him come down here."

The Great Degustator decided to play an honest game. He wanted to look like a decent person in his own eyes. He called.

"Listen, Zalyzin, your love is with me in the restaurant. She's drinking without stopping. And crying. She says she loves you. Come down and take her away, I guess."

"No," replied Zalyzin, without a shadow of the sentimentality that the Great Degustator despised. "I'm a man of my word."

What a cruel generation, thought the Great Degustator and shivered. We weren't like that. What causes that? Well, anyway, my conscience is clear.

"What can I do, dearie?" he said gently, as he sat down at the table where Boat waited, her eyes faded blue. "He doesn't want to see you. To tell the truth, the trial year wasn't his idea, it was mine. I admit it was a little harsh, but useful for his soccer career. I haven't done anything to him. But I have to you. But he could have ignored my conditions if you were more important to him than soccer."

The Great Degustator was sorry that he had said the last part—that was probably breaking the rules of being a gentleman. But for the situation that was ripening, it was more convenient not to respect Lyza, so as not to regret it later.

They were interrupted by the maitre d' with sweet black eyes and a pyramid of various tummies — two tummies on his cheeks, one tummy on his chin, one on his neck and one on his belly. He was holding a bouquet of miniature roses, drops glistening on the petals.

The maitre d' whispered in the Great Degustator's ear, "For your lady from Himself. He's inviting the two of you to the private room. A banquet in honor of the arrival of the Moscow writers, here for tomorrow's banquet in honor of the arrival of Nazym Hikmet."

"Get a hold of yourself," the Great Degustator whispered to Boat, feeling a cold shiver of fear in his knees, and in his temples the hot hammers of delight at these sudden, dizzying heights to which fate had brought him. "After all, it's the Boss of Azerbaijan."

The Boss of Azerbaijan, who was rumored to interrogate select prisoners personally, had eyes that resembled the maitre d's, except that they sometimes grew icy cold and turned merciless. He greeted them with open arms.

"I was there, I was at the game today. The friendship of peoples, as they say, won today. You let our team have it. And it serves them right. They've gotten too fat. The fatty tails on those sheep have gotten too heavy. I find your lady adorable. . . . A powerful beauty. A tsar maiden. She's like the song, 'My homeland is broad.' Was the poet referring to you, my dear, when he wrote, 'She can bridle a horse while galloping and enter her cottage when it's burning'? Am I quoting correctly, visiting Moscow poets?"

"Yes," came the eager voices. "What a wonderful memory. And for one so busy."

"Pour our Russian guest a big glass of Azerbaijani champagne, as red as the banner of our country. The French faint with delight when they try it. . . . I drink to the consolation of all the republics of the Soviet Union — to Russian women! The men will stand for this toast."

Suddenly, the Boss of Azerbaijan noticed a bald little poet whose sunken eyes were rimmed with shadows of suffering, but who sported a coquettish bow tie. The poet drank to women, but sitting down. He had merely risen a bit from his seat.

"Who is he?" he demanded softly of the air.

The air rustled with the lips of his assistant, as tender as the petals of the roses of Lenkoran. "Antokolsky. Poet. Laureate of the Stalin Prize."

"Why is he sitting when I am standing?"

"His leg hurts. He has a cane with an ornamented handle."

But the icy eyes filled with ruthlessness could not be stopped.

"Antopolsky!" squealed the Boss of Azerbaijan, mispronouncing his name, probably on purpose. "Get up!"

The old poet, who had read his early poem to Igor Severyanin, the king of poets, who had been in love with the poet Marina Tsvetayeva, who had written a famous poem about his son killed in the war, who had brought up a Pleiades of poets, started to rise with an apologetic smile, clutching his cane.

The private dining room, its walls hung with carpets and daggers, was turning into a torture cellar.

"Antopolsky, sit down!" breathed the Boss of Azerbaijan, apparently satisfied. But as soon as Antokolsky had sat down, he squealed once more, "Antopolsky, get up!"

And without changing his rhythm, he shouted about ten times more, choking the exhausted old man with shame and fear, "Antopolsky, sit! Antopolsky, up!"

Then, tiring of the game, he left the old man alone. Turning to Boat, he murmured, "I'll do whatever you want. I'll give you a motor boat. A house in Lenkoran with a vineyard and garden. Just one night. I want you, giant Russian woman."

But Boat was only half-listening to him.

She drank everything that was given to her, from the banner-red champagne to the forty-year-old intoxicating cognac, to the moonshine *chacha* made from Cornelian cherries, which in the Caucasus is drunk only at weddings (and not even then), to Riga balsam, and even Czech beer. She still was not eating, and as the object of the Boss of Azerbaijan's special attention, the waiters danced around her in vain, filling the table with delicate pink slices of salmon like thin-sliced dawn, steaming *plov*, golden with saffron, marinated eggplant with a crimson scattering of pomegranate seeds, and cutglass serving dishes with the burgundy powder of *sumak* and *nash-arabi* sauce, which resembled bull's blood. The Boss of Azerbaijan was so drunk that he was no longer able to pester her, but his minions still had time to bring her a present, a mysterious enameled bucket wrapped in cheesecloth.

Boat's eyes were swimming, it was all a sticky, bad dream, with only one pain that tore her soul apart: her beloved did not want to see her. She didn't care about the rest.

And she didn't remember how she ended up in the Great Degustator's room, how his hands traveled all over her, and how his face ended up over hers, trying to stick his tongue, smelling of marinated garlic, into her mouth. She was disgusted, but even then she didn't care.

She woke up with a terrible headache and a buzzing that drilled into her already sore temples.

She pried her eyelids apart and saw a stranger, a man who disgusted her, victoriously whistling and using an electric razor on his cheeks. He had been avenged for the lack of pleasure with the floor lady.

Boat froze in horror, realizing what had happened. She had spent the night with a man she did not love and actually hated. She had never been able to understand how this could happen to other women and had been sure that it would never happen to her. But it had.

She threw herself into the shower and washed fiercely, trying to rub off all traces of his hands from her skin.

Then she dressed and rushed for the door.

But the Great Degustator stopped her. "Take this," he said, handing her the enameled bucket wrapped in cheesecloth. "It's yours." And he added, "I hope that this will remain between us. The needs of the team are most important to me."

Boat grabbed the bucket handle and, wanting nothing more than to get away, ran out into the hall.

A gray-haired cleaning woman had rolled up the carpet runner and was washing the floor with a broom wrapped in a wet cloth.

"Granny, dear, tell me, for God's sake, where is Zalyzin?"

The cleaning woman looked up with eyes as huge and sad as Little Karabakh's. "No speak Russian," she said apologetically.

Boat took from her purse a newspaper clipping with Lyza's picture.

The cleaning woman nodded happily, leading Boat to the end of the hall, where she pointed her broom at a door.

"What if he has a woman in there?" The simple but awful thought shook Boat. "But why not? Why shouldn't he? If I could sleep with some guy just because he was there, like a drunken whore, why shouldn't he do the same thing?"

Her hand didn't dare knock, but scraped at the door.

She heard a noise from inside, but the door didn't open.

"He's with a woman."

But the door opened, and he was face to face with her, alone on the doorstep, wearing a raincoat and carrying a small suitcase. The sun from the hall window splashed his face and his hair sparkled and his eyes, as if warmed by the sun, turned from a hard and focused stare into an anxious, tender, loving, questioning gaze.

"What's the matter, Boat?" He backed into the room and threw his case on the floor. "What has happened to you?'

"I love you." She was shivering. "I love you. More than life."

Her teeth were chattering. The bucket handle slipped from her fingers. The bucket fell on its side and a sticky stream of black caviar dripped through the cheesecloth and onto the floor.

And suddenly Lyza saw how he had tormented her, saw what a bastard he had been, saw how much he loved her and pulled her close, for the first time in more than half a year, trying to warm her with his love, to bring her back to life, the life she loved less than him.

He almost missed the plane from Baku to the next game in Minsk. He and Boat agreed to meet in Moscow and never to part.

To Lyza's surprise, the Great Degustator's response was almost humane. "Well, I see a half-year was enough. You managed to give up your love for the sake of soccer. You passed the trial for a Great Player. You will be one. If you need a godfather for your firstborn, I'd be very happy."

The Great Degustator felt that every self-respecting man had to suffer pangs of conscience. He didn't overdo it, but sometimes he enjoyed it.

Three days later, before leaving for Moscow, the soccer team was celebrating the goalie's birthday at a restaurant in Minsk. The Great Degustator had allowed them to drink, but only beer.

Filled with partying and beer, Lyza and the team masseur went to the bathroom. And suddenly Lyza felt incredible pain, he even yelped.

"That's a familiar ring," the masseur said. "Any discharge?"

"Yes," Lyza muttered.

"What color?"

"Yellow."

"Looks like gonorrhea," the masseur said with the calm wisdom of one who knows. "Personally, the first time I had it, the pus was amber-colored. The second time, a dirty white. The worst was the third time, when I didn't notice anything for a long time."

In Moscow, Lyza took a taxi straight from the airport to Dr. Shneerson.

"Well, Mr. Panic of the Copulation Front, are you hopelessly ill again?" The doctor's eyes laughed over his pince-nez. "But actually, your visit is very timely. I just smashed the rear bumper on my car. Do you know how? In my own backyard, when I stepped on the gas instead of the brake as I was backing up. But luckily I have a patient who is prepared to turn the bumps of his love life into a bumper for my car."

But once he examined the weapon of sin, Dr. Shneerson grunted and sat down at the microscope.

"When did you last have relations?" He had switched from jokes to business.

"Four days ago."

"Well then, congratulations. Textbook gonorrhea. You've finally made it. You find what you seek."

"I love her, doctor," Lyza muttered in horror. "And she loves me. I know that."

"That happens," the doctor said with a shrug. "Don't make a big thing of it. You weren't a monk all this time, otherwise you wouldn't have been ringing my bell with trembling fingers so often. But man and woman are different animals. A man can be a good family man and a womanizer at the same time. A man can love one woman but always be ready to sleep with another. Men have rhinoceros skin, and it's hard for a woman to caress her way to his heart. The greatest love of a woman cannot change a man.

"Women are more subtly organized. Even the lowliest whore, once she is loved and respected, can become the most faithful wife in the world. A woman in love gives herself. Gives herself fully. For a woman it is unnatural to love one man and sleep with another. Most often they do it when they have been mortally insulted and hurt, out of revenge. Women sense the world not with their heads but through their nostrils, and they're always smelling the scent of another woman. And then they take revenge. But that does not mean that they were being unfaithful. We force them to be unfaithful. Do not insult this woman of yours. Bring her to me. And now, time for a shot in a soft place."

When Lyza arrived at the Aeroflot dormitory, fortunately no one else was in the room.

Boat had waited all day for him, worried that he would not come.

She was wearing a new dress that she had made, blue as her eyes and with a white collar. Around her neck was a leather thong with a few Baikal stones with holes in them, "chicken gods," which according to legend brought happiness. In the cloud of her white hair was a single cornflower. At the end of her strong, sturdy legs were silvery high-heeled sandals, on loan from a roommate who worked the international flights and so fragile-looking they seemed to be made of frost.

The table was set with a plate of sliced black bread, two glasses and two buckets — one of white enamel, filled to the brim with black caviar and with two aluminum soup spoons stuck in it, and the other an ordinary tin bucket, filled with ice and a bottle of the best Soviet champagne, from the Crimean New Light Winery.

In her chapped red fist, Boat held two tickets to *The Nutcracker* at the Bolshoi Ballet.

When Lyza, eyes downcast, told Boat what had happened, she didn't utter a word. She was stunned. The ballet tickets slid slowly from her open hand to the floor.

Then she leapt for the window, blindly breaking the glass with her face and hands, pulling the frame out of the wall.

Lyza flew at her from behind and held her, not letting her throw herself from the window. They struggled, rolling on the floor, the blood on her face and hands staining his face and hands. Finally, she stopped fighting, crawled into a corner and huddled there, sobbing softly.

Lyza did not insult her with a single word. He did not try to find out who the man was. But he was too young to forgive her.

He couldn't do anything with himself about it.

Lyza took Boat to see Dr. Shneerson and made no further attempt to see her. Then, as he was coming out of the locker room after a game one day, Lyza saw a man he had never expected to see at a soccer game or anywhere near one.

It was Dr. Shneerson.

"I don't know anything about this game, where twenty-two adult men spend an hour and a half kicking around one innocent ball, but I liked the way you play," the doctor said, taking him aside. "But I don't like the way you behave in love. Do you know that your girlfriend almost went crazy? She kept saying, 'I infected him, I infected him.' Who infected whom is still a question. You infected her. You threw her, drunken and miserable, into another man's filthy arms. She is without blame before you. I, Dr. Shneerson, whose bald head and pince-nez delved inside so many women, I tell you this. She is with her mother, at Lake Baikal. Go to her. Marry her."

But Lyza married another woman. The Great Degustator introduced him to a runway model from a fashion house. The Great Degustator needed her because she was the niece of the Chief of Sports. Besides which, she was his mistress, and he wanted to arrange her life and be able to keep her.

She sashayed down the runway, swaying her hips, modeling wedding dresses. Her name was Elvira, or just Elka.

She went to bed with Lyza easily the first time, but resisted the second. Lyza did not guess that she was following the advice of the Great Degustator. The coach wanted to hold on to his Great Player with a woman's arms. Like an experienced playwright, he had even written a line for her that helped her get Lyza.

"Won't I ever get to wear my own wedding dress?" She said it at the right moment, and like a pretty good actress, with a catch in her voice, but not overdoing it. The sentimentality that Lyza had not completely overcome did its work.

He married her, and found himself surrounded by a sports-world-black-market-car-repair-modeling-small-time-acting Bohemia, in which his name was an object of their favorite pastime—making a profit.

Through his apartment passed icons, antique paintings, crystal, porcelain, tape recorders, cartons of foreign cigarettes, mounds of jeans, and one time he found a cardboard box filled with French tickler condoms.

Lyza's real life existed only on the soccer field. His house was a black market trying to pass for high society.

Their son followed in his mother's footsteps and started selling American chewing gum in grade school.

Elka tried to guide Lyza's taste in his choice of friends, clothing, theater premieres and books. She even gave him soccer advice with such aplomb that one would think he had always missed and she had made all the goals.

Sometimes Lyza would recall, like something that had been stolen from him forever, the blue lantern eyes of the Siberian rock climber, who on a snowy night long ago had plucked a crystal icicle for him from a Kremlin tower.

And now she was here again, and in his arms. Slowly she lay down on the bed that had long forgotten women, and the hedgehog Chunya scrambled out from under the lacy white bra that fluttered over him as though made of cherry blossoms.

Boat, her still youthful breasts untouched by treacherous wrinkles, moved the two tiny mouths of her nipples towards the suddenly dry lips that had almost forgotten how to kiss. They loved each other with that special poignancy that comes only after a long separation and before another separation that might be forever.

And then his eyes became different, as if the blue lanterns had imparted their youthful sparkle, and cheerfully he broke the glass in the place of honor, pulled out the yellow Brazilian shirt with Pele's unwashed sweat, and put it on for the first time, preparing for the greatest match of his life. He also took his old Paris cap with the gilt Eiffel Tower on the lining, put Chunya in it, carried him to the park and released him in the grass.

"Well, Chunya, goodbye," Zalyzin said. "I don't know what may happen, so we'd better part now. And here's some advice. If you should fall in love with a young hedgehog and she loves you, don't be afraid, marry her, so that she can give you many little hedgehogs that look like the two of you. Don't repeat my mistake, when I missed the chance many years ago to marry this woman. But if we win today, I'll correct that mistake."

"Lyza, do you mean it?" Boat asked, hardly believing his words.

"Yes, I do," he said. "But please don't think that I don't love you. I've loved you all these years, and more than ever today."

Zalyzin put on the Parisian cap and, with the same street swagger as his plumber neighbor Van Gogh, strode off quickly to defend the Russian Parliament, far from perfect but still the Russian Parliament, arm in arm with a woman who had blue lanterns glowing in a white cloud of hair.

And only after their figures dissolved in the distance did Chunya cautiously enter the bushes, his little heart beating fast with fear of the outdoors which had become so unfamiliar, his button nose sniffing, searching for signs of other hedgehogs.

The First Day
And Other Days:
Fear

MY DOG WAS HOWLING LOUDER and louder, trying to jam TV announcements about the coup not very far from the Minsk highway. I heard the roar. It was armored fear crawling to Moscow.

Two things had caused me physical fear ever since childhood—the dark, and heights.

The dark was always like a huge shaggy beast ready to grab me in its clawed paws and suffocate me in its embrace. But if there were the tiniest bit of light in the dark, a person's eyes, a glowworm or *tsitsinatella*, the red tip of a cigarette, a star in the clouds or even a swamp light, however pale, then the fear passed.

Heights sweetly, murderously tugged at me, whether we came face-to-face on a cliff or a balcony, and they made a trembling chill grip my knees. Only a bird flying through that yawning emptiness could allay my fright.

But now, with the television spewing the nauseating past that brazenly and cravenly wanted to become the future, the fear was resurrected in me, the dark without a glimmer of a star and the drop at my feet without a single lark fluttering in it.

I did not feel that fear under Stalin because, fortunately, I was saved from it by my youth and stupidity. But I saw the fear in others, and they breathed it into my lungs. Just as one can have a predisposition to tuberculosis, our entire generation has a predisposition to fear. The people of the sixties, the *shestidesiatniki*, are a generation genetically predisposed to fear and have yet to begin to conquer it.

I felt that fear with my own skin in 1956, when on the morning after my birthday, my head throbbing with a hangover, I heard a brief, neat ring at the door, then another, longer one, a tactful reminder, and then yet another, an imperial demand for the door to be opened.

Opening the prerevolutionary iron hook in the entry, I saw on the porch of our wooden house on Fourth Meshchanskaya Street a sweetly smiling, round face, as shiny as a buttered pancake, with whitish eyebrows and a raspberry bald spot surrounded by whitish fluff.

The uninvited guest, remaining on the porch, stuck his closed fist into the entry and then opened it with a triumphant smile, like a magician very pleased with his own tricks.

In his pink palm lay the red identification book, the sight of which turns people, when faced with the identification of a snake, into rabbits, and causes them to lose the ability to resist. The book opened and closed so quickly that I could not remember the name.

"Happy belated birthday," the little man drawled sweetly. "We didn't want to bother you yesterday. But we need to talk. Could you visit us today?"

"When today?" I managed to say, feeling my legs turn to cotton at the edge of a cliff with so many bones at the bottom of the canyon.

"Right now," he replied energetically. "I have a car. We'll be there in ten minutes."

"Where?" I muttered.

"Lubyanka. The entrance is from Serov Alley. It's not far at all. Ten minutes and we're there."

My hungover brains barely functioned. Someone must have turned me in. For what? Must be for what I said the day before yesterday at the shash-lyk joint near the Literary Institute, when I called our tanks in Hungary a shameful thing. . . . But there were only a few of us at the table, and we were all friends, students. Or maybe it's because of that night last week when, after many bottles of Xhvanchkara at the Georgian restaurant—Aragvi, Volodya Gneushev and I were straggling home along Stanislavsky Street, and we saw a woman in a window beyond a cast-iron fence, slowly, seductively brushing her hair, and after we had climbed that fence with uncontrollable intentions, to our horror we saw a white, enameled sign in German on the building, and a foreign flag. Then, looking around, we saw the sentry box at the gates that we had managed to overlook. It was obviously an embassy or consulate. Luckily no one saw us and we slipped off. But what if we were seen, by cameras in the bushes, and now they had found us?. . . Or maybe it was for my poems? Which one? There was much hidden between the lines, yet not really hidden. It stuck out anyway. . . . Would they put me in jail? Would I vanish like my grandfather Ermolai in 1937? I don't know how and when he died. He must have been shot or tortured to death . . . by people like this one, with round, pancake faces and raspberry bald spots. They smile sweetly now. But what if it all starts again? I have to refuse to go now. At least, everything will be clear then. If they're going to arrest me anyway, they'll do it and bring me to the interrogation by force.

"I have a headache," I muttered.

"There can be no Russia without drink. . . . Understandable. If you didn't have a headache after your birthday, it would be ungodly somehow," the little man said with understanding, hinting at his own frequent miserable mornings after. "Then let's say noon, all right? I'll come by . . ."

"No, no," I said quickly. "I'll get there myself. Whom do I ask for?" My little ruse to get his name failed.

"Don't worry, you'll be met at the entrance," he drawled, glowing in anticipation of his imminent hospitality, and dissolved into the air of the era, the stuff of which he was made.

But that little man didn't know I was not alone.

In the next room, one of last night's guests was snoring soundly, a war poet who had played on the Stalingrad Traktor soccer team and who stayed the night, after his slightly Kalmuk eyes had shut tight at the table, rendering him unable to drive himself home. All my friends were older than I. He belonged to those rare few who are not boring during prolonged evenings of drink. If someone was talking too much, showing off too much or, on the contrary, panicking, he usually said with friendly, soothing mockery, "Take a rest."

I loved the way he talked and even the way he was silent and the way he sighed. His sigh was a coloratura, with many interruptions, like the creak of a well chain bringing up water from deep, mossy depths, reluctantly giving itself up to the bucket. Even now, in his sleep, he was not simply snoring, he was snoring in sighs.

I shoved him awake, told him my rambling story about the morning visitor with the red book, and that I had to go there, a place from which many did not return, at noon.

Will they put me away? I asked, not exactly with chattering teeth, but not joking either. We lived in a country where the arm of the institution that gave out red identification books could pull any person out at any time, as though he were a card in a deck, either a six, or an ace that immediately turned into a six.

He smiled heavily, hung over. "Ah, how they scared you. Not a drop of blood in your face. Take a rest. Don't be afraid, they won't arrest you. It's your luck, the times are different now. They are going to proposition you . . . ordinary recruitment."

My eyes popped. "Me? Recruit me?"

A vile relief played in my heart. They won't arrest me. But that joy was squashed by the thought that recruitment is worse than arrest. "Snitch" was the worst thing you could call someone in the eyes of my mother and father and friends on Fourth Meshchanskaya.

"They're recruiting everyone, renewing their cadres," my older friend informed me. He had written about war: "But it's better to come with an empty sleeve than with an empty soul." "They tried to recruit me, too. With the same method. The morning of New Year's Day. They know that a man with a hangover can be twisted however they want. You just listen to what they say. Let them talk. You keep quiet. Nod your head, like a Chinese mandarin. Let them think, 'Well, we got 'im, and with our bare hands, and still warm.' They'll want to break you, but you break them instead. And when they offer you work, don't give them a finger. They'll take your whole arm. Play the dumb lamb and bleat at them, 'Thank you for your priceless trust in me, but I am not worthy. If I happen to see a dastardly spy crawling through the rushes over the border into our Soviet Union, I'll come running to you, dear comrades, but you know writing poetry and also writing something for you at the same time, sorry, but it's too confusing, I'll screw it up for sure. . . . So please fire me.' In other words, put their famous vigilance to sleep. Get everything that you can learn out of them, and then scram. . . ."

At the entrance on the corner of Lubyanka Square, a hospitable and friendly face was waiting for me, a female one this time.

She looked like an ordinary, middle-class Russian woman, in a colorful print dress of crepe de Chine, white sandals and simple red earrings that were too big to be rubies. But her cheekbones were, I think, on the heavy side, like a boxer's, and I couldn't catch the expression in her eyes.

She started chattering instantly, but her voice was thick and military, and the prattle that was supposed to charm and tame me did not gibe with the timbre, and therefore it sounded rather false. She behaved as if back in the early days of her career she had been in charge of the children's room at a police station, where you had to use both clucking noises and a strong state arm. As she led me down endless corridors and opened a door leading into her small office with two jars on the desk—one containing a few pink and white carnations and the other a wide variety of candies—she never stopped her patter.

"We're so happy to see you here, Zhenya. . . . Believe me, you have more friends and admirers here than you do in the Writers' Union. They all envy you there. And why not—so young and already so popular. Have some candy, don't be shy. I'll confess a secret. I have a sweet tooth. Just recently we were all thrilled by your poem, 'Fighting for Soviet Power.' What memorable lines: 'You want to die for Grenada? Why don't you live for Grenada?'"

Her chatter lulled and relaxed me. She seemed like a close friend, practically a relative. It was all carefully calculated. First play on one's fear of the word "Lubyanka." It had been only three years since Stalin died, and "Lubyanka" was synonymous with torture, executions, disappearances. A summons to Lubyanka does not bode well. And suddenly, this homey friendliness. Instead of executioners, you find well-meaning fans. I'm certain that many people summoned to Lubyanka, terrified at first, fell for the unexpected tenderness. It was my great fortune that I had been warned by my friend about the meaning of that tenderness. Therefore I was prepared for the friendly approach, could play the game with the hidden advantage of knowing the enemy's next step.

The candy atop all the others in the jar was special, and certainly didn't sell by the pound. It looked like a little round chocolate hill and lay on a lacy paper ring, and was probably the last from a box. Of course, the box would have had a picture of birds pecking at juicy cherries hanging from a branch. Inside the chocolate was a real cherry, blissfully swimming in aromatic liqueur. My grandfather Ermolai had brought us a box just like that the last time I saw him before he was arrested.

Maybe he had been interrogated and beaten in this very room where I was being offered candy?

The crepe de Chine lady, apparently certain that she had prepared me to agree to anything—just as long as they didn't arrest me—led me to another, much roomier office. Seated at a desk was a man who was much higher in rank than she, because she stopped her chatter and stood at attention, which showed her officer training beneath the crepe de Chine, and then vanished.

The man didn't chatter at all and didn't practice any compliments. He studied me, not in a friendly way and not in a frightening way, but his two steel-blue eyes, heavy with information, drilled into me and made me very uncomfortable.

"Here in the Lubyanka, like everywhere else in the country, we are seeing great changes," he said, spacing out his words and maintaining the intensity of his gaze. "New people are in power. We are helping the Party fight with the remnants of the cult of personality. We are rehabilitating the unjustly convicted. This is something close to your heart, is it not? But among the people who give us information there are too many of the old cadres. They are used to saying only what people want to hear. Now they are at a loss. They do not understand what is wanted from them. And the only thing we want now is the truth because it is on the basis of our reports that the most important government decisions are made. We do not need informers. We ourselves despise them. We don't want denunciations, but what Pushkin called 'the mind's cold observation and the heart's bitter notes.' We need fresh, bold, sincere people, who could share their bitter notes on what people are thinking and thereby help the people. Is there anything shameful in that? What do you think?"

"I don't think," I said hastily and senselessly and then, remembering my older friend, I nodded like a Chinese doll.

"What don't you think?" The man was disturbed by my vagueness, and I felt his steel-blue drills cracking my ribs and piercing my intestines.

"Well, that it's, uh . . . shameful," I mumbled, and suddenly, in my fear as sticky as pond scum, I felt the play and flash, as though I were a strong fish trapped on a hook, as though I were back on the Siberian train platforms where, pretending to be an orphan, I sang for a piece of bread, "In a quiet town, Columbine lived with her friends." My desire to play with him and win flashed like a knife pulled from the top of a boot, like a soccer player who feints to the right in order to lure his opponent that way, and then suddenly rushes to the left and scores a goal past the welcoming, spread legs of the confused goalie. I decided to find out everything I could from him, and I started to play the game.

I straightened my shoulders and lowered my voice so that it had a confidential thickening and said, with a readiness that surprised the man, "How can there be shame in doing one's civic duty?"

The man, trying to hide his shock at such a swift turn of events and even, I think, disappointed that fine jeweler's work would not be necessary for this kid, grumbled, "It's nice to work with people who understand."

Then he paused and, apparently having lost all interest in me, promised casually, "We can help you, too."

"How?" I asked with heightened animation.

"Well, for instance, trips abroad. I don't believe you've been anywhere yet. . . . By the way, the people keeping you from traveling are your fellow writers, who blame it on us. Even your poems howl about not being allowed out: 'Borders bother me. It's embarrassing not to know Istanbul, Tokyo, New York.' Is that the quote?"

"'Not to know Buenos Aires, New York,'" I corrected.

"Is that it?" he said with a smirk. He had more trouble with smiles than with smirks. "But I hope you'll have no objection to seeing Tokyo and Istanbul?"

"How?" I asked, with unfeigned curiosity and with the feigned air of a man prepared to do whatever was necessary to get outside the country at least once.

"For a start, we'll help you get a job as a waiter on an international cruise," he offered, completely bored. Apparently, he liked cracking tough nuts. His teeth, though not blindingly white, were strong and big.

I suddenly remembered that some students from the Literary Institute had gone as waiters on a cruise to India last year, and immediately entered them on my presumed list of snitches.

"But the flow of information, naturally, must begin on solid ground first," he added and tried to smile pleasantly. "Like a publishing house. . . . You give us a manuscript and we give you an advance."

His dulled eyes showed some curiosity. How would I react to a direct sale?

I borrowed a bit of boredom from his face and played at hidden disappointment of a too-modest evaluation of my agreement. I began to bargain delicately, hinting with my facial muscles of an expectation of a raise for my patriotic readiness to inform the Homeland of dangers threatening it.

The man saw, not without professional pleasure, that I hadn't been bought as easily as he had disdainfully anticipated. He seemed to be interested once more, probably because he enjoyed playing only with a mouse that tried to escape his paws. Falling for my acting exercise and fearing that I might slip away, he added to the price, testing me with his steel-blue drills.

"You have an eloquent line: 'But where will I carry you?' Yes, young people sometimes have no place to go for love. Many people don't have a private apartment until they're old, and sometimes not even then. . . . But you're a poet, and judging from your poems, you tend to fall in love. . . . We could let you use a room at the Tsentralnaya Hotel from time to time. It's right near the actors' restaurant. You could feel completely free in that room. You could do some writing and have time for recreation. What's the point of youth if you won't have anything to remember? We're fighting against corruption, but corruption and hypocrisy are just two sides—"

"— of the same coin," I completed his thought, confidentially, as though we were like-minded men. I pretended to be delighted, looking forward to my modest orgies in the hotel, where the golden key to a private room would be handed to me by the KGB itself, the only institution in the country that had a sympathetic solution to my tormented question, "Where will I carry you?" now slightly expanded from the original to "Where will I carry them all?"

"And what will I have to do?" I asked, playing at being a bought informer-intellectual.

The man, who had just carelessly blown the cover of his snitches from the Literary Institute, went on revealing his cards, certain that we had a deal. "First of all, we want steady information on the mood of writers as well as scholars and students with whom you are close. There's a concrete job as well. Next year Moscow will host a World Youth Festival. It's time, of course, to take down the iron curtain. But . . . it's too soon to turn it into scrap metal. There will be more foreigners here all at once than there were in the USSR over the last thirty years. Some will bring their socialist hearts"—here he chuckled—"and some will bring syphilis and still others, disgusting literature. We are not against a thaw, just against slush. The more freedom there is, the more control over that freedom is necessary. You can't let history take its own course. Who will deal with all the festival's guests— the black, yellow, brown and polka-dotted? There will be young writers from the capitalist countries among them. Take care of them. Join them in restaurants, have heart-to-heart talks with them. We are interested in what they think. As Mayakovsky used to say, 'Communism is the youth of the world, and young people are the ones to build it.' By the way, you'll have an expense account . . . for champagne. I believe that's your favorite drink?"

"How did you know that?" I feigned shy simplicity.

"Well, we're supposed to know a thing or two," he joked glumly, and no longer respecting me now that he had a done deal.

He hurried up our conversation, pointedly looking at his watch. "So . . . for mutual convenience you will receive a new name, and when you contact us, use it. We'll be in touch." He stood, letting me know the audience was over.

His steel-blue drills stopped working. He was certain that they had drilled through me.

I rose also and also did not offer my hand. But I saw that I had overdone the acquiescence, and it was time to turn the chess board before I was pushed into a corner.

"Excuse me, but I have a question," I said, still very docile.

"Well?" He sensed something was wrong, and the cartilaginous wings of his nose twitched and tensed.

"Is the new name you want to give me a code name?"

"Why put it so coarsely?" He shrugged and tried to allay my fears with a warm, friendly smile. But the smile couldn't break through to his face, now frozen with the realization of his unforgivable mistake. "It's a professional usage, a type of password."

"No, it's a code name," I said. "Nothing else. And I'm a sensitive person. I can go off my nut and forget which is my real name and which I'm supposed to use to call you and which one I use to sign my poems. Besides which, I'm absolutely incapable of keeping secrets. I'm right off that poster, 'A chatterbox is a find for a spy.' I'll never be a spy."

"We're intelligence agents, not spies," he said grimly, trying to keep this from going wrong, drilling his eyes into the floor since there was no point in drilling them into me.

"I'm sorry," I said. "I'm afraid that I'll be so proud to have your trust that I'll be shouting about it from every rooftop. I know myself. Modesty, alas, is not one of my many flaws."

"Well, we never suspected you of modesty," he said, irritated but still trying to joke.

"Really, thank you for your trust. But I must refuse because I am afraid that I will not be on the level of your . . ." —and I stopped to find the right word— "your high demands. Let me add one thing. You insulted me. You really did."

"How?" he asked, his eyes still lowered with the sadness of being outdone by a boy.

"Do you really need to pay in order to save Russia from danger—with cruises and hotel rooms and champagne money? Aren't there any people who are ready to save their Homeland for free?" I asked seriously.

This time he couldn't even manage a smirk. He replied with a sad, multi-stepped sigh, which resembled the sigh of the former soccer player from Stalingrad who had coached me for this game with the KGB. Judging by the sigh, his life wasn't easy either.

He understood that even though I had overplayed, I had won, and when he looked up, I saw something like rueful respect in his eyes. He knew that further persuasion was useless.

"Sign that you will not reveal anything about our conversation," he said dryly. I signed because I didn't know that you didn't have to sign.

As I left, he unexpectedly offered me his hand. He was more angry with himself than with me. He tried to smile.

But it didn't work.

That day I had conquered my own fear, the fear that made my knees freeze at the word "Lubyanka," the fear of the gigantic foot of a giant state, calloused from squashing people, near which, as in *The Thief of Baghdad*, was a hot frying pan on the desert sands.

I once wrote, "Fears are dying in Russia." But I was wrong. Fears inculcated in childhood do not die. They merely hide. There is nothing more humiliating than the fear of your own fear. I never hated anything in my life as much as my own fear.

This hated fear of mine returned in 1962 when, in order to keep the intelligentsia from being too free and easy, a risk-taking but sly and fearful peasant shook his fist at it.

It happened at a banquet — itself a form of mockery — held in the government's reception palace following an avant-garde art exhibition. Khrushchev had frightened himself. It was as though the first, green shoots of his "thaw" were really devilish faces, peeking up through the soil that had been trampled by the boots of guards. While avenging himself for the cream pie that the Boss with his shaggy, dried-up left hand once slipped under his rear end, Stalin's posthumous exposer from time to time still clutched at his trousers with the generalissimo stripes as if they were his mama's skirts.

The raised fist and the furious face were both the color of crazed borscht. Even his warts filled with blood and jumped with anger; at artists; at writers and all others who got in the way of major politics; at politics; and even at himself, because he shook his fist but politics shook him. The fist resembled his face, and his face the fist. The fist, so infuriated that the reddish hairs on it stood on end, smashed into the cloth of a banquet table, greasy from shashlyk, upon which his toadies had set up dangerous sculptures, and the face roared to sculptor Ernst Neizvestny: "If you don't like your country, get your passport and get away! Only the grave will straighten the hunchback!"

It was scary because the fist wielded enough power to send missiles to Cuba aboard grain ships or to build the Berlin Wall. But I conquered that fear too, and banged my own fist on the table and managed to shout through the viscous clay that sealed my mouth, "No, the time has passed when people were corrected by the grave!"

Was it the fear of a former slave who had become master of one-sixth of the planet that made him bang his fist on a banquet table, making the sculptures tremble from the blows, or bang his shoe on the table at the United Nations, the metal tips of the laces painfully lashing the fresh-shaven cheeks of his own minister of foreign affairs and shocking the spoiled nostrils of diplomats with the strong odor of peasant feet?

Khrushchev's fear was not misplaced.

He was pensioned off by the very people he had tried to impress with his show of severity toward the intelligentsia. While he had shouted like an oaf, he did not allow new trials or psychiatric hospitals for dissidents. That was done by the imposing, teary-eyed Brezhnev, who never raised his voice in public, and Andropov, who wrote sonnets.

When the coffin of the most celebrated *muzhik* (peasant) in history, who had dared to remove Stalin from the Mausoleum and who, drunken and proud with damp eyes, had kissed the first earthling to return from space, was placed modestly and without fanfare in the funeral hall beside the Kuntsevo Hospital, only relatives, foreign correspondents and KGB agents came to honor him. However, across the asphalt path that led to the hospital, a small crowd had gathered, primarily people who worked in the government hospital where only the select few could be treated or do the treating.

There were nurses, wildly made up and smelling of French perfume, which they could buy cheaply at the kiosk in the hospital; red-faced cooks, who carried away as much leftover sturgeon and black caviar as did Bulgakov's *maître d'hôtel* Archibald Archibaldovich during the fire; full-breasted, medal-bearing masseuses with the hands of tender stranglers, specialists in osteochondrosis and in elevating the limp towers of Pisa of the *nomenklatura*; gray-haired nurse's aides with varicose veins on their legs, who spoke three or four languages; former KGB beauties from embassies; janitors, retired majors and colonels who swept sand from the paths of the still-walking remnants of a glorious past; boiler stokers, who secretly chugged fifteen-year-old Eniseli cognac, stolen from the hospital warehouse, which the doctors prescribed for improving circulation; dishwashers who drove to work in their own Zhigulis, stuffing the trunks with feed for their small, private pig farms. They all stood in a herd, pressing close and shuffling their feet, whispering, but not moving closer.

It wouldn't have been any trouble to cross the path and enter the funeral hall, to create the appearance of a crowd and to bid farewell to the peasant from Kalinovka, who had recently been heard around the world to promise to catch up to and surpass America and to bury capitalism. But instead, they were burying him, stealthily, looking over their shoulders, without the state honors that were due him.

The distance from the curiosity seekers to the entrance of the funeral hall was no more than ten yards, but there was no sign of any attempt to buck up and take those few steps, to stand at the coffin's side in silence and think, for there were things to think about.

But those few steps could bear a heavy price. While the militia was not stopping anyone or asking to see documents, and while there were no barriers, no signs, nor even a hint at a ban, there were no orders to enter the funeral hall, or even permission to do so. And those people were used to living by the principle that what is not expressly permitted is forbidden.

Those ten yards were asphalted with an even, gray, fine-grained fear and flattened by many steel rollers.

All the people composing that craven crowd were workers in *nomenklatura* health and had to go to work the next day, where their friend, the administrator of the Taganka Theater, who promised a couple of tickets to *The Master and Margarita*, had asked for some Swiss medicine from the hospital's self-service pharmacy for his long-suffering prostate; and the chief of the shoe department at GUM—where, by the way, they were expecting a shipment of crocodile shoes from Brazil—was hinting openly for a French silver spiral for "down there"; and the sovereign of the *kvass* kiosk at the Kiev Station demanded a dozen cans of crab meat from the hospital's canteen for her sixtieth birthday; and their well-read nephew was nagging for a novel about the corruption of the tsar's court from the hospital's book outlet. The last Bolsheviks enjoyed reading about the last Romanovs.

But what if you come to work in the morning with all those requests on your mind, hand your pass to the guard, and he says with the creak of a robot speaker, "Your pass has been rescinded. Sorry."

And that could happen simply because you crossed a ten-yard road. Why cross?

Fear was stronger than curiosity. Fear was stronger than Christian charity to forgive and to bid farewell. This was an unknown unconscious fear, inexplicable, not inculcated and not instructed—a fear of the absence of instruction, of not being told what to do.

But they wanted to see, at least from afar. Who wouldn't want to feel part of history by looking at it from a safe distance?

In general, I consider fear to be a normal human feeling. The fearless fanatic is a pathological manifestation. Overcoming fear through your conscience is a greater exploit than being a fearless kamikaze. But there is a special fear that is in your spinal column, a servile fear, and there is something servile even in overcoming it.

And that damned servile fear lives in me and in all of us, like an infection that will be under our skins forever. Our blood must consist of red and white corpuscles, and black corpuscles of fear. Servile fear may masquerade as politics, or ideology, or patriotism, or romanticism, or life wisdom or so-called love of life; but whatever you call it, it is animal fear, the instinct for self-preservation trying to replace conscience. Even victory over your own servile fear does not bring happiness, because the fact that you have to keep fighting that fear is not heroism but humiliation.

And on the morning of August 19, 1991, after my dog Bim, howling over his shaggy love separated from him by a fence, did not let me sleep all night, I was picked up by the scruff of my neck by the casual thieving hand of history and tossed into the fear of a modern-day Akaky Akakiyevich, from the short story of Gogol—whose freedom, still unaccustomedly new and uncomfortably tight in the arms, is being stolen like a much-longed-for overcoat.

". . . To run the country and efficiently establish the emergency measure, a State Committee on Emergency Measures (GKChP USSR) is formed with the following members . . ."

I always have a quick run at dawn with my two dogs. The morning of the coup was no exception. As usual, I took the simple-hearted, piebald heavyweight Bim, exhausted by his unrequited love, and Moroz, the borzoi aristocrat who was almost indifferent to the ladies and who resembled a four-legged snowy cloud, as thin as a bookmark in the hunting pages of Tolstoy or Turgenev.

I ran, through the still-wet morning forest pierced by stripes of shadow and morning light, the golden rays between trees occasionally peopled by bent old women wandering in search of mushrooms. Their gray sticks, rustling in the fallen leaves and pine needles, also began to glow, and the mushrooms they pulled from beneath aspens and birches glowed in response through the needles, leaves and ants adorning their caps.

A silvery web with butterflies trapped in it swayed noiselessly between peeling trunks, and the only sounds were the soft footfalls of the old women, the crunch of the path beneath my running shoes, the panting of both dogs, the businesslike rattle of a woodpecker, the chirp of crickets, the light buzz of a few gnats, the soft roar of tree tops, the distant cry of a baby and the even more distant horns of commuter trains.

But I still heard the names, listed by the television announcer, of the men who had taken on the illegal right to decide the future of that invisible child crying beyond the trees.

Damn it. . . . There was the fear again . . . not because of the names, but their positions. Those people had the army, the KGB, the MVD, the Council of Ministers and the military-industrial complex in their hands— the whole web of the state, in which all our hopes, like trapped butterflies, might end up struggling. It was a conspiracy of mediocrities. And the President had appointed all of them himself.

Gorbachev had been so stubbornly adamant that his vice-president be that brazenly craven, former Communist Youth League busboy, who used his eyebrows with Brezhnevian coquetry and who, incapable of handling dishes with his shaking hands, had now appointed himself *maître d'hôtel*. During the confirmation hearings he was asked about his health, and he replied with a gross chuckle, "Well, my wife hasn't got any complaints." Twice he failed to get a majority in the Parliament and was then pushed through by some backstage machinations.

And the President had so stubbornly held on to his cloying, insinuating, rosy-cheeked head of the KGB, nicknamed Cherubino. Was he afraid of the dossier they had on him, left over from his university and Stavropol days?

And he had played up so pathetically to the talentless generals, who hadn't even had a plan prepared for bringing back the troops from the Baltics and Eastern Europe because, with their meager imaginations, they couldn't even imagine that this, and not Communism, was the inevitability. Had the President really forgotten what came of Allende's self-assuring vows about how much he trusted the Chilean generals?

But what if he had decided to step aside for a while, and get everything done by their hands? No, that couldn't be. . . . But why not? He had given such an ugly answer when asked about the bloodshed in Lithuania, when the Black Berets took the television tower in Vilnius. He said he didn't know who had given the order. He had to know. And if he really didn't know, that was just as shameful.

And he must have known about the order to send tanks into Tbilisi, when teenaged Georgian girls died trying to escape from gas and soldiers' shovels. But he said that he had been asleep after a trip abroad and knew nothing. And maybe this was the same thing. There was no conspiracy, but an agreement, and the President was merely removing himself to the sidelines to appear uninvolved. . . .

But wait a minute, what was happening to me? What right did I have to be suspicious without any evidence? Hadn't I been suspected of things of which I was innocent? Didn't I know how insulting and painful that was?

Wasn't he the man who removed the atom bomb from the pendulum that swung between the United States and the USSR, saving us all from a third and probably final world war? Wasn't he the man who stopped the Afghan intervention, who returned Sakharov from exile, who did away with censorship and decided to have the first more-or-less-normal elections?

When at the First Congress I idealistically raised my voting card at the podium and called on the others to vote for the repeal of Deputies' Rooms, otherwise known as VIP lounges, in airports and railroad stations — privileged islands in a roiling sea of people sleeping on the floor — to my bitter surprise only a few red flames of other voting mandates lit in raised hands. Moreover, I saw among these "servants of the people," nervous faces, eyes tense with all the perks taken or gloomy from not having had enough perks, who looked at me with such hatred you would think I were all the Trotskyites, Zionists, agents of imperialism and Interregional Group members rolled into one. My mandate, raised almost hopelessly, was beginning to burn my wearying but still waiting arm. It was a pause of defeat.

And then something happened. Those very "servants of the people," who had hissed and booed Sakharov at the congress, suddenly wore faces of obedient, even toadying expressions, reached into their breast pockets and hurriedly waved their mandates in the air. The Kremlin Palace was turned from a barren semidesert into an alpine meadow covered with thousands of crimson poppies. I looked around in shock for the cause of this miracle, and saw that the all-powerful General Secretary, not yet the President, had, with a smile, raised his mandate in support of my proposal.

Even though he could be nasty when angry and did not know how to hide it, charming smiles came easily to him.

Once he called me at my dacha—and not for any political reason. "My wife and I were rereading your selected works, and we found so much there that we still remember from our youth. After all, we're of the same generation. Caught a piece of the war, and sang songs about Stalin in school, and then . . . and then . . . the time came for other songs. My wife and I heard you read the first time in a student canteen. Poetry helped us rethink many things. . . . And then there was an unhappy autumn we had. We went to the seaside out of season and took many books with us, especially poetry. . . . It poured and it was cold, but we huddled in blankets and read poetry aloud to each other, the poets of your generation. Excuse myself, our generation. . . ."

Yes, he did talk like that—"excuse myself" instead of "excuse me" and "lie it down" instead of "lay it down," and he never could pronounce "Azerbaijan." But he was the only man in the entire history of the Russian Empire who allowed his countrymen to criticize him and even insult him, an opportunity that they used with great pleasure.

He turned red with shame, but bore it, when he had to hear this parliamentary pearl from a cabbie who, in a heavy Ukrainian accent, proudly demanded he be called a "transportation provider": "And what can you say, Mikhail Sergeyevich, to the fact that many of my passengers compare you with Napoleon and your little woman, Raisa, with Empress Josephine, whose heel you are under?"

This "transportation provider" had run into the President in the corridor of the Kremlin Palace during a break, and from the calloused hands of the incorruptible defender of proletarian interests fell a package, from which scattered about a dozen pairs of newly purchased socks. The driver defended himself from any imagined suspicions of his corruptibility and aggressively attacked the President. "Well, Mikhail Sergeyevich, you probably think that I'm getting all this for me, using my deputy badge for profit?"

"I don't think anything," said Gorbachev, trying to pass the driver from one flank or the other, but either way bumping into his outspread arms waving the South Korean one-size-fits-all socks, which he had hastily picked up as if they were proletarian signal flags.

"No, you *are* thinking, and thinking nastily, and in vain. We are the working class, not any of those cooperative speculators. I bought these socks not in some Party shop or from under the counter, but in Iraq, with my hard-earned deputy travel funds, and brought them with me to the Parliament because I'm off to Kharkov on the train right from here because the voters are waiting for me. And all these socks aren't just for me — I've only got two feet! — they're for the guys down at the taxi park. These yellow ones with Mickey Mouse are for my cab partner, Sevka Andryushchenko, and these green ones with cowboys are for Levka Pridykhalsky, the electrician . . ."

"Uh-hum," muttered the President and, backing away from the implacable reality of the people he had awakened politically, ran with grim concentration in the other direction.

"Now these white ones with tennis rackets are for the cleaning woman, Manyukha," said the driver, hurrying after him. "She has to lose fifty pounds and the doctor told her to take up tennis. I brought her a racket from Libya, but they have a problem there with tennis balls, like we do. Why is it that whenever a nation rises against world imperialism, they have one problem after another with goods? It's sabotage, that's what it is. . . . Mikhail Sergeyevich, where are you going? Can you help me get at least a couple of tennis balls for Manyukha? Are you avoiding an answer yet again, Mikhail Sergeyevich? . . . Oh no, Comrade President, you can't turn your rear end on the working class. . . . The mouse's tears will haunt the cat . . ."

How can we wonder why the proclaimer of democracy, mud flung at him from all sides, sometimes feared only one thing — that by some freak accident his proclamation would come to pass.

And that fear made him make his biggest mistake. He was frightened by universal, direct elections, and became president by bypassing the people, and he lost his last chance to be elected by all nations.

And he had had that chance.

I have two tiny notes from him.

At the Second Congress a rising young general attacked me with full firepower from the podium, accusing me of disrespect for Parliament and my own people. I was furious and, forgetting that this condition is contraindicated for speeches, sent a note to the President, who was chairing the congress, in which I asked for the floor.

He sent me a reply on a piece of paper from a pad. It was very brief. "Tomorrow! M. Gorbachev." His eyes smiled soothingly.

I worked on my speech all night, trying to let the young general have it — artistically.

The next day the President called on one speaker after another, but I did not seem to exist.

I wrote again, "Mikhail Sergeyevich, where is your 'tomorrow'?" He sent me a sly, and perhaps even symbolic, message. "Your tomorrow will be tomorrow! M. Gorbachev."

That gave me another chance to have my speech in full battle readiness. I came up with a new opening, one that was not annoyed but politely telling: "Esteemed young general!"

So Mikhail Sergeyevich had helped me, by reasonably allowing my anger to cool. And where was he now? How could I help him?

No, he couldn't have conspired with these men. He was different. They must have interpreted his indecisiveness and ambivalence as approval, and probably they had hoped that he would join them as soon as they had done their work. They must have counted on him to join them and, if he didn't, they had one way out — to announce that he was incapable and to use neuroleptic injections to bring him to a condition that would make any U.N. medical commission drop its hands. They wouldn't dare kill him — though, who knows. . . . The world community? No, they'd squirm and then swallow it. The damned world community would be chided, simply and confidentially, as an atom bomb (created by Sakharov, incidentally) tapped delicately upon the table: "After all, he's our president, not yours. And we can do whatever we want with him . . ."

What reformer in Russia did not become either the victim of his reforms or . . . or their destroyer?

These were my thoughts as I ran through the woods in Peredelkino that morning, jumping over the powerful veins of roots crossing the path. Suddenly, in a green tunnel of trees I saw a figure running towards me in a red, faded T-shirt and shorts that had lost all semblance of color, legs pumping away, not bulky but impressive, covered with a golden pelt, and huge feet in sneakers.

There was a radiant glow around his head, as in illustrations from the prerevolutionary Christmas issue of *Niva*. As he came closer I saw that the light didn't surround his head, but reflected off it, and therefore wasn't a halo.

It was a reddish, shiny bald spot, onto which nature had tossed a handful of freckles and surrounded them with the remains of once-luxuriant curls like a golden wreath.

There was only one such bald head in all of Peredelkino, and it represented a direct threat of a goal when it came in contact with a soccer ball when we played with the local kids in the meadow. The owner of the bald head was called Bubukin because of his resemblance to the once-famous head of a player of that name on the Moscow Locomotive team.

As he came even with me, Bubukin did not stop as he usually did, but merely said, as if it were so obvious that there could be no doubt, "Sorry, old man, I'm rushing for the train. So, I'll see you at the White House, on the barricades."

Is It Far
To The Prison?

A LIVE BUTTERFLY ORNAMENTED the dead hot-line, its wings—chocolate, with white, gold and emerald swirls and a peacock eye—stirring.

"Grandpa, look what I have." His youngest granddaughter pressed close to him, a deck of cards in her hand—a guard's idea of an appropriate toy. "This is the king, and this is the jack, and this card is, oh, I forgot . . ."

"A ten," the President prompted.

"What's that, Grandpa?"

"It's a way of counting." He pointed out the window. "See, there are navy ships in the sea. Let's count them. One ship, two ships . . . ten ships makes a ten."

"Grandpa, there are more than ten ships," his granddaughter said.

"You're right, there are. Sixteen in all," the President told his granddaughter, and thought, Isn't that too many? If the coup succeeds, they'll say they were guaranteeing my isolation to keep me from fleeing by sea. But if it fails, they'll justify it and say they were protecting me from attack by sea. . . . Double accounting. And what politician hasn't done double books? If I hadn't, I wouldn't be president.

The butterfly flew off the telephone that never did come to life.

From outside came the sound of hands slapping a ball. The off-duty guards were playing volleyball.

Well, and what are they supposed to be doing, praying? They're actually behaving rather well, he thought. And if the order is given to liquidate me or to pump me full of drugs, I wonder if they'll defend me? They seem to enjoy keeping the ball in midair too much. . . . Jack London wrote about love of life. But he forgot that love of life could turn into cowardice and betrayal. . . . After all, I loved my Czech friend, my roommate in the college dorm, Zdenek. We stayed up so many nights talking about how things had to change. But they started perestroika in Prague, and we squashed it with our tanks. And I never spoke up then. I hid all my progressive thoughts in a dark trunk, and later, when I came to Prague in a delegation, I drank Pilsner and ate Spekacki with the people who betrayed Dubcek and my friend Zdenek. I was afraid to stick my neck out. Actually, I did, but only in the general direction. And if I hadn't been careful, I'd never have been a politician. Of course, that might have been for the better. I wouldn't have had this good luck of being neither president nor — what am I now? — prisoner. It's like the song we enjoyed singing in our youth: "Payment for mistakes is also hard labor." What is it that's rotten in the very nature of politics? You have to betray in order to stay in the game. . . . Maybe my comrades, sensing that they were about to be tossed out, decided to betray me before I could betray them, and that's the whole secret of this coup?

"Grandpa, this morning I heard Grandmother tell Mama that we were in prison and then she cried."

"Grandmother is exaggerating."

"What's exaggerating?"

"That's when things are not as bad as they seem," he replied and patted his granddaughter's head sadly, thinking, will they have to live in their childhood everything that we lived through in ours?

Suddenly he heard an exhausted, almost forgotten voice that always lived within him. Is it far to the prison?

A hawk careened over the hot Stavropol steppe, waiting for a groundhog or field mouse to peek out of its hole.

But in the thirties, people vanished in uncounted numbers and so did mice, like water into parched soil. People and mice had nothing to eat; people because almost everything they had down to the last grain was taken by the workers' and peasants' state, whose long arm reached even here, to the former refuge of runaway serfs; and mice because people couldn't leave anything in the fields or granaries.

Therefore people sometimes trapped and ate groundhogs and mice, and then the hawks, the eternal patrollers of their mother steppe, had nothing to eat.

This hungry hawk, high over the steppe, was losing sight of the horses that until recently had raised merry sparks with their shoes on the road. The horses, without which the very concept of steppe was impossible, were also vanishing. Horses, like people, were being forced into kolkhozes, where the people somehow survived, but the horses were dying, because if a horse is not your own but everyone's, then it is no one's, an orphan. Now there were new "iron horses," tractors, lauded in the newspapers and in song, but they didn't neigh beautifully or stretch out in the wind when they ran, their flying manes braided with wild flowers. They couldn't rest a smart face on a farmer's shoulder and rub a silky equine cheek with trembling veins against the man's bristly beard. The iron horses also were held in common—that is, were no one's—and they broke down often because they were made clumsily and driven by careless hands.

And now, the hawk saw a solitary tractor crawling along a field near the village of Privolnoe, which had gotten poorer during collectivization, but was still alive, unlike many neighboring villages. The tractor sneezed, jerked and stopped.

"Well, sonny, it looks like we're done for," said a still-quite-young tractor driver with a boisterous pompadour beneath his greasy cap to his little boy, three or four years old, sitting in his lap. The boy put his little hands on the wheel next to his father's, which seemed huge and black.

"Pa, I want to drive," the boy whined, holding onto the burning hot but enticing wheel.

"You want many things," his father said with a chuckle, gently but firmly unfastening the scratched and pockmarked fingers holding tight to the wheel. "What's the point of driving something that's not moving?"

His father pulled him out of the cab and set him down barefoot on the hot steppe soil. The boy's feet were not city feet and were used to the ground.

"Get back, lad."

The father opened the steaming hood, wrapped a cloth around his hand and pulled the cork from the radiator. He barely managed to jump back before a fountain of rusty steam burst forth.

"The machine is mad," his father said, shaking his head.

"At who, Pa?"

"At us, boy. We overheated it. Looks like the motor's stuck."

When the tractor's roar, which had obliterated everything else, stopped, the music of other sounds was resurrected—the vibrating hum of bees, crickets, cicadas and all sorts of other tiny flying creatures not collectivized, the chirp of skylarks, the piteous croak of frogs in dying ponds, the crackling quiver of immortals, the light trembling of gray stands of wormwood, the rustling movement of tumbleweed which needed almost no wind. They could hear snakes rubbing their skins over dry ground and the soaring hawk occasionally moving the shimmering heat with its wings.

It seemed that somewhere close a *bandura* (lyre), forgotten a few centuries ago by a wandering blind musician, lay on the ground and its strings, intertwined with dodder vines, softly played the remembered songs of the Cossacks who had sought freedom here since the days of Catherine the Great.

But that barely restored soft music of the steppe was drowned once again by the clanging and creaking of humankind.

The father had stuck his head into the gleaming metal innards of the tractor and worked there with his wrenches.

The son was not interested in the innards. The only thing he was interested in was the wheel, which he stared at longingly with greedy eyes. The black circle of the wheel was the most desired sweet of his childhood, and he liked licking it with the tip of his tongue, even when it was hot. The wheel was so simple and so wise. You turned it to the right, and the whole big tractor would obey the comparatively tiny wheel. If you wanted to go left, it would obey that, too. And if you held it straight, it would go forward and knock down everything in its path.

The father, tugging at the shirt sticking to his tanned body, tried to start the tractor with a metal crank, but no sounds came from the apparently dead machine.

And suddenly there was a sound, alien to the triumphantly resounding music of the steppe. It did not emanate from the tractor, though, but, mockingly, from above, in the sky shimmering in its own heat.

Low over the steppe a crop duster flew, without any reason but the banner hanging from its belly—"Kulak agents to Siberia!"

"Pa, what does that say?" the boy asked.

"Learn to read. Then you won't bother your father all the time," his father replied reluctantly.

"Pa, do planes have a wheel, too?"

"Yes. Let's walk home." The father took the boy by the hand and led him, feet sinking in the plowed earth, to the road.

First the boy's bare feet were in black socks of soil, but when he stepped onto the road, the socks changed color. They were ashen with dust.

"Will somebody steal the tractor?" The boy looked back with a sigh.

"Nowadays nobody has the strength to steal a chicken, much less a tractor. And you have to find a chicken first."

But the boy kept up his questions about wheels. "Pa, does a ship have a wheel?"

"Yes, it does."

"And a steam engine?"

"Steam engines, too. Not a wheel exactly, but like . . . levers."

"Pa, why does a train need a wheel? It's on tracks, and you can't get away from them."

"The tracks have forks and sidings. The engineer is the driver. One can't manage without wheels and drivers anywhere."

"Does the world have a driver?"

"The whole world? No, not yet. But our country does. You're a big boy. You should know that."

"Uncle Stalin."

"Right. And who was the driver before him?"

"Lenin."

"Good boy. When you grow up, you'll be a driver, too. First of a tractor, and then, maybe of a *kolkhoz*, like your grandfather, and then . . . and then. . . . Who knows? It's all up to you."

And so they walked down the road. The boy stopped his father and pointed to another rusted tractor, obviously abandoned a long time ago, cannibalized and resembling a skeleton covered with weeds.

"Pa, did that iron horse die?"

"It did, poor old thing."

"But why isn't it buried in the ground?"

"You only bury real horses in the ground. Unless they're made into sausage, the way they are now."

"And what does the ground do with the horses?"

"They turn into earth themselves."

"And then?"

"And then grass grows out of them."

"And other, living horses eat that grass?"

"I guess so," replied his father, amazed that he hadn't thought of this before.

"But grass for horses won't grow from a buried tractor?"

"No, it won't," his father said with a smile and patted his son's curls, which didn't completely cover the dark birthmark on his head, which caused the local kids to tease him. "But you can make another tractor from an old one. Or a tank."

And they stopped talking. Coming straight at them and taking no notice of them was a rickety old man, barefoot, with his used but still-useful boots slung on a pole over his shoulder, wearing blue trousers with red stripes rolled up his shins, a Cossack cap with a band that showed an unfaded oval where the cockade had been, and carrying on his back a pack, worn by time and events, that seemed empty.

Only when he bumped into the father and son did the old man notice them, stop and ask, "Is it far to the prison, good folk?"

"Which one do you want, grandfather? Are you carrying a parcel for someone?" the father asked.

"Doesn't matter which, just so it's close. I'm the parcel myself. I'm handing myself over to the authorities. I've got a pass."

"You're not mixing things up, are you grandfather?" The father couldn't understand.

The old man took a linen cloth from his shirt pocket. In the cloth was a neatly folded district newspaper, with two photographs on the front page; at the top, a large one of Stalin raising a warning finger and, smaller and lower down on the page, the threatening regional Party secretary, Sheboldayev, waving his revolutionary fist ruthlessly at kulaks he still hadn't destroyed. His name was used as a bugaboo for children. "Watch it. If you cry, Sheboldayev will come and send you to Siberia." And inside that newspaper was the important document, a heavily lined page from a school notebook. On one side were mathematics problems, and on the reverse side were illiterate scrawls made by a pen that left many blots.

TO ANY PRISON IN NORTH CAUCASUS REGION

In view of the loss of horse and manpower the vicious kulak agent Iona Shikhirev (b. 1861) is being sent on his own recognizance to prison in the class struggle. This agent of the world bourgeoisie treacherously kept his noninventoried colt named Gnedko from the happy labor at the kolkhoz, provocatively wore tsarist medals on revolutionary holidays and despite the shame of his Pioneer grandchildren, who bravely alerted us about this, kept a picture of the enemy of collectivization, known under the name Jesus Christ, in his house. Therefore I ask he be put in any institution with free space.

— GPU executive Skrynuyk

"But, grandfather, this must be a mistake," he said, returning the letter.

"No mistake, good man," the old man said and smiled kindly, as if the driver were just as little as the boy holding onto his greasy pants. "They're going through our village for the third time. The first time was with a rake, then with a fine-tooth comb — like when you look for lice — and now with a scraper. Sheboldayev came and shouted, 'We'll send whole villages to Siberia until we're rid of all the kulak contras!' So I'm getting rid of myself. But why did they expel my grandchildren from the Pioneers? They had denounced me already. They're clean in the eyes of Soviet power in that case. . . . Will they take them and exile them, too? . . . So, is it far to the prison? I'm wandering around for three days, and all the jails have people stuffed in them like fish in a barrel. No room, they all say. I have to get behind bars quickly. I have to or they may take me for a fugitive, and it won't be any easier for my grandchildren."

"Go to Stavropol, grandfather," the father said in a small voice. "They'll figure it out there." Then he lowered his head and strode off silently, without looking up, not wanting to see anything except dust and his son's little feet trying to keep up. And suddenly he heard the same question, asked by a different voice, "Is it far to the prison?"

Barely looking up, he first saw a scrawny mutt, all skin and bones, sniffing at his boots, and then a man, also skin and bones with bottomless, faded blue eyes set deep in that skin and bones, so huge that they seemed to go beyond the confines of the exhausted face. The man was hitched to a cart in which sat two skinny children — skin and bones — younger than his own son, atop bundles and belongings. Behind the cart came a woman, so transparent and wavering that she seemed part of the heat shimmer, knitting for a child not in the cart as she walked and whispered to herself, "You'll fool them all, my dearest, most precious, my third child, and when the bad people fall asleep, you lift the top of the coffin — your father only pretended to hammer in nails — and crawl through the ground up to me, and I won't let you go back, and we'll go to Siberia together, and there are lots of mushrooms and berries there, you just have to see them in the grass. . . ."

He did not answer the man's question. The man did not seem to expect an answer.

Taking tighter hold of his son's hand, he backed away. He remembered how his son, two months old, barely survived when his mother's milk stopped and the child's grandfather, the fierce organizer of the kolkhoz, had given their cow to the general herd. The cows had stopped giving milk, because they were unaccustomed to the new place and to strangers' hands and because they were underfed. And then he, the father of a dying child, forgetting about the class struggle, ran with a pitcher to one of the last private farmers. As he ran into the farmer's yard, he saw that the man, with one withered arm, was horribly drunk and with his good hand was pulling the trigger of the gun the authorities had given him and was killing his ducks, geese and pigs. Neither the cries of the women nor the shouts of his comrades could stop him. The farmer's face contorted with the lust of a destroyer. He shot his cow, black with a white blaze on her face, which fell on its knees before him, its eyes, as blue as plums, pleading for mercy. But he laughed and shot again, and the cow slowly sank to its side, stretching out its legs, which jerked one last time.

Crazed with the realization that this was the only cow in the village that could save his son, the father rushed over to its dead body and hysterically began milking the still-warm teats. White streams of life pouring out of death rushed into the pitcher.

The father remembered this and picked up his son, holding him close to his chest, afraid that he might die from hunger and end up atop bundles in a cart headed for nowhere, when he heard the question again, "Is it far to the prison?"

This was yet another man, and the father didn't even look at his face because he ran, to save himself and his son from the question of the damned.

But he tripped and fell with the child. He had caught his foot on a white cattle skull with a bullet hole, perhaps the very cow that had saved his son even after its death. And he pounded his fist on the parched earth, as if it were to blame for all the injustice and cruelty that people did upon it. The question that was eating away at him returned, in total contradiction to what he had been saying to his son. Did some people have the right to drive other people like cars and force them into kolkhozes or prisons or to shoot them, the way the one-armed man had shot the innocent black cow in the white blaze between its eyes?

The boy could not understand why his father was beating the earth and why his shoulders were shuddering and his face was screwed up as if he were crying, even though no tears came out of his eyes, as if the eyes were as dry as salt flats. And the steppe rustled and swished, and creaked around them, like tumbleweeds arising in the shimmering heat waves and vanishing over the horizon, with disembodied human voices asking the same question. The question contained that slippery, cold, ratlike word "prison," which the boy would fear for the rest of his life.

The boy looked around and saw that all the voices had shape, resembling humans. Either he imagined it because of the unbearable heat, or it was true, but along the road and off the road came people, looking more like clouds of dust twisted into whips, or like sheaves of wheat burned by the sun and now alive and walking; they came in ones and twos and threes, some pulling carts or wagons with children and they all asked, their cracked lips as dry as the soil, "How far to the prison?"

The President stood by the window and silently looked at the ships. He knew how many ships there were now: Sixteen.

But he didn't know how many ghosts there were tormenting him, and perhaps no one knew. As president, he could have found out, but avoided it. You couldn't revive the dead anyway, so why dig around in your soul for nothing?

The fear of prison lived in him and in millions of people like him, who grew up in a country where the nameless door to your peasant hut or the mahogany door with a name plate gleaming gold could be kicked down any night by the secret police and you could be hauled out of bed and declared a kulak, saboteur, Trotskyite or spy. Some hid from this fear in vodka, trying to become less noticeable, more insignificant. Others scrambled upward, breaking their nails, in order to be no longer one of those who fear, but one of those who are feared. But things got all mixed up and the ones who were feared were also afraid.

Power—small, medium and big—did not save you from the biggest power of all, and that biggest power did not belong to someone, it was something even bigger than Stalin himself—fear.

The peasant son who lived within him had a secret fear—that someone might learn he had been in occupied lands. The question: "Were you ever on occupied territory during the Great Patriotic War?" was in every application form, like a trap in the snow. Even someone who, at the time, had been only a child could get caught in it. What if he had cleaned the boots of the occupiers, thereby humiliating the dignity of a Soviet Pioneer? What if he had amorally accepted chocolate from enemy hands? Or what if his mother had played hanky-panky with the Fritzes?

Two of his friends in Privolnoe had run with him to the hilltop well to watch the Germans enter their village. First, far down the road, came a huge ash-colored cloud of dust. The cloud roared. The cloud came closer, threatening to swallow up the village and the three boys frozen on the hill. Two of them couldn't stand it and ran away. He remained. He was also afraid, but curiosity was stronger than fear. The cloud began to reveal motorcycles and people in helmets. They held the handlebars wearing long gloves with slits. Their faces seemed to be molded out of dust. They were the first foreigners the future president ever saw. Could those German soldiers ever have guessed that a boy pressed in fear against a white shed and coughing in the dust they raised would be the man who would help join divided Germany?

He was scolded by his mother for the dirt and dust from the German motorcycles on his face and the whitewash on the back of his shirt.

There were several bad labels they could brand you with in those days. The first, and the worst, was "enemy of the people." This meant either execution or a hard labor camp. The second was "member of the family of an enemy of the people." You went either to the camps or, if you were a minor, to a special orphanage: a camp for children. The third was "POW." If you ended up as a prisoner of war, you were a coward or a traitor. This meant the camps, or a life under suspicion. The fourth was "occupied," and it wasn't as hot a brand, but even if it didn't burn all the way through, your skin still smelled singed and the mark stayed with you forever.

And it was hard to have a career with a brand. You either had to humiliate yourself, insist that you were innocent or try to make people forget about it. Therefore, two people lived in the soul of the future president: one was the Peasant Son, and the other was the Occupied Kid, who had the burdensome addition of two arrested grandfathers.

His maternal grandfather had been exiled to Siberia back in the early thirties for refusing to join a collective farm. The Occupied Kid didn't remember him at all, and they tried not to mention his name in the family. But then disaster struck his paternal grandfather, too. He had been the organizer of the collective farm in Privolnoe. Revolution, when it stops being a lofty ideal and becomes the reigning power, rids itself of the idealists first.

The idealist grandfather was kept in the Stavropol Prison under investigation for two years, where he was beaten and tortured, and released only when the investigator who tortured him committed suicide. Perhaps he too was a revolutionary idealist, and sensed that it was his turn to switch from executioner to victim. And the scary local Communist, Sheboldayev, when he became unnecessary, was also shot, and perhaps he had been an idealist too, fervently believing that revolutionary cruelty was the new justice.

Despite his "splotchy" personal file, the Peasant Son miraculously got an Order of Lenin for his work on the collective farm thresher when he was eighteen. That miracle actually involved a bit of know-how, because people had advised him to soft-pedal his arrested grandfathers and his living in occupied territory when he wrote his autobiographical statement, or else he might be crossed off the awards list.

Then, when they started dragging the decorated thresher operator into all these committees and presidiums, as a living gilt statue with a medal on its chest, the Peasant Son got bored. But the Occupied Kid, afraid of falling under suspicion and losing the opportunity "to grow," "to move up," applied to join the Party.

The Peasant Son was of draft age. "Not so bad," he thought. "Everyone serves, and so will I. I'll work as a driver or run a tank. I'll start corresponding with a girl. And when I come back, I'll get married right away. The steppe can wait for me."

But the Occupied Kid was urged higher by his fear—to a place where he thought there would be no fear. He figured it was stupid to lose two years in the army, where anyone who felt like it could steer you, especially those fat-faced sergeants. Proud of their trifling service medals, the sergeants would never forgive some snotty kid for having a civilian medal and they would force him to clean toilets. He had to make his way to where the golden gleam of his order would cut like a laser through a crowd of other ambitious men. The order would be helped with a candidate membership card in the Party, a ruby square of light from the red stars over the Kremlin, signaling through his coat pocket to those who mattered: "I belong."

The Occupied Kid, hiding inside the decorated thresher operator, decided to go to Moscow State University, to law school.

Why there? Because it was not so hard to get in. In a country without the rule of law, there weren't many who wanted to serve the law. In the past there had been a lot of Jews in the school. But in 1950, after the "cosmopolites" were destroyed and before the story of the "killer doctors"—Jews who'd allegedly murdered Stalin—there was an unspoken quota for Jews, and the admissions requirements for Russians were eased. And then, there were too many Muscovites and children of white-collar workers. His calculations proved correct: a decorated farmer from the provinces with a peasant and worker background was welcomed with open arms, and he was made leader of the Communist Youth League right away. The Occupied Kid was transformed into the Rising *Apparatchik*, who tried to stuff the Peasant Son into a dark closet, to shut him up.

The Peasant Son, with his common sense, could not believe that the Jewish personal physicians of Stalin had poisoned him, and when anti-Semitism rolled down like an avalanche from the Party heights, he defended one of the few Jewish students from insults. But the Rising *Apparatchik* could not avoid chairing meetings condemning the killer doctors, and could not avoid "brainwashing" the students considered "morally unstable," otherwise he would be considered so himself. The road to major politics is paved with people.

The Peasant Son wondered bitterly why Khrushchev, who had exposed Stalin's crimes, couldn't find the courage to repent of the blood on his own hands. But the Rising *Apparatchik* understood Khrushchev very well: if you repent in politics, it's the end of you, because people consider repentance a sign of weakness and they will never follow anyone they think weak.

The Peasant Son, grandson of two arrested men, felt sorry for Khrushchev when he was overthrown so unceremoniously — after all, he had released so many people from prison. The Rising *Apparatchik* hurried to pledge allegiance to Brezhnev — he didn't have time for pity.

The Rising *Apparatchik*, now regional Party secretary, worked hard to please and satisfy the big bosses from Moscow who came to his area for mineral water and mud treatments of their exhausted glands, gall bladders and livers.

"What have you turned into?" the Peasant Son asked bitterly. "You should be ashamed of yourself, considerately picking up those mummies at the airport, tenderly lashing their flabby flesh with eucalyptus brooms in the sauna and delicately, with two fingers, removing those leaves from their pampered skin, and sitting with them, wrapped in sheets like Roman patricians, gnawing boar or venison bones and smirking at their own dirty jokes?"

"I am ashamed," the Rising *Apparatchik* would reply. "But what can I do? Their bodies may be flabby, but when they close ranks, they become an impregnable wall that will keep everyone from moving up. And I have to get to the top, because that's the only way to change Russia — from the top. You reproach me with sauna brooms? I'm building steps rising upward with those brooms."

"So, you want to use the mummies to become a mummy yourself?" the Peasant Son jabbed. "What makes you any different? They used to tickle big bosses with leaves in the sauna, only so that later someone else would tickle them."

"No, I don't want to get to the top for myself. Do you think I've forgotten my arrested grandfathers or those ghosts who talked to me with barely moving lips: 'How far to the prison?' That's what I'm ashamed of. And if I have to put up with small shame to get rid of the big one, it's all right with me," the Rising *Apparatchik* defended himself.

"When small shame becomes a habit, then you don't feel the big shame, either. And what if you become a different person by the time you get to the top?" the Peasant Son asked warningly.

"I won't. I'll do everything to stop people from being put away and to make people unwilling to go under the knife in an obedient herd."

One time at the Mineral Waters station he met three general secretaries of the Party at once: the current one, a decrepit bon vivant who could barely move his jaw, and two future ones; the first a rather grim-looking man, eaten away by assiduously hidden diseases, the bearer of compromising material on the bon vivant and his corrupt entourage, and the other a frail, faceless bureaucrat, hair yellowish-gray from his eternal fear of being removed from office, choking on asthma which he had probably developed by the constant inhalation of dust from the files and paperwork of a lifetime.

Observing those three mastodons, the Rising *Apparatchik* saw in a flash: they were all ruins and would not last long. His time had come. There was no one at the top in Moscow with his energy and grasp.

Three more sauna brooms, and he was in Moscow.

As he had presumed, the three mastodons died one after the other. Two other mammoths, pretenders to the Party throne—princelings of Leningrad and Moscow—were too ungainly and slow, as well as "besmirched." One had a son who married Beria's daughter, and the other had taken the imperial dinner service from the museum for his son's wedding and it had been smashed. Whether this was true or just a rumor is not known, but the old saying "there's no smoke without fire" did its job. Nevertheless, you need the support of some mammoths in order to fight off others, and the Rising *Apparatchik* was proposed as general secretary by an international specialist mammoth, who did not characterize him as a liberal (no one would have voted for him) but as a Party member "with iron teeth." The military mammoth also supported him, dropping all his tanks and missiles onto the scales at once.

And so the former Occupied Kid became the General Secretary—or the new tsar of an enormous empire.

Could he have reigned, say, ten or fifteen years if he hadn't started changing things? He could have.

But the Peasant Son, not forgetting "How far is it to the prison?" lived on inside the General Secretary.

Before the fiftieth anniversary of the victory in World War II, the General Secretary was flooded with letters from war veterans demanding that Volgograd be renamed Stalingrad once again.

"What will this give me?" weighed the General Secretary. "The army, the veterans, the majority of the Party. . . . I guess I'll have to yield."

"So, you climbed to the top over the sauna leaves just so that you could yield to Stalin?" The Peasant Son would not give up. "Have you forgotten your arrested grandfathers, and those ghost-people in the steppe?"

In his speech on the anniversary of Victory Day, when the General Secretary inevitably mentioned Stalin as commander-in-chief, the marshals, generals and officers filling the Kremlin Palace jumped from their seats, medals jangling. Their eyes, hypnotized once again by the sound of that magical name, filled with tears of nostalgia.

"Stalingrad! Stalingrad!" Was it his imagination, or did he really hear the name in the thunderous applause?

"Say it, say Stalingrad, and we'll follow you through fire and water." That seemed to be the message twinkling from the medals and bright buttons of the uniforms, chests puffed up in anticipatory patriotic zeal.

"What if I do deviate from my text and tell them what they want to hear?" thought the General Secretary. "The Politburo will accept it — they'll probably welcome it."

"Don't you dare!" The Peasant Son blocked the way. "Then it won't be far to the prison for anyone."

It was a pause that lasted less than a minute, but it determined the course of history for at least the next quarter-century. The applauding hands could have molded out of thin air a ghost in the generalissimo's uniform, and it would have filled in with flesh and thrown the country and Europe back into the past.

The Peasant Son won. He went on talking, suppressing the applause in the hall and the General Secretary in himself.

"What's this nonsense you've come up with — this stupid anti-alcohol campaign?" The Peasant Son, still full of common sense, berated the General Secretary. "You enjoy a drink yourself. Why are you listening to those reformed drunks in your ranks, who can no longer drink and are losing their minds with jealousy of those who can? You'll set the people against you."

"Think how many people die from the green serpent alcohol," the General Secretary defended himself. "The people will come to understand that this is necessary."

The Peasant Son was right. The people didn't understand. The people were infuriated by new lines—for vodka. The people, poisoning themselves, started drinking cologne, raw alcohol, callus remover and moonshine—made of anything at hand. The people didn't hate the General Secretary, but they mocked him, calling him not the *generalny* but the *mineralny* (Mineral Water) secretary.

The Peasant Son proclaimed glasnost, which after seventy years of censorship had its dangers for him, ended the war in Afghanistan, liberated humanity from the fear of a third world war, brought Sakharov back from exile and took the risk of having the first "almost free" elections for congress.

The General Secretary, purple with frustration, yelled at reporters, rudely interrupted the stuttering academician at the podium, created a quota of one hundred non-elected "deputies" from the Party, including himself, vacillated during the slaughter in Sumgait, missing the moment when force would have worked and silently allowing the use of force when it should have been avoided and, desperately trying to save the party, avoided a general election for president, surrounding himself with people who eventually betrayed him.

The General Secretary had cornered the Peasant Son in the Crimean trap.

"Grandpa, Grandmother is crying again!" His granddaughter ran into his office, still holding the deck of cards from which she could not be parted.

"What makes me any better?" thought the President, laughing at himself. "I didn't want to give up my deck, with those old faces, and I lost. The greasy cards slip out of your hands and they're hard to shuffle. Well, soon my wife and I will no longer be the President and First Lady, as they say in America, but just Grandpa and Grandmother. If they'll have no pity for me, it'll be even worse for her. They hate her — especially the women. And why? Because she was the first wife of the first man in the country who didn't hide her in the kitchen, because she kept her figure, because she wasn't frumpy and dressed with good taste. Of course, sometimes she lacked the taste not to show off her good taste. In Khabarovsk for a meeting with workers, where there were so many women in overalls, she was decked out in Dior. But when she saw herself on TV, she understood — she dressed more modestly the next time. And she's holding up very well in this trap, even when . . . even when — but that's something I'll never tell. Her eyes are always dry when she's around me — although there's a suspicious amount of makeup under her eyes. But our granddaughter gave her away."

"Grandpa, play cards with me. Go fish!" The girl kept pestering him.

"I don't want to play, I'll lose. Why don't we go pick some flowers for your grandmother instead?"

He took her by the hand and went outside.

And he heard footsteps behind him.

The steps were three or four yards away.

The steps did not come closer, nor fall behind.

The steps were not loud, but confident.

The gravel merely crunched under a heavy, but trim and careful man who did not want to be heard too much, but was not concerned about being silent.

"Are they going to kill me now — in the back, with my granddaughter here?" thought the Peasant Son.

But the President did not turn around.

He wanted to pick flowers for his wife.

In the flowerbeds in front of the house there were pansies that looked like the faces of tiny lapdogs, and golden snapdragons with bees working inside, *calla* lilies a red-hot crimson, and some other flowers the names of which he did not know. Along the gravel paths among the smoky green agaves, gladioli showed tender pink. But these were not the flowers the President wanted to give right now — they were beautiful, but too carefully bred, too pampered by three gardeners, each of whom was at least a captain in the KGB.

And then in the distance, the President saw something unexpected and half-forgotten — in a mound of topsoil near a shed glowed a single small sun in eclipse, with a dark center and a flaming crown of yellow petals. It was an ordinary sunflower, accidentally finding itself in the government paradise, probably growing from a seed uneaten by a guard or cook.

The Peasant Son went to the sunflower as if it were a childhood friend, and caressed the stem with its rough skin and silvery fluff.

The steps following the President stopped by the sunflower.

The Peasant Son pulled out a seed from the center, just turning black, and bit into it.

The seed was not quite ripe, soft, with a sour milky taste, but it was the taste of his long-ago Stavropol childhood.

The Peasant Son remembered a time at the university when he was out of money and had to last until his next scholarship payment, and all there was to eat was a canvas sack of sunflower seeds sent by his mother from Privolnoe, and he and his wife had chewed on the seeds while sitting on a bench in the dormitory yard, as if they were at home in the village.

"Well, pal," the Peasant Son addressed the sunflower. "Do you mind if I give you as a present? Otherwise, who knows who'll be eating your seeds."

The Peasant Son had not lost his touch and he deftly twisted the sinewy stem.

"Grandpa, does it hurt the flower?"

"Yes. But it knows that I'll be giving it to Grandmother."

The girl's right hand was holding the deck of cards, and he placed the sunflower in her left. "Take it to Grandmother."

"When will we play cards, Grandpa?"

"Later." He slapped her bottom gently to get her going.

The girl ran off, and the President was left face to face with the headless sunflower stem, and with his back to the breathing of the man who had walked behind him.

Well, the child's gone. You can shoot, sighed the President, still not turning around.

The fresh break in the twisted stem oozed a transparent, milky blood, marking the last seconds of the flower's life.

And instead of a shot, there came a voice. "May I ask a question?"

The President shuddered. He had never heard that voice before. Yet only people he knew were supposed to be at the residence.

The President turned slowly.

Before him was a familiar guard. But the President had never heard his voice. Guards do not speak. They follow orders. A guard's face should not be memorable, but this one was. Blue eyes, like faded cornflowers, had an Asiatic slant, and the tanned skin was tight on Mongol cheekbones.

"I was born in Irkutsk," said the officer.

"Well then?" the President asked coldly, trying to be polite.

"But my grandfather was born in Privolnoe. He was a friend of your grandfather on your mother's side. They were arrested together and sent to Siberia. My grandfather told me that when his cow had been shot, you were given its last milk, taken from her by your father after she was dead. And your grandfather used to dandle me on his knee. And sing a song:

> The ship has sunk, has sunk, has sunk.
> And with that ship, a sailor's trunk.
> What was within, within, within?
> Just one sailor's sin.
> So have the sails.

The President was quiet. The Peasant Son asked, "How did my grandfather die?"

"Natural causes—maybe homesickness. My grandfather missed the steppe. Yours must have, too. My father married a Buryat woman and stayed in Siberia. So may I ask a question?"

"Of course."

"I guarded you during many of your speeches and I often heard you say that even your grandfather made the socialist choice, and so on. It sounded as if the entire nation in the person of your grandfather had voluntarily made that choice."

"My grandfather—my father's father—actually was the organizer of a collective farm," the President muttered hastily, stunned by this unexpected confrontation with history, especially in the form of his own bodyguard.

"Why did you forget that your other grandfather did not make that choice?"

"I didn't forget," whispered the Peasant Son.

The President said nothing.

"Grandpa, I gave Grandmother the flower." The girl tugged at his sleeve, trying to make him take the cards. "Come on, let's play!"

"You don't even know the cards," the President said, trying to fend off her gaming passion. "Well, for instance, what's this card?"

"Queen!"

"Which one?"

The girl frowned, and then happily pronounced, "Spiders!"

"Spades, not spiders," corrected the President, and then gave a bitter laugh. "Politics is the queen of spiders."

"Politics? What's that, Grandpa?"

And the President suddenly realized that he would not be able to explain it to her.

The President Of Russia
Loses His Socks

IN THE EARLY MORNING OF August 19, the President of Russia wore house slippers on bare feet — his socks had disappeared somewhere, and he didn't have time to look for them.

Apples neatly sliced by the President's wife were drying on the windowsills, and the whole house was filled with people at the crack of dawn, people with a special, military anxiety. Yet the apple smell, soothing, sweet and sour, winy, was in the air.

"Help yourself." The President nodded toward the windowsill to one of the men coming in and, feeling how tensely the man shook his hand in his own two, added soothingly: "We dry them ourselves."

"We dry them ourselves" made the visitor feel cozier and more secure, as if that dacha near Moscow, protected only by a few guards with pistols and automatic rifles, was for a brief time defended from the tanks — naively, fragilely, but still protected by the glass barricades of Russian pickles and jams, erected by women's hands and wrapped by threads of dried mushrooms and apples instead of barbed wire.

"Join in. We're writing an appeal to the people," said the President, slapping at a mosquito that had reached his blood through a hole in his old T-shirt, and turned to his aide, sitting with a draft in his hands. "Read on."

The aide continued: "We call on the citizens of Russia to give a worthy response to the coup leaders and to demand that the country be returned to normal constitutional development. Without a doubt, it is necessary to guarantee that President Gorbachev be able to speak to the people."

"We don't need a second mention of Gorbachev," came a gloomy and irritated voice from a corner. "He's mentioned in the beginning, and that's plenty. It's all his own fault anyway."

"Is there anyone who's not at fault for something?" came a quiet but persistent voice from the corner opposite the source of the grumbling.

That voice, creeping out of memory, was not heard by everyone, but the President heard it.

It was the voice of Academician Sakharov, who had died a year and a half ago. He had gotten past the guards and now sat on the edge of a chair, and the question he posed gently swayed in the air, like the sound of a piano with the pedal down. And between the President and Sakharov, separating them, rose a granite stoop, its textured steps covered with dried and fresh flowers from the Urals, and a lone apple, rosy on just one side and with a few bird pecks in its skin. This was not a simple stoop, and it appeared before the President not often, but from time to time: in his sleep, or as it did now, seeming almost real, and reminding him of one of his greatest guilts.

When he had been Party governor, he was bombarded with tons of secret packets from the Center. Most of it was nonsense not worthy of being stamped "Top Secret." But once, he received a special packet, with a secret decision of the Politburo calling for the instantaneous razing of the Ipatyev House, where the tsar's family had been shot long ago.

In the twenties, at the height of the revenge mania, the square had been renamed Square of the People's Revenge, and the house was proudly turned into a Museum of Revolutionary Justice. Guides discoursed at length on who was killed there and how, triumphantly thrusting school pointers at the rusty stains left intentionally on the walls and floor of the cellar. But the bloodstains of that cursed day of July 16, 1918, began to spread across Russia, turning into so much blood that the bragging madness scared itself and gradually turned into cowardly silence. The square was renamed yet again, removing all mention of the people's revenge. The museum was shut. The executioner's shamelessness evolved into the executioner's shyness. And some people even felt stirrings of conscience. The Great Rehabilitation had begun.

It was no accident that the first people to be rehabilitated after Stalin's death were criminals — the rehabilitator, Beria, was a criminal himself. Then they rehabilitated the "Reds," those "enemies of the people" who, before their own arrests, had shot other "enemies of the people." The slowest was the posthumous rehabilitation — a psychological one — of the people who had been called "Whites" for so many years.

The first Whites to be rehabilitated were those of song.

Around campfires, the grandchildren of former Reds began singing a long-forgotten song by White émigré singer Vertinsky lamenting the officers killed by their grandfathers. A famous bard, the son of an executed Communist, now plucked his guitar strings and switched from the romance of "commissars in dusty helmets" to nostalgia for the emperor and the officers of his retinue, hoofbeats clattering down the alleys of Tsarskoe Selo, which had sunk to the bottom of time like an Atlantis of the Russian nobility. The editor of a Leningrad journal was fired for the "ideological myopia" of publishing a nostalgic ode to the murdered royal family. However, the scandalous poem was feverishly copied by weeping female members of the Communist Youth League, even though their heaving breasts still bore red badges with the profile of the chief tsar-killer.

In some intellectual apartments a portrait of Nicholas II was hung next to the traditional photo of Hemingway in turtle-necked skipper's sweater, and in Bohemian circles the only acceptable form of address was "Gentlemen!" which replaced "Comrades!" When compared to the portrait of Brezhnev, with his jaw drooping like that of an overaged turtle in funeral surroundings, the image of the melancholy face of the last tsar, with his neatly trimmed beard and mustache and an aureole of martyrdom, elicited sympathy bordering on veneration. The fact that people called him "Bloody Nicholas," after his troops shot into a peaceful workers' demonstration in 1905, seemed like a lie, as did everything written in history books.

People came on pilgrimages from all over Russia to the Ipatyev House. That was why the Center relayed a secret packet to the Party governor instructing him to raze the house.

The Party, like a toothless old she-wolf, wanted to use its mangy tail to sweep away any traces of the blood spilled by the wolf's then-young teeth.

The Party governor had not known much about the "Ekaterinburg Case" before his assignment there, and why should he have known? The *nomenklatura*'s knowledge was selective—anything that would complicate clear theory or add a burden of conscience was contraindicated. Pasternak's novel *Doctor Zhivago* was shortened to thirty-five pages for the Politburo version. But there wasn't even a tiny brochure for the *nomenklatura* to read on the murder of the tsar's family.

The Party governor displayed cautious curiosity. He went down to the special archives in Sverdlovsk (as the city of Ekaterinburg had been renamed) and turned the yellowed pages of the files with his own hands. He had known that the tsaritsa had been killed along with the tsar, but he had never heard that the heir and four daughters and Dr. Botkin had been killed too.

In the special archives, in mildewed vinyl-covered files tied with the drawstrings from longjohns, those murdered children—the clear-eyed boy in a sailor shirt and four snowy angels with aureoles of wavy hair—looked right into his heart with a silent reproachful question: *Why?* They had not had the time to be guilty of anything. And what had the family doctor done to be shot along with them?

From the archives, the Party governor learned with disgust that, on orders from Moscow, the bodies were cravenly covered with sulfuric acid to make them unrecognizable.

The peasant-worker soul of the Party governor, which could be expected to be imbued with class hatred of the tsar's family, filled with disgust, not toward the victims but toward their killers.

The Party governor was no big poetry lover, but he remembered the poem written by the tsar's daughter, Grand Duchess Olga, in her diary before she was killed.

> Lord, send us patience
> In the year of stormy, grim days
> To bear the wrath of the people
> And the torture of our executioners.
>
> On the threshold of the grave
> Bring to the lips of your servants
> The inhuman strength
> To pray humbly for our enemies.

He understood that the Ipatyev House ought to be preserved, not as a museum of justice but as a museum of mindless cruelty, a reminder that everything built on blood will end in blood.

But would he have become president of Russia if he had refused to obey orders then?

Of course not.

He would have been nipped in the bud.

The powerful walk down the bloody red carpet of the Kremlin Palace, when in a beautiful gesture he slapped the podium with his Party card and left it there picturesquely, that eloquent gesture completely winning the hearts of those who later elected him president—it would not have happened.

He would not have had anything with which to make a beautiful gesture. His Party card would have been taken away from him as soon as he refused to obey the secret orders of the Politburo, and all his air holes would have been squeezed shut. They wouldn't have broken his spine, they would have stifled him with the simple absence of air.

The era of public executions on the block was past—now was the time of quiet strangulation in offices. Anyone who did not want to be strangled had to strangle the human inside himself.

The Party governor obeyed the orders of the clan.

They decided not to use dynamite, which was too noisy. An army of bulldozers and excavators attacked the Ipatyev House by night, like thieves. The huge steel ball flew up to the top of the crane and then fell, breaking through the roof and walls. But there was one thing it could not turn to rubble—the stone stoop of the house, three steps made of some special, Bolshevik-resistant Urals granite.

The Party governor drove past in the morning and had his driver slow down.

A few passersby were staring at the spot where the house had disappeared overnight. The more enterprising were grabbing pieces of stone or bits of masonry as souvenirs. The rubble was being carted away. The asphalt was already being prepared. Only two parts of the house survived. One was invisible: the cellar, which had been leveled and filled with garbage. The other was visible: the stoop.

The Party governor was not happy to have even a tiny reminder of either the crime in the Ipatyev House or his own crime. But inside of him there lived a Barracks Boy from the Urals.

The Party governor angrily pointed at the stoop and growled at the workmen, "What is that? When will you ever learn to finish what you start?"

But the Barracks Boy felt a secret joy that it was not so easy to pave over everything and turn it into a docile, boring flatness. They had tried to flatten him out many times, and always failed.

The Barracks Boy had always hated the barracks in which his family lived with so many others, and the corner where he was forced to kneel on dried peas for punishment, and his father's strap that danced on his back and the teacher's ruler that struck his fingers.

When he rose against one vicious teacher, he was thrown out, with a piece of paper on which was written, in rheumatic red letters, that he had been through seven years of school but was not allowed "to enter the eighth grade anywhere on the territory of the country."

But the Barracks Boy, who was used to beating on the ice with a pickaxe until he could get the long-awaited stream of water into his bucket in the winter, did not give up.

He hung around the Party headquarters and butted his head against the door until the Party condescended to pity him and reinstate him in school until he was ready to join the Party. Ever since then he knew that, as long as they were in power, you had to become part of that power if you wanted to get somewhere. And so he did. But that did not mean that he came to like that power. He secretly hated the Party because it had seen him in the humiliating role of ragged beggar, asking for protection from the vicious teacher, and the Party had helped him. The Party, growing older and stupider, did not realize that it was helping its future gravedigger. But as long as he was Party governor, he had to do everything that had once been done cruelly to him. He had to make others kneel on peas, use his father's strap on other people's backs, and be a ruler on someone's knuckles. Having become one of the vertebrae of the Party, he came to hate it even more for making him raze the Ipatyev House, using an old criminal trick of trying to smear him with the tsar's blood that he had not spilled.

But he turned out to be a special kind of vertebra — he dared to rebel against the backbone of which he was part.

When he was in bad but not dangerous grace with the Party, and he came to the scene of his crime, like Raskolnikov from *Crime and Punishment*, to run for president, none of the voters reminded him of the Ipatyev House. But some did remember a few things.

The election campaign meeting was chaired by the editor of a Urals magazine. He looked liked a starving but still sturdy artisan, with long straw hair and, under straw eyebrows, eyes of granite like the stoop. The chairman did everything he could to get his countrymen to support the former Party governor in his attempt to become the first president of Russia. And then a note came to the candidate, which he read aloud from the stage: "Do you remember that ten years ago you chewed out the chairman of this meeting for 'ideological mistakes'?"

"I don't remember," the future President admitted honestly, and he was telling the truth. The Party was the worst of teachers — it taught not only to do evil, but to forget it as soon as it was done.

But still, he did not forget the stoop.

And now today, August 19, 1991, it materialized again, in his summer house near Moscow redolent of apples lying on a windowsill.

And suddenly, right behind Sakharov, a clear-eyed boy in a sailor suit came into the room and sat down on the stoop, and uncoagulating streams of blood poured and poured from the bullet holes in the sailor shirt. Four snowy angels with aureoles of wavy hair flew in behind the boy and joined him on the stoop, and blood dripped quietly onto the floor from their mortally wounded wings.

These were innocent, murdered children, whose faces the President had seen for the first time in a mildewed vinyl file tied with the drawstrings from longjohns. He recognized them by name.

The one called Olga reminded him softly:

> On the threshold of the grave
> Bring to the lips of your servants
> The inhuman strength
> To pray humbly for our enemies.

"Will I be able to pray, humbly, for my enemies?" thought the President. "I don't even know how to pray."

He signed the appeal to the people and his aide read it on short-wave radio. Suddenly, the President smelled another odor in the air besides that of apples and tanks—the gunpowder smell of expectation of action, action not from just anyone—but from him.

He wasn't sure himself why history had picked him. History did not idealize him, but no one else was handy in that hour of need.

His wife waited, standing at the door with a white shirt for him.

His driver waited, holding the key ring in his hand and dangling it beckoningly.

Sakharov on the edge of the chair waited, shyly cleaning his cracked glasses.

The boy in the sailor shirt waited on the granite stoop and so did the four snowy angels.

The Urals' Zyryanka River waited, where the President used to jump from log to log as a child, enjoying his first death-defying game with danger.

The President, wearing slippers on his bare feet, rose quickly, kicking them off and rubbing one foot against the other to soothe his itchy mosquito bites: "Ladies, could you at least find a pair of socks for the president of Russia?"

Palchikov And The
Python's Whisper

THE ROMANTIC OF THE COUP resembled both a romantic and the coup itself.

He had the concentrated pallor of an earthworm, the insecure confidence of a nightingale trilling praise for the general headquarters and the proud and self-sacrificing nervousness of a racehorse that has harnessed itself to History's chariot — that is, to the tanks.

His face was contorted by hysterical love for the military-industrial complex; tanks, submarines, jet fighters, atomic bombs, chemical and bacteriological weapons and especially war missiles, which in his socialist-colonial novels he described with militaristic eroticism:

> And when the edge of the moon peeked from behind the cliffs, like a
> dushan's turban with a bullet hole through it, for an instant I felt fear
> beneath the black veil of the Afghan night. But not far away lay some-
> thing, radiating saving light. I reached for it and felt my hand touch the
> feminine snowy white body of a rocket. At first it was cool, but as I
> caressed it, it grew warmer, it seemed as if its sides were panting with
> unexpressed desire, and I thought that my fingertips would soon feel
> nipples, straining in anticipation of my touch, on the missile's body.

The Romantic of the Coup was a not-untalented and not-at-all-unknown writer. But at some point in his life, he realized that he was not turning into a great writer from a not-untalented one, nor into a world-famous writer from a not-at-all-unknown one. With increasing frustration he thought of the source of the fame of writers better known than he: "Well, all right, they're talented, I accept that. But I'm a Mozart, too, not a Salieri. I've never stooped to black envy. So why are they more famous? They must have achieved fame outside literature. They exploited boldness sanctioned from above, they traded cautious freedom for love of hard currency, all the while maneuvering, toadying and conforming offstage. They say that there is always a crime behind every fortune. And behind every famous man there is something sneaky. And not just something, but someone. . . . The Masons. The Elders of Zion. Professional conspirators, who can destroy or create a reputation. They have the world press in their hands, the Nobel Prize committee. Now that's a real party! Not like ours. You can't get anywhere in politics or art without an organization behind you. And where do we have organized power today? Only in the army."

He decided to ride an armored personnel transporter to glory. He had never been a soldier himself, but he had played with tin soldiers when he was a boy.

And now he would play with generals.

He rubbed himself so persistently against the generals' shoulderboards that telltale traces of gold remained on his own, confidentially offered shoulder. He whispered apocalyptic predictions into the generals' ears, with a threatening creak hammering into their lumpy purplish napes the idea that the country's only salvation lay in the only existing power—the army.

The army became his Dulcinea in khaki. He had always been terrified of flying, but now he begged with tears in his eyes to be taken along in helicopters spraying rounds of machine-gun fire on Afghan villages. He had a fear of water, but now, trembling in horror, he went down to the bottom of the sea in a submarine. He fainted when he heard thunder. But he was almost orgasmic when he watched an atomic bomb go off at a test site that he had penetrated by hook and by crook. He even wanted to embrace that mushroom cloud, as though it were a voluminous ruffled gown over a mighty and tempting giantess with red stars for beauty marks and the golden tassels of military banners for hair. He had an allergy to alcohol, but he overcame his disgust and heroically downed vodka with the generals in saunas, making those belching sounds of pleasure the way they did, because that fit his conception of masculinity. He even forced himself to use swear words from time to time, to strengthen his army image, but his cursing was so subtle, so amateurishly feeble, that it elicited condescending smirks from the generals, who nevertheless did not diminish their patronage.

He was very bad with Jewish jokes, if only because he looked so much like a confused Jew cravenly pretending to be anti-Semitic. He knew about this resemblance, which may not have been coincidental, and it brought him to frenzied fits of superpower patriotism.

Beneath his eyes, exhausted by longing for extraordinary measures, were not simply bags, but duffle bags with full army supplies and three days of rations.

He was so enervated by his love affair with the army that he had nothing left for ordinary women, and in order to be effective he had to play military marches during intimate moments and imagine military parades on Red Square: missiles constantly erect, an avalanche of tanks rumbling along the paving stones, blindingly white gloves at temples swaying in rhythm with the steps of blindingly black boots shaking the planet. It was almost the only thing that aroused him now.

He was also electrified by the shag of the red carpet-runners in the corridors of power, on which he walked lustfully, signaling, prophesying, warning.

Actually, he was not a chauvinist by conviction. He became a chauvinist because he lacked self-confidence, as perhaps do all chauvinists.

He could not see a place for himself in a world where the borders were open and there were no invented enemies. And that is why he went to the generals, who were like him. They too suffered from an inferiority complex, complicated by a military-industrial one.

They were not evil men, but they feared the future that had no room for them. It's different playing a leading role in an open society. They feared not only democracy, but their own coup. They did not want to kill anyone. But they wanted to survive at any cost, and not just as people, but as bosses of people. They did not know how to do anything else.

He was the Romantic of the Coup, not they. He was a reactionary intellectual, but an intellectual nevertheless. But they did not treat intellectuals — even their own — quite seriously. They decided on the coup not out of bravery, but out of fear of the future. Their coup was a coup of self-preservation.

"It's happened!" The Romantic of the Coup cried eagerly, bursting into the office of the Crystal-Clear Communist and opening his arms. "The country is saved!"

His nostrils trembled like butterfly wings.

However, there were no answering embraces, and the Crystal-Clear Communist's nose was not fluttering. His lumpy nose, with nostrils as hairy as swamp moss, sniffed grimly.

It's that psycho patriot again, he thought with a grimace. Why do we attract all the psychos? Well, the democrats get their share, too. Maybe the only surplus we have in the country is of psychos.

The Romantic of the Coup trilled like a nightingale and trumpeted a bugle before the attack. "Do you know what the crime of the Russian classics is before history? They idealize parasites, sissies, namby-pambies and wastrels! Onegin, Pechorin, Chatsky—they're superfluous men, consumed by their own irony! Oblomov is a sentimental layabout!"

The Romantic of the Coup did not notice that his rapturous entrance had tactlessly interrupted a conversation—there was another man in the office.

The man was unshaven, unkempt and he smelled of trains. Seeing that the monologue would be a long one, the man took out a toy moonwalker that must have been bored in his briefcase and let it walk around the parquet floor.

The moonwalker wandered with delight, stepping softly but determinedly, even though it tripped on an almost invisible wrinkle in the red carpet. Of course, many have tripped on those carpets. A curious detail of the toy was that a sock, not very clean, was flung over its shoulder like Porthos's bandage, a sock that must have kept it company in that long-suffering briefcase.

"I'm unlucky with socks. They keep betraying me," thought Palchikov sadly. "Even though I wash them myself—ingrates. And this guy is as ungrateful as the socks. Listen to him complain about the classics."

The Romantic of the Coup went on exposing them. "Akaky Akakiyevich is a cowardly nothing! Alyosha Karamazov is an idiot! Pierre Bezukhov is a wimp in a tuxedo! He should have played golf on the battlefield of Borodino. Doctor Zhivago hangs around the Civil War like shit in a sewer. And Russian literature stupidly made heroes of these antiheroes!"

The Crystal-Clear Communist coughed meaningfully a few times, trying to stem the flood. He couldn't care less about the Romantic of the Coup's relations with the classics. He already knew what the Romantic of the Coup did not yet know.

The coup was stuck—not on the streets yet, but in the minds of those who had decided upon it so indecisively. Two of them were already hitting the bottle.

They seemed to lack a small thing needed to save Communism—enough Crystal-Clear Communists. The decades of training in cowardice had taken its toll among the trainers themselves. They did not know what to fear more—action or their own inaction. So they half acted. As cowards, they did not count on their own courage, but on the assumed cowardice of their foes.

Meanwhile, the Romantic of the Coup, to show that he at least was not a coward, fearlessly dealt with the heroes of Russian literature. "All those mealy-mouthed men leapt from the page into life, crawling through it like bedbugs, breeding. Literature flooded Russia with heroes who were really premature babies—feeble adults. And that's why our people are so literary and feeble. Down with the cult of helplessness! There is no shame in glorifying strength! We need our Soviet Rambos! The heroes of the new Russian classics will not be humble stationmasters, reflective Uncle Vanyas, but ones who squash the hydra of democracy with tanks, not the sentimental whore Anna Karenina, but the army! And our names will be written on the remains of the rule of swine!"

The eyes of the Romantic of the Coup gradually took on a drugged glassiness. Foam flecked the corners of his mouth.

A helpful manic is more dangerous than an enemy, thought Palchikov, jumping after the escaping moonwalker and removing the ill-starred sock.

"Do you have a concrete question?" The Crystal-Clear Communist got tired of the tirade and stood up abruptly.

"I do," the Romantic of the Coup said, coming to his senses. "I . . .

I . . . request that I be armed." He coughed. "I mean, give me permission for a personal weapon."

"Take care of your job, and we'll take care of ours," said the Crystal-Clear Communist unceremoniously. "You writers are too impressionable. Your weapon is your pen. Leave the pistols to us." And for the first time in his life, he shivered from the unpleasant sensation of his own revolver under his arm. The revolver felt like a rat in a holster inside his suit, tickling his armpit with a cold steel tail.

He was so manly and rough with me. He was so imperially majestic as he ousted me from his office, almost without insulting me, thought the Romantic of the Coup masochistically as he hurried down the corridor, his feet conducting the red carpet's electrifying inspiration for, perhaps, a coming speech on the occasion of victory over democracy.

Gasping with anticipatory delight, he pictured silver bugles, with golden tassels hanging from them like icicles, raised high above the cobblestones of Red Square; the heavy, almost granite figure of a marshal in a shiny convertible limousine resembling a statue poised atop a black grand piano; troops at attention, from whose open throats, along with a thunderous "Hurrah!" cascaded down the ranks, there seemed also to burst jet fighters, their mighty roar making the crosses on the onion domes of St. Basil's tremble. He pictured the freckled peasant soldiers with cornflower-blue eyes at last throwing down the defeated slogans of the democrats, like war-trophy banners. He pictured the St. Georges of August on the Mausoleum, the men who had finally liberated Russia from freedom, and he was among them, the unbribable chronicler and fearless knight without reproach for the great struggle for unfreedom, standing out among the peasant-like comrades-in-arms with his enlightened patriot's intellectual eyes and sensitive profile.

Down below his feet, among the crowds on Red Square who now understood, repented and were even more confused, he pictured a wild mishmash of pictures of Ivan the Terrible, Nicholas I, Muravyov the Hangman, Bulgarin, Arakchev, Pobedonostsev, Lenin, Stalin, Dzerzhinsky, Zhdanov and other outstanding leaders in the struggle for unfreedom, and swaying among those portraits were pictures of him, with his Semitic black-velvet eyes tactfully changed to blue.

But then the Romantic of the Coup felt cold: What if they don't take me up onto the Mausoleum? What if they won't forgive me for being the only one among them to have read *The Brothers Karamazov* and for knowing what "convergence" means? . . . I'm too refined for them, too talented. They're just peasants. Politicians need people more talented than themselves until the victory. Afterward, they get rid of them, like an unflattering background. If you want to look smart, you have to surround yourself with people who are stupid.

But the Romantic of the Coup suppressed those tormenting thoughts with imperial masochism. But if that is your wish, my great superpower country, well then. . . . Crush me, country, kill me. Crunch my bones. I still love the smell of your boot polish. Walk all over me, my country.

And the nose of the Romantic of the Coup, as he walked out into a Moscow filled with tanks and fears, fluttered again like butterfly wings, directing him toward the encouraging smell of army boot polish and tank fuel.

"Second childhood?" the Crystal-Clear Communist regarded the moon-walker in Palchikov's hand.

"Better than playing with tanks," Palchikov replied. "May I consider my resignation accepted?"

"Too bad that you're not with us," the Crystal-Clear Communist said. "You could have had a great future."

"I don't need a great future that doesn't fit me. I'd rather have a small one that's my own," Palchikov joked.

"The future is a collective concept. No one has a separate future."

"The future must happen, create itself, be. But you want to herd people into a future that you make up in your minds before it is born naturally," Palchikov said, shaking his head.

"But people are stupid and often do not know what is best for them," the Crystal-Clear Communist defended himself. "People who are drowning often kick and fight off their rescuers."

"It's time to stop saving people who do not ask to be saved. Who gave you the right to understand what's best for people? What will you do with them if they do not follow you? You'll have to shoot the ones you are planning to save. It's better to shoot yourself than to shoot your own people," Palchikov said bitterly.

The rat in the Crystal-Clear Communist's holster lay hidden, waiting, and it flicked its tail again.

As Palchikov left the office, he set the moonwalker down on the red carpet of the corridors of power. "Let's get out of here," Palchikov told it. "Forever. We'll find something to do on this earth."

The moonwalker marched forward, and Palchikov followed.

When he'd nearly reached the ministry doors, a hand came down on Palchikov's shoulder. He turned and saw the Crystal-Clear Communist's assistant.

They had been born and raised on the same street in Pavlov Posad. Back then it had been a street that resembled a village road, overgrown with nettles and wild flowers, covered with mounds of steaming manure in which black-gold roosters, their red crowns passionately trembling, pecked for grains of wheat, and puddles in which ducklings floated like yellow beads of mimosa. The red carpets of the corridors of power could not make the two former bare-assed kids forget their street.

The Crystal-Clear Communist's assistant used to be called Fang when he was a kid, because once in a gang fight all his teeth except one were knocked out by a chunk of lead hidden in a fist. The lone tooth stuck out beneath his small but feisty sparrow-like nose. When he got a job, Fang had steel teeth put in and later, when he joined the embezzlement squad, he heedlessly had them replaced with gold crowns, forgetting Chaliapin's warning, "People die for metal!" His broad smile resembled an open accordion of pure gold. A smile like that in a member of the embezzlement squad looked like a mouthy bribe. He couldn't explain to his colleagues that he had spent his great-grandmother's treasure (she had been a merchant's wife) on his teeth. The Party organization in the ministry passed a special resolution, making Fang replace his gold crowns with ceramic ones in order to avoid rumors that discredited the men fighting corruption. At the moment Fang, like the whole country, was in a transitional period, toothless and nervous, his gold crowns gone, his new ceramic ones not yet in place.

His one tooth, the sole survivor of the dental perestroika, shone in the black abyss of his mouth, justifying his old nickname.

"What's up, Fang?" Palchikov asked, surprised to see him again, having just parted in the Crystal-Clear Communist's reception area, where his childhood friend had been markedly standoffish and officious.

But now his face had changed, and he no longer tried to cover his gaping mouth with the solitary tooth.

"Hippies," Fang confided in a whistling whisper. "In wigs. With guitars."

He didn't have time to say any more, because two army generals, in a haste unbecoming to their rank and with shifty eyes, rushed through the ministry doors.

Fang clicked his heels, saluted, gave Palchikov a farewell look and led these apparently expected guests to the Crystal-Clear Communist's office.

Hippies, Palchikov repeated to himself as he left the ministry. In wigs. . . . Not real hippies then. With guitars. What's dangerous about that? If it's not dangerous, he wouldn't have told me about it. After all, we come from the same street.

The street of his childhood was nothing like the Moscow street on which he now stood. Ministry Mercedeses raced wildly from the gates, their rooftop lights flashing. But alongside several armored troop carriers an old Pobeda chugged along, obviously bringing things back from a summer house; a bed, a couple of stools and an ancient television set strapped to the aluminum trunk, its screen like a memory that held the faded images of television's first announcers, adored by one and all — the legendary Valya Leontyeva and Nina Kondratyeva.

Moscow lived as several cities. In one, there was triumph and anticipation, chuckles and rubbing of hands. In another, there was fear and hiding. In a third were preparations for storming the White House, in case the democrats didn't roll over, and the compilation of lists for arrest. In yet another Moscow, people were headed for the White House, turning buses over, creating barricades out of slabs of concrete, armatures and garbage cans.

But there was also the City Where Nothing Was Happening, and that was the biggest of all the cities inside Moscow.

Palchikov was shocked to see that on Pushkin Square, near the American McDonald's, even on the day of the coup there was a line of Russians who didn't give a damn about anything but getting a Big Mac, a piece of long-awaited capitalism slathered in ketchup that resembled Hollywood blood and created from the flesh of Russian beef. Those people merely turned their heads, not budging so as not to lose their place in line, when tanks moved slowly down Gorky Street, from Mayakovsky Square to the Moscow City Hall.

And from there too came a crowd of people, covering the entire street, linking arms and chanting: "United we win! Yel-tsin! Yel-tsin!"

Between the crowd and the tanks inexorably coming toward them, there was only Pushkin and a man with a video camera, who was everywhere. With a gray mustache and childlike astonishment, he battered through crowds with his powerful belly, resembling Balzac or Pierre Bezukhov—who did not panic on Borodino field—but dressed in jeans and a black jersey with "Guinness" imprinted on it.

Why, it's the film director Savva Kulish, Palchikov thought. I hope he doesn't get squashed by the tanks. The Russian coup could turn "no less meaningless and ruthless than a Russian rebellion." So Pushkin had put it, the bronze bard of "secret liberty" who now sadly regarded his fellow countrymen from his pedestal.

The tanks, trying to obey at least traffic rules, stopped for a red light. Who knows what would have happened if they hadn't stopped then. But once they were immobile, even for an instant, the tanks seemed less threatening, in their immobility resembling hundreds of tanks that had been in battle and were now standing on pedestals in hundreds of Russian cities, covered with flowers on Victory Day.

A plump middle-aged woman with rollers peeking out from her kerchief ran out into the crosswalk in her checked house slippers, waving a stuffed shopping bag and shouting at the tank drivers:

"Children, what are you doing fighting your own people! Children!"

The woman's string bag caught the steel treads of a tank, tearing a paper bag of macaroni, which fell onto the tank in a white shower.

The hatch opened with a creak, and two huge "children" in helmets climbed out.

Perhaps the woman reminded each of them of his mother in some faraway town, each with her string bag, in line for macaroni. This woman certainly did not look like an enemy, and the image of *enemy* fell apart, like the macaroni. Knowing how hard it is for our women to find any food, the "children" gathered up the pasta, which flickered like pieces of light here and there on the armor plate, and poured it back into the shopping bag.

"Hurray for our tank drivers! The army is with us!" came the shouts, and in an instant everyone who had been on the sidewalk rushed to the tanks, surrounded them, climbed up on them, shaking the boys' hands, taking out bread, sausage, apples and bottles of kefir from their own shopping bags. The soldiers were shy, but they ate and looked with childlike interest at Moscow, which many of them had seen only on television during military parades.

These provincial village lads, used to the solemn voice of radio announcing: "Attention, this is Moscow speaking," listened from their own tanks with surprise and curiosity to the real Moscow speaking. This was the Moscow of people who did not want all the houses in the country ruled by the most menacing house in the capital, the house that, according to rumor, had three stories underground—the gray stone monstrosity on Lubyanka.

There were several orators upon each tank. Everyone was yelling enthusiastically, but it was impossible to make out what they were saying.

The crowd heading for the White House unlinked hands in the middle and flowed around the tanks. Palchikov went with the crowd. His right hand was tucked into the hairy paw of a driver of a sewage-disposal truck, who had abandoned it along with its aromatic contents. The insignia of the Soviet Union was tattooed on the driver's arm, and it was impossible to imagine that this seemingly indestructible superpower, one-sixth of the planet, would soon vanish from the map. With his left hand, Palchikov carefully held the thin hand of a pretty, brown-eyed, dimpled girl who was living illegally in Moscow. She wore a button with John Lennon's picture on her down jacket, and a rakishly angled captain's cap, adorned with a silver crab, on her head.

If Palchikov did not have Alevtina, he would have made a pass at her. But he was an almost faithful husband. And when he felt guilty toward his wife, he became faithful without any almosts.

Palchikov went with the expanding crowd to the Krasnopresnenskaya metro stop, but when the crowd turned toward the White House, he slipped away quietly, with the face of a man on a special mission.

Palchikov went to the zoo that was part of the City Where Nothing Was Happening.

A few people who apparently lived in an enviable world without politics, newspapers, radio or television were feeding bread to the swans and ducks and pointing at the monkeys, who always and especially today had the right to point back at them. They put their children on the pony-cart ride, the children whose future was being decided some thousand paces away.

"She's with Pitey," the elderly cleaning lady in the invertebrate house told Palchikov.

"Who's this Petey guy?" Palchikov asked.

"Not Petey, Pitey. And it's a she, not a he," the cleaning lady explained patiently. "That's what we call our python. She's sick. And she's so long that it's hard to figure out what part hurts."

Palchikov found Alevtina in the back yard of the invertebrate pavilion. She was wearing a blue work smock and rubber boots and looked more like a cleaning woman than the chief of the snake house. He noticed that she had not dyed her hair in a long time, because she had an inch of gray at the roots while the rest was solid black. A large run was visible in her stocking above the boot. Alevtina was wearing dark glasses to hide her mood. Her hands, as usual, were covered in ink.

Oh, Alevtina, sighed Palchikov. We're both neglected. But I still love you, Alevtina, even though I'm the most incorrigible snake in your life, one who caused you so much pain. It was I, with a big brush, who painted the silver in your hair. But I also know the beautiful black berries under your dark glasses. I used to love to lick your eyes around your lashes. Have you forgotten all that, Alevtina?

Alevtina was so involved that she did not notice her husband two feet away from her.

Everyone in the yard was busy with the body of the mighty spotted python, held up by about ten people, spread out full-length and looking like a crossing barrier. The python clearly was not enjoying it. Alevtina was palpating its body, her nails with chipped polish digging gently into the muscular, unyielding flesh covered with a golden-brown armor.

"Relax, Pitey, please darling, relax. Why are you so tense?" Alevtina cajoled. "I promise I won't hurt you. I have to find the spot where you're stuck and massage it. What could you have swallowed, Pitey?"

"She could have swallowed a cat, and the cat is scratching from inside," said a little girl with black eyes like Alevtina's, even though she was adopted by the Palchikovs. Nature seemed to have known that Nastenka's mother, a single parent, would be killed by a polar bear at the zoo when she was cleaning its cage, and had given the girl eyes resembling her future adoptive mother.

For Nastenka the zoo was like a kindergarten, the snakes like Alevtina's other children. She was not afraid, and she massaged Pitey with her tiny hands.

"Pitey isn't stupid. Cats don't taste good," said Alevtina, trying to pour a laxative into the python's mouth from a tin soupspoon.

"Mama, let me," Nastenka said. "I'll whisper to her first. She likes that."

Nastenka kissed the snake's head fearlessly and, petting it with one hand and holding the spoon in the other, she whispered to the snake.

Pitey licked Nastenka's cheek with its forked tongue and hissed a response into the girl's ear, which was translucent as a mandarin section.

"Pitey says that she just ate too much, and won't do it again," Nastenka translated for Alevtina. "And now, because she is a good girl, Pitey will open her mouth and drink this most delicious medicine in the whole world."

And to everyone's amazement, the python obediently opened its mouth and swallowed the medicine, almost taking the spoon with it. It went back to the girl's ear and whispered with a slight whistling sound.

"Pitey says thank you, but asks that you don't keep her straightened. She prefers being coiled up."

Alevtina signaled her assistants to release the python. The former crossing barrier rolled up into a form so complicated that it could have been a sailor's knot.

The assistants, seeing that they were not needed, hastily made their escape — you never know what a big snake like that might do.

Among them were two new zoo employees — Levchik and Vovchik, fired from the Vagankov Cemetery, where they stole flowers from Vysotsky's grave and used little old ladies to resell them.

"They're selling ginger vodka — no lines," Levchik said.

"Can we find someone to pay the last third?" Vovchik wondered.

"There's a problem in Russia finding someone for the first third, but never for the last," chuckled Levchik, and they sucked in their stomachs and slipped between the bent bars of the zoo fence right opposite the wine store. Earlier members of the zoo's proletariat must have done the bending.

"Mama, who gave snakes such beautiful skins?" wondered Nastenka, still stroking Pitey.

"Nature," Alevtina replied.

"And where does she live? In Africa, where the snakes live?"

"Nature lives everywhere, in Africa, and in Russia. It makes the skin on snakes, and the flowers, and the clouds, and people," Alevtina replied, smiling, although her voice was still sad.

"Nature must be a very busy lady," Nastenka decided. "Can she turn a dead person into a living one?"

"She can't," sighed Alevtina.

"Too bad," Nastenka said, also with a sigh. "I used to have two mothers. One is dead and the other is alive . . . you. I'd like for both of you to be alive forever. I didn't have a father at first, and then I got one. But now he's lost . . ."

"I'm not lost."

They saw Palchikov at last.

Nastenka ran to him and flew up in his arms, chattering happily, "Papa, I don't want to be an actress anymore. I want to be a snake doctor. I can already speak snake."

Alevtina said nothing, hiding behind her dark glasses.

Holding Nastenka in front of him and hiding behind her hot, happy body as if it were a living shield, Palchikov managed to say, "Well then . . ."

"What?" Alevtina asked, without any particular signs of pleasure at his appearance.

"I've quit," Palchikov announced.

"So what? You'll work yourself to death wherever you go, forgetting your family, disappearing for weeks at a time—you're a workaholic. You know the old adage: 'You don't have to be a husband, but you must be a citizen.' When you have a husband but he's never there, it's better not to have one at all," Alevtina declared.

"Mama, don't blame Papa! He's nice. We should buy him some ice cream!" Nastenka defended him.

"I'm off to the White House," he said, looking down. "If anything should happen to me, give all my rods and lures to Fang."

"Wait a minute here. Didn't you just tell me you quit? Was this a final order from your chief that you have to obey? Don't tell me you're with those fascists from the Emergency Committee? You're off to storm the White House, with the rest of that crowd? How low can you get, Palchikov?"

"Papa isn't low. He's standing up straight!" Nastenka kept on defending him.

"Alevtina, how could you even think that. . . . I'm not going to storm the White House, I'm off to defend it," he tried to explain.

But she blew up. "Ah, so you're defending so-called democracy! It's full of the same ugly faces from the Party, they're just inside out! I notice they've stopped fighting against privileges now that they've got them. The old ones at least had their limit. But these new ones are grabbing everything they can. A fine cultured lot they turned out to be. I remember how one of them got Sakharov's name screwed up when he was making a speech about his death, all teary-eyed. While the jerks with good hearts are rushing to the barricades, the real decisions are being made behind the scenes by whoever can outsmart everyone else. And people could die. And you're hurrying to defend this democracy that will get rid of people like you tomorrow?"

"Who else is there to defend, Alevtina?"

"Defend your soul, defend me, Nastenka. Everyone keeps shouting, 'Russia, Russia!' and striving to save her. Why doesn't anyone strive to save the family? Can you have Russia, a nation, without families?" Alevtina asked bitterly.

And suddenly the python crawled out into the space between a bewildered Palchikov, Nastenka in his arms, and the irate Alevtina. It lifted its head, forked tongue flickering. Its emerald eyes had a familial rebuke in them.

"Papa, let me down," Nastenka said. "Pitey wants to tell me something."

Pitey moved to Nastenka's ear and whispered. "Pitey says not to argue," Nastenka translated. "We must love each other, because Nature doesn't know how to make dead people come alive."

"I'm not arguing," Palchikov said. "I love you, Alevtina. I love you, Nastenka. I have a present for you—this moonwalker. Be careful with it—it might run away."

Palchikov kissed Nastenka, patted Pitey, and said goodbye with his eyes to Alevtina, because he was afraid to touch her, and strode off past the cages filled with animals upset by the rumbling of the tanks.

Levchik and Vovchik, having finished off the vodka, were sweeping up after the deer and exchanging business ideas.

"That viper would make a good souvenir," said Levchik.

"About seven yards of snake skin. . . . Would be easy to sell," Vovchik mused.

"But do you know how to skin it?" Levchik worried.

"We had the first Sputnik in space and we don't know how to skin a snake? There's more than one way, you know," chuckled Vovchik.

The Tadjik
In The Tank

THEY SAY HIS GRANDMOTHER WAS the most beautiful woman in their mountain village.

But he had never seen her.

When she was young, women on both sides of the river that separates Tadjikistan from Afghanistan wore the parandjan, and taking photographs was considered a sin.

But those who had seen his grandmother when she bathed in the spring in which tender petals of mountain roses floated, said that the skin of her face was as fine as a moonbeam penetrating a crack in a harem wall, her eyes were like lacquer and elongated like dates and her lashes were so long that butterflies could rest on them.

In the early thirties, her husband was killed by men from the valley because he had too many horses and sheep, and she was left alone. Thrown out of her former house, she lived in a dilapidated adobe hut with her three daughters.

All that remained from the former homestead were the chickens, who wisely fled to the hills during the revolutionary confiscation and then loyally returned to their mistress.

The daughters ran on sharp stones and their shoes soon wore out, and their mother decided to cross the river to Afghanistan, to the Sunday bazaar in a neighboring village, to sell an old silver amulet that she had hidden from the men from the valley and a few chickens, and to buy her daughters some shoes.

But that Sunday the men from the valley came back with rifles and a red flag. They blew up the bridge across the river, and put up a post, with a sign reading "USSR" and sentries.

The poor woman ended up alone in a foreign country, without the right to return to her own, and she ran up and down the bank, shouting and waving her arms, three pairs of children's shoes dangling from her hands. On the other bank of the river, now a locked border, her three orphaned girls ran up and down, also crying and screaming.

But the cries of the mother and the daughters did not reach the opposite shores and fell impotently into the middle of the river, rolling downstream with the white flecks of foam.

And one night the mother, having lost her reason, climbed desperately to the top of an Afghan minaret, even though that was strictly forbidden, and howled and cried until morning, trying to reach her daughters' ears. The infuriated mullah and his faithful came running to pull the blasphemous woman from the minaret, but they froze at its foot, stunned by howls of maternal grief, and let her cry until she could no more.

She went mad and jumped into the river, swimming to her daughters, but the border guards with red stars on their green caps shot her. The corpse floated to her native shore and with it, three pairs of children's shoes, tied around her neck on a rope.

But she saved her daughters by her death, because the other residents of the village were shamed by her fearlessness, and took the girls in and kept them from starvation and brought them up.

And one of those girls was the mother of the Tadjik tank soldier who on August 19, 1991, drove his tank along Kutuzovsky Prospect, past the triumphal arch erected in memory of the Battle of Borodino and straight for the Russian parliament. And the Tadjik's helmet had the same red star as the ones on the caps of the guards who had shot his still-young grandmother, carrying three pairs of children's shoes in the stormy waves of the mountain river.

They say that when the shoes were taken from her neck, in which there was no pulse, they found a live silverfish in one of them.

As a child, he had worn the patched but still-whole shoes that his mother had worn on her orphaned feet, her legs covered with scabs and mosquito bites.

Those shoes had hung on his grandmother's neck when she tried to swim across the Pyandzh.

There were even more scratches, cracks and wrinkles in the leather, the soles had been changed three times, but his mother would not allow these long-lived shoes to be discarded, and now they were waiting for his return from the army, in his native kishlak, or village, at the bottom of the family trunk woven out of willow branches.

"I want your son to run around in these shoes, too," his mother had said.

The Tadjik tank driver did not yet have a wife, but the future mother of his future sons already existed.

Before leaving for the army, he had gone to say goodbye to his old friend Waterfall.

Waterfall lived not far from the village, in the mountains. Waterfall had a long silvery beard and his face, way up high in the clouds, had never been seen.

Waterfall talked not with his face, but with his beard made of many streams, a beard that rustled, rang and roared.

But that day when the young man came to say goodbye, Waterfall paid no attention to him.

Waterfall was busy with someone else, and his beard was whispering with great tenderness.

The first thing the boy saw was a lonely peach.

The peach lay in a small crevice upholstered with velvety moss, importantly, as if this granite bed had been made by nature especially for it.

The peach was fuzzy, and the Waterfall's moist breath sparkled on the fuzz.

Next to the peach was an earthen pitcher with a long swanlike neck, not yet filled with water, holding down light, colorful trousers with mountain burrs stuck in the fabric, to keep them from flying off in the wind.

The peach was pale pink and one cheek was red, embarrassed by something it saw.

The peach didn't have a second cheek, because someone had taken a bite out of it.

In the open, golden flesh of the peach ran the impression of even teeth, filled with glowing juices. The pit looked like an ossified brown face that had lost all its features except for wrinkles.

The boy looked where the peach was looking and saw the white pitcher of a woman's body, with which the beard of the Waterfall was playing, embracing it.

The boy knew the girl whose hair, freed from its braids, had turned into a small black waterfall within the big silver one.

As children they had played, and he used to pull her braids, and then she began lowering her eyes when they met.

Her shyness was born before her beauty, but the beauty peeked out from shyness like the tender green shoot of a future tree from inside the peach pit.

Now the girl seemed like a stranger to him, as if, upon entering Waterfall, she had been born anew within it. The boy thought with jealousy of Waterfall embracing the girl, and saw Waterfall not as a friend but as a rival.

The boy quietly took the peach and impulsively pressed his teeth against the impression of the girl's teeth—their first kiss, through the peach.

He forced himself to look away from the forbidden sight. He went down a few spirals in the path and waited. Only when the pitcher floated up around the path, filled by Waterfall and swaying on the girl's shoulder, did he appear, apparently by accident.

The girl did not stop but merely lowered her eyes.

He could not walk next to her, because the path was too narrow, and so he followed, seeing only the braids on the back of her head, dividing up her tamed hair into black streams. He saw the pitcher on her shoulder, held by a hand with softly jangling bracelets, on which drops of love from the silver Waterfall evaporated and died. But the fact that the girl had lowered her eyes saved her, because she saw a viper at her feet, crawling across the path.

The snake froze, a muscle of anticipation. It started swaying, preparing to strike in the direction of danger and sink its fangs into its enemy, the fangs full of poison deadly for everyone but itself.

But the boy had known from childhood how to deal with snakes. He formed a flute with his hands and whistled a tune that an old shepherd had taught him.

The melody worked on the snake — it realized that these two did not wish harm to it or its children. The snake hissed something maternally beckoning and went calmly on its way, and the path was crossed by several tiny snakes that then disappeared with their mother in the brush.

"Would you like a drink from my pitcher?" asked the grateful girl. It was really another question: Do you love me?

"I do," he said, and that was his answer: I do.

And when he drank from her pitcher, he remembered that he was drinking the water in which she had just been swimming, and he could not tear himself away from the clay mouth for a long time.

"I'm leaving for the army tomorrow," he said.

"I know," she replied. "Where are you going?"

"To Russia," he said.

"Russia has big houses," she said, and that was a question: would he return?

"But we have big mountains," he said, and that was his answer: he would.

And on August 19, 1991, he, a man from the big mountains, looked out in fear from his tank as if from a boulder on steel treads rolling along the asphalt at the people from the big houses, whom he did not understand.

And the people from the big houses looked with fear and hostility at the man from the big mountains in the tank.

The tank was lost in the streets of Moscow, separated from the others, and his head poking out of the hatch, twisting around, felt hemmed in by the buildings that were like unfamiliar cliffs, boding no good.

From far, far beyond these rooftops with spires he thought he heard a voice that he had never heard before.

His mother had told him about that voice.

It was the voice of his half-crazed grandmother crying from the minaret, separated from him forever by the river.

And when he looked through his binoculars here is what the Tadjik saw.

The tanks were caught in a living human trap.

The tank drivers were peaceful, cursing a bit or joking with the people climbing up on the tanks.

The tank drivers were eating ice cream that was being offered to them from all sides.

The tank drivers had allowed Muscovites to stick flowers in the muzzles of their guns.

But a shot through the guns would easily spit out the flowers stuck in them.

The tank drivers could not understand a thing: they had been told to defend the bridge and wait for orders. But they could not foretell what the orders would be. And they were more afraid of the orders than of the people on the tanks.

The Raincoat Of Yevtushenkologist Number One

WHEN I GOT BACK TO my dacha in Peredelkino after my run in the woods, Yevtushenkologist Number One was already waiting for me in his red jalopy, splashed with mud by the tanks headed for Moscow.

First we stayed glued to the radio, greedily trying to catch the latest news from abroad, as we had done in the recent past of radio jamming and psychiatric prisons. But then we looked at each other and understood.

It was time to go.

"Let's take my jalopy," said Yevtushenkologist Number One. "Yours is newer, shame to get it banged up."

Yevtushenkologist Number One knew by heart the Yevtushenkiana, which was composed primarily of exposés of me. He did not idealize me, but he did not like people who did not like me.

The Union of Yevtushenkologists is a touching and slightly funny brotherhood of specialists and idealists, slightly jealous of one another and "in acute need of qualified psychiatric help," as one of my wives put it, pestered to death by their requests for my rough drafts.

The founder of Yevtushenkology, who preceded Yevtushenkologist Number One, was a fellow countryman, like me from a tiny Siberian station, and when still a student he appeared on my Moscow doorstep, like the materialized ghost of a Trans-Siberian Railway car, in which somebody's foot, hanging down from the upper berth, scratches the other foot and knocks off the rabbit-eared hat of someone in the corridor, asleep standing up like a horse; and of the train station, where on the saliva- and sunflower-shell-covered floor, beneath the crooked portraits of Politburo members, Gypsy women offer their tanned breasts to infants with curls like bunches of black grapes; railroad canteens, with flypaper strips hanging down from the ceilings, where a man rests the four wheels of his wooden platform on a chair, a monument to the war that chopped off his legs, and pays for vodka with a heap of copper coins.

When, with provincial tact, my countryman removed his raggedy shoes so as not to mark the floor, the smell made me reel backward.

He ate and drank hungrily, without distinction, and his eyes suddenly grew glassy, as if his head were about to roll to one side and he would start snoring. But his almost dead eyes suddenly filled with phosphorescence, his prematurely balding head jerked, and from his throat poured poem after poem . . . he knew hundreds of my poems.

He read poetry the way woodcocks sing in the spring, eyes shut and deaf to the stealthy steps of the hunter aiming at his love song. He read my poems, even old ones, as if he had just written them himself, and I, the author, were simply someone who had come along to listen.

And suddenly I felt that it was I, young and hungry, with worn elbows and rundown heels, in socks sticky with travel, who had come to read poetry to another self—fortune's favorite, who had traveled the world. And it wasn't clear who was the real me—I, or this Siberian lump clumsily formed by nature from hunger, frustrated desires and a feverish love of poetry.

When we grew closer, something similar happened to him: he began to think he was me. He even developed a complicated love life, like mine. Having studied my technique, he tried writing his own poetry, but they were doubles of mine. He started drinking a lot and often, like me, but I drank only wine and champagne, and he drank whatever was handy.

He couldn't take being me, and he was the first of me to die.

When he got drunk and wept, he would wag his finger at me and tell me, "Yevgeny Alexandrovich, just don't . . . I beg you, just don't!"

He never told me what it was I shouldn't, but it was something that I was never to do. Perhaps it was that I must never betray those who, like him, believed in me once and for all and wanted to continue believing in me forever?

When he died, he left behind an enormous, unorganized archive of my manuscripts, clippings, notations and photographs, and also the membership list of the Union of Yevtushenkologists, which he had founded, and whose first conference he had even managed to run. There were members from Moscow—the chairman of a chess club, a submarine man, a cyberneticist, the chief guard in a printing house, an anesthesiologist and his cardiologist wife; and from Leningrad—a pharmacist and an engineer; and an architect from Donetsk, a militia captain from Irkutsk, a journalist from Zima Junction, a philologist from Altai, a People's Deputy of Russia from Murmansk . . .

The Yevtushenkologists read my poetry all over the Soviet Union: at dance halls, animal farms, maternity homes, drunk tanks, village clubs, "post office boxes," resorts, colonies for juvenile delinquents, schools, dry cleaners, recruitment offices, breweries, Pioneer camps and VD clinics—anywhere that they were allowed.

Yevtushenkologists were walking volumes of my poetry. When I was in disfavor, none of them stopped performing my poems, even though it had its danger. Some Yevtushenkologists, to the horror of their families, turned their modest apartments into mini-museums or mini-archives. They gave me invaluable help in putting together books, because they knew my poetry better than I did. They collected any scraps of paper that had anything to do with me.

One Yevtushenkologist, a respected lady, faked a lower-back attack to get into the Gulripsh Hospital where my wife, Masha, was an intern—an innocent prank, played just to collect for her archives a medical certificate signed by my wife. She didn't turn it in to her workplace like any normal patient, in order to get her sick pay.

And yet the Union of Yevtushenkologists was not at all like a rock star's fan club.

For one thing, their attitude toward me was not at all idolizing. Rather, I was but a desperately selected figure to whom they could apply the remains of their idealism.

I knew that they would read every line of my verse from left to right and right to left, every word in every interview, and I was afraid of the noble censorship of these idealists.

Yevtushenkologist Number One entered my life about twenty years ago, when he was still a top-secret specialist working on perfecting submarines.

It was in a submarine, unexpectedly sent to Cuba during the missile crisis, that he became a Yevtushenkologist, because while he was under the water for a very long time, a two-volume collection of my poetry became the stand-in for all literature.

One morning, a stranger in a black naval uniform appeared at my house and placed about ten very impressive volumes, bound in leatherette, on my piteously creaking desk. All those volumes he had typed personally.

I opened the first and saw what I had immodestly been dreaming of since my literary adolescence:

YEVGENY YEVTUSHENKO
COMPLETE COLLECTED WORKS

I agitatedly thanked the stranger and gladly saw him off, eagerly anticipating the pleasure of going through the leatherette pyramid on my desk. I lay down on the couch with the first volume. But I was horrified to see how many bad poems I had written, like Pinocchio in the Land of Fools, tricked either by his own tiny thoughts, or by the advice of crooks to bury gold coins deep in the ground and wait for a tree to grow.

With even greater horror I thought that if after my death some evil enemy pronounced me a genius and published everything I ever scribbled, it would be the most terrible exposé in the history of literature.

The stranger had bopped me on the head with the full collection of my works and, without knowing it, had knocked a lot of foolishness out of it, although not all of it. Sometimes you don't want to lose your own foolishness. At least it's yours.

This is the role that Yevtushenkologist Number One had once played in my life.

Now, my friend drove his crooked red Zhiguli down Kutuzovsky Prospect toward the White House, parallel with a lost tank, a Tadjik tank driver sticking his head out of the hatch in confusion.

Yevtushenkologist Number One, as a military man, knew better than I what a mush the tracks of the army and KGB vehicles could make out of people if they went at top speed. He had to be afraid. But he helped me to overcome my fear, just as my neighbor had done on the path in the woods, and he overcame his own. And we also overcame our joint fear of our wives, who gave us hell for our revolutionary intentions, under the general heading, "If you get killed, you idiot, don't you dare come home!"

If it were up to me to name that day in the Russian calendar, August 19 would be the Day for Overcoming Fear.

Yevtushenkologist Number One parked on the bridge, since the first barricade was there—two two-car trolley buses, cement blocks and rusty iron railings and bars blocking the road.

Hanging from one of the trolleys was a sign: NO PASARAN!

On the roofs there were people armed with pieces of metal, sticks and their own fists.

The trolley-buses were empty but for one, in which a noble-looking, gray-haired lady sat by the window, a passenger in no hurry, calmly reading *Le Monde* through a mother-of-pearl lorgnette on a gold chain, as if this were the natural thing to do in a Soviet trolley, especially one that is serving as a barricade.

"Foreign citizen, this ain't no reading room," grumbled the mighty sewage worker, gruffly but with concern, as he hauled a garbage can to the barricade, the emblem of the USSR and his own nickname, "Mishanya," tattooed on his hand.

"*Excusez-moi*, but I'm not a foreigner at all," the old lady replied with dignity.

"Hey, you can speak a foreign language? Wow!" Mishanya was impressed. "Where'd you come from so smart?"

"From Paris, *jeune homme. Je suis arrivée* for the Congress of Compatriots," she explained patiently.

"But you'd better get out of here anyway, lady, even if you are from Paris. If a tank comes now, there'll be nothing left but a wet spot and a newspaper," Mishanya warned.

There were people walking and running from all directions, but they were frighteningly few. The White House was huge and vulnerable from all sides. The barricades were like chain mail with huge holes.

By the irony of history, a statue depicting a proletarian of Krasnaya Presnya who had risen up in 1905 under the red flag against tsarism, today held in its bronze hand the Russian tricolor flag, stuck there by someone, the flag that, during the Civil War, had fought with the red Bolshevik flag.

"I don't understand *quelque chose* in this *situation*," the Parisian Russian Lady complained to Mishanya. "Inside the White House are Bolsheviks who just recently decided against being Bolsheviks. Other Bolsheviks are trying to overthrow them in an attempt—*comme je comprends*—to save the old tsarist empire that the early Bolsheviks had hated. I, *par exemple*, am against all Bolsheviks. *C'est impossible* to figure out this masquerade, as Tsar Peter liked to put it. But still, *mon coeur* is on this side of the barricades, because even though I am from *l'aristocratie* I support *la democratie*. I was a nurse in *La Resistance. Probablement*, I'll be useful here, too. And why are you here, *jeune homme?*"

"I'm not even in Moscow legally," Mishanya said. "I'm from the country. But I support that . . . what do you call it . . . liberty."

"Liberty," sighed the Parisian Russian Lady. "Does anyone know what it is? That holds for *democratie* as well. My late friend Georgi Ivanov wrote:

"Up with . . . ," yells the patriot,
"Down with . . . ," comes the rebel's roar.

"I don't get it," Mishanya said apologetically, scratching his head. "Can you repeat it, granny?"

The Parisian Russian Lady repeated it.

Mishanya made an effort, got it, and felt depressed. "I got it. Then there's nothing a working man can do?"

"Not only the working man. Man, in general," sighed the Parisian Russian Lady.

"Then what's the point of living, granny?" Mishanya wanted to know.

"Well, if only to have a conversation like this," the Parisian Russian Lady said with a smile. "I'll get out of the trolley bus. *Vous avez raison.*"

In the distance, beyond this first line of defense on the bridge, we could see tanks and armored personnel transporters stopped by other barricades on the embankment. But between here and the main barricade was the crowd— still not large, but serious and, fortunately, not angry at the tank drivers.

Apparently the marooned tank we had seen, with the young driver poking his head out, had fallen behind that human barricade.

The Tadjik tank driver went down and closed the hatch, having decided to get through the barricade and rejoin his group.

[1 5 2]

The lost tank, angry, butted the trolley bus just where the lady had been sitting, and the impact was so strong that people fell atop the trolley off its roof. But the barricade held.

The tank backed up to get more speed and strike again. But suddenly, next to the tank was a man with a wrench in his hand and fiery red swirls of hair sticking out like a sunflower from his greasy black cap. He jumped up acrobatically onto the tank, didn't let it throw him off, and jumped at the last moment onto the tank's roof, banging his wrench on it.

"Party's over!"

The tank braked abruptly, trying to throw him off.

"Hold on, Van Gogh!" Now a tall, middle-aged woman, agile in a youthful way, with blue eyes in a cloud of white or gray hair, jumped onto the tank.

"Tarpaulin!" she shouted. "We need tarpaulin!"

Yevtushenkologist Number One selflessly started removing his raincoat, but his excessive consciousness of the historic moment got him tangled up in it. The raincoat was that of a navy officer, with a burn mark on the hood since 1962 from the cigarette of the submarine commander, his last smoke before starting the long underwater road to the shores of Cuba.

"Well, do you think there'll really be a war?" the commander had asked, and at that moment a gust of sea air broke his cigarette and the glowing tip struck his subordinate's hood. There was no war and the raincoat survived. And now it was coming in handy. Someone's helping hands assisted Yevtushenkologist Number One and pulled him out of his own coat and his memories.

This was a man with a neat gray pompadour in a yellow T-shirt that said BRAZIL.

Taking the Yevtushenkologist's raincoat, the man in the BRAZIL T-shirt clambered up on the trolley-bus roof, holding the coat ready, like a toreador taking aim at the racing tank.

The tank had no intention of giving up.

This was not the aggression of anger. This was the aggression of despair, the aggression of loneliness.

This was loneliness for your own kind.

The tank backed up once more to pick up speed. And when it butted the barricade a third time, the man in the BRAZIL T-shirt jumped from the trolley roof onto the tank with the raincoat in his arms. The raincoat of Yevtushenkologist Number One fluttered in the wind, filling up like a sail, not allowing itself to be spread out, and clattered change from its pockets onto the tank.

"Boat!" shouted the man in the T-shirt. The woman jumped onto the unruly coat and they both fell onto the fabric, holding it down with their bodies against the observation slits and laughing and kissing like very young people, as if life had turned from slow dying back into a funny and risky game.

"I love you, Lyza! Even more than before!" Boat whispered and her lips bumped into the tank armor.

The tank was blind.

The tank rushed about.

The tank stopped.

"Get out!" shouted Van Gogh, banging his wrench on the hatch.

The hatch creaked.

It opened.

From the hatch came the raised hands of the Tadjik.

Zalyzin laughed and put a cigarette into the Tadjik's fingers.

"I don't smoke," the Tadjik said, shaking his head and returning the cigarette.

"Then here's an apple," said Boat. "Eat it, don't be shy."

The Tadjik understood that no one intended to kill him, and looking around in a badgered way, he sank his teeth into the apple.

It seemed sour. Back home the apples were sweeter . . . not to mention the peaches.

I wondered where I knew this man in the BRAZIL T-shirt from. And suddenly his crumpled face began to change, ridding itself of wrinkles and smoothing out. The pompadour with the neat part changed from gray to raven black, sparkling and getting thicker and cheerier. The yellow BRAZIL T-shirt turned into a red one that said USSR.

My God, it's Zalyzin—Lyza. I'd heard that he'd become a wino. Someone else said that he had died. I recognized the great soccer player at last. He had not been as idolized as his peers Bobrov and Streltsov, who always had spear-carrier boys to carry their suitcases. He had always carried his own, but he had always been respected.

When they let Lyza loose, to replace someone in a losing situation, the fans sighed in relief—he wouldn't let them down.

And now I also sighed in relief, seeing him there at the White House barricades. But who's that woman with hair that's either white or gray? Look how they love each other, they're kissing on the tank. I'd like to be dead like that. . . . So this is how we meet, idol of my youth. . . . What were you doing all these years after you left the game? Where have you been?

Twenty Years Earlier: Lyza At The Beautiful Spring Café

THOSE MISERABLE POLITBURO GUYS. They can't have a beer on the street, or hang out with their pals, or spew their guts out at the base of a statue, or bring a broad to our café. Of course, I'm sure they drink, probably with their own aides—who are no friends but half-guards and half-informers—and they have sex on the side with their own nurses and maids, whose insignia you can see on their shoulders even when they're naked.

So mused Semyon Palych, the coatroom attendant of the Moscow ice-cream café Beautiful Spring, as he watched workmen on top of the Riga Train Station across the way hauling up gigantic portraits of Brezhnev and his comrades for the coming anniversary of the October Revolution.

That one day in the near future this holiday would be done away with, as would the Politburo and the Communist Party itself, never occurred to him or the majority of Soviet humanity.

Semyon Palych, like all coatroom attendants in the world, had a professional way of summing up his customers. Much depended on faces, manners and clothing as well as a multitude of intangibles unknown to people who did not work in the business. Hand luggage played an important part in his assessments. A suitcase was good for a ruble, and if you grumbled that you weren't supposed to take suitcases, maybe a couple of rubles. A shopping bag would get you no more than a penny, and you'd have to wipe up the mess left on the floor from leaking frozen meat. A string bag of oranges usually meant zero since the people who had stood in line for hours to buy them had no money left for tips. A backpack was five kopecks, or maybe nothing. Lately people paid well for the safekeeping of a garland of rolls of toilet paper on a string, more than for an opera score or a rolled-up architectural drawing. A box of dishes — at least three rubles. He recently got five for a folding table with rubber wheels from Leningrad. And once he had to stow a car bumper, and not just any bumper, but a Mercedes bumper. The Georgian gave him a tenner for that. The mysterious world of acquisitions came and went from the coatroom of this café near the station, sometimes in the form of a gas-powered saw, going to Czechoslovakia with Russian tourists, or of a chandelier returning from there, inside of which were ten other chandeliers. To be fair, Semyon Palych's attitude toward his customers was not determined solely by mercantile considerations. With sincere altruism he watched over baby carriages, and tricycles, and a crate of paper diapers, and he never took a penny for anything held for children because he loved children and unfortunately didn't have any of his own.

Semyon Palych knew fur as well as a professional furrier and summer hats as well as any cap seller. Like many of his colleagues, he enjoyed guessing the professions of his clients, as a form of mental and spiritual exercise. In general, he was good at it. But sometimes he failed. Once he was rather rough in getting rid of an old man in a shabby jacket with black elbow patches. The old man, who was trying to tell him something in Ukrainian, had struck him as a petty bureaucrat from some provincial hole and instead, damn it, had turned out to be a Canadian millionaire of Ukrainian descent, and a major peacenik at that. That was a serious lesson for Semyon Palych, and a certain caution entered his evaluation of people based on the way they dressed.

On this hot August day in 1971, Semyon Palych was rather gloomy as, before opening the café, he wiped away a few dried tomato seeds that had somehow stuck to the coatroom counter. The gloom could have come from the fifty rubles he lost the night before at the Ostankino billiards hall, betting on Ashot, the shaggy wizard of the cue (on the advice of the sergeant whose precinct was in the same building as the hall). Ashot lost to the chairman of an Uzbek kolkhoz, who turned out to be a hustler. The Uzbek kept pulling out pieces of dried melon from the bottomless pockets of his striped robe and sucking on them as he pocketed one ball after another. And then the wizard Ashot blew the decisive shot. Or Semyon

Palych might have had the blues because early this morning, as he was chipping away at the shell of his daily soft-boiled egg, accompanying himself with slow, thoughtful sips of kefir like majestic chords, into the window of his bachelor apartment flew a blackbird, which was bad luck. It wouldn't leave, flitting from his wardrobe to the orange lampshade and from there to another spot and accidentally messing up the framed photograph on his bedside table of the idol of Semyon Palych's youth, Vsevolod Bobrov, breaking through to the goal of Arsenal in unforgettable 1945.

Life passed like the smoke of white apple trees, thought Semyon Palych, quoting the poem of the father of one of the people he admired most in the whole world, the soccer announcer Konstantin Esenin. And really, were there ever any apple trees at all? There was smoke. Lots of it. Then he looked at his watch, which showed ten o'clock, and went to open the doors of the Beautiful Spring Café with a sense of being doomed to open and close them to his grave.

There was no crowd, but a few people waited, basically young people in jeans, without headgear or baggage. One had a guitar in a cloth case. But Semyon Palych had an old superstition: Whatever the first customer was like, so went the day. And the first one in line, standing away from the others, was a man of about forty, wearing a cap, green with red and yellow speckles, a classy cap. His face seemed strangely familiar. There was a touch of fame or celebrity in that face, although perhaps it was celebrity long in storage, as there was nothing special about the face. The nose was a real folk nose, on the large side and at the same time tilted upward. You couldn't call it red, but it wasn't white either. The eyes were blue and watered down with vodka. The face, to be frank, was not memorable, but nevertheless it awakened vague memories.

"Enter in the order of the line, comrades. . . . Don't push. . . . There are seats for everyone," Semyon Palych said happily, and thinking where do I know him from? as he took the cap from his first customer. He had a laborer's hands, big, but unnaturally white for a laborer. They belonged more to a bathhouse attendant. Semyon Palych's fingers felt that the cap wasn't some cheap double-knit but real tweed, though not brand new. As he hung the cap on the metal hook, Semyon Palych took a peek at the lining, which was greasy but gold-stamped with an Eiffel Tower. Was he one of those famous exhibition laborers who were transformed into union bosses and got to travel abroad? Just in case, Semyon Palych gave him a respectful smile.

"Don't need a number for your cap. . . . Please don't worry. . . . We haven't seen you here recently. . . ." The last, almost beseeching phrase was a test, but the customer didn't bite. He muttered something and headed for a table. Semyon Palych's eyes slid down his figure, palpating and evaluating. No, he wasn't someone who traveled abroad too often. Other than the cap, nothing else matched the Eiffel Tower. The faded pink shirt with the old-fashioned, too wide and pointy collar and mismatched buttons sewn by a bachelor was domestic. The shiny trousers were made of bright blue Aeroflot twill and had long lost any hint of a crease. The behemothlike shoes with thick and porous soles left scuff marks on the parquet floor.

He took an empty table, under a colored mosaic depicting a young Russian peasant wearing white footwear resembling the spats of British colonial India, and playing a flute. The customer didn't fit in with the mosaic or with the melodic tinkle of ice-cream spoons. There was something about him; of back alleys stinking of cats, of chipping in for a bottle, of lines at beer stands, where the counters shake under the thumping of dried fish and glow phosphorescent from yellow fish scales.

The waitresses floated haughtily past the lone customer, like majestic dreadnoughts past a rusty tugboat moored at the wrong spot. The only thing about him that was neat was his highly cultivated pompadour. It was showing gray, but it was thick and coarse and had a precise part. The hair gave him a noble wholeness. He was a strange customer, down on his luck while retaining his dignity.

His face had come out of the past, and it kept worrying Semyon Palych, tickling the depths of his subconscious, tormenting him, as if he were the Russian craftsman who once could shoe a flea and now couldn't remember how he did it. He couldn't place it. He wondered whether he should tell those horrid waitresses to serve the poor guy or not. The waitresses didn't like being told they were serving a nobody, but they wouldn't forgive him if he didn't point out someone exceptional. He was about to tell them when he happened to glance into the cracked mirror, held together with tape after someone had thrown a bottle into it last year, and realized with relief that the face reminded him not of some celebrity but of himself, coatroom attendant Semyon Palych Trufanov. They had come off the same conveyor belt, with the same nose, neither small nor white, and the same eyes, vodka-watered blue. Of course, Semyon Palych didn't have such a well-tended hairdo, just a few glued-down hairs. . . .

Almost my double, Semyon Palych chuckled sadly. A mysterious phenomenon of nature. . . . We're getting old, my unknown brother. . . . Blackbirds are flying into our windows. But we're still holding on. And then I had this dream that your face was familiar. Of course it's familiar! After all, I shave every morning, and even though it makes me sick, I look in the mirror.

And he changed his mind about warning the waitresses. Looking like Semyon Palych wasn't such a big deal. It's not that Semyon Palych underestimated himself, but he didn't overestimate people who looked like him, which is typical of most people. And suddenly he shuddered.

Someone had casually stuck a cap in his hand. Semyon Palych's shudder came from the Eiffel Tower that was in the lining of the cap. He had the sweet, dangerous recollection of all the old Italian movies about the Mafia, like *Under Sicilian Skies* and *No Peace Among the Olives*, which he had cut classes to go see in the little cinema, now torn down, in the old prerevolutionary red-light district.

The Beautiful Spring Café suddenly filled with the invisible shadows of great Italian movie actors — Massimo Girotti and Raf Vallone. It was just like the scene in which a bloody hare, shot by an unshaven mafioso, was tossed onto the banquet table to signal a new vendetta. Semyon Palych slowly looked up in fear, as though waiting for someone to hand him the torn half of a thousand-lira note and ask for the missing half. What two Eiffel Towers in one day could do to a modest Soviet coatroom attendant!

But nothing of the sort happened. Something much more amazing did. Before Semyon Palych stood a clumsy, sturdy, stocky man with slightly mismatched, deepset brown eyes. Like the other lone customer, he was also around fifty, and he too sported a carefully tended, graying pompadour. The shoulder of his black leather jacket was supporting the textured strap of a Nikon camera case.

Semyon Palych was thunderstruck. Reeling, he whispered, "Alexei Petrovich! Tiger? Is it you? Alone?"

Alexei Petrovich's pompadour lost its gray for a second and shimmered with an anthracite gleam. Goalie's gloves grew over his hands. Instead of the leather jacket, a black sweater covered his firm, vibrating body. The entrance to the Beautiful Spring Café turned into a soccer goal, where the great goalie like a caged tiger leaped about, stopping the ball or getting it away from the heads of Stanley Matthews and Tommy Lawton.

"I'm meeting someone here," Tiger explained, snapping his chewing gum youthfully. "An old pal."

Semyon Palych figured it out instantly and informed him, "He's here . . . waiting, Petrovich. . . . He has the same cap as you . . . but I'm sorry, I didn't recognize him. . . . His face seemed familiar, but I didn't know . . ."

"The years," Tiger sighed. "You think many people recognize me anymore? It's Lyza, you know."

"Zalyzin? Prokhor Timofeyevich? Himself?" Semyon Palych gasped. "He's a great player. But he never had a good team. He was always stuck with the Wings. But people in the know appreciate him. Oh, boy, how could I have missed him. Will you check your camera, Alexei Petrovich? It's like putting it in a safe with me."

"No." The great goalie pushed aside his anxious hands. "My camera was stolen at a hockey game with the Canadians. This belongs to TASS. They lent it to me temporarily . . . out of respect. Some people still remember."

"What do you mean, *some people*, Alexei Petrovich! Everybody does," Semyon Palych assured him.

"Don't exaggerate, *everybody*," Tiger cut off his rapture. "Half the country was born after we left the scene. How can they remember? . . . So, where's Lyza?"

Semyon Palych, touching the great goalie's leather elbow as if it were ancient Saxon porcelain, led him to the table where the other great player, still unserved, sat waiting. The two great men embraced and kissed. You could tell that they had not seen each other in a long time. Semyon Palych was melting with the thrill of being present at this historic moment. Looking around proudly with a heightened sense of participation, he suddenly saw that the young laborers in jeans were not impressed. They weren't even looking. Semyon Palych reflected bitterly on how you couldn't explain the importance of this moment to the new generation, since the era when these two men were national heroes was long gone. Now these heroes couldn't even get served. Semyon Palych rushed into the kitchen and grabbed the first waitress who came to hand. His teeth were chattering and he was too excited to make sense.

"What's the matter, eating loco weed?" With her powerful arms like a judo master, she shook him off as if he were a feather.

"Ariadna!" Semyon Palych moaned and wailed. "Serve them! First class! Champagne! The director's special—the black label Abrau Durso! Hungarian chocolates! Ice cream! Bananas! Oranges! I'm in tears! It's Alexei Petrovich himself! The Tiger! Do you understand, Ariadna? It's Zalyzin! Prokhor Timofeyevich! Understand?"

"Who?" Ariadna didn't understand. "You mean from the rock group?" Just in case, she fluffed up her hair and leaned her heavy bosom on the counter to get a look at the mirror. "Zoya, let me have a half kilo of bananas . . . VIPs, get it? Either a rock star or a man from the embezzlement squad. . . ."

"So, how are you, Lyza?" Tiger asked with a touch of condescension, following a sip of champagne with a spoonful of purplish ice cream that had a real blueberry frozen inside.

"I'm all right," Zalyzin answered calmly, unused to the biting bubbles of the weak golden liquid.

"You've vanished. Have you changed apartments? I had a lot of trouble getting your phone number. I heard someone say you're divorced?"

"I am," Zalyzin said tersely.

"What happened?"

"Incompatibility."

"After three decades? You've remarried?"

"No."

"You mean you're alone?"

"Yes."

"Do you drink?"

"I do."

"Do you work?"

"I do."

"Where?"

"At the sports store."

"Doing what?"

"In the warehouse. And I see you've become a photographer. . . ."

". . . just for *Soccer and Hockey* magazine. First they offered me the job of caretaker of the diamond collection. But I couldn't handle it. The electronic alarm system was enough to drive you batty. People used to photograph me and now I'm doing it to them. . . . A reversal of fortune. But I keep up my training. I've lost my leaping ability, of course, but the ball still sticks to my gloves. . . ."

"What for?" Zalyzin asked softly.

"What do you mean?"

"Why do you keep training?" Zalyzin repeated, just as softly, twirling the champagne glass by its thin stem.

"Why? Why, to keep in shape. . . ."

"And why the hell do you need that shape at the age of forty?"

"For my self-respect. And then I organize these veterans' games . . . exhibition games. People are interested. They come."

"I went to one. I'll never go again. . . . Stinking, rotten shame." Zalyzin's pompadour shook intractably.

"What's the matter with you?" Petrovich was taken aback by his harshness. "The guys don't have the speed, but their signature style remains. . . . It's to prolong the traditions of our soccer."

"Stuff it. Don't try to impress me with that. If you want to keep in shape, you can run. If I had the beer belly your exhibition stars have, I'd run only at night down dark alleys. But you shake your bellies in public, shaming your good names. And you get money for it, too."

"We can't get by without money, you know!" Alexei exploded. "It's not like it's exploitation."

"It is!" Zalyzin's head shook. "You're exploiting your names."

Tiger turned purple and stood up. Sparks came from his mismatched eyes. Semyon Palych, watching the mysterious conversation of the soccer giants from afar and mentally biting his nails because he couldn't hear, froze in horror — would there be a fight? The light mustache over Ariadna's gold-toothed mouth twitched in hope of a scandal breaking out in the café. But there was no grabbing of lapels or throwing of dishes. The tigerish sparks turned to friendly sparkles of reminiscence, and the great goalie sank back into his chair and clapped Zalyzin on the shoulder with his paw, claws retracted.

"You were always a great fighter against exploitation, Lyza! I remember how you took the ball away from Malyavka, and he lay on the field pretending to be in his death throes, and you gave him a slight kick and said, 'Get up. Cut out the exploitation!' And remember in Paris, when you found that the left winger, Goshka, had three two-kilo cans of black caviar and you roared at him, 'What are you, a soccer player or a black marketeer, exploiting things?' And then with your provincial purity you forced him to flush the caviar down the toilet. And Goshka, the son of a bitch, wept, but he kept flushing. You made him use the clothes brush from the hotel room to scrape out the last egg from each can. I wonder how many future guests walked around with Russian caviar eggs on their suits? . . ."

Tiger kept himself from softening too much in reminiscence and kicked the ball back out onto the field.

"You're wrong, though, to throw that word around now, Lyza. If I didn't know what a disgustingly moral stickler you are, I'd punch you in the nose. Of course, money plays a part in these veterans' games. But the guys have a hard time of it, they do. . . . There aren't enough coaching jobs for all the ex-players, you know that. And not everyone can get a job on TV, at a newspaper, or even like you, in a warehouse. . . . But it's not just a question of money, Lyza! Don't you have any feelings at all, man? Don't you feel a longing for the ball? Don't you find yourself kicking whatever comes your way — a tin can, a cigarette box, a chunk of ice, a piece of brick, an orange peel? And don't your guts ache when you see kids playing in a yard and the ball rolls right toward your foot, round and scuffed and teasing you with its rounded cheeks like the loaf to the fox. . . ."

"The fox ate my loaf a long time ago," Zalyzin hissed.

"You mean, old age is the fox?"

"Life is," Zalyzin summed up curtly.

"It may swallow us up without a trace, but it'll choke on a soccer ball." The great goalie spoke, and his mismatched eyes got that tigerish glow and danced so wildly that they became completely different from each other. "That little loaf got away from grandpa and grandma and it'll get away from us — from any old gray fox. It's rolling toward kids, Lyza. A childhood without a ball is no childhood. . . . Do you know why our phony soccer stars are so boring nowadays? Because they've lost the child in them. They don't play soccer, they work at it. More exploitation, in your terms. But soccer came out of back yards and alleys, out of childhood. The ball, it's . . . how can I put this . . . it's like the globe, I guess. . . . When kids kick a ball, they're trying to send the earth in the right direction."

"Well, you've managed to hold the earth in your goalie's gloves," Zalyzin joked sadly.

"Well, at least we saw Paris. . . . Remember our matching caps, from the store of that little old Jew from Odessa near the Père Lachaise Cemetery? Remember how that old man asked us, 'Well, how are things going in Odessa, have they put away the Duc de Richelieu for being a kulak yet?' I put on that cap today for old times' sake. How about you?"

"I don't have any other caps."

"Listen, Lyza, are you expressing class hatred for me?" Tiger asked patiently but strictly. "We're players of the same class, understand? How was it put in that book of the jungle about Mowgli? 'We're of the same blood, you and I.' That's our soccer clan. And as for the fact that our lives went in different directions, it could have been the reverse, you know. The important thing is that we're both masters. The rest, to use your term, is exploitation. But not the veterans' games, Lyza. . . ."

"So that's it. . . . You're recruiting?" Zalyzin frowned.

"Why are you treating me like a cheating shopkeeper?" Tiger got angry again. "You're the exploiter here, Lyza. You're exploiting your pride and loneliness. Do you think you're better than everyone else? Take a look at this. . . ." He opened the Nikon case and took a packet of airline tickets from one of its many pockets. He pulled out a ticket and handed it to Zalyzin. "Read it."

"I can't see without my glasses."

"Moscow–Kishinev," Tiger read. "August 16—tomorrow. Eight forty-five, Vnukovo Airport."

"I didn't give my approval," Zalyzin interrupted.

"The ticket's not for you. It's for Lekha Sbitnyov." The great goalie watched him, waiting.

"What's the matter, he won't play and you're trying to get me?" Zalyzin was angry.

"Don't you know?"

"Know what?"

"He's dead."

"Lekha!" Zalyzin couldn't believe it. "How could—why he's—was maybe only five years older than we. . . ."

"Well, not five, maybe a bit older than that. But still. . . ."

"He didn't drink or smoke. He collected stamps. How can it be?"

"A stupid death. . . . He was knocked down by a bicyclist."

"Is that possible? Can you be killed by a bicycle?"

"I guess you can. We're getting fragile, Lyza. . . . He was coming home from the vegetable store with two bags of potatoes, and was crossing in front of a standing trolley when a kid rushed out on a bike. Lekha hit his head on the sidewalk and died on the spot. . . . Klavka cursed herself for sending him out for potatoes."

"Why didn't anyone tell me?" muttered Zalyzin.

"How are we supposed to tell you when you don't exist anymore? When you don't exist for your old soccer pals?"

"I exist." Zalyzin hung his head. "I do."

"We'll see. . . . Now do you understand why I'm holding Lekha's ticket for you? We had planned this trip a long time ago. They sent the tickets for all of us—including Lekha. And they're promising good money—seventy rubles for the game. And fruit, of course. And we've decided that the entire take will go to Lekha's family. Klavka has heart trouble, and she has three children. They're not little, thank goodness. The oldest is in his second year of college, the middle one is just finishing high school and the girl is in seventh grade. But they're still children. They're not on their own yet. And believe it or not, all Lekha had in the bank was fourteen rubles. So, will you play for Lekha?"

"I will," Zalyzin replied, still in shock.

"When's the last time you touched a ball, Lyza? Be honest!"

"Yesterday," Zalyzin said in embarrassment.

"So. . . ." Tiger drawled reproachfully. "And you give me a hard time because we play. . . . And where did you touch the ball?"

"Back home . . . in the yard with some kids . . . just playing around."

"Lyza, Lyza, you're a straight arrow." Tiger emptied his champagne glass abruptly and switched to business. "The trip is for a week. One match a day. In the evenings we meet with the fans in the clubs. I'll handle your factory bosses. I'll go to the office now and get on the phone. *Soccer and Hockey* is the most respected newspaper there is. I'm not going to give you the ticket because you'll lose it. The team is meeting at Vnukovo Airport tomorrow at 8:45 in the morning, at the information desk."

Tiger put the tickets back into the pocket, zipped it up and, as he rose, added paternally, "Just don't stay too long here, Lyza. Pack and get a good night's sleep. See you tomorrow."

Zalyzin's gray pompadour nodded.

Semyon Palych noted that the two great men did not even shake hands. Did they have a fight? This late in life? He felt sick, but he quickly handed the great goalie one of the caps with the Eiffel Tower.

"Thanks for your respect," Tiger said. "Keep an eye on my pal. See that no one bothers him."

So they didn't have a fight, Semyon Palych thought with a relieved sigh. Thank God. People like that shouldn't ever fight. You can count them on the fingers of one hand. And then he asked, "How is he, Alexei Petrovich? In good shape?"

"He's okay!" the great goalie said without a shade of doubt, putting a new piece of gum into his still strong and clean teeth. Almost forgetting to leave a tip, which, under the circumstances, would have been an insult, he ducked through the door of the hospitable Beautiful Spring Café, and into the huge and dangerous world filled with bicyclists.

Semyon Palych picked up the gum wrapper with almost religious awe.

Prokhor Timofeyevich Zalyzin was alone, staring dumbly at two champagne bottles, one half empty and one full, with black labels reading Abrau Durso. The labels also had a word Zalyzin did not understand, "*brut.*"

"You don't want anyone to join you?" Ariadna asked sympathetically, taking away the second glass and the second metal ice-cream dish in which the great goalie's spoon had drowned in white liquid.

Zalyzin did not reply, and Ariadna tactfully withdrew.

Along the edge of the plastic table came a tiny Lekha with his inimitable dribble, keeping the tiny ball on the edge, just inside, not letting it go out, and jumping over feet in his way. Lekha was wearing a shirt without a number, the way he did in 1945, and those knee-length shorts that made the London fans howl with laughter until the defending Chelsea players had to grab on to them, and the first ball in history from a Russian boot flew into the goal of soccer's homeland, past the helplessly spread suede gloves of Woodley, the goalie. Lekha was one of the "eleven mysterious unknowns in identical coats"—as they were described by the English press—who scored nineteen goals in four matches on British fields in the foggy autumn of 1945. They were children of the barracks and communal flats, where several bicycles at a time hung on the corridor walls and several women stood in the kitchens, each guarding her own soup, and dressed, to save face, in those identical coats with velvet shawl collars by Zatirka, the only fashionable tailor in Moscow then. They learned to play with rag balls on empty lots, their knees scraped by brick rubble from bombed-out buildings, their hands held the violet-colored numbers of their places in bread lines. They were the fox cubs of the crooked alleys of Moscow, and they burst into British stadiums, a hungry, fiery, fearless gang that shattered the soccer-uniformed stockholders and owners of farms, bars and sports stores.

"Just a second," said Ariadna sweetly in warning, and in the second it took her to wipe the table, she swept away all the tiny soccer players that Zalyzin's loneliness had placed there, as if they were tin soldiers.

"Shall I open it?" Ariadna asked, her plump, freckled fingers holding the body of the second bottle. It was only then that Zalyzin noticed that the first bottle was empty.

"I'll do it myself," Zalyzin said, probably only to have something to do. He had never learned in his forty years to open champagne bottles, and feeling with some trepidation that the bottle was already warm, he pulled off the silver cap and started undoing the wires. Naturally, the wire broke and Zalyzin had to wield his knife. The champagne exploded and the foamy stream shot out like a fire extinguisher, hitting the people at the next table.

"Sorry," Zalyzin said, biting his lip and redirecting the stream into his glass. "Very sorry."

"It happens, pops." A young man in glasses with a peeling nose laughed in a friendly way. He didn't even wipe off his college jacket that said "Filfac MGU," which stood for Philology Department at Moscow State University.

That casual "pops" hurt Zalyzin, and he thought about his own two children, now grown, whom he almost never saw since Elka put his battered suitcase out the door. Elka had been stunned by the fact that he had lost the coaching job she believed she had arranged for him, in order to work in the jungles of warehouses. As far as Elka was concerned, former ballplayers fell into two castes—the higher category included those who became bosses in soccer, and the lower those who simply went down, returned to being unknowns, to the life of no travel and no privileges. The higher caste did not betray Elka. They found a spot for her, and now she swayed her spreading hips with the professional gait of a former model down the halls of the Sports Committee, where she was the secretary to the former half back who had once made a rough interference against Lyza during the semifinals, in the pouring rain, when the referees couldn't even see the straight leg he set out under Lyza's boot.

Out of politeness, Elka invited Zalyzin to his daughter's wedding to a young and promising diplomat with whom she was moving to Zambia. Taking her ex-husband off to a corner and redoing his tie with an embarrassed expression, Elka said, "This is the wedding, but after this I don't want to see you around, Zalyzin." And he had stayed away. The last time he saw his son was behind the wheel of a silvery Volvo, which had stopped at a red light near the beer truck where Zalyzin was drinking with his old pals from the factory, lovingly cutting up dried fish on a newspaper and sharing touching soccer reminiscences. Zalyzin thought that his son had recognized him and turned away. His son worked somewhere in the upper spheres of the agency that serviced cars for Intourist travelers, and apparently he wasn't thrilled by the prospect of contact with shabby relatives. However, he did call him at work one day and asked if the warehouse had any Australian underwater spear guns.

"What, are you leaving?" Ariadna asked in a sweet voice when she saw Zalyzin standing up.

"I have to make a phone call," Zalyzin muttered, hating the embarrassment he always felt when talking to waitresses.

At the pay phone in the lobby, Semyon Palych's helpful hand offered him two kopeks shiny as gold.

"Boat, it's me," Zalyzin said, hoarse with nervousness when he heard the voice, aged but still the dearest in the world, which once whispered tender words that he had never heard from anyone else.

"Lyza," the voice gasped, the way it used to when they had loved each other in a distant, completely other life. "You finally called, Lyza. And it's only been twenty-five years."

"I did call all these years, Boat. Just to hear your voice. But I'd hang up."

"I knew it was you, Lyza. I was calling you, too, and hanging up once I'd heard your voice. Did you know it was me?"

"Yes."

"Has something happened to you?"

"Lehka Sbitnyov was killed. By a bicycle. Come to me."

"I know, I was at the funeral. I've buried three of your old pals. I kept hoping I'd see you at the funerals. You've started drinking again. Where are you, Lyza?"

"At the Beautiful Spring Café near the Riga Station. Please come."

"I'll be right there, Lyza. But . . . but I'm old and ugly now. Your Boat has dried up."

"And I'm sodden with booze."

"Don't get soggy. I'm on my way."

And suddenly Zalyzin felt scared.

Told by Zalyzin that he was expecting "a friend," Semyon Palych recognized her immediately, even though he had never seen her before.

He liked everything about her—her blue eyes that would find the way in any fog, the white cascade of hair, the high cheekbones on her weathered face and even her red fists—rough but reliable.

"I'd like to marry her off to Zalyzin. Oh, that would be fine," he practically moaned, just thinking about it.

There used to be a profession in Russia—rainmaking. It was extinct now. But another profession flourished—matchmaking. Most often, matchmakers were people who did not have families of their own. Semyon Palych considered it a great injustice that often the people who gave the greatest pleasure to others—famous writers, musicians, actors and athletes—were unhappy in their private lives. He had understood long ago that everyone in the world was more or less unhappy—if only because they had to die.

What were the happiest moments of Semyon Palych's life?

He was happy at the end of the war, in Berlin, when, in a shower of bullets from the Hitler Jugend, he and a couple of other young soldiers — without any officers at all — climbed the roof of the Reichstag and stuck the red flag between the contorted metal bars of the rafters. Then, the officials from the Army Political Directorate and the KGB's SMERSH* division showed up, surrounded by photographers, and they jostled the soldiers with unchecked biographies from the flag and rehearsed cultural compositions around the flagpole using selected, politically correct heroes — a living compendium of the friendship of peoples — while the cameras clicked.

That was the photograph seen around the world, but no one could have taken away Semyon Palych's happiness when he stood on the rooftop with tears in his eyes, one hand waving his cap with its red star and the other, which was wounded and never healed right, holding onto the pole with its fluttering flag, like the red mast of a ship on which you could sail wherever you wanted.

But the ship did not go far. The true victors were pushed away from the sail and from the rudder. They were no longer needed after the victory. After the victory came the conquerors of the victors. But the happiness of the moment of victory remained.

After the victory, the last happiness of Semyon Palych and many other war veterans became soccer.

The only pedestals upon which the country placed its many heroes were wooden platforms made of a few rough boards and four wheels. The invalids, truncated by war, turned into their own busts, rolled noisily to soccer matches, pushing off from the sidewalk with hand supports that resembled irons. The applause of artificial hands was louder than that of living hands. It would be shameful to play badly for such people. Perhaps that is why Russia's soccer was so great right after the war.

The veterans were the freest speakers in the country — you could not frighten men who had lost their legs with the threat of cutting off their tongues. The veterans did not accept filthy hands getting into soccer and

---

* SMERSH (Death to Spies!) is the acronym for the Russian Army Reconnaissance Special Division.

hockey—areas the veterans considered their own, their last happiness.

The veteran fans hated General Vasili Stalin, son of the country's leader, who bought up the best hockey players for his personal air-force team, VVS. They called him "Fritz," and he really did look more like a German general, with his wolfish, mean face, and in a gray overcoat with a wolf collar. The other Soviet generals wore coats with the traditional karakul collar.

When three former Spartak team members—Novikov, Zikmund and Zhiburtovich—skated out onto the ice in front of the roaring crowd, wearing the brand-new, tiger-striped uniforms of the VVS, for a game against Spartak, the veterans exploded.

A furious crowd surrounded the former Spartak players and Vasili Stalin after the game. The invalids on roller platforms swayed above the crowd, held up by their comrades. The invalids without hands or legs spat into the faces of the "sell-out traitors" and their patron. The veterans with hands grabbed the players' sticks and used them to hit the players and the leader's son, who hid his alcoholic, trembling face in his wolf collar tinged with hoarfrost.

Probably not on Stalin's orders, since he was not very pleased with his son's alcoholic and athletic interests, but more likely because of Beria's animal fear that the aging tyrant might consider the beating of his son with hockey sticks to be not just a mere oversight but a conspiracy on Beria's part, the war veterans on wooden platforms were expelled from Moscow, since they spoiled the look of the city anyway.

Semyon Palych came to see off an old war buddy, without legs and one arm, who was being forced out of his apartment by the militia and sent to the northern island of Valaam. And his buddy, wiping away a drunken tear with his prosthesis after they had finished off a pint for the road, told him, "The war took away my legs. And one arm. Now they're taking away my soccer. So you'll have to go to Dynamo Stadium for both of us. Keep your eye on a new guy, Lyza. Fedotov is retiring, but that kid reminds me of him."

And so Semyon Palych first heard Zalyzin's nickname, later to become famous. His buddy, exiled from the capital because he was not a pretty sight, had recognized a great player in that gawky teenager with wild and clever feet.

Lyza had brought many happy moments to Semyon Palych and to all other soccer lovers, playing a game that represented the last vestige of freedom to do what you want—albeit only with your legs. Running away across the border was not a freedom that extended even that far.

Semyon Palych, seeing his aged and neglected idol at the café, wanted justice to triumph, and for Zalyzin to have some happiness at the end with this large and reliable woman, who came the minute he had telephoned, a call that took place thanks to the coin from his faithful fan, Semyon Palych.

Boat had understood even over the telephone that Zalyzin was drunk and unhappy. This was not a surprise.

She knew that he drank.

She knew that he was unhappy.

The hardest part for her was that he did not want to be happy—with or without her.

He was sitting alone, head down, twisting an empty champagne glass in his sinewy hands.

She came up behind him and put her red, weathered hands on his pompadour, gray but still thick. On her wrist she still wore the watch with the scratched crystal.

"Thank you," he said, rubbing his head against her strong and tender hands, feeling all the lines and bumps in her palms.

"Don't turn around," she said. "I'm afraid I've gotten old."

But he didn't listen and turned sharply, putting his arms around her but not pulling her close. He pushed her away a bit, the better to see her.

The blue lights had not been broken. They were whole. Her flaxen hair had taken pity on its mistress and hidden the gray in its midst, so that it was hard to tell her former flaxen hair from the gray.

Wrinkles? Of course there were. But the blue eyes, like two living pieces of the Baikal in which the pupils swam like silvery fish, were so blinding that they did not allow one's gaze to rest on the wrinkles. It was she: his woman, whom he had not seen in twenty-five years.

"Don't look," she said, but she did not lower her eyes because she wanted to see his face, which she had missed for many years.

When he was still playing she could see him, at least from afar. Even when he became a coach, she could see him as he sat on the bench or stood at the goal. But when he vanished from soccer, all she had left were photographs and her memories of his face, unknown to the fans, beginning with the boyish and suffering face she had first seen on the victim of homemade cocktails, throwing up by the ficus on the balcony in Izmailovo.

Now, he had thrown up all his fame and money and was empty. And he filled the emptiness inside with the cigarette smoke of loneliness and a drink of whatever was handy.

He was as weak and turned inside out as he had been on the balcony and he needed her help again. But it was he: her man.

The waitress Ariadna floated up to the table with a new bottle of champagne and, following Semyon Palych's instructions, said, "This is from admirers of your talent, who wish to remain unknown."

"Can he take it with him?" Boat asked.

"Of course," Ariadna replied with a smile, even though she was disappointed. She liked serving pleasant people and she was sorry to see them go. They were always replaced by nasty ones. It was some law or other. And nasty people were rarely replaced by nice ones.

But Semyon Palych was happy that the woman wanted to take the champagne home—that was the way people acted when they did not want to part, and that meant she would not leave Zalyzin alone tonight, thank God.

Zalyzin fell asleep in the taxi, wheezing like a baby. But Boat was happy anyway, because his head had not rested on her shoulder in so many years.

When they arrived at his apartment, Zalyzin could not find his key. He woke up the super and asked her for an axe, terrifying her with his request, even though she was unlikely to have read *Crime and Punishment*. He tried to force the blade into the crack. Chips flew but the door did not open. The struggle with the door sobered and cheered him up.

"Come on, let's do it together—with a running start!" he suggested to Boat.

Holding hands the way they did long ago, they ran and struck the door, padded with torn vinyl, next to which hung a mailbox labeled with the only newspaper to which Zalyzin subscribed—*Soccer and Hockey*. The door, loosened by the axe, cracked, creaked and breaking the hinges, collapsed inside, along with Zalyzin and Boat who were laughing uproariously.

They bumped heads and kissed—their first kiss since the time, twenty-five years earlier, when Boat had tried to commit suicide by jumping out the window.

The door had crashed right into the trophy case, filled with cups, statuettes and pennants, and Zalyzin's gloried past went flying along with the smashed glass.

Boat opened the champagne and poured the golden, dancing bubbles into a steel cup engraved with a cruiser, a soccer ball and congratulations "From the fans of the Black Sea Fleet—Happy Birthday! 25 forever!"

They sipped from either side of the cup's cold steel edge, passing the dance of golden bubbles from mouth to mouth, and Boat whispered, "Is it possible to be twenty-five forever?"

And then she gave him a pleading look. A significant one. He remembered what that look meant—he hadn't seen it in a long time. He knew that there was no resisting it, and with a sigh he nodded. Boat happily filled the cup with the rest of the champagne and, like a little girl given permission to be naughty, ran out into the night with the cup, gesturing for him to wait.

"Where's she off to?" Zalyzin thought anxiously, unable to guess what she had in mind.

But soon he heard a knock at his window. That had never happened before, since he lived on the fourth floor.

He turned and saw, sparkling with the lights of Moscow in the dark, the cup filled with champagne, knocking on the window in the hand of the rock climber. The other hand held her large and nimble body to the ledge.

Zalyzin rushed to the window and tugged at the frame, unopened all summer, tearing away last winter's sealant, and pulled Boat into the room. Then he wailed, "So, you're still just as crazy?"

"Worse," she replied. "I've been climbing up to you for twenty-five years, Lyza."

In the morning they were beside each other, in the plane flying from Moscow to Kishinev.

Palchikov And
The Long-Haired
Guitarists

ALEVTINA, YOU'RE RIGHT, THOUGHT Palchikov, nevertheless searching, with a professional eye, for long-haired hippies with guitars amid the crowd headed for the White House. It's been beaten into our heads since kindergarten that we must serve the homeland. But what is the family if not your homeland? When this mess is over, you and I will start over, fresh. But where does that line come from, 'Where it won't be better, there it will be worse, and it's not far back again from bad to good'? Where? And where are the long-haired guitarists?

There were long-hairs in the crowd, but without guitars. And the ones with guitars didn't have long hair.

But the crowd itself was not large. The handcuffs they had ordered would be more than enough.

The vulnerability of the White House horrified Palchikov. Of course, there were barricades, but the people who'd built them were not armed.

The main entrance was covered by a few bewildered militiamen, who let people in or refused access only by instinct.

About six men in civilian clothes, who looked like boxers or karate experts from the Alex Bodyguard Service, stood with automatic rifles behind the glass doors of the side entrance, giving themselves a sense of insouciance, like that of the Americans in the movie *In Old Chicago*, by chewing gum.

Palchikov recognized one of the guards as a former racketeer who had extorted money from the new cooperative restaurants and who was now unexpectedly defending democracy.

"People are maturing," chuckled Palchikov.

A couple of old fishermen were driving wooden stakes into the White House lawn and stretching nylon nets on them.

"What are you up to here?" Palchikov asked.

"Well, I'll tell you," an old man readily replied. "It's like this. If they try to storm the place, they'll trip on the nets and we'll get 'em."

Palchikov didn't know whether to laugh or curse. He settled for a silent curse. And he thought, All that's needed to take the White House is about a hundred Blue Berets. Thank God this is a coup of cowards. But where are my guitarists?

Suddenly he saw in the crowd the back of a head, with long hair like tangled wire, and a black leather guitar case covered with foreign labels.

Palchikov hurried up to the figure and quietly put his hand on the shoulder, also covered in black leather. "I wonder, is your guitar six-stringed or seven-stringed?"

The man turned and Palchikov, embarrassed, recognized an aging rock star of the sixties, the leader of a once-famous underground group. He was the First Soviet Long-Hair.

"Six-stringed," replied the First Soviet Long-Hair, shrugging off Palchikov's hand with irritation.

"Could I please have your autograph?" Palchikov said, thinking quickly and pretending to be an ordinary fan.

"Autographs after the victory," replied the First Soviet Long-Hair, leaning toward the black reed of someone's microphone, to make sure the historic aphorism would not be lost.

And then Palchikov saw four long-haired guys in denim jackets, carrying guitars in camouflage canvas cases. They walked in single file, with concentration.

Palchikov noted that the jackets and the canvas cases were all alike and brand new, as if they had all been issued from the same stock. Their faces also were identical and new, from the same warehouse. No identifying features except their military bearing. And they kept a small military distance between one another. Were they the ones? Palchikov didn't want to make another mistake.

He got close to them, to overhear their conversation. But they walked in silence and you could tell they knew where they were headed and why.

One of the men scratched his head. Maybe several thoughts had gathered in one spot.

But he had an interesting way of scratching—not through his hair, but under it. Palchikov got very close and stared at his head. Under the flaxen hippie hair, Palchikov could see a shaved head, with short black hairs. The long hair was definitely a wig.

Palchikov walked beside him, brushing his hand against the guitar case. Whatever was in there was certainly no guitar.

One of the men moved at an angle to the general flow of the crowd and slipped into a telephone booth. The three other clones surrounded the booth, blocking off his sight lines.

Palchikov approached as if he saw nothing wrong. "Hey, guys, got a coin?"

The hairy clones shook their heads, without even pretending to be friendly.

Palchikov rummaged through his pockets and with a pleased cry, pulled out a two-kopek coin, from which he blew off tobacco crumbs.

While performing this act, he had glimpsed the "hippie" in the phone booth between the powerful shoulders of his friends. The man was not on the phone, but was using his walkie-talkie.

Now Palchikov had no doubt that these were the "hippies" his old friend Fang had warned him about, back on the red carpet.

"Young man, you're not the only person in the world," Palchikov complained loudly, reaching across the shoulders of the guards to knock on the glass of the booth with his coin. But one of the shaggy clones clamped his iron fingers on Palchikov's wrist and the coin fell with a jingle on the ground, next to someone's torn-up Party card.

That day many people tore up or burned their cards.

"Our Kolya's having complicated family problems," the clone said with a phony smile, nodding towards the telephone booth and releasing Palchikov's hand.

Apparently sensing that something was up, "Kolya" came out of the booth, a shiny antenna tip peeking out of his jacket. He looked Palchikov over.

"Please, go ahead," Kolya said, not doing a very good job of appearing polite, and holding the door open hospitably.

Palchikov bent over to pick up his coin and felt a terrible blow on the back on his head.

He woke up hearing voices: "Shameless lout. Getting drunk on a day like this and falling down and banging his head."

"But what will be left if we take away the right to get drunk?"

Palchikov felt his head. There wasn't too much blood, the wound wasn't deep, but his head was spinning.

They hit me with the guitar case. Must have been the gun stock. Must be a sniper rifle in the case. Palchikov had trouble thinking straight.

Unable to stand, he sat on the curb and listened to abuse from passersby. "Lousy wino, you mother . . ."

"*Excusez-moi*, if you've had intimate relations with this man, it doesn't seem very polite to tell him about it. What he needs is a bandage." The delicate voice belonged to another era. In a fog, Palchikov saw something flash blindingly in front of him. He focused with difficulty on the dancing light. It was a diamond, a big one, probably three carats. It was cut in the old Russian style of Catherine's day. They say Prince Potemkin had sent three serfs to Paris to learn how to facet diamonds. He gave the first ring cut in Russia to the empress. Palchikov had been involved in a major jewelry case and had learned quite a bit about diamonds.

This one, set in a ring that looked like a golden net, exploding in the sunlight and then fading in the shade, was on a well-tended hand, wrinkled and with age spots, that had pulled a bottle of Madame Rochas from a purse and was unscrewing the cap.

"Turn your head, I'll disinfect the wound," the Parisian Russian Lady said. "Who did that to you? They could have killed you."

"I think that's what they're programmed to do," he replied, or rather mused aloud. Then he yelped, "Ouch! That burns. . . . But it smells nice."

"There's a saying about Russian poetry related to this perfume," the Parisian Russian Lady said with a smile, but without getting soft and mushy with the memory. She was tearing up her initialed, lace-trimmed batiste hankie with surprisingly strong teeth. She tied up the pieces and wound them around Palchikov's head. "Guess who wrote these lines: 'I, I, I! What a crazy word! Could that really be me? Did my mother love him, grayish-yellow, half-gray, and omniscient like a snake?'"

"If I'm not mistaken, it's Khodasevich," Palchikov said, groaning.

"No, you're not mistaken." The Parisian Russian Lady suddenly burst into tears, repeating through her tears of joy, "You're not mistaken, you're not."

Palchikov felt uncomfortable. He warned her, "To tell the truth, I'm not a specialist in poetry. It's my wife, who's educating me. She's tops in invertebrates and poets. She said that Khodasevich was the best émigré poet. Is that true?"

"I'm glad Georgi Ivanov didn't hear her. I'm afraid she wouldn't have been able to convince him," the Parisian Russian Lady said, shaking her head. "But in my opinion, they were both the best. But let me tell you about the perfume. It was Khodasevich who gave me my first bottle of this perfume — secretly, of course, from his wife, Nina. She would not have forgiven him, especially since I was younger than she," recalled the Parisian Russian Lady.

"'. . . grayish-yellow, half-gray, and omniscient like a snake.' That's great. It almost describes me," Palchikov said, gradually feeling better. "But is omniscience possible?"

"No, and that's probably for the best," replied the Parisian Russian Lady. "Otherwise life would be very scary. But boring too."

"But sometimes I'd really like to know what all the villains are thinking," muttered Palchikov. "It would be scary, but useful. Life is so short, and there are so many good books, and even more villains." Palchikov sighed and asked, on the off-chance, "Would you happen to remember where this comes from: 'Where it isn't better, there it will be worse, and from bad to good is not far again'?"

"Sincèrement, I remember the words, but not where they come from. . . . Somewhere far, far away . . . the classics. My memory is beginning to give out on me."

And then, through the crowd of people walking and running to the White House surrounded by tanks, out of the 1930s came Vladislav Felitzianovich Khodasevich, still a bit in love with her despite his all-seeing and cast-iron wife, Nina. In his hands were a nosegay of Antibes violets and a gold-wrapped box with red ribbon, holding that first bottle ever of Madame Rochas. His haughty exile's eyes peered over his glasses, and he asked, seemingly unperturbed, "Happy Saint's Day! Just think, you're twenty now. Can you love an old dying pedant? Hurry up, or the Nazis will eat up our escargots and drink our Chablis at La Coupole!"

And she, his young admirer and student, burst into laughter, teasing him with her rustling white ruffles and her wind-blown chestnut hair, into which she stuck one of his violets and said, "Don't be silly! How could I love a monster like you, who in his own words, 'inspires revulsion, spite, and fear in yellow-mouthed poets'?" After a pause, she whispered in his ear, "I would consider it an honor." And her rustling was all around him and he, who had wanted a rejection as a new justification to feel miserable and alienated, grew embarrassed, mumbled something and she realized what had been hidden by his tough shell as the acerbic and pitiless legislator of Russian-Parisian literary style: he was shy.

She did not become a famous poet, as had predicted another legislator of literary fashion — Georgi Adamovich, a tiny, sweet man with porcelain skin and a brilliantine, perfect part in his hair, an incredibly gentle walk and soft, almost feline paws that could become ruthless tiger claws capable of shredding a reputation. He had written, "When will we return to Russia? It's time to pack and set forth. Two copper coins on the eyes, hands folded over the chest."

The White émigrés died out, poets included. Khodasevich died like Alexander Blok — of death. Getting ready for the funeral, his student touched her temples with the stopper of the bottle of Madame Rochas. She wrote a poem about his death, which began, "The love between us almost did not have time to happen."

At the funeral she came up quietly to Nina, who kissed her and forgave her, even though the next time they met, thirty years later at a bookstall on the Seine, the two proud old women pretended not to notice one another and, at a distance of approximately twenty books, cast sidelong glances at each other while studiously leafing through De Custine's book on Russia on the one hand and Spengler's *The Decline of the West* on the other.

During the war, she joined the Resistance, not because she was very brave but because she felt not joining would be dishonorable. She had not been brought up to be a hero, but she had been brought up not to be dishonorable.

After the war she buried Georgi Ivanov. Elegant even when his trouser cuffs were frayed and charming even when he was tipsy, now he was elegant in his coffin, and it seemed that his mocking eyes would open wearily beneath his severe hair and he would ask about her poetry, "Well, are you still doing that hopeless business?"

But he was only pretending when he had joked bitterly that poetry was hopeless. He had predicted that he would return to Russia in his poems: "There are no dear graves in Russia anymore. Perhaps there were once, and I have forgotten. I don't remember the borders, or the seas, or rivers. I know that Russians are still there. Russian in heart and Russian in mind. If I were to meet one, I would understand him. Right off the bat and then I would begin to make out his country in the fog."

Then went Father Alexander Turintsev, a handsome phrasemonger, a talent, a hussar in a cassock, a priest rather than a poet only because he liked talking more than writing—especially with the lovely half of humanity.

Kirill Pomerantsev held out the longest. He dried up slowly, contracting more with each literary funeral, eventually looking like the wrinkled skeleton of Russian émigré poetry itself. Just before his death, he left a little testament puzzle: "Gorbachev does not rule the country, nor does the Central Committee. Perestroika will not change the result of seventy years." He felt that nothing would change while "an embalmed corpse rules us from the grave."

Then Irina Odoevtseva, the widow of Georgi Ivanov, crawled by plane to die in Russia.

And Khodasevich's student stopped writing poetry because everyone to whom she might have wanted to read her poems was dead.

Only Nina survived.

Nina had visited Moscow and then sent a postcard from America to her former rival in Paris: "Go to Russia. We will never return, but we have all returned already."

And the Parisian Russian Lady went back to her homeland for the first time at the age of seventy-four—as old as the October Revolution, which had flung her from her cradle into exile. But the October Revolution, judging by the signs, had died of old age, while the Parisian Russian Lady had not.

The first thing she went to see in her homeland was not the Kremlin or the Pushkin Museum or the churches. She went to the bookstores. She was looking for what she had lost—the dead poets of the dead emigration. She was unpleasantly surprised by the mounds of mysteries and sex books, and she thought bitterly that the most widespread forgery of freedom is the freedom of bad taste.

But then, in an underground passage, she found a used book stall, and between Ian Fleming and James Chase was Khodasevich. She opened the cover and saw the Teacher's cruel and shy eyes. He had come home after all.

Would Vladislav Felitzianovich ever have thought in Paris in the thirties, when he had only fifty or a hundred readers, that a half century later, in his homeland that had apparently rejected him, a man in a crowd would have no trouble recognizing his work?

For that alone, just to hear someone say, "If I'm not mistaken, it's Khodasevich," it was worth coming back before her death. Not everything came back, but everyone was back—some before they died, others after.

Even in those underground passages where they sold puppies, *matryoshka* dolls and books, you could see Berdyaev haul himself out gasping from beneath *The Art of Oral and Anal Sex among the Tuaregs*, or Lev Shestov climb out from behind Dale Carnegie, or Zamyatin peek out sadly with one eye from under Edgar Rice Burroughs and Edgar Wallace—all of them resurrected by profligate freedom.

The Parisian Russian Lady thought, So, there is hope. Of course, they killed so many wise and talented people, buried them in prisons, exiled them abroad, but if they all come back to their homeland at least posthumously, then maybe will they help Russia become wiser and more talented? Oh, Alexander Turintsev, Sasha, so generous in conversation and so criminally lazy when it came to writing about yourself, why didn't you take my advice and write your memoirs? Then you could have returned to your homeland as a book, too. And how about me? Why did I give up writing? I thought that Russia was dead. It was true, Russia had died, but then it was resurrected. It was unlike the old Russia, a stranger, but no matter how we cursed it, it was ours. It killed so many of its own, but it also defeated Hitler. Now even that Russia is gone. A new one is being born. What will it be like?

The Parisian Russian Lady had gone to the White House not to defend the Yeltsin she barely knew but to defend her good friends, the dead Russian poets, who had just returned to their homeland and who were in danger of being exiled again if the coup succeeded.

It would be sad to have generations of Russians from whom the poetry was stolen.

And suddenly, the Parisian Russian Lady recalled the lines that the man with the head wound had quoted. "Where it is not better, there it will be worse, and it's not far back again from bad to good."

"*Mon dieu*, I know where that's from! Of course I do," she exclaimed, turning to Palchikov. But he was long gone.

Palchikov went to the militiamen guarding the main entrance and showed them his CID card.

"You need a special pass," said the captain and then, lowering his voice, added, "I wouldn't flash that around too much today. Don't you know that our minister is on the side of the coup?"

Palchikov went to the side door patrolled by the bodyguards from Alex, including the racketeer-turned-defender-of-democracy, and rapped on the glass door.

His old acquaintance was drinking from a can of Heineken and breathing heavily. His automatic rifle bounced on his belly with every swallow. His right leg, encased in a Brazilian crocodile boot, leaned comfortably on a cardboard box containing more beer.

The Former Racketeer heard the knock, recognized Palchikov, and cracked the door open. "I'm perfectly legal, chief. Everything's okay," he said, smiling radiantly. "Anyone brings up the past loses his eye. The putschist's no Maupassant! Wanna beer?"

"I need to see the President," Palchikov said. "Important information."

"Chief, I'm full of respect for you, but how do I know which side you're on? Everything's confused in the Oblonsky house, as bearded Turgenev so wisely put it," he answered, generously misattributing Tolstoy.

"And you — whose side are you on?" Palchikov queried.

"The one that has canned beer," the Former Racketeer joked.

"And what if they see the file I have on you in my computer?" Palchikov said, doing a teeny bit of blackmailing.

The Former Racketeer thought and grunted. "Wouldn't you like to make me a present of the small stuff you have on me in there?" the Former Racketeer gave it a shot.

Palchikov didn't like to make empty promises. He considered and weighed. The game was worth the candle. "Fine," he said. "But you have to throw in a can of beer."

Within moments he was sipping a beer and walking down a White House hallway, chuckling bitterly. I could have been sent with the same mission as those guitar players, and that defender of democracy would have let me in.

About five minutes later he was at the door of the President's outer office. Two young guards, who looked as if they came straight off the Communist Youth League recruiting posters, blocked his way. They had both automatic rifles and full shoulder holsters.

One of them grabbed the almost empty beer can from Palchikov's hand and peered into the hole with his penetrating eye.

The other frisked him impolitely and almost sexually.

Behind them, stepping softly, appeared a third man, with a well-tended gray brush of a mustache, a smashed boxer's nose and the special eyes from Lubyanka.

The eyes pressed, the eyes drilled, the eyes tried to push him into a corner.

He and Palchikov were old friends—they had met at conferences on organized crime. Palchikov had noted back then that the man always doodled labyrinths on his note pad.

"Well?" the Labyrinth Lover asked.

"A few minutes with the President," Palchikov asked modestly.

"He doesn't have even one," the Labyrinth Lover replied. "What's the matter?"

Palchikov knew that he would not be allowed to reach the ear of the tsar and would have to settle for the boyar's ear. But to whom else's ear was it connected?

"There's an assassination threat," Palchikov said.

"We're taking all precautionary measures," the Labyrinth Lover answered warily. "We're professionals."

Palchikov thought of the fishermen's nets around the Parliament, but did not laugh—this wasn't the time.

"It's a concrete threat," Palchikov said. "Four snipers wearing wigs to look like hippies. They have rifles with scopes in guitar cases."

"Where did you get this information?" the Labyrinth Lover asked too quickly. He seemed more interested in the source of the information than in where the snipers were at that moment.

"I got the information from a blow on the head." Palchikov pointed to his head, bandaged with batiste strips embroidered with initials.

The Lubyanka eyes tried drilling into him, but they struck metal, pulled back and started running back and forth.

Are you tied up with them, you bastard? thought Palchikov, and now it was his eyes and words that started drilling into the Labyrinth Lover. "If the President speaks from the balcony, he has to wear a bulletproof vest or he has to be protected with shields."

"Those are details," the Labyrinth Lover said in irritation. "I doubt that will look very good on TV."

"How will it look if he's killed?" Palchikov roared.

"Thank you for your information, comrade," came a deep voice, pushing aside the Labyrinth Lover who jumped at the unexpected arrival, and the President of Russia appeared in the doorway, offering his hand to Palchikov. "Sorry, I can't seem to say 'mister' yet. Even though I'm fighting the Party *apparatchiks*, I was one myself, you know."

" 'Comrade' is a word Pushkin used," Palchikov said.

"Really?" The President was sincerely surprised.

" 'Comrade, believe that our star will rise,' " Palchikov reminded him.

"Right! We had to study that in school." The President laughed in happy recognition and then moved on to business. "I'm not going to wear a bulletproof vest—not that I'm a fashion model without one. But I think a shield is necessary, just in case. Will you hold it?"

His question had an edge of uncertainty, in himself and in the people around him, and Palchikov felt the loneliness of the big, clumsy, rather crude

Bolshevik who thought that the word "comrade" had been invented by the Bolsheviks to refer to people like him and who nevertheless was rising against Bolshevism, in essence rebelling against himself. Following Bolshevik tradition, he had climbed up on the tank in front of the Parliament that morning, like Lenin on the armored car, and asked, half-jokingly and half-seriously, "You're not going to shoot your president, are you, boys?"

The ground beneath the tank had seemed to swell up, lifting him and making him visible to the entire world, on millions of television screens in Paris bistros and English pubs and Italian trattorias. From that tank he declared illegal the past to which he himself had belonged.

The President did not imagine that the hardest and most daunting job still lay ahead.

Over his rough-hewn face, which seemed determined, until you looked closer and saw that it was bewildered, fell a gray lock of hair resembling a clump of foam in a whipped-up history that had taken him to the crest of a stormy wave from the bottom of a barracks floor. History helped him, but history does not offer its help for free. He would still have to pay a price.

Palchikov realized that he could not allow the first President of Russia to be killed, even if he wasn't a man one could ask about the provenance of the line "Where it won't be better, there it will be worse, but from bad to good is not far again."

"I'll hold the shield," Palchikov said, despite the fact that he had never held a bulletproof shield before any presidents before.

The Balloon In The
White House

"IT'S YEVTUSHENKO. LET HIM THROUGH," spoke the mask with a basso like that of Chaliapin.

The hooded mask was black wool, with three thin slits for the eyes and mouth.

The eyes were young but piercing. In the mouth, slipping from one corner to the other, was a childish candy.

The mask and the voice belonged to a giant in a camouflage paratrooper's uniform, who stood with an automatic rifle at the small service entrance of the White House, like a museum knight with lowered visor.

He was one of the paratroopers who had switched to the side of the Russian Parliament, and the mask was not a theatrical device. No one knew how it would end and these men could end up court-martialled — either for following orders or for not following them. It all depended on which side won. So they wore masks.

The hand that had just rested comfortably on an automatic rifle came down majestically on my shoulder, and thanks to its patronage, I found myself inside the tank-encircled White House.

I had expected to see almost anything except what I saw:

The White House was almost empty.

In the central lobby, on the marble stairs covered with a Party-red carpet, there were only about thirty armed paratroopers, clearly not knowing what to do. Their faces were bored and uncertain.

The newspaper and book kiosk was closed, but under the glass display

I saw Nabokov's *Lolita*, Yeltsin's *Autobiography*, Bulgarian toothpaste (a relic of other days) and a French perfume called Salvador Dali, behind which I thought I saw the Great Magician himself, twirling his already twirled moustache in astonishment, failing to understand the surrealism of history in its Russian variation.

A sparrow had somehow gotten into the White House, and was hopping around the empty coat racks, its claws making the numbered tags jangle softly.

A ladder spattered with white paint leaned against a wall with peeling plaster and next to it, on an old newspaper with a picture of Gorbachev and Reagan shaking hands, was a bucket with paint and a brush, belonging to a painter who had apparently thought better of showing up for work today.

The parliamentary cat, which had once saved the day by jumping on the Presidium table during a boring speech, was scratching at the door of the cafeteria, which was not yet open.

The corridors of power were a ghost town.

Gone were the applicants, holding between two fingers an envelope of politeness which they would place shyly on the corner of the desk.

Gone were the clerks who, with equal shyness, were tactful enough not to notice the envelope.

Gone were the clerks' wives who carried from the cafeteria, which the cat was trying to enter, shopping bags stuffed to overflowing and resembling a horror film—with German sausages in cellophane wrap peeking out like severed fingers, and Cuban bananas like the green noses of drowned men.

It seemed as if the tanks had surrounded, not the last bastion of democracy, but only emptiness.

And suddenly I saw a red balloon.

The balloon floated out from a corner of the seemingly endless corridor of power.

The balloon danced lightly over the carpet runner, dragging the string someone had released.

After the balloon a boy of about three came bounding around the corner, trying to catch it.

The boy's face was as round as the balloon, as if someone with a merry brush had drawn curious eyes, a tilted freckled nose and a kewpie-doll mouth upon it.

The draft drew the balloon to the open hall window, where on the windowsill stood a round metal Danish cookie box, probably bought at that cafeteria, filled with yesterday's cold cigarette butts.

The boy reached the balloon at the windowsill, but merely brushed it with his fingertips instead of catching it.

That was all the balloon needed. It jumped out the window and flew up into the blue infinite sky, high above the tanks and the barricades with the still-unfamiliar tricolor flags, high above the city which did not know what lay ahead for it.

The boy wept bitterly.

"Don't cry. You will have lots of balloons," I said to him. "And whose boy are you? How did you get here?"

"I'm with my grandmother."

"And where is she? What does she do?"

"She's the most important one here. Do you hear her, mister?"

I listened.

Off in the distance, at the end of the corridor, was the tapping of a lone typewriter.

I took the boy by the hand and we went towards the only other human sound, besides the boy's weeping, that I had heard in the White House.

His grandmother was at her typewriter, retyping several crumpled and heavily edited pages.

His grandmother was smoking, letting the smoke out through her nostrils—something women very rarely do. Her nostrils were finely shaped and slightly angry-looking.

She was beautiful and almost young.

Her eyes were enormous and very green, like two Easter eggs carved out of malachite.

She had a ballerina's swanlike neck, but the collar of her blouse came up to her chin, to hide her wrinkles. It was impossible to hide the crow's feet around the malachite eyes, though. She wore her graying hair with dignity, like a crown of silver and ebony.

The grandmother, not stopping her typing, gave me a quick blast of cold malachite flame over the rims of her glasses and then stunned me, as she spoke with a slight tinge of mockery. "Thanks, Zhenya. I'm touched. I didn't expect you to be nursemaid to my grandson."

I couldn't take my eyes from her face, as through the wrinkles the face of a fifteen-year-old girl slowly surfaced, the way she had been when I first met her. She had the same malachite eyes, but now there were many more black flecks in them.

She was the granddaughter of my first son's nanny, who sometimes brought her to our dacha. The girl looked like an angel whose one desire was to become a fallen one. Her nostrils, not angry then but only impatient, trembled with the need to become a woman.

Catching the female seductiveness in the malachite eyes of that girl, I would look away. Lolitas always scared me. Or was I scared of myself? Once we took her swimming with us. She didn't have a bathing suit, and my wife lent her one. While everyone else was swimming, she came out of the pond, and, encased in the wet, sparkling suit as in a stranger's borrowed skin that gave her rights to me, she took a step in my direction. I saw blue-red bruises on her fragile, thin arms and legs.

"What's that?" I asked.

"The neighbor's dog bit me," she said insouciantly.

Fearlessly, with undisguised meaning, she looked me in the eyes, and I stepped back. She took another step, and so did I. And then I saw how angrily her nostrils could flare. After that she stopped coming to our dacha.

Five years later she called me, which she had never done before. As I drove up to the corner where we agreed to meet, I barely recognized the angular teenager in the twenty-year-old beauty, slightly made up and slightly angry, and I saw how many new black flecks there were in her malachite eyes.

Pulling open the car door and getting in quickly, she said off the bat, "You can congratulate yourself. Your conscience no longer has to bother you. I'm of age. I've had a man. And I can't even get pregnant because I am pregnant."

And then she wept, but without tears. I had never seen anyone cry so long without shedding a single tear.

"You didn't understand then," she said, weeping through her dry tears. "You were frightened by my love. But I wanted to be with you as soon as possible not because I was a crazy kid, like you thought. My stepfather was after me then. I didn't say anything to my mother — it would have killed her. I built barricades in my room every night, but he got in anyway and tormented me. I was all beaten up, remember? I wanted the first man to be someone I loved. Didn't I have the right to that?"

She smoked, inhaling deeply, and that's when I saw her exhale like a man through fine nostrils.

I had not seen her since that day. Twenty years had passed until the red balloon danced down the carpet of the empty corridor of the besieged White House, and her grandson led me to the solitary tapping of her typewriter.

Now she was barely over forty, but she was Grandmother.

"It's good that you came here today," Grandmother said. "Very good!"

"And why did you come, and with your grandson?" I couldn't keep from asking.

"Someone has to type the decrees and make tea," she replied with a chuckle. "The clerks chickened out today, but we secretaries came in."

The door flew open, and a fat man with goggling eyes entered the room. The lower buttons on his shirt were undone, releasing a belly pampered by so many stagnation-period and post-stagnation government banquets, of which the belly's owner had been in charge.

"Where is the President's decree?" roared the Banquet Master.

"Working on it," Grandmother replied calmly, her hands flying over the keys.

"You're killing me," he half-squealed and half-grunted.

"Take it easy. This isn't just retyping," Grandmother warned him honestly. "I've improved a few things here and there."

"In what sense?" the Banquet Master gasped.

"In the sense of grammar and the sense of sense. There are so many people hanging around the President — couldn't they hire one surviving intellectual to read these things? By the way, button your shirt, or God knows, I might get excited by your body. . . . Here's the decree."

The Banquet Master exploded as he stuffed the typed copies into his gold-imprinted burgundy leather case. "What is this folk creativity around here? What's going on here, anyway? Strangers hanging around while presidential decrees are being typed. Unexplained children crawling around underfoot. . . ."

"I'm explained. And I don't crawl, I walk with my own two feet," the boy interrupted.

"These 'unexplained children' is my grandson. And do you know why I brought him?" Grandmother said, angrily moving on the Banquet Master, blocking his path to the door. "So that if those bastards decided to storm the building in the night I could stand in front of the tanks with a child in my arms! Understand?! I won't be defending you, because all you're worried about is stealing the banquet leftovers. I will be defending these children you find incomprehensible, and the people you find incomprehensible, and myself—a woman you can't understand but under whose skirt you try to get at every possible opportunity."

The Banquet Master cowered in the corner, the case under his arm, and obediently buttoned his shirt with trembling fingers, getting his belly to look decent.

But the furious grandmother could not stop. "And do you know who this stranger is?"

The Banquet Master finally took a good look at me, and pressed the file with the future decree to his chest. "I'm sorry that I didn't recognize you right away. I had no idea that you knew my girl . . . I mean my secretary. Is there anything I can help you with?"

"I need to see the President," I replied.

"You'll have the President," he snorted the promise, putting his arm around me and pushing me toward the door ahead of him. "We'll organize it. You'll have the President."

He reminded me of a wandering-eyed waiter from a tea room in Zima, who screwed up his face in mysterious ways when given the order: "Jellied meat, borscht, ragout, fruit salad" — even though the greasy menu had no other choices — and whispered confidentially, "We'll arrange it. For you, we'll do it."

But the Banquet Master, once he had slipped away from the frightening claws of his rebellious subordinate, instantly changed and began complaining, "Everything's upside down. If the President yells at me, don't I have the right to compensate by yelling at my secretary? But if both the President and my secretary yell at me, then where are my human rights? By the way, I wonder if you should bother the President now? I'm just a little man. . . . You'd be better off going to the speaker of the house. He's a mysterious man. He can do anything." And the Banquet Master, snorting, wandered down the corridors of power, which were as crooked as he.

In the waiting room of the Mysterious Speaker, his young, neatly ironed assistant stood looking out the window with his foot on the sill.

He turned sharply when the floor creaked under my foot, reached for his armpit, looked me over, recognized me, calmed down, and shared information, as if he was required to report to me. "We have information that there are snipers in the crowd intending to shoot the President."

A guard with an automatic rifle at the other window—a handsome man of medium height, apparently from Chechen, and resembling a young Clark Gable—added, "And there are more tanks coming down the Leningrad Highway. They're going to storm us tonight."

At that moment, the Mysterious Speaker came in.

He was mysterious because no one could understand who was behind him, how had he gotten into politics in the first place, and what he wanted. No one knew who he was—right or left. He was to the right of the left and to the left of the right. But you couldn't call him a centrist, either. To use soccer terminology, he was a wandering center.

I had never seen his face before. But his face was hardly there.

He walked within a millimeter of me, and looked through me with unseeing eyes.

"I guess I'll be rich," I joked to the assistant, referring to the old Russian superstition. "He didn't recognize me."

"He didn't see you," the assistant said with a sigh. "I'll tell him you're here."

The Mysterious Speaker stood by the window and looked down.

"People are coming, but slowly. Not enough people. Ca-ta-stro-phically few," he mused aloud. At last he turned toward me and reacted, without fake delight but with what I would call intimate officialness. "Thank you for coming, Yevgeny Alexandrovich."

"What can I do?" I asked.

"You've already done it," he said. "Would you like me to give you my book?"

He signed it and handed it to me, saying, without even a smile, "This may be my last autograph."

At the time, I think, he was being sincere.

At that moment neither I nor the Mysterious Speaker himself would have believed that in December, he would be drinking whiskey with the President of Russia in the Kremlin office of the President of the Soviet Union, whom they had in effect overthrown and who, like a poor relation, would come in and be humiliated by the sight of new masters seated at his desk.

And even more incredible would it have been, at that moment, for the Mysterious Speaker to learn that someday, someone would accuse him of being an opponent of reform and the free press and that, just two years from now, he would be arrested by the very men with whom he had stood on the barricades.

The people who make history do not know what history will make of them. But all the people who rose that day against the tanks, against the past, must be given their dues. No matter how bad the present may be, a return to the past would have been worse.

"I'd like to see the President," I said to the Mysterious Speaker. "Could you ask on your internal phone if he would see me?"

The Mysterious Speaker looked huffy and, with a shrug, replied reluctantly, "We have our etiquette." Seeing my surprise, he added more softly, "Just go in. He'll be happy to see you."

"If I don't see him, would you please give him a note from me?"

"I'll try." It wasn't a promise, but the Mysterious Speaker didn't refuse, either.

I wrote a brief note to the President of Russia on a slip of paper: "Thank you. I wish you endurance, courage and wisdom."

Going down the halls of the White House to the President's office, I flipped through the pages of the Mysterious Speaker's book, *The Bureaucratic State*, and came across this:

"An act of violence is a gesture of weakness," was the brilliant formulation by Nikolai Berdyaev and probably, if the Bolsheviks had considered themselves strong, they would not have disobeyed their own teaching and would not have taken the path of terror, even terror justified by History. However, I doubt that there is any justification for terror.

The irony then was that this book had been given to me on a day when its main protagonist, the bureaucracy, had surrounded the White House like a green armored plasma, threatening to stifle infant democracy.

The irony later was that the bureaucracy became one of the protagonists of the White House itself, stifling democracy from within, with paper and red tape.

Then I turned to the title page, to the autograph of the Mysterious Speaker, and I almost gasped. There was a mistake in the inscription, a typo. Three letters were missing.

"To Yevgeny Alexandrovich Yevtushenko, with admtion. 19 August 1991."

I have a collector's psychology, and my first thought was that the superhuman weariness and tension of that day, which made him drop three letters of the word "admiration," made the autograph even more valuable.

And as I walked to the President's office, I noticed that the halls of the White House had become more animated.

There were clusters of deputies from various cities.

Some looked determined, others whispered nervously, still others whispered with an expectant gloating.

A man who looked like a drunken toadstool in a blue workman's jacket passed me in a cloud of alcohol fumes, with hurried steps and lots of backward looks, too furtive for an honest man and carrying a bag, with the word Puma on it, so heavy that it almost dragged on the floor.

After him came a round little Mushroom Lady, in white coat and chef's cap, waving a broom.

When she caught up with him, she mercilessly smacked his hand with the broom and the Puma bag fell from his fingers.

The man, as craven as a jackal, ran off, around the bend in the corridors of power, filled with deputies like Shakespearian ghosts, deciding whom to support.

The Mushroom Lady fell to her knees in awe and feverishly felt the bag, unzipping it, and relaxing only when she saw the Chatka cans of crab and the shiny brown sticks of Finnish salami.

"He should be ashamed of himself. Using even this, whatdoyoucallit, putsch, to steal," the Mushroom Lady complained. "Mister, could you help me get the bag back to the cafeteria. We're opening soon, come for a cup of coffee. I'll give you some Brazilian. . . ."

Each holding a handle, we dragged the Puma bag, clanging with cans and redolent of foreign smoked delicacies, to the door, through which the parliamentary cat followed the Mushroom Lady for its belated breakfast.

Soon, I was in the room where two of the President's assistants were shouting into telephones, their hoarse voices traveling over the thousands of miles of Russian land, now like a swamp ready to swallow up the White House, like a chip of marble, in its crumbling, treacherous scum.

The country that day was divided into three countries. One was frightened and wanted to return to yesterday. The second did not yet know what tomorrow would be like, but did not want to return to yesterday. The third was waiting.

The first country, which welcomed the coup, was small from the very start of the putsch. The second country, which resisted the coup, was not so very big, either.

The biggest country was the third, which waited. But the tanks on the streets of Moscow had done their work. They intimidated—but not in the way that those who had sent them intended. They were scary because they reminded people of the past, and the past, like a tank, could return and squash living people. And so the fear of the return of the past helped people overcome fear *per se*.

While some republics vacillated and plotted, Russian cities joined the territory of resistance quickly, like helmets arising beyond the horizon. The telephone lines of the President's assistants were filled with voices; drawn-out o's from Yaroslav, drawling ones from Irkutsk, singsong voices from Novgorod and clipped tones from St. Petersburg, still called Leningrad.

There were calls, not only from cities, but from villages.

There were calls from the Comandor Islands.

There were calls by radio from a fishing trawler in the Barents Sea.

There was a call from a retired major of army engineers who had defused the mines in Berlin. He offered to mine the approaches to the White House.

There was a call from Academician Likhachev, who asked them not to shoot at the Kremlin and other historical buildings, and not to shoot in general.

There was a call from a Moscow taxi garage, offering a dozen cars for errands.

There was a call from a retired actors' home, where the residents were prepared to entertain on the barricades.

There was a call from the Russian Commodities Exchange, to say they were delivering fifty tricolor flags and wanted to know how many hot lunches would be needed for the defenders of the White House.

There was a call from fifth-grader Vitya Filyushkin, who knew a secret passageway that could be used to attack the White House.

There was a call from a state farm near Moscow, to say that they were sending a tankload of milk and two truckloads of potatoes.

There was a call from construction workers, who were sending five cranes.

There was a call from Yuli Krelin, a surgeon at the Kuntsevo Hospital, sending bandages and iodine.

One of the President's assistants was a small stocky man, an Executive of Politics, who, his face raspberry with tension, strained his voice as he hammered away on the phone for political support, as if it were a product in short supply.

The other, a retired colonel who looked like a general, decorously strolled around the office with the phone on a long cord, pushing not with his voice but with the confident, almost marshal-like tones of a military leader wisely pretending that he was sure of victory. They both spoke on the telephone so firmly that one would think that they were in an impregnable fortress, with innumerable warriors behind its walls.

But I knew these marble walls were no stronger than a paper curtain. I had the feeling I was in La Moneda palace during the Pinochet coup. Unfortunately, we did not have an Allende, but fortunately this coup had no Pinochet, either.

And then the Executive of Politics, picking up the phone yet one more time, beckoned to me with a smile in his eyes and handed me the hot receiver.

"White House?" The words were hard to make out over the hissing, crackling and snatches of other conversations. It was a hoarse voice, yet thin as a spider web, shouting across thousands of miles: "White House? This is Zima Junction in the Irkutsk Region. We are with you. Do you hear us, White House? We are with you. . . ."

"The White House hears," I replied, out of breath with agitation and the pain in my eyes, as if a diamond had slashed my pupils.

I think it was the voice of my pal Kolya Zimenkov, or maybe the voice of my late uncle, Andrei Ivanych, driver of all Siberia who, during the war, would put my child's hands next to his axle-grease-stained ones, on the wheel of his truck fueled by birch chocks, as we splashed through the wet roadless expanses of the taiga on wheels wrapped in chains.

The voice vanished, but I held on to the phone, as if I could hear ducks quacking in the puddles of the little streets overgrown with the smoky feather grass of my childhood; the murmur of spurred pigeons in my uncle's coop; the farewell moos of Zorka, our black cow with the white blaze, whom we had to butcher during the war; the cabbage crunch of the snow, sparkling like crystal, under the runners of sleds and the ornamented felt boots of kids; the creak of the wet well-chain hauling out of the dark depths a pail that looked like a silver crown of icicles; the white moons of frozen milk brought home from the market in winter under your arm; and the ditty that flew with white puffs of breath out of young women's frost-kissed lips:

> I don't want to die
> In the morning with the dew.
> I want to trample hay
> Barefoot with you.

Both presidential assistants seemed to sense my momentary absence, but they pretended not to notice.

"Ask the President what I can do to help," I asked the Executive of Politics.

He came back out and said, "Speak out. The President hopes you will be heard throughout the world. Right now the President is going to speak from the balcony and invites you to be with him."

The Executive of Politics led me down rows of corridors and suddenly, coming toward us, as if from a wall that had opened up, hurtled the

President of Russia with his heavy but swift walk, like a striding Urals boulder; and next to him the Prime Minister, as white as a birch mushroom, with his unpanicky face that showed a canny peasant's understanding; and the Vice-President, a heavenly hussar with bushy mustache and broad chest open to bullets and embraces.

I had never been a swooning fan of the rough-hewn man from the Urals who was not meant to be an exquisitely honed instrument of history. But Russia had elected him president and history had elected him battering ram. For that role, a lack of nuance was a plus — for a short time, at least.

That day I admired him. Not as a politician, but as an elemental force.

There wasn't enough room in the narrow corridor of power to pass. I automatically offered my hand to the President and, to my horror, burst out with the sincere, but ridiculously high-flown, "Thank you from the Russian people!"

I hoped the earth would swallow me, I was so ashamed of my operatic words, which the Russian people, naturally, had not asked me to convey. Without slowing down, the President of Russia shook my hand and smiled broadly with a merry wink. "Well, looks like we'll fight together."

He put his arm on my back and pulled me along, and so I ended up with him and his entourage on the balcony facing the Moscow River.

The President had planned to speak from the opposite side of the White House, but at the last moment the security service asked him to switch.

When the President reached the microphone, two men raised bullet-proof shields in front of him — up to his chin. I immediately worried that someone would shoot him in the head.

I looked down and I couldn't believe it.

There, below the balcony, was no mass uprising of the people, in whose name I had just thanked the President. There were about fifteen hundred people, who looked like a pathetic handful of grain against the background of the embankment covered with tanks and caravans; against the leaden river with indifferent barges floating by; against the background of the bridge covered with buses blocking the way, where that morning the Parisian Russian Lady had read *Le Monde*; and against the background of the Ukraina Hotel on the other bank, where hard-currency prostitutes and loan sharks hung around the monument to Taras Shevchenko today, as they did every day, and from the windows and balconies of which foreigners took home videos of the picturesque events in Russia that Stolypin had once urged the country to avoid.

In the crowd I saw the nervously convulsive face, with its unhappily noble eyes and gerbil ears, of the economist and academician who seemed to have dropped the futile attempts to turn Lenin's formula: "Communism is Soviet power plus electrification," into "Capitalism is anti-Soviet power plus privatization."

I also saw the blessed gray beard, sprinkled with the ashes of Prima cigarettes and quotes from Dostoyevsky, of the aged Alyosha Karamazov of the Party, who the year before had been the first to suggest allowing the embalmed Lenin to rest in the earth.

I also saw the chronicler of the Leningrad blockade and the partisan tragedy of Belarus, his glasses flashing signals, his face red and burning from inside with the steady flame of civic nobility.

I also saw the fighter for Russian wheat, whose face was so charred by agricultural passion that it began to resemble a badly burned baked potato.

There was nothing strange about these people appearing here. But there were some people who did not seem natural here. As if present in accordance with some scenario, they surrounded the crowd, like foam. They greeted the appearance of the President of Russia so loudly, and for so suspiciously long, that they made it impossible for him to speak. Once he started speaking, the President had to stop several times. At first he was touched, accepting the enthusiasm at face value. Then he stopped in confusion.

The huzzahs paralyzed him. He did not understand what was happening. He pouted like a child. He resembled a bear that had bumped into a mirror and could not get past its own reflection.

The screaming fans looked drunk. That in itself was not surprising — the junta had given orders to bring out all the stockpiles of vodka in the stores that day. But when I looked closely, I saw that the drunkards had sober eyes.

And among those sober drunkards I saw one face that I could never confuse with any other.

The face was sweetly smiling, round and shiny like a buttered pancake, with blond eyebrows, and a rosy bald spot fringed along the sides with light fluff. Over three decades ago he had tried to mesmerize me with the red

ID inside his sticky palm, held as if he were a magician. Wasn't he retired yet? Or did they never retire?

"Yel-tsin! Yel-tsin! Yel-tsin!" they chanted with unflagging Komsomol energy, clapping and not letting the President speak.

I noticed that the band of sober drunkards followed the rhythm set by those probably still-sticky hands.

The President finally got it. He didn't wait for the fake fans to quiet down. He raised his voice until it was like the trumpet of Jericho, and used it to overwhelm the shouts and applause.

The voice's echo, bouncing from loudspeaker to loudspeaker, reached the tiny tanks standing by the bridge, and the turret of one flew open, raising a new tricolor flag to flutter like a moth.

And I also saw the service door of the White House open and the Mushroom Lady slip out, no longer wearing the chef's hat but carrying the Puma bag. It didn't look as if the delicacies taken away in outrage from the thieving workman were on their way to polio-stricken Soviet orphans. The Puma bag looked even more stuffed, as if that jungle predator had swallowed a couple of heavy sturgeons and a dozen cans of black caviar.

The Mushroom Lady plopped the Puma bag on the seat of her export model Lada and drove off, straight at the protruding rusty bars of the barricades. But the barricades were an illusion. An almost invisible passageway had been left in them for the insiders.

Python On The Barricades

THE METAL SIGN, READING "PYTHON reticulatus," shook as the tanks moved near the zoo.

The pythons have as much respect as the Spaniards for an after-lunch siesta, but today Pitey wasn't sleepy.

She recalled her native island of Solebabo, where there were so many tasty frogs and mosquitoes; where, having digested some inattentive lemur, she draped herself luxuriantly and majestically on a tree limb that resembled a finger bent under the weight of several precious rings; or she swam in the river, her beautiful and dangerous body bumping into recoiling fish and lotuses that looked like white lanterns with yellow flames.

And Pitey remembered once creeping up to a watering hole, where the clay on the bank showed imprints of goat hooves and tiger paws, filled equally with chocolate-brown water by nature's amiable generosity.

A lovely nanny goat, knee-deep in the river where the water ran clear, her velvet lips greedily sipping her own reflected beauty dappled with sunlight, was unable to quench her thirst.

Her skinny kid stood on shore, its coat licked clean by the mother. It was learning to walk, and its thin legs splayed out from beneath its belly. The sun was behind it, and its black, smoky fur seemed outlined by the light, as if drawn in charcoal and then cut out.

Pitey took a moment to admire the kid, but the hunting instinct was stronger than appreciation of beauty or mercy.

She crawled over to the kid and, shooting toward it, instantly encircled it with many rings.

The baby kid bleated so piteously, and with such a high pitch, that it could have been the golden contour of light on his coat singing. Pitey tried to loosen her own muscles to let the kid finish its farewell song, but the muscles would not obey.

The nanny goat, hearing its kid, ran with desperate maternal fearlessness to save it, but at that moment a tigress, like the goat emaciated after giving birth, grabbed it in order to feed its cubs, who were also learning how to walk.

When the kid was inside Pitey, moving under her skin, she thought that it was still singing.

Pythons never touch humans.

But when a crazed, thirty-foot python suffocated and then swallowed a Malaysian boy, Pitey sensed that trouble was on the way. People started catching the snakes, and Pitey, trapped in nets, ended up in this country, so far from Solebabo, where the chilled clouds fell onto the earth not in drops of rain, but in white flakes that looked like frozen lotus blossoms.

In the big city zoo Pitey felt helpless, like the kid squashed by the granite-like rings of a gigantic snake.

She had become unaccustomed to freedom, but had not yet grown accustomed to captivity, and the most difficult part was the humiliating necessity of allowing herself to be viewed in exchange for being fed.

Pitey had come to like her two protectors, Alevtina and Nastenka, and was always happy when they came to visit. But when Vovchik and Levchik came into the cage, stinking of vodka as they did now, it reminded Pitey of a hyena's smell, and she sensed danger.

"Try some of our Russian treats, beauty," Vovchik sang sweetly, pouring out a pile of toxic-yellow patties from a greasy bag.

"With meat, my darling, meat. Don't be picky, have some," Levchik crooned.

But Pitey did not stir.

"Come on, dearie, don't waste good food," Vovchik cajoled.

"You'll hurt our feelings," whined Levchik.

But Pitey coiled its rings more tightly and did not succumb to suspicious treats.

"She's no fool, that crawling viper. She's a snake, but she's like a person, she's worried about her skin," Vovchik said, lowering his voice. "We'll have to try plan number two."

They returned in a short while, this time armed. Vovchik had a wooden rake that was used to sweep hay into piles for the antelopes, zebras, deer and yaks. Levchik had a sledgehammer.

The doomed kid bleated anxiously within Pitey. Pitey strained and prepared, her quick emerald eye noting that Vovchik and Levchik had not shut the door.

"Wait, I'll get her neck with the rake and you hit her between the eyes, and then on the back to make sure. But don't mess up the skin," Vovchik whispered in Levchik's ear. Then he came close to Pitey, gently murmuring as he took aim, "Well, what are you afraid of, ingrate? We feed you, we take care of you, you know us."

Levchik, performing ballet steps around her with the sledgehammer, crooned in a coloratura, "We're modest workers. You shouldn't distrust the working class, citizenness. . . . It's not democratic. We come to you with our laboring heart on our sleeve, and you . . ."

Vovchik was waving the rake near her head, and Levchik was taking aim with the sledgehammer, when Pitey slipped away from Vovchik's rake and struck Levchik in the stomach with her head, knocking him over.

She made a headlong dive for the open cage door, and streamed down the zoo's paths like a winding golden-coffee river.

Seeing the freely rushing python, caged parrots and hummingbirds squealed in horror, while a huge baboon, envying Pitey, tried to push aside the metal bars of its cage with its shaggy hands to join in the escape.

Pitey slipped beneath the closed gates of the zoo and froze in confusion and fear.

Enormous green reptiles with heads on their backs and long, scary noses were moving down the street.

They crept with a lot of noise.

People watched them grimly, not noticing Pitey.

Pitey backed up and looked around.

Vovchik and Levchik were running down the path, waving their rake and hammer.

"Comrades, hold that anaconda!" Vovchik appealed to society.

"Come back, all is forgiven!" promised Levchik.

Pitey realized that these "modest workers" were the most dangerous animals, and she practically threw herself under the tanks to get away from them, turning at the last second to avoid the steel treads and slipping through the arch of an old, peeling house.

A boy, playing in the sand under a wooden mushroom hut, squealed with delight and horror, pointing with his toy shovel. "Granny, look! It's a giant snake!"

His grandmother looked in the direction he was pointing, saw no one and nothing, and shook her head. "Oh, what an imagination."

Pitey's trail was cold.

Alevtina knew something was wrong the second she saw the open door.

"They've stolen Pitey," Nastenka cried.

Alevtina saw the toxic-yellow patties on the ground and picked one up. It was broken and there was a pill inside it.

Alevtina took it out, rubbed it, sniffed it, tasted it. "Why, it's phenobarbital." Alevtina recognized the sleeping pills she herself had needed ever since she had thrown out Palchikov. "Did some bastards put her to sleep and kill her?" Alevtina muttered.

"Pitey is smart. She'll never take anything from a stranger," Nastenka defended Pitey.

They ran all around the zoo. But all sharp-eyed Nastenka found was a golden coffee-colored scale dropped on a path, and a thin trail through the sandy path leading to the exit.

Alevtina had her suspicions when, at the exit, she bumped into Vovchik and Levchik, with their rake and sledgehammer, their treacherous faces. But their faces were always treacherous.

"Have you see Pitey?" she asked anyway.

"I'm not required to keep an eye on your vipers and asps — may I never set eyes on them — out of working hours," Vovchik snarled. "And it's past working hours."

"Snaky's gone for a ride, Snaky's gonna hide," Levchik rubbed it in.

Alevtina left the zoo, saw the crowd hurrying toward the White

House and heard a voice coming through the loudspeakers. The crowd was not large, but it was growing.

"Have you seen a snake?" Alevtina asked.

"Snake? What snake?" People stared at her as if she were nuts.

"A python." Her explanation merely confirmed their diagnosis, and they increased their pace to get away from her.

Alevtina did not like crowds, especially political ones, but now she had to "join the ranks" she so despised.

The voice from the loudspeaker was getting closer. The voice was coming from the balcony that faced the embankment. The voice called those who sent out the tanks "state criminals."

Alevtina and Nastenka looked for Pitey under trolleys, trams and trucks blocking the road, and even under the tanks on the embankment, but the fugitive was nowhere to be found.

Suddenly, Nastenka cried out, pointing at the balcony, "Papa!"

Alevtina shuddered and looked for the first time at the guardian of Russian democracy, in whom she believed about as much as she did in Russian reactionaries.

On the balcony she saw the husband she had kicked out of the house.

Papa was holding a bulletproof shield in front of the President, who kept banging his chin on it during the emotional moments of his historic speech.

"What's Papa doing there?" Nastenka asked.

"He's protecting the President's precious chest from bullets," Alevtina answered angrily.

"And who's protecting Papa's chest from bullets?" Nastenka asked in concern.

"Your father is not a national treasure like the President, so no one is protecting his chest. To my misfortune he is our family treasure. He doesn't give a darn about us, and that's why he's endangering his life. There are family criminals as well as state ones. That's what he is. He's wrong to think that I'll forgive him if he gets killed. And if he doesn't get killed, I'll divorce him," Alevtina announced.

"If you divorce Papa, I'll marry him myself," Nastenka said, defending her father.

Just then, during the thunderous, historic speech, came historically insignificant but nevertheless important cries from the embankment.

"Look, a snake!"

"A big snake! What if it's poisonous?"

"Maybe the co-op guys are growing them to make shoes, wallets and bags."

"You could make a couple of suitcases out of this one."

"I'll bet the putschists are letting the snakes loose from the zoo to attack us. It's a diversion, citizens."

"What if the KGB trained the snake to attack democrats? Surround it, kill it!"

"Have no pity! They have no pity for us!"

"Rocks! Throw rocks and stick at it! Come around from the back!"

"Don't let it get away!"

Alevtina and Nastenka grabbed each other's hands and rushed to help Pitey.

The poor snake was atop a barricade, swaying among metal bars and the staffs of tricolor flags, and trying to avoid the stones and blows. But her lovely patterned skin was wounded in several places.

Her pursuers were climbing the barricade to finish her off, but Alevtina managed to get between them and Pitey. She flung her arms open and shouted, "Don't touch it!" Her deep voice, almost like that of Chaliapin, stopped the crowd. "It's unique! This is the only Malaysian python in all the zoos of the Soviet Union."

"I'm unique, too, an only child," muttered a big fellow, tattooed with the seal of the USSR and the nickname "Mishanya" and wielding a piece of iron in his huge fist. "But if it bites me with its poisoned tooth, my mother won't have her only son."

"Pitey doesn't bite! Pitey isn't poisonous! Pitey can speak in a whisper!" Nastenka shouted.

But those scientific and sentimental arguments had little effect on Pitey's pursuers.

Then Alevtina had an idea. "Stop! This snake costs twenty thousand dollars!"

That amount paralyzed the attackers. The raised bars, cudgels and sticks froze in the air and came down slowly.

"That's an expensive creature," Mishanya said, scratching his head. "I'm a cheap creature compared to that snake. I get about fifteen hundred rubles a month working on my shit carrier. How many rubles to the dollar today, anyway?"

The hard-currency topic interested the crowd, and it came up with contradictory answers. Other people moved closer.

"It depends where, Pops. The banks give one price, the stock exchange another, and the black market at Izmailovo Park has its own rates," spoke an authoritative voice belonging to a kid firmly packed in denim — a jacket with a dozen zippers, a shirt with pearl buttons, Wranglers with artificially worn knees and even a denim cap with zippered pockets. "My personal rate comes from the Pushkin monument market. The price there at the present historical moment is fifty."

"*Pops?* You called me *Pops?*" Mishanya was shocked, and then he frowned. "Well then, help me figure out how many months I have to work to pay for that snake."

The denim kid whipped out his solar-battery calculator. "Two thousand months, or a little over one hundred and sixty-seven years."

"You mean if I haul shit for a century and a half, I still won't make enough!" Mishanya was angry. "A snake at the zoo has the real good life. Doesn't have to moonlight to survive, doesn't need to stand in line, all the food is served on a saucer with a blue rim. You just lie around exhibiting yourself. Well, there's the rather unpleasant fact of the cage, but a lot of people — lots and lots of people — would rather be fed and live in a cage than have freedom on an empty stomach. I'm surprised our people don't demand to be kept in a zoo."

By then Pitey had vanished again, finding an opening inside the pile of scrap metal and concrete blocks.

Alevtina and Nastenka kneeled at that opening, where in the dark depths of the barricade two emeralds, swaying on the patterned stem of a neck, shone warily.

"Pitey, it's me, Alevtina. Come on out. No one will touch you, I promise. Let's go home," her deep voice begged.

"Pitey, it's me, Nastenka. I miss you. I have a lollipop for you. You like them so much, you swallow them stick and all," begged a tiny voice.

But badgered Pitey feared that Vovchik and Levchik had stolen Alevtina's and Nastenka's voices and were using them to lure her out.

Suddenly a small Tadjik tank driver, wearing a huge helmet much too big for him shading elongated eyes resembling shiny dates, with eyelashes long enough for butterflies to rest upon them, jumped onto the barricade.

The Tadjik tank driver gestured the others to stay back, crouched before the opening in the barricade, curled his fingers into a pipe and played a tender, spellbinding, exotic melody. As if by magic, Pitey's wounded head appeared from the bowels of the barricade, the eyes still suspicious, and then the rest of the snake followed.

"What have they done to you, poor dear?" Alevtina said and kissed Pitey's head. "Let's get away from here."

And Pitey's recent persecutors stepped aside to make room for three females — one adult, one child and one snake that loved them both.

"Mysterious are the ways of the Lord. A python on the barricades," the Parisian Russian Lady said with a smile. "Only snakes shed their skins — " But she did not finish the quotation.

A high, ringing voice did it for her. "We changed our souls, not our bodies."

The Parisian Russian Lady turned and saw a young man who resembled Bryusov's line, "Pale punk with burning gaze."

That burning gaze came not from his eyes, but from an invisible depth that must have burned constantly.

She was not mistaken — they were the eyes of a born poet. A poet of the twenty-first century. But those eyes did not belong to him alone.

They were also the eyes of the poets of the Paris émigré community — who had loved her, who never did make it home, who weren't embraced by their homeland because when they were alive, her hands were tied.

They used to play Poetry Memory within their narrow circle in Paris. One person would start a poem and another had to pick up the recitation. The Parisian Russian Lady had not played that game in a long, long time. All her partners had died. But suddenly, she felt that she had found a partner again, and as she returned to the game of her youth, she grew younger.

Of course, now the game was a sorrowful one, because everyone she wanted to quote was dead.

She threw a trial pebble:

> I do not fear the rebelling nation
> It will avenge the years of blindness.

The Poet of the Twenty-First Century returned the pebble:

> And for your bells, Liberty,
> Will tear open bellies with a slingshot.

And rushing happily on, as though taking oral exams in a favorite subject, he added, "Don Aminado. Real name, Shpolyansky. Dates, 1888–1957. The poem was written in 1920. But it seems to be about today."

The Parisian Russian Lady tested her partner again.

"Who am I, Lord? A pretender . . ."

"Squandering grace," continued the Poet of the Twenty-First Century.

". . . Every scratch and scrape," she barely got in the third line.

"Tells me I am a mother," he finished up. "Elizaveta Kuzmina-Karavayeva, Mother Maria. Born in 1891. Died in 1945 in a Nazi concentration camp, going into the gas chamber of her own will. As did Raisa Blokh."

"You know her poems too?" The Parisian Russian Lady was stunned. They recited together, his voice loud enough to be heard on the barricades, hers a whisper.

> In the resounding hour of morning prayer
> Sink softly to your knees,
> Do not call, do not wait, do not contradict.
> Pray to be forgotten,
> Like those who came before,
> Like those who will come after.

"She was my best friend. And I could not save her," the Parisian Russian Lady said with difficulty. "I thought that no one but me remembered her. That means she's alive . . . she is here . . . in Russia. May I kiss you?"

The Poet of the Twenty-First Century blushed and grew embarrassed but, looking away, allowed himself to be kissed on the forehead and blessed by a hand wearing a diamond cut in the original Russian manner of the days of Potemkin.

"Tell me," she asked, holding her breath in fear. "Do you remember this?"

And, her lips suddenly cold, she mumbled, "The love between us almost did not have time to happen."

"Of course I remember," the Poet of the Twenty-First Century replied with condescension, and recited the rest of the poem.

I whimper like a she-wolf over her cub in a trap,
Ready to lick all your rusty wounds,
To graft meadow fogs to your sides with missing fur.
But you are already dead, caught in a Paris trap,
and you can't be pulled out, whole or in pieces.
Farewell my dead, shy, wild wolf cub.
You will always be dearer to me than any domesticated ones.
But there are none that are not trapped, and in the world all countries —
softer, harsher, smaller, larger — are traps.
Farewell, my wolf cub, fierce wolf for so many.
There may be some with fewer teeth but none kinder or purer,
and I howl over the lupine and canine fighting by your grave
no longer a she-wolf, but simply a beaten dog.

"It was written on the death of Khodasevich. It was printed only once, in *Contemporary Notes* in 1939. The author is Antonina Korzinkina. Member of the French Resistance. Born in 1917. Date of death unknown."

"Why do you think she's dead?" the Parisian Russian Lady asked, barely breathing.

"She's old enough," the Poet of the Twenty-First Century replied with the unrancorous cruelty of children. "She was born the year of the Revolution."

And the Parisian Russian Lady thought, Maybe it is time? No, it's not. A person dies only when his memory goes. Then there's nothing to pass on to others and nothing to talk about with oneself. Life without memory is meaningless. But while we still remember things that are important for others, it's not really decent to die.

Unloading sandbags from a truck, a strongly built woman, no longer young but with young, blue lantern eyes, and a man with a neat gray pompadour and a yellow T-shirt with BRAZIL on it, listened to the poem.

"If I could write poetry, I would write something like that about you," Boat said as she easily picked up a sack and passed it to Zalyzin.

"But I think I'm still alive," Zalyzin joked, grunting as he lifted the bag to the top of the barricade.

"Oh, Lyza. Do you know what the test of love is? The fear of the person you love dying," Boat said and she went on working. "You've died many times inside me, Lyza, I was so worried about you. You can die for a while, but it's not nice to die for good when someone loves you. It's a betrayal. You'd better not die while I'm alive. Remember how Alexander Grin used to end all his stories? 'They lived long and happily and died the same day.' Let's die on the same day, all right, Lyza?"

"You already tried to persuade me to die together once, and then you changed your mind. Remember?" Zalyzin asked slyly, taking another sack from her hands.

"Of course I do," she sighed. "It was in Moldavia, in the city of Drokia, after a game of the veterans of the All-Stars USSR against the All-Stars of the local wineries, when you made your greatest goal. Lyza, wake up! I'm holding this heavy sack. Be careful, don't strain. It's wet."

Twenty Years Earlier:
The USSR All-Stars
In Moldavia

THE POSTERS, PUT UP ON the streets of four Moldavian cities, read:

USSR ALL-STARS
(old-timers)

It was a grape republic, and they were playing winery teams in every city, with the proceeds going to the family of Lekha Sbitnyov, and the wine to the team.

The team's captain and oldest member was Alexei Petrovich, the great goalie known as Tiger. At first he was not pleased by the unexpected appearance of a woman with Lyza. But then he realized that it was for the best — she would not allow him to get drunk before the game. As for after the game, especially in Moldavia, where the wine seemed to flow from the ground, drinking seemed to be God's plan.

Watching Lyza play for the first time in so many years, suddenly she realized that soccer played Lyza too, and how beautiful it was. Soccer was a living, ever-young creature that shared its youth with those who played it and with those whom it played. She realized that you could play soccer all your life.

And she also realized that people who are great in what they do have no age. If the great professional can no longer do what a young man can, he will still be able to do things that no one else could ever do, because he is unique.

The forty- and fifty-year-old players—balding, gray, with emaciated cheeks or bouncing beer bellies, suffering from old injuries to the kneecaps and ankle bones, operations, sciatica, gout, hemorrhoids, infections, funguses, prostate problems, high blood-pressure, drinking binges and the shakes—played circles around the young bucks on the winery teams, despite the marvelous aromas of the medal-winning Negru de purkar, Cabernet, Fetasca and Lydia awaiting them at Lucullan post-game feasts. They ruthlessly scored one goal after another, the clusters of grapes hung from the goal posts—a generous but ill-considered gesture—falling with every blow.

Of course, they no longer had the speed—the veterans played in tango rhythm, while the home team played at the speed of rock-and-roll mixed with the Moldavian folk dance *Zhok*. But the ball stuck to the slow and gentle feet of the veterans, and did not want to leave them, and seemed to dribble on its own, without their help, and to go around the young wine makers, who were angry and bewildered that these senior citizens could beat them.

Interestingly, the years had changed the faces, figures and weights of the players, but not their signature playing style, and the overflowing stands held quite a few elderly Moldavians who rooted for the guests more than for their own youngsters, and who wept tears of joy in recognition of their own youth, whenever Kostya Krizhevsky did his famous "scissors" in the air; or when tireless Valya Bubukin jumped not higher but smarter than the young winemakers, attracting the ball with his shiny bald head as if it were a magnet; or when Seryozha Salnikov, admirer of the poets Pasternak and Gumilyov and a passionate cardplayer, who back in the finals of '44 had scored a goal from the corner, elegantly repeated that trick in Moldavia so many years later. They wept when the still gorgeous Lyokha Paramonov, with the birthmark on his cheek that his female fans had adored and which still had three wiry hairs sticking out of it, now silver instead of wheat, took a ball in the chest as if he had a special spot for it between his ribs, and the ball halted for a second and then slid down his body to the boot that was gently waiting for it; or when defenseman "Uncle" Kolya Senyukov, who looked like a metalsmith who enjoyed drinking but knew his work, and who in his day had blocked many a famous forward, and was now a great-grandfather, still stuck tight to the impetuous Moldavians like a tar baby. They wept when the man who had made the Olympic goal in Australia, the ageless, rosy-cheeked Tolya Ilyin, still slipping out of every soccer trap like a watermelon seed from your fingers, scored a goal even though his big toe was so swollen with arthritis that his boot had to be slit before the game; or when the ball seemed to glue itself to Tiger's gloves when he dove for it, landing so hard that his agitated kidney stone made him throw himself against the wall in pain all night after they won the game.

Zalyzin played almost as easily and youthfully as he had long ago at the Stormy Petrel Stadium, when the girl with blue lantern eyes handed him a single dahlia, which she had picked from the flowerbed, and said loudly in front of everyone, "You are a genius."

But she alone, that gray-haired rock climber, knew what happened to him after these games, in the stuffy hotel rooms, their walls hung with still lifes of fruits and vegetables and portraits of Brezhnev, of whom the local officials were as proud as of anything grown on Moldavian soil.

Zalyzin would jump up in the middle of the night, his lip bitten and bleeding, to hop around on the floor on one bare foot or the other, trying to get rid of the painful cramps in his legs, and Boat would massage his leaden calves with the republic's best cognac from the ten-liter gift jug.

The soccer old-timers were buried under flowers and bottles.

For the beauty of their game, they were forgiven the fact that, instead of showing their gratitude for Moldavian hospitality, they got eleven goals in the first three games, and that Tiger and his backup, the relatively young old man named Pshenichnikov, did not allow a single goal.

But of course the crowds really wanted to see the legendary King of the Heel Pass, "Elephant." He was the blue-eyed Pele of Russian soccer — and probably as talented as the Brazilian. After the genius Bobrov, whose underwear was pulled off by defenders desperately trying to hold him back, Elephant had gotten the most kicks in the legs. He combined Bobrov's rough-and-tumble break with an unpredictable, elegant heel pass. The King of the Heel Pass did not like to run without the ball, and at those times irritated his fans by seeming to nap as he slowly ambled along the field. But the touch of the ball on his boots aroused him, as the kiss did Sleeping Beauty. He really did resemble an elephant in the zoo who, asleep on his feet, awakens. Then the King of the Heel Pass turned into a fighting elephant from Hannibal's army, destroying enemy lines.

Unlike Pele, who was in charge of his own legs, the King of the Heel Pass was told by everyone and his kid brother how to use his legs — they all gave him advice and lessons. He was sent to collective farms to harvest potatoes, where his frozen fingers, along with the fingers of professors of philosophy and mathematics, of surgeons and computer experts forced to do their patriotic duty and not get stuck up, pulled potatoes from the wet, cold soil. Envy of his universal fame and anger at his independence, his indifference to the lectures given him, turned to accusations of "star sickness." Then he was framed on rape charges, even though girls were all over him, practically raping him. The King of the Heel Pass spent some of the best years of his life behind barbed wire (although not the most barbed variant — he went on playing soccer, but now with murderers, thieves, crooks and camp guards).

When the King of the Heel Pass was allowed to return to the game, now with the halo of martyrdom around his balding head and noticeably heavier after life on the inside, he still played well, though heavily. But for years he was not allowed to travel abroad with the team — what if he ran off. . . .

He differed greatly from many of his teammates because he was not interested in foreign clothes and all kinds of stereo equipment. The only thing he cared about in a woman was that she be a good person, and he liked the cheapest, black-top vodka, and he was willing even to drink it warm, as long as there was a pickle and a damp twig of dill weed and a black currant leaf to chase it.

His "uppityness" was an envious lie. He knew his own worth, but he was always amiable, like the elephant that did not take advantage of its strength. His legs trapped in the chains of gossip, unhappily he lugged in his clumsy trunk the log of his fame.

At the beginning of the first Moldavian game, the King of the Heel Pass pulled a leg muscle and was taken off the field by local fans unable to believe their luck, that their sweaty shoulders were embraced by their idol, hopping on one foot.

He was so adored that he didn't even have to play — it was enough for him to appear before the game and wave, for the fans to fall into religious ecstasy at the sight of the European Golden Boot winner and virtual prisoner of conscience.

And so he traveled with the team from city to city, nodding tipsily in the bus, a living souvenir that could be touched and even gotten drunk. He was happy to be photographed with people's arms around him, and it happened so often that he could have been a cardboard cutout of himself.

On the whole, all the players in the USSR All-Stars (old-timers) were harmless and friendly. With one exception.

The exception's nickname was "Numero." As an offensive player, he was not so much talented as effective, and he made goals thanks to two qualities that have no direct bearing on talent—speed and arrogance.

Numero gave off a whiff of shit even as a teenager, and with age the smell got stronger. His eyes did not improve—they went from wandering to shifty. The only thought process they reflected was how to steal, speculate, swipe, cheat, spoil. His only relatively positive quality was that he didn't even try to appear a good person.

Numero was not a disguised bastard but a sincere one.

Zalyzin discovered that Numero was among his teammates only when they were airborne to Kishinev. Otherwise he would not have gone. Numero had once pulled a very dirty trick on him.

Zalyzin was the assistant coach of the USSR All-Stars for a series of games with Latin-American teams in pre-Allende Chile.

The King of the Heel Pass was at long last included in the team, his first time abroad after doing time. This was due to Zalyzin's insistence and made his personal responsibility.

"Honest, I won't run away," the King said with a sigh as he scratched his head. "All you guys would get into trouble if I did."

The games were friendly but, following tradition, the bosses kept the Soviet team to a Draconian regimen; at least three people together when they went for a walk; no making friends with men or especially with women; 10:00 p.m. beddy-byes; and of course, the dry law.

It was made worse by the fact that the Brazilian All-Stars were staying at the same hotel and the Soviet players saw the Brazilians drinking after every game—moderately, mostly piña coladas—dancing the mambo with girls as supple and clinging as the lianas from Amazon jungles, and then taking them up to their rooms.

And the Brazilians were not the least bit scared of their coach, who differed from his players only in that he drank Mexican tequila instead of piña coladas, licking the pinch of salt from the soft spot between the thumb and forefinger of his left hand, and instead of liana girls he preferred giggly, plump ones, who looked like a Latino version of the short-order cooks in Moscow.

The Soviet players glumly watched their own head coach, the team commander and the KGB agent (posing as assistant masseur) put a bottle of vodka on the table and sadistically drink it in front of them, while they themselves had only Borzhomi mineral water brought from home in crates, because foreign mineral water might have had an adverse effect on their goal-making.

Zalyzin was against this kind of torture, but the head coach merely laughed. "It's all right. It builds character. And it'll make them meaner."

Zalyzin knew that as soon as the management troika got drunk and went to sleep, the Soviet players in their rooms would pull out their open bottles of vodka, their Soviet smoked sausages and pasteurized cheeses and secretly drink and play twenty-one and poker for money or peanuts.

One evening, when a forward did not answer Zalyzin's knock at his door, Zalyzin tried the doorknob and the door swung open. Through the partly open bathroom door Zalyzin saw the young forward, who had made so many female fans swoon over him in Moscow, standing over the sink with his pants down, a photograph of a naked woman propped against the mirror, his face grimacing not so much with pleasure and relief from his pain but with disgust at himself.

Zalyzin knew that this would lead to no good. And he was right.

Zalyzin's phone rang at three in the morning.

"Comrade Zalyzin?" asked a polite male voice, in Russian with a slight foreign accent.

"Well, yes," Zalyzin replied cautiously, remembering all the rules about possible provocations.

"Please forgive me for the late hour," the voice continued, a bit too fancy for a foreigner but with that accent. "I'm Chilean. A graduate of Lumumba University in Moscow. I must see you immediately. I'm downstairs in the lobby."

"It's late," mumbled Zalyzin, wondering whether this was or was not a provocation.

"Unfortunately, it has to be right now. Otherwise it will be too late. But don't say a word to any of your people."

It must be a provocation, decided Zalyzin, if he doesn't want me to mention it.

But the voice persisted. "I feel that you do not trust me, Comrade Zalyzin. I can understand that being excessively trusting in capitalist surroundings can be dangerous. But Comrade Zalyzin, when I was a student I went to all your games. Do you want proof? Here is my favorite goal of yours. Luzhniki Stadium; the quarter-finals with Spartak. It's one-all; the forty-fourth minute of the second half. Spartak attacks. Simonyan shoots a high pass across the entire field to Tatushin on the right wing and moves, unattended, to the penalty zone along the center, waiting for the ball. And you, Comrade Zalyzin, you come up, your legs in the trajectory the ball must follow. Tatushin falls, barely getting the ball to Simonyan, but the ball, blocked by you, rolls very slowly. Tatushin, on the ground, waves his arms in outrage to the referee to show that you knocked him down. Simonyan, thinking that the referee has blown his whistle and he hasn't heard it over the roar of the crowd, has also stopped. And then you, Comrade Zalyzin, storm the pause, as a Russian poet put it. You jump up, as if propelled by a hidden string. You manage to remove the lazily rolling ball practically from Simonyan's boot and move forward in a slalom, going around all these men — Parchin, the almost impenetrable Netto, then that redhead, what was his name — "

"Tishenko," Zalyzin said, impressed.

"Two furious defenders are stepping on your heels behind you. The goalie rushes out of the goal and throws himself at your feet. It was Kavazashvili, if I'm not mistaken? And you jump over his spread gloves and land with the ball in the net an instant before the final whistle, hanging on the net and swaying happily. The goalie is sitting on the ground, crying and banging his fist into the earth in frustration, but you help him up and you leave the field together, arms around each other's shoulders. . . . Right?"

"Yes, it's all correct. You could work for *Soccer and Hockey* and write as well as Lev Filatov. I believe you. I'm on my way. I won't say anything to anyone. But are you really Chilean?"

The lobby of the Hotel Carrera was empty at that time — it was either too late or too early—except for the desk clerk and a neatly dressed police officer with the traditional Latin American mustache worn by professional tango dancers and card sharks and presidents. The policeman must have come in to warm up, for the nights in Santiago were getting cool.

Zalyzin looked around the lobby, searching for his caller who spoke such good Russian, but the policeman approached him, saluted, and then offered his small, friendly hand.

"I called you. Don't be surprised by my police uniform. It's not a masquerade. I really do work in the international police force of Santiago. I did not want to tell you this over the telephone so as not to scare you off. I really am a linguist, specializing in Russian and the Slavic languages. But it's not easy finding a job with that profile in Latin America."

The apologetic smile on the Slavicist Policeman's face was replaced by concern. "Do you know where your players are right now and what they are doing?"

"They're right here in the hotel, sleeping," replied Zalyzin, surprised and anxious. "Where else would they be?"

"Comrade Zalyzin, I have to disappoint you—the entire USSR All-Stars team is in a brothel, except for the goalie Lev Yashin, who overcame that capitalist temptation. To use Soviet officialese, which I employed in writing my dissertation, a signal proceeded from the house of ill-repute," stated the Slavicist Policeman, neither mockery nor tragic tones, in fact taking professional relish in the linguistic opportunities. "There's nothing awful about it. Both Pushkin and Blok did not deny their fallen sisters the benefit of their compassionate attention or any other attentions, either. I doubt that when Kuprin was working on *The Pit*, his novel about prostitutes, he avoided direct study of the material. . . . The guys are young, their blood is hot. After all, you keep them wrapped tight in, how do you say it in Russian? Kiddie gloves?"

Zalyzin didn't correct him. This wasn't the time for linguistic nuances.

"You don't have to worry about their health," the Slavicist Policeman consoled him. "As they say, the more a glass is used, the more it is washed. But your knights of the leather ball have forgotten that the contents of their wallets are more modest than their Slavic generosity. However, didn't that happen with Dostoyevsky in Monte Carlo? Your boys did pay for the lovemaking, we have to give them that. But then—I think it was a guilt complex at work—they started drinking and sentimentally buying drinks for the girls, which is very expensive in such establishments. The madame has called us to complain that her clients do not have enough money and has asked us to come so that she can file a complaint. But if one is filed, a copy will go to the Soviet Embassy. And there will be stories in the press. Your boys might get into a lot of trouble. Do I, as a Slavicist, now in the police force, have the moral right to allow the discreditation of the All-Stars team whose members speak the language of Tolstoy and Chekhov? Forgive the direct question, Comrade Zalyzin—do you have any money?"

"How much?" asked Zalyzin, gradually becoming accustomed to the elaborate verbal style of his unexpected new acquaintance, a contact that was definitely not recommended in the memoranda for Soviet citizens traveling abroad.

The Slavicist Policeman lovingly checked the time on his watch, made at the Moscow Watch Factory Number Two. "Exactly one hour ago, according to my information from the madame, they owed three hundred dollars," he said with an unhappy shrug and, with professional precision, added, "and a bit over."

"I have three hundred," Zalyzin said happily, trying to forget that the sum was his per diem for the whole month, and that his wife, Elka, had given him strict orders to buy a maxicoat or two of llama shearling with it.

"I'll take care of what's left over," the Slavicist Policeman said, a real *caballero*.

The police car with its flashing light drove up to the Latin American den of iniquity that was quietly corrupting Soviet soccer. The brothel, with its innocent-looking white columns, looked quite proper from the street and reminded Zalyzin of the Writers' Union building on Vorovsky Street, where he had once had coffee and cognac before a conference called "Masters of the Pen Meet Masters of the Ball."

The madame, in black-lace mantilla and resembling a wonderfully restored ruin of former beauty, met them at the door, a silver tray with two thin-stemmed glasses in her ring-covered, wrinkled hands, one of which bore traces of a removed tattoo.

A bouncer with a boxer's broken nose, wearing a raspberry-colored tuxedo with a matching raspberry bow tie, synchronized the cork's explosion into the predawn sky from a bottle meant to represent champagne, its label carefully hidden from curious eyes by a not-very-fresh napkin, with the arrival of the police car.

"Bienvenido, jefe," the former priestess of passion said methodically, offering the tray, where a liquid too toxically lemony to be Veuve Clicquot or Dom Perignon valiantly tried and failed to bubble. "Como modesta administradora del amor, estoy a sus ordenes. . . ." *

"We have to drink," whispered the Slavicist Policeman. "To get things done."

A provocation? Zalyzin wondered again, but sighed and took the risk. The drink reminded him of the infamous cocktail he had made when he was very young.

Zalyzin and the Slavicist Policeman followed their hostess into the brothel's lobby, and the Administradora del Amor put her finger to her lips and pushed aside the theatrically heavy curtain of deep-red velvet with gold tassels.

The first thing one saw in the living room was the cracked wooden statue of Christ with a bent crown of thorns made of wire, a butt from a Krasnopresnenskaya cigarette on one of the barbs and a clip-on tie with a label from Dnepropetrovsk hung from another. Against the clumsy, pseudo-Baroque walls — with plaster cupids, fake bronze cupids as electric light fixtures and pink cupids on wallpaper the same shade of red as the bouncer's uniform — was a picturesque scene that reminded the Slavicist Policeman of Vasnetsov's painting about the Tatar invasion, *After the Battle of Kulikovo Field*.

On the floor, on couches, love seats, cushions and pillows lay members of the USSR All-Stars in the embrace of their newfound girlfriends, like the dead, wounded, or simply exhausted by love, with invisible cupid's arrows sticking from their bodies, snoring innocently, already dressed but some with their trousers not completely buttoned.

Only one, Numero, was not asleep. Sitting tailor style in his black, knee-length, Soviet underwear, on top of the chipped, once-white grand

---

* "As your humble manager of love, I am at your service . . ."

piano — also ornamented with cupids, this time with triumphantly raised trumpets instead of bows — and laughing vilely, he poured the so-called champagne, apparently the house drink of this respected establishment, into the pink shells of two women's lipstick-smeared mouths. When he saw the assistant coach and an unfamiliar police officer and the madame he thought he now knew well he shouted, "Welcome to our party! Lady, more champagne for my friends and local cadres! Move your ass, mother! . . . Numero's treat!"

"And what are you treating with?" Zalyzin asked quietly, trying to control himself.

"Stop it, Lyza boy. Stop showing off. Do you think you're better than us?" Numero's eyes grew shiftier. "We paid. And they cheated us. I told the old broad, 'Let's have the complaint book,' but she doesn't understand."

"Shut up!" Zalyzin hissed and Numero faded instantly.

"Reveille!" Zalyzin ordered loudly to the rest.

The USSR All-Stars started waking up slowly. The players who were rough on the field and therefore less talented were rough here too, unceremoniously pulling off the girls. The players who did not allow roughness on the field were better here, carefully freeing themselves from embraces, trying not to wake up the girls. Zalyzin recalled the words of Arkadyev, the famous coach, "Why are you being rough? No talent?"

"The total bill, please," the Slavicist Policeman asked the madame in Russian.

"Perdoname, no lo entiendo, jefe,"* the Administradora del Amor said in confusion.

"La cuenta, por favor," the Slavicist Policeman switched to Spanish, realizing that not all brothel owners had mastered the language of Tolstoy and Chekhov.

And then Zalyzin noticed that the King of the Heel Pass was missing.

His stomach lurched.

Had he decided to defect after all?

But where would the fool ever find fans like his, or a bottle of blacktop, or such pickles, or sprigs of dill weed, or leaves of black currant?

---

* "Sorry, I didn't understand you, chief,"

"Where's Elephant?" Zalyzin heard his own voice, which sounded like a stranger's.

And from above, "Here I am."

Zalyzin looked up and saw the abashedly smiling, tipsy King of the Heel Pass coming down the spiral staircase, with a young pretty Chilean girl hanging on him and covering him with kisses. She had wiped off her professional colors, loosened her black hair, and looked like a wild, long-legged horse from Tierra del Fuego.

The girl dragged Elephant over to the madame and babbled something tearfully, pulling a gold cross and chain from her neck and offering it to her boss.

"What's going on?" Zalyzin asked the Slavicist Policeman.

The Slavicist Policeman replied with a smile. "What's happening is that the *muchacha* seems to have fallen in love with him. He kissed her and that was the first time she was ever kissed. . . . You don't kiss women like her. . . . She knows that the guests don't have enough money and so she wants to give the madame her most valuable possession to pay their bill — her childhood cross."

The *muchacha* threw herself on the King's chest and started telling him something, kissing his hands, which he tried to hide in embarrassment.

"She says that she comes from the mining city of Antofagasta. Her father died in a copper mine, leaving her mother with five daughters, and she was forced to give her eldest to this house so that the other daughters did not starve to death. The *muchacha* is asking him to take her away from here and says that she will be his and his family's faithful servant all her life and his wife will never learn that he had kissed her."

The King of the Heel Pass shifted from foot to foot, blushing and not knowing what to do with himself.

None of the soccer players laughed. Only Numero giggled weakly.

The Administradora del Amor bit the cross and shrugged as she returned it. "No vale nada." At her signal, the weeping girl was taken away by her friends.

The bouncer in the red tuxedo brought the bill on a tray. The "bit over" three hundred had grown magically.

The Administradora del Amor reduced that amount somewhat

with a stroke of her gold Parker pencil and, bending toward the Slavicist Policeman, whispered with the creaking smile of a coquettish crocodile, "Solamente para usted, jefe. Porque usted no puede vistarnos qualquier dia despiues del trabajo para un pequeno massajito?" *

Zalyzin threw three one-hundred-dollar bills onto the tray and the Slavicist Policeman added a pile of Chilean pesos in approximately the same amount.

There were too many players for one car, so Zalyzin sent some of them back to the hotel in a cab.

The Slavicist Policeman drove the rest of them, with two forwards bouncing around in the trunk. Zalyzin had determined who would ride back there—Numero and another forward, Bunya, just as unbearably sincere in his brazenness. Even from the front passenger seat Zalyzin could hear them shouting and cursing—probably the usual stuff about who didn't let whom get a pass, and when. And suddenly Zalyzin saw something incredible in the rearview mirror—scrunched up on the backseat, between players sleeping in cramped quarters like sardines, the King of the Heel Pass was crying.

But one couldn't even call it crying, because crying is an action. The tears were flowing by themselves from his unmoving, seemingly paralyzed, eyes.

"What's the matter?" Zalyzin asked quietly, so that the others would not hear.

"She . . . she . . . kissed my hand," the King of the Heel Pass squeezed out the words. "But I'm . . . I'm not worthy of that."

Dropping off the team around the corner from the hotel, so that the doorman would not see him unloading the two forwards from the trunk, who were now stifled not so much by the absence of oxygen as by each other, Zalyzin thanked the Slavicist Policeman with all his heart. And so the story with the Chilean brothel ended relatively well.

But when Zalyzin returned home, he was fired as assistant coach of the USSR All-Stars.

Apparently worried that someone would snitch on him for his initiative behind the cultural field trip to the brothel, Numero decided to act first and reported to the not-unfamiliar KGB, which had once helped him out when he killed a pedestrian while driving drunk.

* "Only for you, chief. Why don't you visit us one day after work for a little massage?"

He turned out to be quite talented in the fantasy genre. His denunciation involved a fake Soviet consul, a brothel disguised as a restaurant and the threat of blackmail. Zalyzin, called to the scene by Numero, appeared with a man in the uniform of the Chilean police, who spoke Russian suspiciously well (perhaps actually a CIA agent) and tried to bribe the Soviet soccer players with allegedly friendly help, even paying part of the bill. The other half was paid by Zalyzin with bourgeois flagrant extravagance and with mysteriously gotten funds that humiliated the ordinary team members, instead of expressing a categoric protest against the shameless financial blackmail of the USSR All-Stars by the administration of a brothel.

It was unlikely that anyone in the KGB or the Sports Committee took Numero's composition seriously. But a report was a report, and they had to react to it, especially if it came from a whorehouse.

Zalyzin was out on the street. The only job he could find was in the warehouse of a sports store.

His wife, Elka, did not forgive him for not bringing her a llama shearling coat, and she did not need a warehouse guard for a husband.

Zalyzin was completely alone.

And that is why, many years later, when he ended up on the same team as Numero in the Moldavian tour, he did not pass to him once.

And whenever he heard that old envious song about the uppityness of the King of the Heel Pass, Zalyzin nipped it in the bud, remembering how he had seen tears rolling down that bewildered face in the rearview mirror of the police car in the faraway and long-ago city of Santiago de Chile.

They were down to their last game in Moldavia, with the team from the winery of the charming green town of Drokia. Boat and Zalyzin wandered with their arms around each other, carefully stepping in the lacy shade of trees, going down shiny stone steps into cool cellars where winemakers, handling dark green bottles stoppered only with fern leaves so that the bottles would not explode, filled glasses with young, sparkling pink Lydia for this not very young couple, the stormy lilac foam rising over the edges.

People here were friendly, but in one wine cellar they were attacked by a man with eyes red either from insomnia or alcoholism. In fact, his whole being seemed inflamed. He shouted, "Why are you ruining our Moldavian wine? You don't appreciate it anyway! Why don't you stay in Russia, lying around and drinking your vodka?"

"If we don't appreciate Moldavian wine, why don't you teach us about it?" Boat asked gently, not taking offense. "And maybe we could teach you something, too."

A born nanny, Zalyzin thought, as he had back then when she threw several victims of his cocktails into his aunt's bathtub as if they were piglets.

"You've taught us enough," the inflamed man hissed with hatred. "There was never a people called Moldavians. We are Romanians. You force us to rewrite in Cyrillic the Romanian literature written in Moldavia which, until you interfered, had been written in the Latin alphabet. But now, when we so-called Moldavian writers are published in Romania, our Romanian words, written in Cyrillic are — just think of it! — transliterated! Back into the Latin! That's what you've taught us."

"We didn't do that. Not me and not him," Boat said firmly, but not angrily. "We didn't force you to write in Cyrillic. We ourselves were forced to write in Cyrillic. Things we didn't think. . . . And that makes it a foreign language, too."

But the inflamed man did not want to hear what she was saying and he moved away, muttering and waving his arms.

"I can understand him, Lyza," Boat said, watching him go. "But why doesn't he want to understand us? Are you and I to blame for Stalin and Beria?"

"What about Brezhnev?" Zalyzin asked, answering himself. "If we put up with him, then we are to blame."

"You know, Lyza, I'm afraid that all this friendship of the peoples is held together with chewing gum," Boat said thoughtfully. "And beneath the gum there's blood. And the ones who are going to pay for the blood are those who are not responsible for it. 'Their ancestors ate green grapes, but their grandchildren have sores on their lips.' Come on, Lyza, guess where that's from."

"I don't know. There's a lot I don't know," he replied.

"The Bible!" she said triumphantly, pushing the tip of his nose with her forefinger, as if he were a child.

Before the game Boat and Zalyzin, worn out by the heat, lay on the singing metal bed with knobs on its posts, on top of the blanket with its creaking, highly starched blanket cover—lovingly embroidered in a provincial stitch that looked like a forest of circles, appliqués and ruches—and made love. The mountain of pillows was so chaste that to rumple it didn't seem right, and Boat put it on top of the TV, a pyramid of sugar.

From the wall, beetle-browed Brezhnev puffed out his green chest, but they did not notice him. He was part of the furniture. Boat rubbed Zalyzin's body, exhausted by the heat but still strong, with an ice-cold bottle of Borzhomi mineral water, and he had only to reach down from the bed to find the straw basket filled with cool, golden pears, clusters of violet grapes with a pale blue cloudiness and big-cheeked red apples, too large to fit in one hand.

"Forgive me with wine, refresh me with apples, for I languish with love," Boat whispered to Zalyzin. "And where's that from?"

"Why do you keep pestering me?"

"From the Song of Songs," she said, popping a grape into his mouth.

"I have a couple of song books," he said. "But I don't seem to remember the Song of Songs in there."

"It's not from a song book," she laughed. "It's from the Bible, too. By the way, it's not such a bad book. . . . Haven't you ever opened the Bible, Lyza?"

"I did," he confessed. "But not for long. When we played in Amsterdam, all the guys on the team were given a Bible in Russian by some young Christians. But books were confiscated in customs. Why—have you become religious?"

"In my own way," Boat evaded the question. "But I've read a lot in these years, Lyza. And I'm grateful to you for that."

"To me?" Zalyzin asked suspiciously.

"You gave me the gift of solitude, and solitude gave me books. You know, books are like mountain climbing. To keep from being dizzy, you have to hold on tight to books the way you do to cliffs. Then you won't get hurt. I've read a lot, I think I've gotten smarter. But what am I supposed to do with my brain now? I'm trading it for happiness. I'm happier with you than I am with books. I love you so much, Lyza." And she grabbed his hand and started kissing it.

And suddenly something appeared over the hotel bed, swaying and blinking, out of nowhere. Looking closely, Zalyzin saw that it was the rearview mirror from the police car in the city of Santiago de Chile — only this time, instead of the King of the Heel Pass, he saw himself in it, with paralyzed eyes, unstoppable tears flowing on their own. It was he, but different, forcing out words of shame and repentance — "She . . . she . . . kissed my hand. But I'm . . . I'm not worthy."

"I feel so good now, Lyza, so happy," said Boat, caressing him with her body and also crying — but at long last they were tears of joy. "God may have done the right thing in separating us for so long, otherwise we wouldn't be so . . . so . . . I don't know how to put it. You know, I think that I've climbed the hardest, tallest mountain . . . and not alone, but with you, my love, and I will never ever see anything more beautiful than what I see from this peak. And if that is so, then why do we need to keep climbing, seeking something else? Maybe it would be better to hold each other and jump off? Only our bodies will be shattered against the ground because our souls will go right through it and end up on a different plane, where there is no death and no end to love. . . ."

"That's beautiful," Zalyzin said. "Beautiful, but scary. Do you mean that you have to die in order to never die? But no one's ever come back to tell us how it is. What if there are no books there? I, for one, would like to read the Bible. I don't think the Bible has made anyone a worse person."

"Except the Inquisitors," Boat corrected.

"And what if there's no soccer in this place you're so hospitably inviting me to?" Zalyzin went on with a sly smile. "I'm sure there won't be. It's hard to imagine dribbling in weightlessness, or a penalty box for incorporeal beings. And most importantly, there won't be a ball to kick. No playing, no watching soccer . . . and I can't live without the game. If I'm ever paralyzed, I'll want to be brought in a wheelchair out to the goalposts. I don't care if I seem immobile and useless. I'll still be able to inhabit the feet of the young players and I'll continue making goals — even if it is with someone else's boots. I don't want to jump from some peak into an abyss I don't understand and from which I'll never get out. Even with you, Boat."

Reaching down, Boat found the coolest apple, took a bite, and offered the apple, its bite filled with juicy foam, to Zalyzin. "Sorry for my stupidity. It was just a mood for a moment. Death is postponed, forever! If you ever decide to betray me and die, I'll slap you around and bring you back to your senses, even if I have to beat you up! Look at my fists! And if I start planning to die, tickle me, tickle me so that I don't. You know how I hate being tickled! Maybe love is not letting each other die? Since we're going to die anyway, why the hell organize your own death? It's better to organize marvelous wild times for ourselves! Everyone who was incapable of beautiful wild times died before his death. Isn't being terminally bored a form of death? Let's not die before our death! Huh, Lyza? Give me five!"

Zalyzin gave her five. And with the side of her left hand she cut through their two right hands pressed together in a pact not to die.

But she had scared Zalyzin again. He felt relief when there was a knock on the door and he heard Tiger's grumbly voice. "General meeting! The whole team in my room."

They were all there, including the King of the Heel Pass, who was tipsy again. But of course, he needed only to be seen, not to play.

Tiger's face was tragic. "Bad news, guys. I'm afraid there's an ethnic conflict brewing. What do we have as we face our fourth and last game? To the shame of our sports conscience, we have three wins in three games. Eleven goals against such hospitable hosts. Isn't that too cruel? I really didn't expect that of you."

Guilty sighs all around.

"Couldn't you make a few less goals?" Tiger asked belatedly.

"We could have, Alexei Petrovich, we could have," Numero tried to please. "I tried real hard, I held up the ball, or dropped it over the line, but the rest wouldn't even give me a messy pass, not once! It was always right at my feet, every time. Never a mistake—that's unacceptable! If you like, you could say that it was a discreditation of professionalism. It's impossible to work in that atmosphere. And we have to have respect for national feelings and know how to lose for the sake of friendship of the peoples. Shattering three local teams could have political consequences."

Tiger hid his unmatched eyes, so as not to reveal his scorn and mockery of a man who took even black humor seriously.

"I've come to the upsetting conclusion," Tiger summed up, "that our performance is certainly not an example of humanity toward our hosts. I also mark the shameful fact, of which I am personally guilty, that we haven't been scored against yet. We'll never be invited back to this republic. We have to mobilize and make sure we lose the last game. Let's leave a positive memory, at least at the end. By the way, the center forward of the winery team is the winery's young and generous director. Getting ahead of myself, let me tell you a secret: It was he who has given orders for us to receive, after the game, two bottles each of their twenty-five-year-old cognac in souvenir boxes, a Moldavian embroidered blouse for our womenfolk and a crate of fruit for our grandchildren."

"Let's help that young director to someday tell his grandchildren with pride that once he personally got a couple of goals off the goalie of the USSR All-Stars, Tiger himself!"

"We'll do it, Alexei Petrovich! We'll help the winery youth!" Numero offered readily.

"If they can't hit a goal, I'm ready to knock a few into our own goal," Bunya offered.

"I'll knock *you* if you try!" Tiger said, waving a fist at him. "The elegance is in opening up the local talents like budding flowers. Don't forget that our main bud is the young director. We must resist at first and then tactfully expose an opening, and allow the man who has done so much for us to break through. We have to show an elementary bit of gratitude."

"It's selling out," Zalyzin said disdainfully. "I won't participate in it. You can expose yourselves all you want. But I'm no whore."

"And I'm not going to expose myself either!" Kolya Senyukov banged his fist on the table. "The striptease hasn't come to my hometown yet!"

But the rest were torn. On the one hand they wanted to play a good game, and keep sending the ball into the other team's net. But on the other hand, they wanted to be tactful and avoid ethnic conflict.

"What does it matter?" Seryozha Salnikov said with a melancholy shrug. "It's no skin off our noses if we lose."

His opinion swayed the others. They thought: Really, it doesn't hurt — we're not creeps, and it's not like we're losing the family cow. Their age helped them stifle ambition and substitute magnanimity.

They voted on a compromise. They would play at full throttle for the first half, show their stuff, but without traumatizing the hosts by scoring goals. They would start the second half with stormy attacks, but then — using the Stanislavsky acting method — run out of steam, making errors in their passes and creating corridors for their opponents toward the goal.

If that wasn't enough, they would force penalties by using their hands or being blatantly rough—but without hurting their hosts, especially the director.

If their hosts still couldn't score from the penalty spot, then they would pretend to attack passionately, moving to the hosts' side of the field and "expose themselves" enticingly—making sure, of course, that their hosts didn't get offside.

The score was voted on several times, and they eventually settled on 1:0 as a final score.

But things did not go according to plan.

The oppressive heat broke with a brief, but powerful, rainstorm. The field turned into a swamp.

Despite the muck that called itself a soccer field, the stadium was as packed as a cob of Moldavian white corn.

It was the final game, it was a Sunday, and the fans of the living relics of Soviet soccer came from Kishinev, and other towns and villages, on new Ikarus buses, shabby old local buses, trucks, tractors, bulldozers, caterpillars, cranes, cars, motorcycles, bicycles and creaking coaches unchanged from the days of Pushkin, when he tasted the wines and in a red shirt wandered the marketplaces with Gypsies and a bear on a chain.

Outside the stadium it looked like a Gypsy camp and a marketplace, and it was a shame that there was no Pushkin.

A cart hitched to a white horse and filled with aromatic, fresh hay held a beautiful handmade carpet—black with huge red roses, like the mouth of a giantess opened for a kiss.

The carpet's owner, a tall peasant woman with large earrings, must have used her own lips as a model for the roses. She stood, arms akimbo, enveloped in a thundercloud of hair, and shot lightning bolts from her eyes, as dark as overripe cherries, at potential buyers who pinched the carpet but did not purchase it.

"A carpet is not a chicken. No matter how hard you pinch it, it's not going to lay an egg."

The teams came out for practice.

When the young goalie from the winery team fell in a puddle, it elicited only sympathetic laughter.

But when it was Tiger who slipped and fell face down in the mud—gray-haired Tiger, who crouched in the goal not so much to be prepared for the kicks but because he was stooped with age—the fans were broken-hearted. The greatest fans were, as always, the veterans.

Traveling over the heads of the market crowd, passed from hand to hand, came a surviving member of the once-huge army of legless veterans that rolled on their platforms out of the long-ago and almost forgotten war, out of Stalin's "socialism in a single, separately taken country" and right into Brezhnev's "developed socialism."

Once upon a time the veterans who cheered young Bobrov and Tiger also had young, boyish faces. They were the Survivor Veterans. Now they were the Almost-Extinct Veterans. They had come to the soccer game on their clattering wooden carts to see their idols, who were also dying out.

The veteran who floated over the market crowd was not wearing a torn, striped sailor shirt or an old field jacket like the veterans right after Victory Day. He had a straw hat, three medals for valor and a snowy shirt that was embroidered by him personally.

He was known well in Drokia because when he lost his legs, he taught his hands to embroider Moldavian folk patterns, and one of his pieces was exhibited at the World's Fair in Brussels.

The veteran invalid made a sign to be lowered into the cart with the handmade carpet, and he waved a violet twenty-five-ruble note as if he were sounding an alarm. "Citizens of Drokia! Our guests today could be called the Heroes of Soviet Soccer. And can we sit by calmly while the world-famous goalie, Alexei Petrovich, Tiger, flops around in our mud? Esteemed veterans! Let's all chip in to buy our Moldavian carpet, let's spread it at the goalposts for our guests!"

The seller spread out her skirt to catch the money tossed at her—rubles, threes, fives, tens and twenty-five-ruble notes made a rainbow hill of crumpled bills—and the fans were already picking up the carpet by the edges, as if it were their unquestioned property, and running onto the field to spread it over the mud at the goalposts.

Tiger accepted it as his due, as if he had spent his life tending goals carpeted with red roses. He walked along the carpet, smoothing it out with his feet so that there would be no wrinkles to trip him, and then took his classic goalie's position, tugging at his pants with gloves electrified by anticipation. Rumor had it that the gloves were a gift back in 1945 from the young Princess Elizabeth, the future Queen of England.

The photographer from the local paper, who looked like a wet sparrow, obligingly dropped to one knee right in a puddle near the posts, delighted by the Nikon that Tiger, a newspaper colleague, had lent him for the duration of the game. It was his first time with a Japanese zoom, and the photographer couldn't get enough play time with it, endlessly bringing the great goalie's face closer and then sending it back.

When Tiger, grunting and moaning a bit, got up from the carpet that had softened his fall and gratefully patted the embroidered red rose on its shaggy threads, the photographer zoomed in on the famous face and saw something in the viewfinder that the thousands of spectators could not see. Tears were running down the wrinkles of his face, like spring rivulets in the foxholes after the winter blockade of Leningrad.

When the heavy, soaking-wet ball, almost unmanageable, flew toward the visitors' goal from the boot of a winery player, who looked like Pushkin's Aleko, Tiger raised his weary body into the air with difficulty, but still managed to deflect the ball to the corner with the tips of his gloves.

The carpet in the goal lay like handmade proof of the fans' respect for the old-timers.

The plans for hypocritical mercy toward their hosts were shot to hell. It would be indecent to play badly when you were so respected. Pride would not allow them not to make goals.

And so it happened.

Salnikov made the goal. He behaved as if he had been so engrossed in his own depression during the general meeting that he had not heard. Perhaps that was true.

He got the ball through the puddles to the penalty area and kicked. The young, inexperienced goalie, certain that the heavy ball would go low, rushed to the lower left corner. The goalie had guessed the direction, but not the height of the ball's flight.

The score was 1:0, but not in favor of the hospitable home team.

The violator of the group decision not to get any goals so as not to traumatize the hosts headed toward center field with the grim but noble face of an individual who has done his duty against the ignoble will of the collective that has tried to suppress him.

At half-time, Tiger roared with the no-less-grim and no-less-noble face of a leader fulfilling his international duty. "Guys, we've satisfied our vanity. It's time for honor. Let's screw up our courage and lose."

Everything then went according to plan for a well-rehearsed defeat.

They attacked wildly—and grew tired.

But they couldn't provoke a penalty kick into their goal. Even though they grabbed the ball with their hands and were demonstratively rough, the Moldavian referee sensed that the fans were completely on the side of the visiting grandpas and did not blow his whistle for fear of a lynching.

So then they tried "exposing" themselves.

They all went over to the hosts' side of the field.

Only Zalyzin and Kolya Senyukov remained on the visitors' side, since they did not agree to the exposure.

Tiger would leave his position to go beyond the penalty area, presenting the ideal opportunity for the ball to get past him, or stand invitingly near one of the posts, turning half of the goal into a dead zone.

Numero and Bunya tried very hard to get the ball accidentally to the young director for a breakthrough.

Eight members of the old-timers' team had either stopped playing or, even worse, were playing up to the opponents, trying to retain the appearance of resistance.

The fans could see that something strange was happening on the field, but attributed the obvious drop in the old-timers' play to their age.

It's much easier to play-act deathly exhaustion than boundless energy.

But if incorruptible Zalyzin and Kolya Senyukov were only "acting" at boundless energy, then they were the equals of Jean Gabin and Innokenti Smoktunovsky. Left alone, those two continued to fight against seven or eight attacking winery players, not letting them get a single goal, even though the goal was practically unprotected. They turned into two Shivas, with uncountable legs instead of arms, defending against the greater strength of the opponent.

The young director's foot, seeming enormous, dangerously took the ball from Zalyzin's head.

The referee, morally groggy, accounted for all the uncalled hand action earlier by not calling this violation.

When the referee's whistle did not stop him for obviously dangerous play, the young director got a surge of power, took the ball and, spraying fountains of mud, splashed through the puddles toward the All-Stars' goal.

He wanted to score a goal against Tiger much more than he wanted to fulfill his five-year plan.

Tiger pretended to be hassling with his allegedly untied laces, hospitably opening the goal.

Cutting off the director and catching up with him was Kolya, exhausted but still game, and suddenly Numero came rushing to help.

Could he have suddenly developed a conscience? thought Zalyzin, who had taken up a position by a goalpost just in case.

But he never expected anything like this, even from Numero.

Numero, "accidentally" hitting Kolya from behind, knocked him off his feet, pushing the great-grandfather of two into the slurping mud.

This time the referee almost blew his whistle, but unfortunately there is no penalty for rudeness to your own teammates.

The young director was barreling into the goal. With him on the same line, panting like shiny steam engines, stormed three of his teammates.

Tiger, seeing that time was up for his lace trick, pretended to get into position. He spread his legs, creating Siberian expanses — *get the ball in, it's as wide as the Arc de Triomphe.*

But Zalyzin was there, too, and he was determined to protect the goalposts from the young director and the old goalie, softened by a false understanding of internationalism.

The young director, breathing heavily, was already in the penalty area, but for some reason he wasn't kicking.

Tiger left the goal unguarded, offering it on a tray, and meandered toward the director.

But the young director was too scared to make a goal on Tiger, and passed the ball to one of his employees for the kick.

Tiger rushed to his feet with intentional inaccuracy — a half-yard off.

The winery player's eyes bugged out in horror, because he had to act quickly and independently. But his nerves gave out because his boss, next to him and panting heavily, might not forgive losing the glory of personally scoring a goal against the USSR All-Stars. The employee sent the ball back to his director, now almost exactly lined up with the goal, and the director kicked it into the lower corner.

But Zalyzin, seeing where the ball would go, launched his body over the black-and-red carpet and, tipping his gray, wet head, knocked the ball away.

The ball did not go far and got stuck in a puddle next to the post. Zalyzin jumped up and tried to send the ball to the edge of the field, where Uncle Kolya was reborn, like a phoenix out of the mud.

But the ball was mired in the swamp, waterlogged, and died without getting out of the penalty area.

Two other winery players, angered by the frustrated goal, ran towards the ball.

And here Tiger's heart, which had been above the fray so to speak, struck hard, and the player in him won over the diplomat. At last he even used his right to play with his hands. He grabbed the ball and tossed it to Uncle Kolya through the air, which fortunately did not have any puddles.

Uncle Kolya, gently catching the ball with his cozy great-grandfatherly tummy, sped towards the goal of the winery team with the drive of a back-lot player, becoming simultaneously all of his grandchildren and great-grandchildren.

It was a difficult raid, crossing the swamp, which sucked up not only Uncle Kolya and the ball, but also the opposing team, who had not calculated the braking effect of the mud on their youthful determination.

Uncle Kolya knew his job and held onto the ball, attracting the defense.

Zalyzin had already crossed the middle line and could be offside any second. It was time to pass to him. But a low pass in that mud would not go far. Picking up the waterlogged ball and passing it through the air was hopeless. They needed an intermediate pass.

And suddenly from the center circle, Salnikov waved a wet sleeve like a bullet-riddled red flag.

Uncle Kolya kicked up as hard as he could. The ball, showering the players with water from the dry air, flew through the air to the gloomy Salnikov, who did not let the ball hit the ground and sent it on to Zalyzin.

Zalyzin easily passed one winery player, then another. Before him was one more defender and the scuttling goalie.

And suddenly he saw Tiger on his left, who had abandoned his goal and was running clumsily toward the winery goal, waving both fists in the legendary English gloves over his head so that Zalyzin would see him.

Zalyzin passed. The winery defender and the goalie thought that Tiger would be kicking in the goal, and headed for his feet. But Tiger feinted and sent the ball back to Zalyzin, who was now free.

And Zalyzin could not resist the childish pleasure of kicking with all his strength, even though it wasn't necessary, and the ball slurped into the wet netting, like a ball of lightning with an aureole of sparkling wet sprinkles.

The beauty of the play captivated everyone. The whole stadium rose to its feet, clapping, and the *cognoscenti* heatedly discussed the tactical innovation played by the old-timers. There wasn't even a hint of interethnic conflicts.

The inflamed man that Zalyzin and Boat had met in the wine cellar burst into the locker room.

"Forgive me," he said. "I didn't recognize you yesterday and took you . . . took you for . . . well, for not you. Yesterday the Moscow censor removed my novella from the journal *Kodri*. Please understand how I was feeling. You played a terrific game."

Long after everyone had left the showers, Zalyzin still stood in the streaming water, snorting with pleasure, like a lathered warhorse in a river after a battle.

And then through the water and steam, beyond the glass partition, he saw a blurry silhouette.

The silhouette scratched on the glass.

"Lyza, it's me."

"I can see," he replied in embarrassment. "This is the men's showers, after all."

"So what. Nowadays it's almost impossible to tell who are the women and who are the men," she said with a laugh. "Lyza, I want to tell you again what I said twenty-five years ago at the Stormy Petrel Stadium. You are a genius. This was your best game. And your best goal. May I come in with you?"

Zalyzin exclaimed as he had so many times before, "Are you crazy?"

"Haven't you gotten used to it yet, Lyza? I am, you know, and there's no changing it."

And he saw that the silhouette was undressing.

"What are you doing? There are people here!"

"What people?" she asked calmly, taking off her clothes and with a finger drawing her silhouette in the steamy glass.

"What do you mean, 'what people'? The team, the fans, the reporters."

"They're all gone. No-bo-dy here at all. They're all gone. I said I'd give you a massage. And I didn't lie." She jumped into the shower and wrapped herself around him, playing with him like a soft but dangerous Baikal wave that had appeared here in Moldavia against all the laws of nature.

And then she led him away to the banquet that was held in the carved-wood restaurant next to the local television tower, and pleaded, "May I, Lyza?"

He had guessed what she would want to do and he just shrugged.

He remembered what the Great Degustator had once said of her: "That is a dangerous woman. She's not even a woman, she's an element."

And she climbed way up high on the TV tower, to the blinking red lights that warned away planes, and shouted down something to him that blended with the wind, the noise of the trees, the warble of the nightin-gales, and suddenly he was afraid of her again — this time even more than before.

It was not fear of her silly maniacal desire to climb everything she saw, just as long as it was tall. Rather, he was frightened by his guilt for having betrayed her, for having left her for twenty-five years. Abandoning a woman with love in her arms like an infant was the same as abandoning a woman with an infant.

He knew that he was not a scoundrel. But he felt like one with her.

He was frightened that his guilt, if they stayed together, would destroy him.

He was frightened that Boat, seeing that he was miserable, would also be miserable, and then he would feel guilty for this new cruelty to her.

He was frightened that if he were no longer the young man she had fallen in love with but the worn-out drunkard who had almost lost all faith in life, a shell of his former self, she would stop loving him and lose the meaning of her life. And he knew that just as she had no fear of climbing up, she would have no fear of jumping down.

When they returned to Moscow he told her, as he had twenty-five years ago, that it would be better if they did not see each other anymore. He lied and said that he wanted to make up with his wife for the sake of his son.

Boat knew he was lying but she did not let him know it.

She continued to be the boat always waiting for him.

Zalyzin lay low. The only thread connecting him to the past was soccer. But now he only attended funerals for old-timers and did not play in their games.

The King of the Heel Pass. He had been Bobrov's heir. But who would succeed the King?

Then Tiger passed away. Who got his English gloves?

Zalyzin rarely attended games.

He thought that the ball no longer rang the way it used to. The air it was pumped with was not the same.

There were new fans who called themselves *fanats*—fanatics. And these fanatical teenagers supported only "their" teams, not soccer itself.

The *fanats* were "children of Russia's boring years," according to one poet of their generation. They marched to the games in columns and wore scarves and ski caps in their team colors.

They did not want to be a helpless herd. So they became a herd with fangs.

At the stadiums the fans clapped in rhythm, chanting the names of their teams, and insulted the opposing team.

They enjoyed the cheapest pleasure—the pleasure of hatred. It is always easiest to fill emptiness with enemies.

The militia hauled the *fanats* out of stadiums, beat them up, shoved them into police buses, wrote denunciations to their vocational and technical schools, after which they were expelled and thrown out onto the street, unable to get a job. This was called "educating them."

But what else could their homeland offer them? The boredom against which they were rebelling? A lisping, gasping turtle with the position of general secretary—Brezhnev?

The teenagers were embittered by the persecution. Some wore pictures of Hitler around their necks and gathered on his birthday, right across the street from Pushkin's monument.

Once at a stadium Zalyzin tried to quiet down a couple of kids who were shouting, eyes red with hatred, "Kick 'im in the balls! Slit his throat! Hit 'im between the eyes! Break their ribs! Beat, kill, smash, turn the old into hash!"

Zalyzin tried to shut them up, but it didn't work. "Shut up, asshole!" said a pimply kid, with a tiny homemade swastika in his pink ear with its blond down.

After the game, Zalyzin walked down the street, thinking about where to get a drink. Almost everyone he liked to drink with was dead.

He knew only two or three telephone numbers—the sum total of his life.

He tried to use a pay phone, but all the receivers had been pulled out. He finally found a working phone in a booth with broken glass.

He dialed the number he was afraid to dial, because it was the number of his guilt. With the years his guilt had increased rather than decreased. Only the time left to live decreased.

Usually, he would dial the number and hang up when he heard the voice.

Every time, the voice knew. "Lyza, is that you?"

You would think that no one else ever called her. Maybe that was true.

This time he didn't even know whether she had answered, because the stadium gates opened and a wild crowd came roaring out.

Down the embankment they came, horns blaring triumphantly, banging on stolen garbage-can lids, twirling scarves over their heads, throwing rocks and empty bottles at cars and windows, knocking over ice-cream stands and even baby carriages. They chanted, "Beat, kill, smash, turn the old into hash."

It was impossible to hear a human voice over that din. Zalyzin hung up and made his way along the sidewalk, trying to stay away from the column of fans, skirting the buildings.

But the crowd seemed to be kicking and hitting his eardrums anyway. "Beat, kill, smash, turn the old into hash."

At the head of the column, with personal bodyguards to protect him, strode the gang leader, with a face like a ham and the muscles of a body-builder bursting through the T-shirt of his team. A plastic skeleton dangled from a chain around his bull-like neck.

He was clearly older than the teenagers he was leading, and unlike their eyes, which burned with stupid hatred in search of an enemy, his eyes belonged to a cold and calculating agitator-organizer.

Zalyzin suddenly remembered seeing him at the market, chopping up beef carcasses with an axe and wiping the bloodied blade on his white apron, while ladies beseechingly buzzed around him, the Butcher-Master, like flies drawn to fresh blood.

"Dima, dear, did you remember to save me some filet?" "Dima, dear, could I order some bone marrow, but without the bones?" "Dima, dear, could you cut me off some from that side there, but only meat, no bones?" "Dima, dear, why didn't you remove the sinews from this leg of lamb?" "Dima, dear, could you help me get some cockscombs? I hear they're delicious when stuffed with chicken livers."

"Beat, kill, smash, turn the old into hash," shouted the marching column of potential butchers or potential meat under future axes.

The human avalanche spilled over the sidewalk and sucked Zalyzin up with it.

"Hey, guys, it's the old asshole who ruined the game for us!" the pimpled youth with the swastika earring cried with unhealthy joy. "Doesn't know a thing about soccer, but he has to lecture us. . . . Let's teach the old fart a lesson, guys!"

The leader heard the voice of the masses. "Dima dear" leaned over to one of his guards and said casually, but significantly, "Do it. . . . But keep it clean." He chuckled and added, "No blood on the apron."

The order went down the line.

And suddenly Zalyzin was surrounded by a carousel of still-boyish but cruel faces. The carousel turned him, crowded him, and spat him out into an alleyway near a construction site.

It got very quiet, and he could hear the teenagers surrounding him breathing in fear. There were twenty of them against one of him.

If only I had Uncle Kolya Senyukov right now, he thought sadly.

The first blow came, as he had expected, from behind.

As soon as someone strikes, the cowardice of the others vanishes. They beat him for a long time — without splashes — half to death.

But that didn't seem like enough.

They dragged the unconscious Zalyzin to the top-floor landing of a nearby apartment building.

They tied their team scarf to the metal handle of the trapdoor leading to the attic.

They lifted up Zalyzin's lifeless body. The pimply youth with the swastika earring tied the scarf's other end in a noose around his neck.

"Let's go!" he commanded.

The *fanats* dropped the body and ran down the stairs. They were inexperienced hangmen and did not wait to see what happened.

Fortunately, the door was made of Soviet plywood, and Zalyzin's collapsing weight pulled out the handle's nails easily.

Half-strangled, Zalyzin came to late at night, unable to move or call for help, because his vocal cords were damaged.

His head was covered with blood, from falling on the concrete landing.

Zalyzin managed to loosen the noose. His breath escaped with difficulty, and he wheezed like a steam engine.

The apartment on the landing, filled with construction materials, did not yet have a door hung, or panes put in the window frames through which the stars, busy with their concerns, indifferently regarded Zalyzin, just returned from death.

But there was a voice inside the unoccupied apartment.

". . . In these decisive days for the fate of building socialism in one separately taken country, the Soviet people must unite even more closely around our great leader, Joseph Vissarionovich Stalin, completely squash the Trotskyite-Bukharinite hydra lying across the path of our nation. As the great writer Gorky, viciously poisoned by imperialist hirelings, said, 'If the enemy does not surrender, he has to be destroyed.'"

Zalyzin peered in and saw that the voice was coming from the black speaker of a radio hanging on the wall. Zalyzin recognized it because half the face of Andrei Starostin, the famous soccer player from Zalyzin's childhood, was glued to the speaker.

Long ago, when Lyza was a small boy, their cat, Murzik, had jumped from the wardrobe onto the radio, which spoke and sang all day about how happy the Soviet people were. The cat's claws tore the black paper of the speaker, vibrating with the constant stream of happiness coming out of it. Little Lyza glued the torn spots with newspaper strips, one of which had half the face of Starostin, arrested with his brothers, who were also soccer players.

In those days people got rid of pictures of "enemies of the people" because having them could in turn cause their possessors to be branded enemies of the people. They blacked out dangerous faces in group photos, tore them out of family albums and books. But the speaker had only half a face and only little Lyza knew whose face it was.

Beneath the speaker of his childhood Zalyzin saw his familiar iron bed.

On the floor by the bed was a still life—an empty bottle of Triple Seven rotgut, a crumpled can that had held sardines in tomato sauce and now held cigarette butts, two piles of clothing—one male and one female—of indeterminate color, boots smeared with axle grease drunkenly leaning against felt shoes with rundown heels and—for no apparent reason—a lead horseman figurine in a Red Army uniform, still waving a toy sword that no longer knew against whom and for what to fight.

Zalyzin's late mother and father, who hated each other and the rest of humanity because they didn't have enough money for a drink the morning after, sat on the bed, each leaning against opposite ends, and played go fish on the ash-littered blanket. The cards were greasy and torn, so that some of the kings and queens had only half a face, like Andrei Starostin, as if they too were enemies of the people, forced to hide their whole faces.

His mother, who had failed to drown him, held up an ace of spades in her dirty hand with ragged fingernails, turned her unkempt head, and nastily looked at her own son, now much older than she had been, lying in a pool of blood.

"You've heard if the enemy does not surrender, he must be destroyed? And what if your son doesn't surrender?" she rasped.

"The son is destroyed," chuckled his father, reaching with shaking hands into the sardine tin for a cigarette butt which he tried to relight.

"I warned you, Zalyzin," came an almost forgotten, enveloping voice, and the Great Degustator thrust the flame of his black and gold Cartier lighter at the wet and dirty butt in the mouth of Zalyzin's father. "You did not become a Great Player because you did not have the willpower to overcome so-called pangs of conscience."

Looking like a bar of molten Crimean suntan, his aunt walked in with her general, holding a bouquet of feather grass in one hand and a wooden crate of ladyfinger grapes in the other.

"What are you lying around for, nephew, in all that blood? Where's that huge gal of yours? I told you to marry her, but you didn't listen. . . . Who's going to put out the fires on the piano now?"

"Get up, Lyza," whispered Boat. "It's cheating if you die before me. We made a promise, remember? Lyza, I kept trying to take you with me as high as I could go. But we don't need to go very high, Lyza. There's no life there, only the cold and the stars. Climb down, Lyza. There's life here, people, you and I are there, the soccer ball is ringing down there. Crawl, Lyza."

And Zalyzin crawled, smearing his blood on the landing. And as he moved face down on the concrete he heard a quiet but clear patter beside his left cheek.

Zalyzin managed to look up and saw Chunya the hedgehog moving next to him, his concerned eyes sparkling in his prickly face, showing him the way.

Zalyzin crawled to the stairs and lowered both hands to hold onto the steps and pull his body down. But he stopped when he saw that the stairs were covered by a black carpet with red roses and that Tiger in his darned and patched sweater and English gloves was waiting on the landing below, ready to catch his weakened comrade if his body rolled down the steps.

All night, step by step, Zalyzin crawled, head and hands down, from the twelfth floor, and at each landing someone was waiting for him — kids from the suburbs with an oil-cloth ball and shoes of the same fabric, or the coatroom attendant Semyon Palych, his hands full of two-kopek coins sparkling like gold, or the King of the Heel Pass, weeping in shame before the Chilean *muchacha* who had kissed his hands in the brothel, or the

Slavicist Policeman with a Bible in Spanish and Russian, or just a bucket of light-blue paint waiting for Zalyzin to step into it when he was kissing that girl who had eyes like blue lanterns.

And all the steps down which Zalyzin was crawling were covered not only with red roses, but live gladioli, carnations, nasturtiums, asters, pansies, chrysanthemums and forget-me-nots. Boat muttered in her singsong voice, "This is for you from Pushkin. And these taiga snowdrops are just from me."

He crawled down the stairs all night.

From the second floor landing, Zalyzin saw the golden strip of morning squeezing under the doorway, with a horde of dust motes turning golden in the light.

But Zalyzin had no more strength. His heart seemed to have forgotten its place as it fluttered from side to side, or grew still, hiding, as if it did not exist.

"Boat, forgive me for breaking my word. I think I am going to die now," Zalyzin whispered soundlessly.

And suddenly something rattled and clattered on the landing next to Zalyzin. He barely managed to turn his heavy head and saw the invalid from Drokia on his wooden platform, with three medals for valor on the snowy shirt embroidered with his own hands.

"Why are you just sitting there?" the invalid asked.

"Can't go on," Zalyzin said hoarsely.

"Yes you can," the invalid said. "I say you can." And he gave a battle order, "Follow me!"

The platform, controlled by the embroidering veteran's mighty yet gentle hands and the wooden supports they held, bounced down the steps.

"Come on!" the veteran called, his medals bouncing off the sunlight into which he had rolled. "Look at all the people waiting for you!"

Zalyzin looked out the door and saw a crowd of his most important fans on the sidewalk and in the road beyond — the war veterans, living monuments set on wooden pedestals by their homeland, which they loved but which did not always love them.

And in a delirium, Zalyzin crawled until he fell out onto the street, which was empty.

No one came for a long time, as if there were no people in the city or in the world.

Zalyzin passed out again, arms flung out on the sidewalk.

It was when someone stepped on his hand that he knew there were still people on the earth.

The people who had almost killed him had no idea that the boring old man they had hanged with their team scarf was in fact a great soccer player who had defended those very colors for many years in the country and around the world.

But Zalyzin felt that he had died anyway.

He only felt alive again on August 19, 1991, when Chunya tugged at the lace of his shoe and a voice called through the closed window, "It's me, Boat."

The Marshal And The Émigrés At The Barricades

THE MARSHAL RARELY WORE CIVILIAN dress. He didn't like it, and felt like an actor forced to play a role to which he was not at all suited.

And it was with that feeling that, on the evening of August 19, the Marshal wandered in the drizzle around the White House, raising the collar of his old Chinese raincoat with the Friendship Factory label, which he had bought in the unforgettable years when the radio played "Moscow-Peking" every day — "Russians and Chinese are brothers forever. Stalin and Mao listen to us."

Of course, if the Marshal had raised his collar in order to keep from being recognized, he need not have worried. His military uniform was so much a part of him and of the image that others had of him that he was unrecognizable without it. Only his heavy black shoes belonged to a general.

In the old-fashioned raincoat and just as old-fashioned bouclé cap, and in a short, tight suit and checked shirt, he looked like an elderly shop worker; one of those old men who play dominoes in the green bosom of Moscow courtyards, marking the final hours of socialism that has conquered itself; or who bustle in and out of shop doorways, intent upon realizing that profoundly Russian idea (which had never occurred to the Slavophile philosophers, however) of splitting a half-liter of vodka three ways.

So without his black limousine and officer-chauffeur, without gold epaulets and red braid and with his ordinary, slightly pockmarked face of a workman of peasant stock, the Marshal looked like one of those proletarians who had pulled the rebellious Party *apparatchik* from disgrace, as if from a leech-filled pond, and made him President of Russia and was now here to defend the tank-encircled White House.

Actually, that was not the case at all.

It was true that the Marshal's signature was not next to those of the conspirators. However, he was the secret link between the open conspirators and the covert ones; between those simple-hearted people who had no idea that they were on somebody's strings and the puppeteers behind the scenes who, before stepping out on the ice, tested its strength with tanks.

The wisest participation in a conspiracy looks like nonparticipation. As in love (which is a conspiracy of two), you need only unspoken words, unfinished glances, the barest nod. In a conspiracy, the orders to those who command the tanks can be silent.

Neither the open nor the covert conspirators trusted each other completely, but both trusted him fully because, while they were saving their own vanishing power, he was protecting the concept of power.

No one ever knows everything, particularly in conspiracies, but the Marshal still knew too much to hope to survive if the conspiracy failed — or, even, if it succeeded.

But the Marshal himself never thought for a minute that he himself was taking part in a conspiracy, and the word "putsch," which he heard on foreign radio, offended him. The Marshal truly believed that this was not a conspiracy but the salvation of Russia.

He took the risk with what he considered a clean conscience. He was not a coward and he was always prepared to give his life for three words — "Homeland, State and Communism." When the Afghan veteran who had accused Sakharov of treachery shouted these words that, like a hypnotic spell, raised almost all the People's Deputies at the Congress to their feet, the Marshal also stood up, applauding and shedding purifying patriotic tears.

"For the Homeland!" was the sign on his tank in 1941, when he jumped out of its flames, his jumpsuit burning, and into a shell hole filled with rainwater.

Of course, it was no longer appropriate to write "For the Homeland!" on the tanks that under his command entered Czechoslovakia and later Afghanistan, but the concept of "on the orders of the homeland" still existed.

And now his homeland — the Soviet Union — was falling apart, like the

Tower of Babel, burying under its rubble the superpower's main support—the army—and that lovely dream of universal justice—Communism.

The Marshal had never read Marx or Engels, even though he kept their collected works in his office, and he had only a very foggy idea of what Communism was. But people of his high rank were not tested. It was somehow assumed that they were Communist. The Marshal had no other faith and it was too late to change faiths now.

The Marshal was always proud that he had come from the people. Therefore, he assumed that the people thought the way he did. But both he and the people had become very different long ago.

The people had stopped believing in the dream of Communism. That dream was like a pure German Gretchen in a starched apron—the love child of Marx and Engels—who curtsied as she served beer to her fathers. And she was deflowered by the filthy murderers in Ekaterinburg right in the blood of the imperial family. Then she was raped by Stalin on a bed of concentration-camp barbed wire. Then she was mounted by an oinking Khrushchev. Then Brezhnev squirmed around impotently on her almost lifeless body, losing his false teeth in an attempt at a passionate kiss. Andropov and Chernenko carefully scrambled up onto the cooling body of that dream, panting like mountain climbers out of their league and age group and died on top of her, as she was dying. Gorbachev got her when she was dead.

The deceased dream could not be resurrected by the conspirators into Delacroix's bosomy girl with red banner. Besides which, the conspirators only thought that they were communards, but they actually belonged in Versailles with the Thiers government. They needed fear to help them win.

But when the putsch began, the ones who started it were the ones who were most afraid.

It was a putsch with trembling hands.

In the morning the White House was surrounded by tanks.

That evening the White House was defended by those same tanks.

Gladioli and tricolor flags stuck out of the gun muzzles.

Resting beside a tank, as if it were a grassy hill in some village, the young soldiers sat with their arms around girls living in Moscow illegally, singing out of tune but with great pleasure Yesenin's poem:

Maple, leafless, oh icy maple,

Why are you swaying in the white blizzard?

One soldier, his cheek pressed longingly to his accordion and his fingers meandering over the buttons, looked so much like the poet, except that his golden curls poked out from his army helmet, but probably not for long because whenever they grew unruly, the army barber's ruthless razor cut his hair back down to the scalp.

The Marshal almost blew up with fury when the tank soldiers did not jump up to attention and salute when he walked by, but then he remembered that he was in civilian dress.

But then he thought sadly, I used to play the accordion. Too bad I forgot how. The Marshal stuffed his fists into the pockets of the unbearable civilian jacket, filled with old crumbs.

Still, he sighed, What nice boys. And the girls are even better. He particularly liked the brown-eyed girl with a John Lennon pin on her down jacket and a silver crab on her captain's cap.

She reminded the Marshal of his wartime love—a brown-eyed signals corps woman with curly hair under her cap, who let the tanks go through.

After the war, he married—not her, because he was afraid of her reputation—but the daughter of a general. His first love turned out to be his only love, and through all those years he saw her secretly, in her cozy nest that he called the "dugout," where she kept their photographs from the front—separate, but in a single frame of Karelian birch. The photographs stayed young, but the two of them aged. However, his aged but still loving love always cooked the same meal that they used to eat in the real dugouts—wheat porridge with cracklings—and sang old Russian love songs, accompanying herself on the German piano that once was almost burned to the ground by her soccer-crazy nephew and his tough crowd.

These were the memories stirred in the heart of the Marshal, weighed down by the medals and orders hanging from it, by the brown-eyed girl sitting on a tamed tank next to the living circle of hand-holding defenders of the White House.

The Marshal expected to see a motley crew of "long-hairs," hippies, punks, drug addicts, black marketeers, hard-currency hookers, dissidents,

Zionists, Baltic nationalists—all the people he considered "enemies of the Homeland"—and to his astonishment he saw people who were none other than his Homeland.

The living circle embracing the White House as its last hope consisted of people who were used to standing pressed closely together and breathing air that consisted of their own breath. The living circle was made up of people from the lines. The living circle was also a line—a line for hope. In store lines, people stood one behind the other, facing the next one's back. But in the line for hope, people stood beside each other, linking hands and facing those who would take away their hope.

The Marshal found himself thinking that he had not seen so many good people in one place in a long time.

There were workers; the ones who hand-built the armored Party limousine that they mockingly called "member carriers," in which the Marshal drove past, while they observed him with class grimness from lines for sausage and vodka; and the workers who made the ruby stars above the Kremlin that the Marshal cherished; and those who built the tanks that were now turned against them.

There were impoverished doctors, lacking drugs and even the right to prescribe them, but who managed to save so many people—including the Marshal when he went out one night in a track suit and slippers to walk his dog, a German shepherd as old as its master, given to him by Erich Honecker to commemorate successful Warsaw Pact maneuvers. Trying to get away from the boring, protected courtyard behind the filigree wrought-iron fence, where only generals' dogs were walked, the Marshal fell unconscious in some badly lit side street. He was brought back from death in the district emergency room by doctors who had to boil their ancient syringes in an autoclave, onto the lid of which plaster fell from the ceiling, and they massaged the stopped heart of that old man without identification nearly until dawn, when the guards of government health without white coats burst into the hospital, causing a panic.

There were schoolteachers, whose history books were taken away by history but who were making history themselves today, and the Marshal imagined he saw in their eyes the golden glint of the kerosene lamp that stood like a pitcher of light on the table of his first village teacher, back in the early twenties when their little church had been turned into a vegetable warehouse and the priest shot. The teacher taught the children what the authorities demanded of him in the daylight and in the evenings, by the light of the kerosene lamp, told the children about the betrayed and crucified father of all people, who had been executed later, too, and whose face was hidden from the people behind pictures of their substituted father, Stalin.

There were Russian engineers, those written about by Garin-Mikhailovsky, who back before the Revolution, without caterpillars and excavators, built in only fourteen years the East Siberian Line, the new tracks sniffed by unfrightened bears; the engineers who built Moscow's metropolitan, the most beautiful subway system in the world, where you could escape for a while from the arrests and killing above ground, down the escalator to the marble fairy tale below; the engineers who opposed the grim military technology of Krupp and his merry, fire-breathing Katyushas; they who, after the war, sent hurtling into the starry, silent infinity a small metal creature that spoke in unilanguage: "Beep-beep-beep." (But of all the engineers, the Marshal remembered best the one that he, as a young and impatient major, wanted to have shot in '43 for criminal slowness in restoring a bridge blown up by the Germans, which tanks had to cross. "Until everything is the way we were taught, I won't let the tanks go! I don't care if you shoot me!" said the engineer, green with lack of sleep, small, unshaven and bristling like a hedgehog, a telephone wire wrapped around a broken-soled shoe. The engineer woke him later in the night and said, "Give me my ration of vodka, major—I've earned it. Now everything is the way we were taught!" And when the tanks crossed the terrifyingly creaking, temporary wooden bridge, the engineer stood beneath it, swaying, sipping from the major's dented aluminum flask and waving his hat. "It's creaking, but it's holding! Just like they taught us!")

Where was that engineer now? Maybe here in this living circle, in this living barricade?

There were physicists who, classified in secret, semiprison installations called *sharashkas*, had saved freedom of thought, who gave the world Kapitsa, Landau and Sakharov, whom the Marshal tried to drown out with foot-stomping and hand-clapping at the Congress when the physicist insulted (in the Marshal's understanding) the army.

There were war veterans, not the ones from special units who fired on their own retreating soldiers, but the ones who were shot at by them.

There were people with the special eyes of camp inmates. The Marshal could always recognize those eyes and he tried not to look into them, because guilt over history complicated his military patriotism.

There were many of the Marshal's favorite actors here, who had canceled performances, and there were one or two writers, too.

There were university students who resembled the Marshal's grandchildren, and schoolchildren who resembled his great-grandchildren. Maybe they were here somewhere, too?

There were young mothers who were not afraid of blocking the path of the past with their baby carriages.

There were the great Russian babushkas, grandmothers whose knitting needles turned the living barricade into something familylike and cozy.

The fiery redhead surrounded by three equally fiery boys the Marshal recognized as the army scout called Van Gogh who had escaped from the Afghans.

And then instinctively the Marshal raised his collar even higher. He did not want to be recognized by the gray-haired but youthfully brown-eyed woman ladling tea into paper cups from a boiling pail over a campfire, and handing the cups to hands reaching out from the living circle.

But that woman loved the Marshal and she felt his eyes on her.

She shuddered, turned slowly and froze, two steaming paper cups of tea in her hands.

She recognized the Marshal even in his Chinese raincoat from the days of "Moscow-Peking," and she went toward him, trying not to spill the tea, as if she had just made it for the two of them in their dugout.

She reached him and offered a cup.

"Don't burn yourself. . . . Thank God, you're here. I was afraid . . ."

"Why were you afraid?" he asked sharply.

"I was afraid . . . afraid that you were with them. But you're not with them, you're with us."

"Tonya, listen." The Marshal tried to tell her something, but she was so happy, she did not hear.

"Do you know who else is here? My nephew, Lyza. And do you know who's with him? That Siberian woman who once sobered up the guys in my bathtub. Remember?"

"I don't remember. Tonya, this is all much more complicated than you think —" the Marshal tried desperately to interrupt.

"How can you not remember her? A big girl. Eyes like two blue cobblestones. And big red fists as if they had just been hammered in a village smithy. . . . I had told Lyza back then to marry her, but the fool didn't listen. . . . Do you know how long she waited for him? Forty years . . . and now they're together. . . . And I've been waiting for you for almost half a century."

The Marshal knew that she was going to cry now.

Tonya cried only when she talked about this. But she kept her tears in her eyes, not letting them spill over. The brown eyes, magnified by the tears, looked very young, just as they had near Weimar, when a storm caught them in the museum park just after the victory, and her eyes had looked bigger then because they were filled with the flickering rain. Tonya, her wet uniform sculpted to her body, sat down on an oak damaged by a shell, and merrily extended one leg and then the other for the Major to pull off her water-filled boots, and she blissfully wiggled her white babylike toes, delighted to be freed of army footgear. And then, laughing, she poured the water from the boots onto the already soaked Major's head. She called the childhood dare, "Bet you can't catch me!" and, wearing the boots on her hands, ran barefoot down the ancient path that might still recall the steps of Goethe, and the Major ran after her, until there was a shot. The Major dropped into a puddle, rolled behind a tree, pulled out his gun and shot back at a blurry figure in the pouring rain. The figure fell. The Major approached cautiously, pistol ready, and saw a blond Hitler Youth, eyes goggling in horror, pulling the trigger on an empty automatic rifle, while a dark-red rose of blood spread in the puddle around his leg.

Tonya ran up and pulled on the Major's arm. "Don't shoot. . . . I feel sorry for him." And she shouted at the youth, "Der Krieg ist voruber. Deutschland kapitulierte."

"Nicht! Ich glaube das nicht!"* the youth muttered, but then he

* "The war is over. Germany has surrendered."

  "I don't believe it."

realized that it was the truth and wept bitterly, dropping the automatic into the puddle.

Tonya kneeled in that puddle and tore open his trouser leg. The wound in his calf was not deep.

"Du kannst glücklich sein,"* said Tonya, taking out her first aid kit and binding the wound.

"How can you do that? He's a Nazi. If he had had bullets, he would have killed us!" the Major cried.

"He's a kid. A miserable, deceived kid," said Tonya, suddenly looking up at the Major. "Will you and I have a son?"

They never did have a son, even though Tonya had wanted one very badly. The Major did not. He was afraid of dividing his life. But life divided them anyway, and now it was too late. Tonya was almost seventy, and he was over seventy. They continued loving each other, and it seemed they would never fall out of love.

But now the Marshal was worried that Tonya might stop loving him toward the end of their lives if she found out he was not with her and not with them, but with the others. And he was even more afraid because he knew that they were planning to storm the White House that night. He even knew the appointed time—3:30 in the morning. He knew that Alpha, the special KGB force, was assigned to do it. If they had done it this morning, the whole operation would have taken twenty minutes: there hadn't been a hundred armed people inside the building then and there'd been only about fifteen hundred unarmed ones outside.

But that time was lost.

The Marshal calculated that by this time, with the military men and blue berets who had switched sides, the armed defenders inside the White House numbered a thousand. There were six tanks by the walls, and there were thirty to forty thousand people in the living circle.

It was still possible, of course, to take the White House and then arrest and deport the President of Russia.

But they needed air support, machine guns and grenades, the gas tried in Tbilisi—and only then hand-to-hand combat.

* "You are lucky,"

The handsome Vice-President, who looked like a nineteenth-century hussar, a daring pilot who had escaped from an Afghani prison camp, was speaking into a bullhorn, asking women and children to leave the living circle and warning the rest of mortal danger. At this moment it was inconceivable that this same man, in two years' time, would be the President's most furious rival, calling for an attack on the TV station from this very balcony.

The Marshal figured that now, in order to achieve the operation's goal, at least two or three thousand people would have to be killed. And Tonya could be one of them.

"Why aren't you drinking your tea? It's getting cold," Tonya said. "I feel so good here. It's like being back at the front. . . . We haven't sat around an open fire in a long time. Let's sit down. Right here, on the barricades."

Even if the campfire is on the barricades instead of in the woods, can it exist without heart-to-heart conversation?

Standing at the fire while blowing on his tea and drinking in little, tender sips, was a large man with hairy, paw-like hands. His endearing nickname, "Mishanya," was tattooed on one of his arms, along with the USSR emblem.

"'Well,' my chick Zarema then asked me, 'Hey, Mishanya, you ain't sick, are ya?'

"'In what way?' I said.

"She answered shamelessly, in a way no girl back in the village could ever do because of embarrassment, 'To be blunt, in a man's way.'

"So I answer back the same way, no beating around the bush, 'In that way I'm healthy as a horse. In the morning I could use it for a car jack.'

"And then like a brood mare, she said right out, 'Maybe I should go out with you in the morning instead of the evenings?'

"So I tell her real smart, 'It ain't the time of day that matters. . . . It's my intentions, and they're real serious. I'm sick of living in Moscow without a woman, getting ulcers in cheap canteens and making love standing up in stinking doorways. Once I even thought I had VD, cause I got a purple spot — you know where — on that prominent, sensitive place. And when the doctor looked at it he laughed and said, 'That's the car-jack syndrome. . . . I recommend that you switch from vertical to horizontal relations with the ladies.'

"So I explained to my beloved with my full dignity: 'In a word, Zarema, I ain't impotent, just a guy from the village, from the Russian heartland, an old-fashioned man. And I want to marry you first, if you, of course, say yes, and then I'll have to endure — suffer — till I arrive in the right place at the right time — on our wedding day.'

"She suddenly starts bawling and says, 'I say yes, of course I do, because decent guys like you, Mishanya, are rare as buckwheat groats in Russia, you can't find one with a lantern in daylight, even if you got a rations coupon. I too want to be decent and I tell you right off that I'm not a virgin . . . so why wait till the wedding day? We can do it right now, vertically or horizontally, whatever you want. Because I've wanted to for a long time, but was ashamed to tell you.'

"So I drive the point home. 'For me you're still a virgin in your soul, and that's more important than being a virgin only in a certain particular place. But I want to stick to my great-grandfather's tradition. We'll bear out the wait together. . . . Before a priest ties the knot, the bed should not be hot.'

"Well, then my Zarema loses it and mumbles through her tears, 'I never thought, never dreamed I'd meet a man like you, pure as the new fallen snow. And right in my hands. And I hope, in time, between my legs, too.'

"I console her, but don't use my hands, of course. I was keeping my distance, or I couldn't have held myself back.

"So then I decide to tell her what I had out of delicacy *avoided* telling her. 'Well,' I say, 'since we're getting hitched, Zarema, I want to tell you, Zarema, the severe truth about my job — '

" 'What's there to tell?' She kept pressing up against me and vulgarly trying to touch my — you know — with her hand. 'I know you ain't a violinist. You drive a truck. I myself ain't no pianist. I work a lathe — '

"I blushed like a virgin. But I overcame it and squeezed out the bitter truth like dried-up toothpaste out of a tube: 'Yeah, I drive a truck, but a special kind. . . . I pump out and clean sewage lines.'

"She stands there like a statue. . . . Her eyes get wide as if she's looking at me for the first time. Like I was a blimp full of . . . excrement. And I couldn't get into her field of vision.

"I understood that her tender soul hadn't been ready for smelly news like that.

"'But take a sniff, Zarema, there ain't no bad smell coming off me, cause I don't come in contact with the fecal matter directly. I deal with it through a hose. I stick it into a septic tank or main sewer hole. And if it's stopped up, I use my rubber corrugator. Working on the principle of a pump, it sucks up everything it needs to. And the sewer hole cover, well, I'd like to emphasize that I handle it only with a little crowbar. Well, there are cases when the hose gets torn up going through the turns, and then what we call accidental leakage takes place. But I got a rubber apron on, wear rubber boots and gloves up to my very elbows. Well, somebody in this here country, Zarema, has to pump out the crud, or else we'd choke on it. Our great poet, Mayakovsky, for example — the one with that big monument on the square — well, he was proud to write about himself, 'I'm a sewer man and a garbage man . . .'"

"Wa-ter man," someone in the crowd corrected him pedantically — the Poet of the Twenty-First Century.

Mishanya answered, "But I decided to correct Mayakovsky, because I know more about that business than he did. . . . A garbage man, well, that's more respectable than a water man. But I'm not talking about Mayakovsky, but Zarema. . . . And I summed up all I had said: 'So, it's like this, Zarema, from a moral point of view that job is the cleanest of work. And from the material point of view the excrement has only a positive effect on my pay.'

"But then Zarema suddenly started shaking and quaking and took off running from me like I had the plague. She had drawn me too perfect in her imagination, too sweet-smelling. But who knows. . . . I tried phoning her, but as soon as she heard my voice, she hung up. Come on, do you think she could smell shit through the phone lines? I was offended. Hell, she wasn't made out of marzipan, and her ass also fed the sewer lines. And if sewer-line guys like us quit working, then all the pipes would get clogged and all that crap would rise up against those who dropped it. It would shoot up like fountains from out of the toilets. . . .

"I took to drink because my proletarian feelings had been hurt. There's a song, 'Fate Plays with Man.' And if my fate is shit, does that make the anthem of my whole working life 'Shit Plays with Man'?

"And then about a half-year later I heard that my tender flower, that sly Zarema, was getting hitched. And guess with who? A cook from a cheap canteen, one of those guys that poison the working class with rotten meat and sell the fresh meat through their middlemen at the market.

"I found out where the wedding reception would be, and it was in that cook's apartment, and luckily for me on the first floor. I got the idea to stage a revolutionary protest. . . . Right when the wedding was in full swing I drove up in my truck, filled to the top with green sludge, bubbly like champagne, from the military barracks. I stuck the hose through the open window where I could hear the guests yelling, 'Kiss the bride!' Out of the jaws of my corrugated, sweet monster came gushing a fountain of the most aromatic justice.

"Well, later, of course, they tried and convicted me. At first they slapped five years on me, but the people's jury, out of a feeling of solidarity with the working class, gave me only two years' hard labor in a chemical plant. But that cook couldn't be helped by any kind of chemistry. No matter how many times he changed the wallpaper, no matter how many times he sprayed the place with deodorant, it kept the scent of that green anguish from the barracks. It stank powerfully, and nobody would trade apartments for that two-roomed asphyxiating orchid. . . . Do you know what politicized me? Shit! And I'm proud of it! On whose shoulders does Russia stand, anyway? On the workers'! And who are the bosses in Russia? The cooks! The crooks! The people who eat what they are supposed to cook up for us. If the bosses have ugly mugs, the cooks have fat, well-fed faces. They get to eat fine granular caviar, and we get the pressed shit. I'm only for the kind of democracy that will finally show respect for the guys who spend their lives honestly hauling other people's shit on their shoulders."

Mishanya fell silent, warming his hands over the fire, and flames lapped uneasily at the tattooed Soviet emblem. And it seemed that the emblem would go up in flames any minute.

"Shit plays with man," the Mishanya repeated with a sigh. "What a stinking game it played with me — other people's shit. Or is it?"

"Read one of your own poems," asked the Parisian Russian Lady of the Poet of the Twenty-First Century.

"How did you know I write?"

"I don't know. I guessed." She smiled.

"I'm an architect by training and I haven't been published yet," he began explaining, and she realized that Vladislav Felitzianovich and the Poet of the Twenty-First Century shared a secret — shyness. "But I'm taking a seminar at *Youth* magazine and there will be a discussion of my poems in September. I'll read you a new work, it's not polished yet. It's called 'Refugees.'"

He did not read his own work as well as he did that of other poets — he was constrained, stumbling, trying to hide his uncertainty about it and thereby making it all the more obvious.

> We walk and walk along the steppe,
> through forests, swamps, and grasses,
> we have far to walk and long to lie,
> many will have to lie in ditches.
> Fate is severe: you will get there, you will not,
> you will tell your grandchildren,
> you will die when the dawn glows
> blinded by a pistol shot.
> But we must walk, walk, tearing calluses,
> without eating, or sleeping, or drinking,
> through forests, hills, and fields!
> Live, we want to live!

"Very sincere," said the Parisian Russian Lady. "Sincere."

"That sounds like a death sentence," the Poet of the Twenty-First Century said, laughing nervously. "But, to tell the truth, I know myself it's bad."

"No, it's not that it's bad, it's dangerous. You wrote your own death sentence in your poem. So many poets were killed by their own prophecies. The very things they predicted happened to them and to others! Please change that poem."

"I'll think about it," replied the Poet of the Twenty-First Century proudly.

The Marshal suddenly remembered, for the first time with fear, when he was very young and had fooled around with poetry. Imitating Esenin, he had written a prediction of his own death:

The Marshal And The Émigrés At The Barricades

My death will come from the back
It will be worse than war's attack.

"And one more question," continued the Parisian Russian Lady. "You call the poem 'Refugees.' I understand what they are running from, but not where they are running to. Yet the most important part is knowing where you are running. Do you know what I think is happening in Russia now? I don't think this is a revolution. It is escape. People know what they are running from — the Gulag, the Party, the slave-owning state. . . . But the trouble is that people don't know where to run. That's why they could end up where they started. So instead of gloomy predictions, predict something happy, all right? Do give it a try, dear. Draw a window of hope on a blank wall, and it will open into different air, completely different air that you have never breathed before. History is a living creature and is susceptible to influences. Don't instill in history a fear of itself, the feeling of being doomed to blood and crime. So many writers have done that. The hell with them! We émigrés are guilty of that too."

"We émigrés?" The Marshal thought he was hearing things. An émigré? How did she get here? So the KGB chief had been right at the closed meeting when he said that this so-called democracy was instigated from abroad, and that even in the highest echelons of power there were agents of foreign services? The Marshal had never seen a live émigré up close before and he was a bit scared by this unforeseen contact. The very word "émigré" meant "antipatriot" to him.

But what the émigré was saying to the lad had touched the Marshal. If we had old ladies like her in charge of propaganda, the army wouldn't have fallen apart, the Marshal thought.

"Don't frighten history. Help history and people to believe in themselves," the Parisian Russian Lady was saying. "Being a pessimist is the easiest way of seeming smart. You must love life, and not be afraid of seeming stupid for that. My dear boy, redo that poem, for God's sake and as soon as possible. Otherwise, who knows . . ."

And suddenly the Marshal felt someone staring at him. Looking up, he saw a stranger leaning against an overturned garbage can, a man with gray hair that had no yellow in it, styled smartly but not in a military way, with icy, hypnotizing eyes, leaning back and sipping Tonya's tea from a paper cup. The eyes had no attitude — neither condemnation nor support nor curiosity nor even studied interest — but there was no indifference either. The eyes participated in everything going on, and they did not participate as outsiders. Those eyes had neither condescending contemplation nor cold observation nor gloating voyeurism. They had a respectful attention to life — the reason God must have made human eyes in the first place. But there was something subjugating in that gaze, something that filled the Marshal's body with an inexplicable readiness to obey, even though there was nothing in the stranger's eyes remotely like an army order. The readiness to obey crawled up through his spine, as if it had been hiding in his bone marrow all along, waiting for those eyes. The Marshal was not used to obeying because, for people of his rank, there were very few people who had the right to give them orders.

The Marshal tried to look away from those eyes, but he still felt their imperious weight.

Is he a hypnotist or something? he wondered in irritation, even though no one could ever bend his will. There was one exception: Stalin.

Once the Marshal, at the time one of the country's youngest generals, was invited to a defense meeting with the already dying leader, and there he met the young Sakharov, then not a dissident but a top-secret atomic scientist. The word "dissident" was unknown in Stalin's day.

Stalin, pipe in his mouth, paced the length of the table's green-topped surface and thought aloud about the possibility of atomic war and exhaled right into the back of the young general's head. The smoke got under his collar and crawled along his body with burning cold, paralyzing his will.

Stalin's pipe had icy smoke.

And that is what the Marshal recalled under the icy gaze of this stranger. Trying to evade that unexpected feeling of subordination, the Marshal took a few steps forward. Then, angry with himself, he asked curtly, "Who are you?"

The stranger held out his hand, and the Marshal had to shake it.

"Romanov."

The hand was also icy, thin, and there were no laborer's calluses on it, as, incidentally, there were none on the Marshal's hands, despite his peasant-worker background.

The Marshal did not introduce himself, nor did the stranger ask that of him.

The Marshal made a joke. "Which Romanovs? Not one of those Romanovs, are you?"

The stranger smiled only with the corners of his mouth. "One of those."

The Marshal was stunned. "What do you mean?" he asked. "Are you a direct descendant?"

"The most direct. My great-great-grandfather was Alexander II, my great-grandfather Alexander III. My grandmother was Ksenia Romanov, the daughter of Alexander III. The father of my mother, Maria, was Illarion Vorontsov-Dashkov. The father of my father, Nikita Romanov, was Grand Duke Alexander Mikhailovich. And I am Nikita Nikitovich Romanov. I was born in London in 1923," the stranger explained scrupulously but with an air of boredom that reflected, not disdain, but that he had told this story many times to the curious.

The Marshal, unable to digest all this, looked at the hand he had just shaken. The veins were blue. The Marshal looked at his own hand, but the veins were blue there, too. What did "blueblood" mean, anyway?

"Excuse me, but how did you get here?" the Marshal asked in a subdued voice, bitterly laughing at himself. That must be why his gaze affected me that way. Genes — servile genes. I'm a marshal from a family of former serfs.

"I'm here for the Congress of Compatriots. That gray-haired lady over there, Antonina Gerasimovna Korzinkina, my dear friend, is also here for the Congress. But she came from Paris, and I from New York. And as you can see, by tragic coincidence the Congress opened this morning, the day of an attempted overthrow," Romanov replied calmly.

"What did you say?" the Marshal demanded. "Why only attempted?"

"Because the coup is a failure," Romanov replied. "I teach history, after all, and — " he smiled "— I have some relation to it."

The Marshal changed the subject. "Is this your first trip to the Soviet Union?"

"No, I've been twice before."

"Have you been to the Winter Palace?"

"Of course."

"Did you feel hurt that it was all taken away from you?"

"No. It's right to have a museum there."

"What *did* you feel?"

Romanov paused. "I'm seeking the right word. I think I have it: I felt *agitated*. It had nothing to do with politics. It's just the first time in my entire life that I was in a country where everyone spoke my native tongue, Russian."

The Marshal was astounded. Even when they played Reds and Whites when he was a child, he was always a Red. And now for the first time in his life, he was talking to a real White. And as White as you could get, a direct descendant of the imperial line. And this White Russian did not hate him, and he, a Red, to his amazement did not hate the White.

The Marshal's upbringing rose before him against his ideological weakness, against his intolerable sympathy for a White émigré lady and a royal scion, who had shown up on the barricades with unclear motivations.

"And how do you like those tsarist generals who had switched to Hitler's side?" the Marshal asked, forcing himself to be hostile and vigilant.

"I don't," Romanov said. "But there were very few. In our émigré circles there was a story about General Anton Denikin, who was approached by a representative of Goebbels and asked to sign an appeal to Soviet soldiers, calling on them to surrender. The elderly general asked his no-less elderly batman to open his old field trunk and take out his white-kid dress gloves. When the batman brought them, the general gave the insulting Nazi a naphthalene-scented but unambivalent slap. There were no collaborators in our family. My two cousins, Duke Mikhail and Duke Andrei, served with my uncle, Dmitri Alexandrovich, in the British navy during World War II. And Prince Andrei was a sailor with a convoy to Murmansk. And Mikhail, the son of Prince Fedor Alexandrovich, fought in the French Resistance with the maquis. And incidentally, Antonina Gerasimovna was a contact for them in Paris."

The Marshal remembered how he had come to Sverdlovsk, formerly Ekaterinburg, right after the war to inspect the troops.

While drinking with the local officers, one of them suggested going over to the Ipatyev House where the tsar's family was killed to show him, their Moscow visitor, this revolutionary site. It was late and they had to wake the guard, terrified by the nocturnal invasion of so many high-ranking officers, followed by young soldiers blinking sleepy eyes and dragging baskets of food and bottles. It was strange for the Marshal to see himself, red and boozy, with a glass of vodka in one hand, top button undone on his uniform, in the mirror with a poorly patched crack before which the last Russian empress may have combed her hair for the last time. The officers noisily descended to the cellar where the killing had taken place, and one drunken lieutenant colonel, in a fur cap that was tipped dashingly onto his not very brainy brow, pulled out his gun and started shooting at the walls. The new bullets cracked the plaster and it fell off, revealing the scars of old bullets on the brick wall. The Marshal strictly commanded an end to the shooting, but he had not experienced any pangs of conscience.

The pangs came now, at the barricade, when he learned that the Romanovs who had survived were not interested in revenge but, along with him, a young soldier, had defended with weapons the homeland that had been so cruel to them.

"Tell me, why are you here on the barricades?" the Marshal asked softly.

Romanov shrugged. "This has nothing to do with politics. I don't really know why. But you don't resemble a man who is interested in politics. We're about the same age, I believe. . . . I just feel that my place is here today. Wasn't it the same for you?"

"Mitya, how about another cup," Tonya offered, shifting the steaming paper cup from one hand to the other.

But the Marshal was gone, as if Tonya had only imagined seeing him on the barricades.

The Scarred General:
KGB Headquarters

THE HEAD OF THE SPECIAL KGB Alpha troops, the Scarred General, also wanted to vanish today, to drop into the bowels of the earth.

It was the worst day of his life since that day in Kabul, when he—already with scars but still only a colonel—commanded the paratroopers who burst into Amin's palace, gunning down everyone in their path.

He remembered two of the ones they killed that day—a young servant who danced down the corridor, carrying a tray with an icy, fogged crystal pitcher of sherbet with rose petals floating in it. The servant thought that no one could see him and he pirouetted unselfconsciously on the honeyed parquet. Perhaps he was in love—say, with a palace kitchen girl—and he had just gotten his first kiss, tasting of kebab and *sumak*. Or maybe it was youth that flowed sweetly in his veins, like rose petals in sherbet, and swirled him in that dance and carried him right to the steel muzzles of the automatic rifles of the mysterious masked men.

Riddled with bullets, the servant fell, miraculously balancing the tray and continuing his pirouette, dying in midflight, after giving his killers a bewildered look with coffee-colored eyes that splashed out their last shimmer of life.

The second person he would never forget was Amin's bodyguard, who ran out from behind a column with a Kalashnikov of his own, shooting "from the belly," as the Alphas called it. And when they got him, and hit him again with a short round as he lay dying, he managed to rasp out, as a crystal pitcher broke in the background, "Why are you killing your own,

[2 6 8]

you sons of bitches. . . ." And the colonel recognized to his horror Petya Mothyl, one of the best graduates of the KGB school, who had been sent at Amin's request to be his personal bodyguard. Petya was famous at the KGB for his Hamlet, which he had performed at the Dzerzhinsky Club. They wanted to show parts of the performance on national television, but the KGB higher-ups banned it—Petya would lose his deep cover, and no one, not even Shakespeare, could be allowed to uncover him. And so he had to use his acting talent in a different field. But the role of Amin's bodyguard was not a lucky one. The directors of the show had decided to get rid of Amin. And in their hurry they simply forgot that he had several Soviet bodyguards, whom they themselves had sent.

The KGB colonel, who became a general after that "brilliant operation," as his bosses called it, tried not to remember the face of the Hamlet from Lubyanka whom he had killed accidentally, but on August 19 it floated up before him, as if from a river bottom, even though he had tied a heavy stone of forgetting to Petya's body. Petya lay, his head with the Russian curls treacherously peeking out from the Afghan turban lying on the silver tray that the dead servant still held in his hand. Crystal shards lay around Petya's head and rose petals bobbed in the sherbet spilled on the tray. He had stood beside Petya's head, his own boots splashed with blood and sherbet, and above them a golden wasp circled and buzzed.

The Scarred General had remembered that scene when he had walked around the barricades in civilian dress like the Marshal, thinking about the storming of the Parliament, set for 3:30 that morning.

The living circle around the White House seemed to be made up of a multitude of Petyas whom he would have to kill. The Scarred General's mood was very bad.

"Some dinky old man is demanding to see you, says he's a marshal. But he has no documents," reported an aide, knocking at his door.

"It's enough of a madhouse here at the KGB, without another loony. I don't know who I'm supposed to serve, the Soviet or the anti-Soviet powers, and which is which," the Scarred General barked. "Get rid of him."

"He looks like the Marshal. Of course, I've only seen him in photographs or up on the Mausoleum. But it looks like him," the aide warned.

The Scarred General nodded irritably. "All right. Send him in."

The moment of nonrecognition was very brief.

The old man who resembled the Marshal walked into the office and headed straight for the credenza, where he pulled open a cabinet door that he seemed to know well. It had glasses and bottles, with a better selection than at the Beryozka store. The Scarred General had once confiscated that entire collection of bottles from the director of the Eliseyev Gastronome, who had been arrested by the KGB, and the General had been working on the collection for several years, unable to finish it even though he enjoyed a drink.

The old man selected a Hungarian apricot brandy, but did not bother with a glass—he drank, his adam's apple bobbing, straight from the bottle and then wiped his mouth on his sleeve, the image of a retired working man in a Friendship brand Chinese raincoat.

But the Scarred General stood at attention, seeing the face of a Marshal of the Soviet Union under the greasy proletarian cap. The aide had turned into a pillar of salt with KGB insignia.

The Marshal sat down, wearily leaning back, eyes shut. The General gestured for the aide to leave.

"Remember the red-haired scout they called Van Gogh in Afghanistan?" the Marshal asked, without opening his eyes.

"Of course I do," replied the Scarred General. "I tried to get him to join Alpha, but he refused. He's working as a repairman or carpenter or something."

"Do you know where I just saw him?"

"I can guess," the General chuckled mirthlessly. "At the White House. Where else would he be? I was just there. I saw Zalyzin, the soccer player. . . . Yes, that one, Lyza. . . . They said he had drunk himself to death."

"Listen, as an intelligence officer, you have to understand faces," the Marshal began cautiously. "How did the people there strike you?"

"Our people are not bad. They've been unlucky in their bosses," said the General, pouring himself a glass of Napoleon brandy from a dark green bottle that seemed to have a shadow of a tricorn on its label.

"But the bosses, that's you and me," the Marshal went on, eyes still shut. "Are you and I so bad? Neither you nor I steal like the one whose booze we're drinking now. We serve the Homeland honestly, I would think."

"Sometimes I think that there's another boss over me," said the General. "Not the Central Committee, not my minister, not the KGB. Fear is that boss and that boss's office is in my guts, that's where. But now I have a new fear, the-fear-of-obeying-the-orders-of-my-boss-fear. To put it more simply, I don't want to be a bastard. But my job is obeying orders."

The Marshal opened his eyes at last. "Then don't obey them."

The General stood up at attention. "Comrade Marshal, I am a military man. Order me not to obey those orders — just between us."

"I do," the Marshal said, putting on his greasy cap again.

After the Marshal left, the aide brought in a melchior tray with a glass of tea in a melchior glass holder.

The aide held the tray too gracefully for a soldier, on his outstretched palm, just like the servant in Amin's palace.

"Don't ever bring me tea on a tray," the General said gruffly.

THE SECOND DAY

On The Balcony:
My Very Best
Bad Poem

THE FIRST NIGHT OF THE COUP was over.

The first night represented the first victory.

Someone had rescinded the order to the special Alpha troops to storm the White House at 3:30 a.m. on August 20. The professionals of para-trooping and diversions were stopped by a fear that they had not expected to feel—the fear of killing. They had realized that they would have to kill too many and that this could be the start of the new Great Killing, which sooner or later would kill them.

The fear of killing turned into something greater than fear: it turned into conscience.

The living circle that held hands and surrounded the White House had saved Russia from the faces of the past.

The living circle fortunately and unfortunately had not yet guessed that in doing so it would not be saved from the faces of the future.

The night air had been the air before a battle.

While there had been no battle, to me the morning air felt like the spring air of victory, miraculously come from the Moscow of May 1945 to the Moscow of August 1991.

In 1945 I, like many other children of the war, was selling Nord cigarettes, which I bought by the pack and sold by the piece on the corner of Sretenka and the Ring Road. The cigarettes were as skinny as the children of the war and we called them "nails."

When we heard the announcement that Nazi Germany had capitulated, all the Moscow boys brought their tobacco reserves to Red Square and handed them out for free. Ice-cream vendors brought their light-blue ice chests on shoulder straps and treated everyone to cold-steaming cones of *crème brûlée* and eskimo pies. The soda sellers drove their carts with striped umbrellas, alas now gone, to the Mausoleum in Red Square and poured free glasses of "plain" seltzer, bubbling a victory dance, or generously added a velvety dollop of cherry syrup from a glass spout to the silver bubbles.

The most unusual music I ever heard filled Red Square.

Several hundred record players, hand-cranked Victrolas, were set up by their owners right on the cobblestones still scarred by the metal rims of the cart wheels that had once brought the rebellious Cossack Stenka Razin to his execution.

And that day, next to the spot where Stenka had been drawn and quartered, he was mourned by the worn records playing a mix of Russian songs full of bravado, the springy Mexican "La Cucaracha," Glenn Miller's "Sunrise Serenade," Deanna Durbin's "Bicycle Built for Two," songs of the British RAF, songs of Jewish Odessa, the Italian "Santa Lucia" and Ukrainian folk songs.

About fifty thousand people danced in Red Square to hundreds of different songs — the foxtrot to "Rio Rita," the waltz to "On the Hills of Manchuria," Argentine tangos to Russian patter songs. There weren't many men, and most of them were wounded, so the women danced with other women and with boys. You couldn't find a single pair of light shoes on the women on Victory Day — all the women wore boots or wooden shoes covered in sateen, called "tankettes."

Arm-in-arm on top of the Mausoleum were a Russian invalid on his rolling platform and a French pilot (probably from the Normandy-Neman squadron), taking turns drinking from a bottle of war booty schnapps. American officers were tossed into the air with loud "Hurrahs!" and boys picked up the coins that fell from their pockets, testing them with their teeth. I still have my first American coin. And that was also the first time I tasted American chewing gum. But I thought it was candy and swallowed mine, causing all kinds of intestinal problems.

Everyone on Red Square on Victory Day thought that this was the start of an entirely new and happy life.

And that's how it seemed to us on the morning of August 20, 1991, when about two hundred thousand people came for a rally at the White House, which had survived its first night of siege.

The orators spoke from the balcony, not the one facing the river this time, but the one facing the Ring Road.

I was accompanied from the President's office, so that I would not get lost among the many entrances and exits, by the Dapper Democrat, who always amazed me with his flawlessly parted hair under the most disheveled circumstances. He exuded a delicate confidence in his every word, his every step. And it was with this confidence that he led me along the corridors of power, empty just yesterday and populated today. And suddenly I realized that he was leading me — without a shadow of doubt on his face — to the wrong place. This became clear when he left the White House and asked for a car to take me to the City Hall.

"Excuse me, but the President's aide asked me to speak here, not at City Hall," I reminded him gently.

He stopped in midstride to the car pulling up and — this is what astonished me! — without missing a beat pirouetted gracefully and, with the same gentle confidence, went off in the opposite direction. His eyes, rimmed with the blue of a sleepless night, showed not a flicker. He had the confident grace of a lunatic.

And I thought with some fear that he had a great future, for politics must be the art of pirouetting into opposite directions with the implacable, wise look of one who had prophetically envisioned that turning in the first place.

The balcony was like the deck of a ship that had survived a terrible storm and returned to its home harbor.

The people on deck and the people below, on shore, waved wildly and happily to one another. I sought the man with the raspberry bald spot surrounded by fluff who twenty-five years ago had tried to mesmerize me with his red ID and only yesterday morning had drowned out the President's speech with hypocritical Komsomol enthusiasm.

It is not hatred that has the most sensitive nostrils, but revulsion. My nostrils sensed that the man was nearby, somewhere in the crowd that was prematurely celebrating a far from definite victory.

"They thought that we were cattle, that we would be frightened. But we are no longer cattle and we will never be cattle again," roared the merciless voice of the gray-haired dissident with the face of an eagle; a woman who, as a skinny prewar girl, had been in love with Seva Bagritsky and had gone to the readings of those poets who would be killed at age twenty in the war; who as a nurse dragged over a hundred wounded from the battlefields, not letting them die; who was called a spy in the Soviet press; the fierce and hard comrade of perhaps the gentlest freedom fighter of them all — Academician Sakharov.

Waiting for my turn at the microphone, I did not know what to say. What was happening was higher than politics. This was history, and history is always higher. But this was history happening before our very eyes, history that had not examined itself.

I went through my poetry feverishly. But nothing suited.

Once again those lines so dear and familiar came to me, perhaps the best embodiment of the best in the hearts of those who not only speak but think in Russia, written by the man with eyes that resembled seeds of a magical African tree carried by ocean winds to the cold northern snowdrifts.

> Comrade, believe, it will rise,
> The star of captivating joy.
> Russia will awaken from its sleep,
> And on the shards of autocracy
> Our names will be written.

For some reason the final line did not sound like a proud affirmation in my mind this time, but like a question: "Our names will be written?" — with a big question mark.

But as soon as I had decided to quote these lines from Pushkin, a People's Deputy of the USSR and a procurator shouted them out. Apparently they were not only in the air, they *were* the air.

What was I to do? I didn't want to make a speech, but I could think of nothing else to do.

There were three speakers ahead of me. I had about fifteen minutes. I dug through my pockets.

I had no notebook, no pad, no pen. There was nothing to write on or with.

I tapped the shoulder of the gray-haired man ahead of me.

"Something to write with . . ."

He turned, and I recognized the journalist and dissident Lev Timofeyev, one of the people I had helped get out from behind barbed wire, but who differed pleasantly from many of the others by never slinging mud at me on the principle that no good deed goes unpunished. He smiled over his eyeglasses with sad but friendly eyes and handed me a thirty-kopeck plastic ballpoint pen, the kind my mother sells in her newspaper kiosk. "Well, now it's my turn to help you out, Yevgeny Alexandrovich."

I had a leaflet, with Yeltsin's decree declaring the junta illegal. I turned it over. The first thing I scrawled on the back was:

Conscience awakens even in tanks.

Then, about the most important defender of the White House, even though he was invisible:

And Sakharov, alive,
again with us,
on the barricades,
shyly rubbing over
his glasses,
cracked by the crowd.

Then came the image of the White House itself:

And the Russian Parliament,
like a wounded marble swan of freedom . . .

"Too high-flown," mocked the little gnome cultivated within me. But this time I did not listen to him. This moment in history *was* high-flown. "Wounded marble swan" was exactly how the White House looked to me. For those three days it had stopped being a bureaucratic institution and had turned into a symbol.

The rhythm of the poem, being born under the pen lent to me by a former camp inmate, was becoming extended, epic, heavy and clumsy—almost a hexameter. I was inside an epic, I was a small particle of it. Modesty has never been my major flaw, and I knew that the poem I was scrawling on the back of Yeltsin's decree would remain in history forever, no matter how it turned out. Of course, I would have liked for it not to be bad. But history ruthlessly did not give me the time to polish. There were only two speakers ahead of me, that is, I had only ten minutes or so.

I continued feverishly scratching words on paper. Now was only one speaker ahead of me. Just five minutes. Please, Lord, let him talk a long time.

But why do you have to read this poem right now and not when everything's been weighed and polished? the gnome asked with a shrug.

Because an Easter egg is a good present at Easter time. And because I'm not one of those who wave their fists after a fight, I snarled.

There are poems that are just that, poems. And then there are poems that are actions. Unfortunately, a well-polished but belated action stops being an action. While, also unfortunately, a timely action sometimes does not have time to be polished. And if I had listened all my life only to the professional polishers, who buffed their verse to such a parquet sheen that your fingers on their pages could no longer feel the roughness of life that sticks splinters of another's pain under your nails, then there would not have been "Babi Yar" or "The Heirs of Stalin."

The speaker at the microphone was coming to the end of his speech mode as if it were the final uphill stretch of a marathon.

The back of the Yeltsin decree in my hands was completely scribbled over with my jumpy scrawls, and there wasn't room for a single word.

I turned the decree face up and went on writing between the lines of text.

During the war, when there weren't enough copy books in Zima Junction, I wrote dictation with a number eighty-six pen, dipping it into a porcelain spill-proof inkwell, writing the words between the war dispatches from the Soviet Information Bureau.

"Conscience awakens even in tanks." That's fine. . . . But who climbed up on that first tank to develop a conscience? Yeltsin. That was the turning moment in history. I have to mention it. Yeltsin climbs up on the tank. Wait, wait, Zhenya—you've vowed never to mention living politicians in your poems. Bad enough that you glorified Stalin in some poems you wrote as a boy. People love to bring it up, forgetting how young you were then. And in 1956 you were so impressed by Khrushchev's speech denouncing Stalin that you were ready to join the Party. Thank God that those tanks that Khrushchev sent onto the streets of Budapest also squashed your illusions. Of course, in 1960 you fell in love with the young Castro — he was the first national leader you ever saw who could speak with inspiration without a piece of paper in front of him. And because he lacked Hemingway, who had left Cuba in time, Fidel invited you to go fishing. You sang his praises with all the sincerity of careless romantic idiocy: "Inspired like Mozart, [!!!] Castro on the crest of music." It's dangerous to mention live politicians in poetry, even if at the given moment of history they inspire your admiration. Who knows what they'll do in the next moment. While you, who sang their praises, will be tied up with them, and you will have to answer for them. No need for the name "Yeltsin" to appear in the poem.

But I interrupted my own thinking. Stop right there, Zhenya. Stop calculating. What about human gratitude? And the truth of an epic about these days? Is it possible without the clumsy but powerful Urals figure on the tank.

I did not cross out his name.

But I did give the poem a title. It was spare and simple: "August 19th," and it stressed that this was only a sketch from nature, and not a final portrait.

As in a fog, I heard the voice of the man running the rally: "People's Deputy of the USSR, poet Yevgeny Yevtushenko."

I went up to the microphone, which seemed overheated from the previous speeches and began reading to the biggest audience of my life — at least two hundred thousand people. But I felt that I was being heard by my two grandfathers, lost forever when they were arrested in 1937, and my father who had taught to me to write and read poetry, and who lay at Vagankovsky Cemetery under a granite boulder engraved with his youthful and brilliant quatrain —

Firing back at my heavy heart,
I longed to run, run far away,
But the stars are too high, too far apart,
And for the stars there is a lot to pay.

—and all my poetry teachers, now gone, starting with Pasternak, who had believed in me and had had time to bless me.

I had been introduced not only as a poet but as a People's Deputy of the USSR, a deputy from the city of Kharkov.

Why from Kharkov?

In 1963, when the newspapers, in a concerted campaign of "the people's wrath," called me a Khlestakov (from Gogol's novel *Dead Souls*) "who bore the unwashable bruises of treason," I was driving back from Sukhumi to Moscow in an old Moskvich car with the Bulgarian poet Stefan Tsanev. In Kharkov my carburetor gave out. At a gas station I was recognized by a Kharkov engineer who was having his car repaired there. He asked me to give a poetry reading at his institute.

I said, "Aren't you afraid of 'explosions of the people's wrath'?"

He laughed. "In what form do you prefer the people's wrath—meat dumplings or jam dumplings?"

Stefan slyly hinted, "He prefers the people's wrath with beautiful legs."

I wrote in my notebook then, "How tender is the wrath of my people."

The tender people's wrath in Kharkov came in all three varieties, and we stayed a week in the city. On Saturday we were invited to the opening of a new bookstore called Poetry, on Pushkin Square. I expected a couple of dozen poetry lovers. When I drove my Moskvich to the square, I was stunned. There were about ten thousand people there. Traffic was paralyzed, and the passengers looking out the windows of stuck trolleys and buses were happy, not wrathful. A wooden barrel was set up as a lectern on the steps of the store. But a policeman politely yet firmly took away the microphone, since no one had applied for permission for a street performance. Reading to a crowd of ten thousand without a microphone is incredibly difficult and my voice quickly gave out. From the second-floor balcony above the Poetry Store came a string bag suspended from a clothesline, holding a Chinese thermos bottle, blue with pink butterflies, containing hot milk for my strained voice.

And that is why, after my candidacy in Moscow was blackballed by my fellow writers and I lost the election in the Proletarsky District, where I live, I chose Kharkov from the fourteen electoral districts of the Soviet Union that asked me to run. And when I came to Kharkov, my campaign chief, the archeologist Valery Meshcheryakov, who was to become one of my closest friends, organized the first rally at that same square. And from that same balcony, a clothesline came down with the same blue thermos with pink butterflies on its sides, now rather chipped, and a gray-haired woman shouted from the balcony, "Zhenya, we kept this milk warm for you for twenty-six years!"

And I read from the White House balcony as if I had just had a sip of the Kharkov milk:

This day will be glorified
                    in songs and ballads.
Today we are the people,
                    not anymore fools,
                                        happy to be fooled.
And Sakharov, alive,
                    again with us,
                                        on the barricades,
shyly rubbing over
                    his glasses,
                                        cracked by the crowd.
Conscience awakens even in tanks.
                    Yeltsin rises on the turret,
and behind him
                    are not ghosts of the Kremlin,
but our simple people,
                    deceptively simple —
                                        not yet vanished —
and weary Russian women —
                    victims of endless lines.
No,
        never again shall Russia be on its knees!
With us are Pushkin, Tolstoy.
                    With us are people,
                                        forever awakened.

On The Balcony: My Very Best Bad Poem

And the Russian Parliament,

           like a wounded marble swan of freedom,

defended by our people,

           swims into eternity.

I had written many bad poems before.
But I knew that this was my very best bad poem.

On The Balcony:
The Human Cello

═══════════

THIS GREAT MUSICIAN, WHOSE GLASSES were constantly dropping and breaking because he kept turning his uncontrollably curious head
with a lusty yet childlike thirst for life, had had many women, but none of
them ever made him as happy as his cello did.

He was desperately lucky with women and with cellos.

Of course, later, some of the women turned out to be bitches, but the
cellos in his hands sang well and didn't turn out to be bitches.

He was vengefully forced abroad because he had given shelter in his
dacha near Moscow to the Great Camp Inmate, who seemed not even to
write but to scratch on paper with a rusty piece of the barbed wire.

But because all the cellos of the world were predisposed to their most
insatiable lover, their strings and wooden bodies vibrating, they arranged
to have one of their sisters, the rarest in the world, a daughter of Stradi-
varius, to become his permanent wife.

The price, two hundred thousand dollars, stunned the musician, who
still had not gotten used to the West. A Swiss music lover lent him the
money. The great musician, who had not yet become a millionaire, was
amazed when the aged, almost transparent hand with spots of pigment,
wrote out a check before his eyes for two hundred thousand dollars and
handed him that narrow powerful piece of paper, a pass into a new life.

He had no idea then how quickly he would be able to return the loan.

Money rained down on him as if charmed by the sounds of the magical
cello.

He wanted to become a conductor, and he did. But it was the cello that made him a conductor. Even when he was conducting, it seemed to many that he was still playing the cello—an enormous one, in which every musician was a string under his bow that only looked like a conductor's baton.

When he played the cello, they turned into one creature, and he became the Human Cello.

The Human Cello was the most Western Russian in Russia, and the most Russian Russian in the West. From his tours in the West he brought home everything that could be carried by plane, train or truck—from cuff links to cars. His shopping passion was almost a woman's. At the dacha he built near Moscow, everything was foreign—the roof tiles, the wood parquet, the doorknobs, the bar fixtures, the toilet bowls and the bath spouts. This must have annoyed the Great Camp Inmate who sought shelter there, since he angrily rejected all Western temptations, which as far as he was concerned included everything from Communism to cocktail shakers.

But when the Human Cello ended up in the West and, as punishment for his "liberties," was stripped of his Soviet citizenship, his buying energies were redirected to everything Russian.

Just as there had not been a single Russian nail in his Russian dacha, so in one of his many apartments on the globe, the one in Paris, there was not a single Western chair or drinking glass.

The windows had snowy lace curtains with the tsarist crest. The family crest on the crystal belonged to Count Golitsyn. The malachite oval table on golden lions' paws came, it was said, from the Winter Palace itself. The walls were hung not with Picassos or Matisses but Levitans, Polenovs, Serovs, Repins and Savrasovs.

The freezer was stocked with Siberian dumplings, *pelmeni*, made by a former army pilot, a ferociously patriotic Russian woman. She had left the country only because her highly enterprising daughter managed to marry a dissident artist, who painted not the patriotic cranes flying to their native haunts every spring, but some unpleasant bright red fat-faces, enough of whom were around in real life so that one wouldn't want to ponder them on canvas.

The Woman Pilot, like a living addition to the Japanese burglar-alarm system, guarded the malachite-and-lace exhibition hall of Russia's former glories in Paris, played the guitar and sang war songs.

For every night she spent as a watchman in the empty apartment while the owners were out of town, the Woman Pilot was paid the same rates as a professional from the Champs Elysées — the ones who pound the pavement in mink jackets with pampered lapdogs on a leash.

The Woman Pilot, just like the Human Cello, had filled her Paris apartment with a lot of Russian things, starting with her Zil refrigerator, sent by freight along with her son-in-law's paintings.

The seen-it-all Soviet customs officer who went through all these things before they were shipped, jabbed an old Vietnamese rice sack stuffed with something soft, and asked, "And what is this?"

"Rags," the Woman Pilot replied.

"What?" The customs agent thought the citizen was making an inappropriate joke.

"Ordinary rags. For the floor, the kitchen," the Woman Pilot explained with dignity. "A woman without rags is like a plane without a propeller."

Certain that she was lying, they tore open the sack and dumped its contents on the floor, looking for hidden treasures among the rags, but found none. And the rags *were* a treasure from the first day in Paris, because while you can buy anything you want in that city, the rags there were nylon, nonabsorbent and unpleasant to the touch, not like the good old Russian rags that, when wiped on the kitchen table or the floor, dragged a button that had not been removed from a former sleeve.

Sometimes, as she downed a glass of vodka with the Human Cello, the Woman Pilot would sigh and tell him, with a familiar tone as befitted her seniority, "I suppose you still have some connections in the Soviet Union, high up, I mean?"

"Well, my wife has a few," he chuckled, remembering how clumsily one of the "portraits" that the people are forced to carry on Red Square with organized enthusiasm had tried to force his attentions on his wife.

"Well then, she should whisper secretly to one of them that it's time to annex France to the USSR. The Frenchies will put up a fuss, just for show, but then they'll just roll over. You know, France is a great country, I'll be straight with you. There are no lines, and they have strawberries even in winter. None of that 'seasonal fruit' nonsense. And the flowers! The only thing wrong with France is the population. I mean, there are Frenchmen all around and they don't speak a word of Russian. They have tons of meat, but they kill miserable snails with garlic and then dig them out of their shells with forks. And those—you know, oysters—they swallow them live, so that they squeak pathetically in their guts. They fry up frogs, and maybe even toads, and then eat them warts and all. I saw a cheese in a shop window— it was full of worms, but they eat it up. Why, do you think our health inspectors would allow such madness in the USSR? And our people wouldn't let cheese lie around that long.

"The way I see it, they should move us Russians to France, and send the Frenchies to stand in our lines, for detergent, children's tights and bananas. Let our people, who suffered being surrounded by capitalists, now get some rest inside capitalism itself, walking along that main street of theirs, the Chimpanzee Ellizee, smelling the violets on Montmartre, getting some vitamins, seeing their museums and canyons."

"Champs Elysées," the Human Cello corrected. "And where in Paris did you find canyons?"

"You know, when they wear black stocking and kick their legs so that you can see their underwear. I thought it was dirty at first, but then when no one was watching, I tried it myself, but I couldn't get my leg past my belly. So now I respect those gals. It's not easy work, let me tell you."

"Cancan." The Human Cello laughed and then defended the French from the deportation that was now threatening them. "If our people become the main population in France, they'll have lines here too. Sometimes I think that if we were moved to the Sahara, sand would become a deficit item very quickly."

On August 19, the Woman Pilot called the Human Cello and said agitatedly, "Heard what they're doing? Tanks against their own people. I'd fly to Moscow right now. I have the wings, but my valves are rusty. How about you, are you going?"

He had been thinking about it, but had not made up his mind. But once the Woman Pilot asked, he decided, maybe because he had thought of Shostakovich.

How they had broken the soul of that genius, forcing him to repent, to sign all kinds of documents! Would those soul-breakers be back now to mock the geniuses of the future, shoving music into the brothel of politics so that it would be like a prostitute, forced to obey the desires of its important clients?

The Human Cello recalled a devilishly talented sculptor, crazed with work and his struggle with the professional forbidders, and how they sat drinking vodka from a tin can in his studio, filled with disgraced sculptures that the state did not want, and how the sculptor had roared, "Let's be honest, old man! We are facing a huge fat ass, and everyone is trying to lick it. But we can do that with greater qualifications!"

Would all that return?

He took his cello with him. It was not only an instrument, it was part of him. He trusted his cello so much that he sometimes felt that if it were ever stolen, it would not play in another's hands.

It was easier with the cello, not as scary. He was human, after all, and scared. But his greatest fear was not being where he ought to be during those days.

It wasn't a question of politics. It was his civic spirit, the citizenship that they could not take away from him.

At Sheremetyevo Airport the Human Cello was stopped by the border guards, because he had a foreign passport and no Soviet visa. And he gave them a virtuoso performance of the more colorful Russian vocabulary — unfortunately not available on tape or video cassette — so that the border guards were forced to accept his curses as an entry visa.

They sent a car and escort for the Human Cello from the White House.

The escort was taciturn, and answered the question, "How are things there?" with a brief "Could be worse." There was a shadow of concern on his face that had nothing to do with his task of escorting the celebrity. He had the beaten eyes of a man with family problems.

Thank God, he did not express his love for the Human Cello and for music in general. But not far from the White House, he unexpectedly asked, "Do you remember these lines: 'Where it is not better, it will be worse, but from bad to good is not far again'?"

"Of course I do. Of course," the Human Cello replied, jumping up in his seat, pleased that the man had spoken at last.

"Where is it from?" Palchikov asked with cautious hope.

The Human Cello looked sad and started wiping his glasses with a crumpled handkerchief, as if the author's signature were etched in the air, and this act of cleaning would enable him to read it. "I just can't imagine where it's from. I'm really sorry." And he wiped his bald spot, maybe hoping to rub his way to the quotation.

Well, if even he doesn't remember . . . thought Palchikov.

"Tell me, I won't look ridiculous on the barricade with my musical instrument?" the Human Cello asked meekly.

"If everybody carried only automatic weapons, it wouldn't be a life at all," Palchikov said with a shrug and a comforting smile. "People will be very happy to see you. And your bass fiddle."

"Have you ever been to any of my concerts?" the Human Cello asked without correcting him.

"To my shame, no," Palchikov said with a sigh. "You haven't been in Russia for a long, long time. When you first came back, my wife nagged me to get tickets, but I couldn't. Almost all of them cost hard currency. And I couldn't afford to buy them from scalpers. And I shouldn't do that anyway, I'm an investigator."

The Human Cello got his pen and a program of his London concert, which happened to be in his pocket. "I'll write a pass for you. Two people?"

"If it's no trouble, make it three," Palchikov said. "I have a daughter, Nastenka."

The Human Cello handed him the program, where it said in bold, flowing letters: "A pass for three to my first concert in Russia after the coup."

"Thank you," Palchikov said. "Now my family life is saved."

And when the Human Cello went up to the microphone on the balcony of the White House, he lost his breath with the excitement, and could not utter a single word.

The two hundred thousand people helped him get past this silence with their applause. People were happy to see their old favorite, forgotten by the newspapers, but not by them. And then they grew quiet, ready to listen to him, but all that came through the microphone were galloping breaths, rasps in the throat, convulsive gulps. It was a speech, not of words but of breath. Probably hearing that speech as being in some animal language, the denizens of the zoo responded with the piercing cries of peacocks and the velvety roars of tigers.

The Human Cello was feeling something he had never felt before, that he knew each and every one of those two hundred thousand people; that he had fought some of them with his school bag in back yards; stood in line with them for bread, kicking snow off his boots; jogged along the rails in a jangly trolley with tickets stuck like pink petals to the windows covered with frost palm trees; shouted in the stands "Kill the referee!" when his idol, Lyza, was tripped and the tripper went unpunished; argued until he went hoarse, talking politics in the traditional Russian place for such talk—the kitchen—unsuspecting that soon politics would take him and throw him out of his own home. But among the two hundred thousand faces below, glowing with a false sense of victory, he actually recognized only one, which had never glowed before and was not glowing now.

It was the face of the cleaning lady at the conservatory, Auntie Pasha, in her polka-dot kerchief tied under her chin, peasant style, the same kerchief she was wearing the first time he ever saw her, when he was a young and unknown student. She was already gray then, and so old that it seemed as if she had not grown any older in these twenty-five years.

Once, he was rehearsing in an empty room while she was gently and noiselessly moving a broom wrapped in a wet cloth along the parquet floor. And then she stopped, leaning her chin on the broom handle, and listened to him. After that, she shyly asked for his permission to attend all his rehearsals, and even if cleaning was not necessary, she listened standing up, out of respect for the music, resting her chin on the broom handle.

And when he had his first performance in the big hall of the conservatory, and he was dragging out his bows to rather spotty applause, he saw Auntie Pasha, at the very back of the center aisle. No one had given him flowers that evening. There was a basket from his family, but that didn't count. And suddenly Auntie Pasha took small, shy steps down the aisle and he saw that she was carrying what must have been a very expensive bouquet of white roses, a gift of a small, tender cloud.

She stood on tiptoe to hand him the flowers, his glasses slipped from his sweaty nose into the bouquet, and he fell to one knee and kissed her tiny hand, the index finger bandaged. She had cut her finger on broken glass, reaching into a corner for rubbish that the broom could not catch.

And now Auntie Pasha was inside that crowd of two hundred thousand, resting her chin as usual — this time on the still unsullied staff of the still-untattered, resurrected, tricolor flag of Russia.

The cello was nearby and the great musician could have played, of course — for Auntie Pasha and the others. But he was a professional and he could not allow the purity of the sound to be distorted by the rally's microphones and loudspeakers. Besides which, the music he wanted to play now had not yet been written. What he was feeling at the moment was best expressed by the music of his breathing. And he managed to breathe a few words into the microphone, to say that today was the happiest day of his life.

On The Balcony:
The Minister Of
Foreign Affairs

THE STORM OF APPLAUSE FROM the crowd of two hundred thousand raised the pigeons from the roof of the new, bugged building of the American Embassy.

The Soviet bugs, like encephalitis-bearing ticks, were in almost every brick. But of course, American bugs — brothers in a common cause — were placed in almost every stone of the Soviet Embassy in Washington.

While the cold war was dying, eavesdropping was doing very well. It was easier to remove the cold war from people's brains than the bugs from bricks.

The scandalous exposé of the Soviet bugs probably caused no one more trouble than the man who was now receiving the applause at the White House rally on August 20, 1991.

At the microphone was the Minister of Foreign Affairs, Global Georgian who had traveled the entire world. His gray hair resembled the Caucasus clouds scattered in transcontinental flights.

The crowd hailed him because it was he who, just a few months before, had warned about the plans for a coup when, in a speech at the Supreme Soviet that stunned everyone, he threatened to resign. The crowd remembered that.

But the crowd, which as everyone knows has a short memory, generously or stupidly forgot that a few years earlier the Global Georgian, along with the rest of the General Secretary's comrades-in-arms, had attacked Yeltsin, the man from the Urals, who had unexpectedly made a fuss trying to knock his head through the Lenin Mausoleum, his own psychology composed of a material as resistant as the red marble with its five untouch-able letters. No one had ever imagined then that this maverick would become the President of Russia. They all thought, the General Secretary included, that he had been knocked out of the saddle for good.

But the man from the Urals was helped back up into saddle of poli-tics, the bucking mare that had thrown him down painfully onto the ground. The Global Georgian had jumped off that treacherous mare in time, but he was not used to being out of the saddle. He approached the man from the Urals whom he had once attacked, because there was nowhere else to go, and he had to go somewhere.

And the Global Georgian missed not only politics, but his homeland, having leafed through so many countries as if they were the magazines on board planes. However, his homeland was the only country in the whole world where he was *persona non grata*.

They say there is no nostalgia stronger than that of the Russian. Why? Because there is nothing in the world that resembles Russia.

But there is another nostalgia, no less painful, even though the country missed is much smaller in size: Georgian nostalgia — *"dardi samshebloze."*

Nowhere else was there hospitality like Georgia's, where a guest could live without taking money from his pocket, where nothing could be praised in the house, because even if it were a precious dagger belonging to a great-great-grandfather back in the times of Queen Tamara, it would be removed from the wall and handed to the guest.

Nowhere else were there weddings or funerals like Georgia's — for a thousand or even two thousand people, with hundreds of relatives, neigh-bors and friends giving money, as much as they could, and all of it neatly recorded in a thick family ledger. Then, when those who gave what they could were having their own weddings or funerals, no one could give them less than they had given.

Nowhere else did there exist the privilege of being the world's only unremovable president — the president of the table, the *tamada* — and nowhere else were there toasts of such irrepressible poetry.

Nowhere else did so many people live in harmony as they had until quite recently in Georgia, even though they did have a way of jabbing one another, usually with jokes rather than daggers.

They say that he took bribes from the shadow economy, because it was the only way to undo the mafia knot, and anonymously sent the money to kindergartens and hospitals — keeping the receipts, naturally. Be that as it may, he discovered that one secret string led to the bedroom of the first secretary of the Georgian Party, the republic's leader. The man was a former general, not a greedy man, a dimwitted follower who was under the heel of his Ukrainian wife. She accepted diamonds in exchange for appointing regional district attorneys and Party secretaries, and also for protecting the kings of the black market.

Risking his own head, the minister of internal affairs, did something unprecedented. He put the leader of the republic (who was a candidate member to the Politburo) and his wife under house arrest. And only then did he report to Moscow. He could have lost, but he won. Brezhnev, who deserved at least house arrest for all the greed and corruption of his family members, strangely enough supported the calculating and risk-taking Gurian.

Now he had become the boss of Georgia. They say that at one plenary session he asked for a vote on a resolution to fight speculation. He asked that they vote with their left hands. Not realizing why they were to raise their left hands instead of their right, the delegates voted unanimously for it. Then, with the charm of a panther in a man's skin, he asked, "I counted several dozen gold Rolexes, Cartiers and Seikos, which are not sold in Soviet stores. How can you vote with a clear conscience, comrades, to fight against the black market with hands that are wearing direct proof of it?"

He confiscated and shut down many illegal and semilegal cooperative ventures, underground factories set up in caves, making chocolates and stockings. Unfortunately, after the closings, the amount of chocolate in Georgia did not decrease — nor of stockings, come to think of it. But when he started ruthlessly making arrests, he realized to his horror that pretty soon the republic's construction industry would be building mainly prisons and there would not be enough materials to do the job.

He made a television appeal, offering amnesty to those who would turn in what they had stolen from the state. Some took him up on his offer, but not everyone.

They set fire to the opera house when he was there.

They took shots at his car, wounding his driver.

They say that once, at a soccer game he attended, thousands of Georgian fans were incensed by the referee who had called a penalty on the home team just before the end of the game.

The crowd poured out onto the field, like lava. The players made a circle around the shaking, terrified referee, saving him from the mob that would have torn him apart into tiny pieces.

Then the Son of a Teacher, now the boss of Georgia, left his government box to go to the referee.

The crowd was full of relatives of the people he had put behind bars. It would have been very easy to kill him. But he was saved by the fact that he went out onto the soccer field without protection, having ordered his bodyguards not to accompany him. He amazed even his enemies with his personal courage. The crowd let him through and allowed him to leave with the referee.

The attempts on his life stopped after that.

Many continued to hate him, but he was gaining popularity. That created another danger for him, emanating from the Center. Moscow feared leaders who were too independent. They were suspected of nationalism and usually removed.

He tossed Moscow a bone, making a beautiful but unconsidered turn of phrase to the effect that, for Georgia, the sun always rose in the North.

It helped in his relations with Moscow. It did not help in his relations with Georgia. The nationalists sank their teeth into that bone, calling him a toady and a traitor.

Meanwhile, another Georgian, the Son of a Writer, became one of the nationalist leaders.

When he was a boy, his teachers came to his house to hear his oral exams, carefully removing their shoes to enter in their socks what would become a museum.

They say that his famous writer father told his son, either seriously or in jest, "You will be the tsar of Georgia!"

The Son took it seriously. He prepared for the part. He spoke several languages fluently, translated English poetry into Georgian, studied world history, philosophy and literature.

He did not hate Russians—he knew Russian culture too well—but he pretended to hate them, because he felt this was necessary to become tsar of Georgia.

Generally, he did not hate anyone, he merely despised them.

But there was one man he did hate—the Son of a Teacher, the boss of Georgia who, he thought, was ruling illegally.

Their relationship turned into a Shakespearean tragedy of many years' duration, entitled "Two Men and Power." They were both extraordinary personalities, handsome and attractive men, and the power in this tragedy was played by a woman, whom neither would yield to the other.

The nationalist leader and his nationalist cohorts began issuing proclamations illegally, calling for Georgia's independence.

The boss of Georgia tried, through third parties and sometimes personally, to persuade his argumentative compatriots to moderate their separatist passion. But they were also Georgians, and Georgians do not like to retreat. Worried that Moscow would accuse him of sheltering nationalists, he gave orders for their arrest. However, his experience in the art of controlling people told him not to create an aura of martyrdom around his foes—they would be more dangerous dead than alive. He knew that the best way to disarm his foes was to discredit them with their own repentance.

It was useless to try to make the nationalist leader and his cohorts recant. They were prepared to go to the stake. Prison was nothing to them—it merely increased their self-respect and conviction in the righteousness of their cause.

But the Son of a Writer was depressed by prison. He was not a coward, but he could not bear boredom, and everything about prison was intolerably boring for him. He was driven to despair that he had to eat like everyone else and dress like everyone else. And he was threatened with spending the best years of his life in prison. He decided to trick his sworn enemy and pretend to submit. He repented, right on Georgian television. He was disgraced in the eyes of his admirers, who had considered him an implacable hero, an incorruptible freedom fighter.

But here the boss had miscalculated in the art of controlling people. He had forgotten that an enemy you have humiliated is the worst enemy you can have.

Then he made yet another major mistake. Several children of

high-ranking Georgian bureaucrats decided to escape the Communism of their fathers. Their scenario of escape was operatically romantic. They dressed as a wedding party, even with a real priest accompanying the bride in her white dress and the groom with bow tie. Thanks to their parents' names, they went unchecked through the VIP lounge at the Batumi Airport, the pistol in the wedding cake unnoticed. In the air they demanded that the pilot land in Turkey at the American military base. The pilot said he had to refuel in Tbilisi. An army squad burst into the plane and opened fire, not bothering with a more subtle and humane approach. It was a crude and senselessly bloody reprisal.

Politics is never worth human lives, but it is hard to convince politics of this.

The Georgian boss started secretly hating the politics he faithfully served.

When Gorbachev had just come to power, before he was general secretary, they strolled among the fluttering *tsitsinatelli* of Pitsunda seashore and breathed in eucalyptus and salty air. The Georgian boss suddenly burst out, "Everything's rotten. It all has to be changed."

He felt a chill and dropped his gaze, because the words could mean his political end.

And instead he heard, "Yes, we can't go on living this way."

He looked up and saw eyes that understood him, glowing like lights that had been turned on.

And that was probably the start of perestroika.

In a difficult double fight against Georgian and Russian Stalinists, the Georgian boss financed the anti-dictatorial film *Repentance*. He wanted the homeland of Stalin to lose its undeserved label as the nation of Stalinists.

He was already Minister of Foreign Affairs when the film was coming out. In order to get approval from "on high," it was first shown, as in the old tradition, at government dachas, eliciting outrage among some big shots and their wives. But even though he was a new man in Moscow and walked the parquet floors as if they were a mine field, he was consistent. He went to the office of the General Secretary's right hand — the brainy *Muzhik* from Yaroslavl, who was also born in a small village, although his father had been not a teacher, but a simple peasant and his mother illiterate. He had a village nose like a potato and sly but kindly eyes. He limped because he had been wounded at the Volkhovsky front during the blockade of Leningrad. But he was not lame in the arts and often helped writers and directors get around the censors.

"I do not feel comfortable as a Georgian asking for help for a Georgian film," he began with his Gurian caution, but he did not need to continue.

The *Muzhik* from Yaroslavl had picked up his thought. "You don't have to. I'll take care of it myself."

And he came up with the idea of having the filmmakers shyly ask him personally for permission to release the film on a trial basis, with just three or four copies. And the celluloid birdie flew out of its cage and it was impossible to catch it. The birdie flew all the way to Cannes and came back with a gold branch in its beak.

The *Muzhik* from Yaroslavl, who just a year and a half later would be called a foreign spy by the chief of the KGB sitting comfortably in his prison cell, had no idea that his Kremlin telephone calls were being recorded and would be found in the sealed archives of Gorbachev's assistant.

Agitated, the *Muzhik* from Yaroslavl would ask the former President of the USSR, "Tell me, how could you work with me all these years knowing that my line was tapped?"

And the former President would look away and shrug. "What makes you think that I knew about those tapes? They were probably tapping my phones, too."

And who can say what the truth is?

And the President of Russia never imagined that in just a year and a half, he would have to fire him without decent warning from his job as head of television, and toss him like a bone to the Deputies who whispered hastily in the White House corridors on the first day of the coup — one of the founders of Russian free journalism, without whom the President would never have become, or remained, president.

But that was all to come, after the coup.

Before the coup that he had predicted, the Global Georgian did everything he could to narrow the ocean between the United States and the USSR. The Soviet army left Afghanistan, the Berlin Wall finally came down. And he had no time left for Georgia.

But the Son of a Writer did not sleep. He was lifted to the top by the wave of nationalist tears brought on in the reaction to a demonstration demanding independence on Rustaveli Boulevard: tanks rumbled, tear gas rose, and army shovels killed several young Georgian women.

He was working on getting what his father had forecast, but more modestly: he decided to settle for being President of Georgia.

During the election campaign, when he was asked by his gloating opponents why he had recanted publicly, he replied that he had done so in consultation with his cohorts, so as to continue the underground struggle on the outside. Perhaps that was so. But the story could not be corroborated by his cohorts, who had been the victims of a mysterious car crash at the start of the campaign.

Nevertheless, he became the legally elected President of Georgia and, hailed exultantly by his people, declared its independence.

And then they learned that independence and freedom were different things. It turned out that the former nationalist leader was too nervous about freedom of speech, especially speech critical of him. He began shutting down newspapers and expelling correspondents — from Moscow and from abroad. Paradoxically, as a freethinking and refined intellectual, he did not trust other freethinking intellectuals, and even came up with a term for them: "the criminal intelligentsia." Major writers and filmmakers gradually recoiled from him. He was not careful in his choice of words about some foreign states and he did not get any support from abroad. His own guards entered into a conflict with him.

He became convinced that this hatred was being organized by his sworn enemy, who watched his every step with a superpowerful periscope.

Perhaps some things were organized.

But the Son of a Writer, who had fought the authorities all his life and then became the authorities, naively had expected to be loved as he had been when he was a dissident. In his youth he had not fully understood all the beauties of being in the opposition. You were watched, of course, and could be arrested, but on the other hand you were considered a hero, adored and cherished.

People idealize those who are persecuted by the authorities and forgive them many things. But people never forgive anything of those who used to be persecuted and then become the authorities. Power, like a cobra, hypnotizes only rabbits. Power is a strong magnet that attracts envy, suspicion and anger.

The Global Georgian had experienced that for much of his life.

He desperately wanted to go home and he was desperately afraid to do so.

And that is why, as he stood on the balcony before the crowd of two hundred thousand, the Global Georgian felt he was standing at the edge of a cliff, that he was being pulled by power, like an inexorable misfortune.

Whom will I call *genatsvale* when I go back? And who will call me *genatsvale*? How terrible it is to be mistaken in those you call *genatsvale*.

And as if in revenge against the one who had raised him onto the bare and cold peak of power, where fierce winds knock people down, he ruthlessly shouted something that made the crowd gasp:

"We must demand from the coup plotters that they give us the chance to see and hear the President of the Soviet Union. If he is under house arrest we must do everything to save him. And if he is a traitor, there is no forgiveness for him."

Suddenly, in the distance, across thousands of kilometers, he saw a green, slender, almost transparent leaf of *tsitsmati*, floating in a spring.

When the Global Georgian, who had traveled the whole world over, came for a day to the Gurian village of Abasha, to his parent's house after a three-year absence, he felt that the gravity was stronger in his old yard than in the rest of the world.

The land of his home, with its prints of chicken feet and dog's paws, with rubber boots in a corner and a fluffy chick trapped inside one, with purple sacs of figs, striped wasps bustling with pleasure in their crimson cracks — this land did not release his feet, but stuck to them, persuaded them not to leave, because no other land can understand us the way the land of our old yard can, where, if you look closely, you can see the shadows moving, seemingly alive, of your long-gone parents and your own skinny child's shadow.

The large room on the second floor, where the whole family used to gather, was empty and the washed wooden floors were covered by nuts, laid to dry in a huge brown square. *Tkhili* nuts, brown with white spots, turned golden in the sun that seeped into the window through the persimmon leaves.

And on the table were photographs, crudely retouched by the bazaar photographer, of his mother and father, anxiously regarding their son, who had caused them so much worry in their lifetime and even after, by taking up something as dangerous, false and ungrateful as politics.

As a child he had loved to unroll the world map on the floor, lie down on it and rest his cheek on Africa, or poke his curious nose into Paris, or rest his elbow on the boot of Italy, or caress Brazil, or cautiously touch the Pole with his small finger.

Once they had a "What Do I Want To Be?" evening at school and he jumped up and blurted, "Minister of Foreign Affairs."

Everyone laughed, of course.

But that's what happened.

"It's time to go," his aide reminded him, delicately whispering into his ear, seeing that the Global Georgian was still staring at the photographs of his father and mother, his lips moving, as if he were talking to them.

His father had asked him when he was small, "Do you understand the meaning of our Georgian word *genatsvale*?"

"Well, a friend . . . more than a friend . . . like a blood brother," the boy muttered.

"You're right, but the ancient meaning of that word literally meant this: 'I will take your place in trouble.' *Genatsvale* is the person you are prepared to become instead of him when his life is going badly," his father explained, and the son remembered this forever.

"Why don't you call me *genatsvale*?" the Global Georgian unexpectedly asked his aide. "You're half Georgian, after all. What's the matter, aren't you ready to replace me in trouble?"

The man gathered his wits and replied, "Subordination does not permit me to call you that. But I am prepared to take on your troubles. Sometimes you may not even notice it."

"What do you mean?" the Global Georgian asked.

"You are too busy," the aide replied, avoiding a direct answer and shifting the conversation's tone. "We'll have to shorten the lunch in Lanchkhuti with the local authorities, even though that is not an easy thing to do in Georgia, as you know. Then to the Tbilisi Airport, and from there, without going into Tbilisi, straight to Moscow."

"What do you mean without going into Tbilisi? Just for a short time, at least to drive along the embankment of restored Old Tbilisi—it's my doing, after all."

"No time," the aide said. "We have to leave at four on the dot. The General Secretary is expecting you at Old Square at six. And tomorrow morning at seven we are leaving for Indonesia with a stop in Thailand."

The Global Georgian submitted with a sigh. Those who choose politics choose slavery to their own advisers.

The Global Georgian went down the wooden stairs that creaked the same song of his childhood but, to the anxious surprise of his guards, instead of heading for the gate with the waiting motorcade of funereally gleaming government cars, he went into the yard. His vigilant guards accompanied him.

The Global Georgian went to the fresh-water spring, paved with cracking granite stones, their mossy crevices home to tender grass and tiny flowers. A pleated stream of icy water gurgled through the zinc pipe.

Someone must have washed herbs recently beneath that stream of water, and a leaf of *tsitsmati* floated on the crystal surface of the tiny pool formed by a basin of pebbles, and a baby bulb of crimson radish with a white underbelly lay on the bottom.

The Global Georgian saw something at the very bottom. Carefully, almost religiously, he reached in and brought out an ancient silver teaspoon, which had been a gift from his grandmother. About fifty years ago she had spanked him for losing it. But the spoon hadn't been lost. It had hidden in the water from strangers' eyes for a half century and now, recognizing even his aged eyes, it sparkled a signal to him, asked him to pick it up.

The Global Georgian bent over, trying to catch the water in his mouth. But he was roughly pulled back by the chief bodyguard, who used to guard Gromyko and now watched over him.

"It's not allowed."

"What isn't?" demanded the Global Georgian, trying to contain his fury.

"Members of the Politburo are not allowed to drink water from untested sources — instructions. You never know what kind of microbes there might be."

"This is the spring of my childhood," the Global Georgian said, choking with indignation. Softly, pleadingly, he added in Georgian, "*Tskharo,* spring."

"In your childhood you were not a member of the Politburo," the chief bodyguard said without a hint of a smile. He told one of his men, "Cool drinks. Step on it."

The man ran to the car and came back with a cooler, filled with neat ice cubes and Soviet Pepsi and Fanta, Lagidze lemonade with a wine cork and Essentuki 17 and Borzhomi mineral waters.

And for the first time in his life, which like that of any politician had been nothing but a struggle for power, the Global Georgian thought wearily, Why struggle for power, what for? So that you can't even drink out of your childhood spring?

But it was too late to change profession.

Lyza And The
President Of Russia

THE EVENT THAT SEEMED TO be a premature victory rally continued, but not everyone there spoke and applauded. Some, even children,
understood that victory was far away.

"Papa, there's a hole in the barricade here," said the biggest little
Van Gogh.

"A tank could get through that," said the medium little Van Gogh.

"Tanks won't go here. All the tanks are ours now," said the littlest little
Van Gogh.

"Tanks don't know who they belong to or where they'll go. Neither do
the people inside the tanks," replied the big Van Gogh. "Let's get to work, guys."

And they filled in the hole left for the "insiders," the one used the day
before by the cafeteria worker, the little mushroom lady with the Puma bag
filled with caviar and crab who drove off in her export Lada.

Van Gogh had not brought his children to the barricades—they had
sought out their father in that maelstrom that could still turn bloody. It was
too late to send them away now, and too dangerous. Here, on the barricades,
the children were at least under his eye.

Besides, it was more fun for Van Gogh with them. Over the bars of
rusty scaffolding, garbage cans and slabs of concrete, his head of red hair
and the three smaller red heads looked like four sunflowers that had grown
right on the barricades.

Boat nodded at the cab of the tall crane and asked Zalyzin a silent
question. Her eyes were asking for permission. Once upon a time in Siberia

she had trained to be a crane operator. It was then that she lost her fear of heights and then took up rock climbing.

Zalyzin couldn't quite understand what she wanted to do with the crane, but he nodded with a sigh. A few minutes later, Boat traversed the metal steps agilely and was in the cab, to the delight of all the little Van Goghs, whose sunflower heads were lifted up.

What is she doing? Zalyzin wondered warily.

The crane moved slowly and the hook came down toward a metal crate on the sidewalk, where tubby watermelons languished behind a heavy padlock, apparently forgotten by vendors scared off by the putsch.

Unhappy that no one was paying them attention, the watermelons were practically bursting with the red juices hidden beneath emerald skins.

Zalyzin understood, and hooked the metal crate.

The crate swayed up into the air, making the green tails of the melons tremble. Then it slowly descended to fill the hole in the barricade. But Boat released it too hastily and instead of settling down gently, it landed with a crash onto the asphalt.

Several of the watermelons cracked, and the fresh red chunks, seemingly tipped with frost, showed the moist eyes of watermelon seeds, staring with curiosity at the world opening before them.

The little Van Goghs ran to the crate with a squeal of delight. It was impossible to pull out the watermelons whole, so they reached between the metal bars and dug into the luxurious, fragrant flesh.

Pulling out the sugary, melting pieces, the little Van Goghs licked them up from their hands.

Their cheeks were smeared with rosy watermelon juice and sprinkled with birthmarks of black seeds.

Boat came down from the crane and watched the kids with tears in her eyes. "I wanted to have a little Lyza for so many years," she whispered with her head on Zalyzin's shoulder.

"When we get married, you'll have your hands full with the big Lyza," Zalyzin tried to joke. "And I'm about ready for my second childhood—so you'll have a little big Lyza too."

And then there came a haughty, demanding car horn blowing on the other side of the barricade—once, twice, three times. Its spoiled voice implied that the car was used to having all gates open before it and as if its horn was the Open Sesame that makes even barricades part.

Through the bars of the watermelon crate, Zalyzin saw a black Mercedes with government plates. The horn kept blowing.

Then came an irate boss's voice: "What's all this self-rule, damn your eyes? Who gave permission to close the entrance?"

Zalyzin climbed up on the watermelon cage and stood at his full height. "I did!"

Below, at the foot of the barricade, a big boss of short stature, his bald head the color of overripe watermelon, was in a frenzy. He had the face of a criminal, with cruel cheekbones and a low forehead, his face shiny, as if smeared with fat. A pointy beard, intended to be intellectual, could not soften those features or add an iota of intelligence to that face.

Maddened by having to look up at Zalyzin, he practically screamed, "You'll pay for this. . . . Name?"

"Zalyzin."

"What organization?"

"The USSR All-Stars in soccer," Zalyzin answered with a laugh.

The little man stopped . . . looked . . . recognized.

Something almost human flickered in his face, which tried to smile in a friendly way, although it wasn't very good at it — even the cheekbones creaked with lack of use. Hostility was much more natural in that face. But something akin to interest glowed in the narrow, Asiatic eyes that were a strange blue — not a natural blue of flowers but the plastic blue of Finnish toilet seats so popular among the Soviet trading elite. This man was not a trader by profession. He was a trader by nature. Zalyzin recognized him.

They called him the Ice-Hole Democrat.

He had never been a democrat, but he was always a "walrus," swimming in the ice holes even when it was forty below. But he walrused only with people he needed — before perestroika with the nomenklatura, and afterward with the demokratura.

"I don't believe my eyes — my favorite soccer player! Idol of my childhood!" cried the Ice-Hole Democrat, switching from being obnoxious to being a toady. He murmured beseechingly, "But could you please open up the barricade so that my car can get through, eh? The President himself is expecting me. He just called me on the special line. How am I supposed to reach him, eh?"

"On foot," Zalyzin replied curtly. "This is a barricade, not the door to the VIP lounge."

Once he saw that this tone wouldn't work, the Ice-Hole Democrat changed records.

He was one of those record players that would play any record at all — the "Internationale," or "God Save the Tsar," or "God Bless America." And if it would be necessary in the future, "Moscow-Peking" or "Artillerymen, Stalin Gave the Order."

However, he still used the informal "you" in addressing Zalyzin. That was the old Party condescension at work.

"You're right, you know. How can a serious line of defense have a passage for special cars! . . . And it's not as if I didn't climb fences as a kid. Come on, Stepa, give me a hand!" the Ice-Hole Democrat shouted to his driver, who helped him climb up onto the watermelon crate, where he embraced Zalyzin picturesquely. "We never met on the soccer field — different generations. But here we are on the battlefield for democracy. I respect people like you — firm principles. Just between us girls, I'm like that, too. But I have to hide my principles. They could be mistaken for inflexibility. Can't have that. Come on, walk with me to see the President."

"Sorry, I don't know him," Zalyzin blurted.

"That can be fixed. I wasn't a pal of his either, but look at us now. History has made us pals. Come on, come on, don't be shy. He must remember you from soccer, too. You don't appreciate yourself. Just think of yourself in the third person. That helps, sometimes. Zalyzin — that name represents an entire era in our soccer. You're a brand name," the Ice-Hole Democrat flattered and condescended, making his way through the crowd listening to the rally speakers and telling the militiamen at the barriers when they had to cross, "Let us through. . . . This is Zalyzin the great soccer player. What's the matter, didn't you recognize him?"

His own criminal mug was part of the window dressing of democratization and no one checked his documents — they merely saluted.

"Too bad that you don't come to our little soccer games. Why don't you play for our team once or twice? How are things with your apartment? Don't be shy, we're among friends. You can be sure we'll help Zalyzin. But you help us out. Play for us, do some coaching. The actors' team keeps beating us. You think movie stars don't trip you? Hah! Dzhigarkhanyan kicked me like I was an Azeri. Good thing our Russian Madonna, Alla Pugacheva, doesn't play soccer — she knows where to kick a man."

Zalyzin knew that a long time ago the Ice-Hole Democrat had wanted to become a soccer player, and even had some talent in that area, though not much. But no one was better at arranging, fixing, wheeling and dealing. His greatest passion was doing apartment and dacha deals. He enjoyed selling and reselling real estate the way a born pimp enjoys selling and reselling his prostitutes.

The Soviet government was a many-armed goddess Shiva with atomic bombs in one hand; factory smoke stacks and rumbling hydroelectric plants in a second; weeping peasants, driving their last cows to be slaughtered for state meat, trudging on a third; brave soldiers marching on a fourth hand; ballerinas dancing the dying swan on yet another; and tiny soccer players, including Zalyzin, chasing a tiny ball on a lamp covered with green grass. There were more hands than could be counted. But one of the most powerful hands in this Shiva state was the one holding apartment allocations in its fist. The political powers sucked up to the housing powers.

Politburo members called on their hot lines, meekly requesting 'a little place closer to work' for their secretaries or masseuses.

High-ranking KGB officials mentioned, as if in passing, that their children were grown and needed their own place as they brought gifts: with a sugary smile, something banned and published abroad in Russian, confiscated at customs: Henry Miller's *Tropic of Cancer;* sometimes even Solzhenitsyn.

The Ice-Hole Democrat, who even during the Brezhnev years was an Ice Hole but not a Democrat, had lived very nicely even before perestroika. But he hated the fact that socialism, with its monopoly on real estate, did not allow him full scope for his talents. And he wanted to expand. He thirsted for a chance to play in the big leagues. Not with apartments, but old mansions, palaces, blocks, and then maybe cities, regions and finally the whole country. He was almost an honest man. He didn't want to steal whatever wasn't nailed down, he wanted to privatize it.

And that was when he had decided to join the people who wanted to exchange socialism for capitalism. For him, it was like an apartment exchange.

A risky move, but with great potential. That was why he was willing to betray the Party that had suckled him, had moved him with a maternal hand from soccer to a more profitable game, apartments, but was now an aged mother that was in his way. That was why he was happily tearing down the socialism that he had helped to build.

Renting buildings on a long-term lease under the aegis of perestroika was a form of sale, on which more money could be made than the stagnation-period bribe-takers had ever dreamed.

He began modestly, with mansions. He didn't take money himself— God forbid. It wasn't even brought to him. It was transferred to him. And not in rubles. And not to Switzerland. That would be an easy cover to break. To Liechtenstein. And Andorra. And the island of Guernsey. And the Canary Islands.

The Ice-Hole Democrat, behind front people, was practically the owner of a small horse farm near Volokolamsk; a quail farm in Alabino; a publishing house in Tula that produced pirated editions of intellectual writers like Tom Clancy, Rex Stout, Gardner and Chase; a joint venture in Nakhodka with South Korea, making fur coats with Russian pelts and brushes of squirrels, beaver and sable hair for artists; a casino at an international hotel in Leningrad; and a salon for erotic massage with a unisex sauna in Sochi; and several dozen video salons that offered new heroes for Soviet adolescents—Schwarzenegger, Stallone and Chuck Norris.

But that was not all.

The Ice-Hole Democrat had some property in the West along with his bank accounts: a couple of restaurants in Brighton Beach; a few apartment buildings on Santa Monica Boulevard in Los Angeles; an art gallery in Seattle, where simple-minded Americans bought Russian abstractionists, conceptualists and other 'ists' the Ice-Hole Democrat despised; a small factory in New Jersey that used Soviet recipes to serve nostalgic émigré stomachs the liverwurst and egg sausage that had vanished in its historic homeland in the stormy waves of perestroika. And he had a still-unrealized dream — to buy a little island in the Seychelles or the Bahamas, where he could go if there were problems back home.

Perestroika brought hope not only to honest people but to the scoundrels, too. Honest people expected freedom of speech and thought from perestroika, and the thieves wanted freedom to steal.

What the Ice-Hole Democrat learned from world history was that all systems die out in the end, but bribes survive.

He saw that the idealist democrats who had come to power were helpless. They needed scoundrels to survive. But they either became their hostages or turned into scoundrels themselves.

Zalyzin was amazed at how easily all barriers and doors opened for the Ice-Hole Democrat, including the President's door, which he dove into confidently, as if it were a well-used ice hole.

The President of Russia was in his shirt, with the sleeves rolled up. His eyes were red with insomnia and cheerful.

The President of Russia was on the telephone with the President of the United States. He had the receiver in his left hand and in his right, a rather unexpected bottle of kefir. The kefir, a kind of yogurt drink, had thickened and was not submitting to the President's attempts to drink from the bottle during the historic talk. The President held the phone between ear and shoulder and slammed the bottom of the kefir bottle hard with his left hand, a trick developed over years that had nothing to do with dairy drinks. But the stubborn kefir resisted brute force.

While the assistants stared anxiously at the telephone, the Ice-Hole Democrat freed the kefir from the President's clumsy fingers with a gentle firmness, took the letter opener — a gift for his predecessor in the White House, with encrusted handle and an inscription on the blade: "To dear Comrade Vorotnikov from the Steelworkers of Urals" — stirred the kefir with the knife, poured it into a thin tea glass embraced by a tea holder adorned with a small melchior worker and kolkhoz woman, and offered it to the President as if that was the special mission that had brought him to the White House.

A slice of lemon freed itself from the tea glass and floated on top of the kefir. But the President of Russia paid no attention to it and swallowed it along with the kefir, at last wetting his throat, parched from telephone calls and speeches. If the American President heard a suspicious gurgling over the wire and—basing his impressions of Russians on the one-sided information that he got from the CIA—thought that it was vodka, this time he was wrong.

As soon as the President hung up, the Ice-Hole Democrat's whispering lips were at his ear which still echoed with the sounds of the superpower.

The President's fastidiously puckered face made it clear that he was not enamored of the Ice-Hole Democrat, but it seemed to Zalyzin that something kept him from recoiling from the man's sticky lips. Something connected them. The Ice-Hole Democrat's lips were too familiar with the President's ear.

When the near-kiss was over, the Ice-Hole Democrat exclaimed, pointing to Zalyzin as if he had personally carried him for nine months and given birth to him in great pain, "Look who I brought you! Do you recognize him?"

The President frowned as he looked at the gray hair and the yellow T-shirt that said BRAZIL, and then melted into a friendly smile as he asked sincerely, but not very tactfully, "Zalyzin? Lyza? You're still alive?"

"Barely," Zalyzin joked.

The President shook his hand heartily and Zalyzin felt calluses on his broad, proletarian palm—from tennis.

The President as always was glad for a respite from politics. "I've never seen so many celebrities in one day as I have today. . . . I just received a musician . . . what's his name . . . you know the one who plays the . . . came all the way from Paris . . . and now you. To tell the truth, I thought you were . . . you know."

"He's not 'you know,'" giggled the Ice-Hole Democrat.

Waxing sentimental, the President interrupted the giggle. "Do you know, Zalyzin, you once cost me a deerskin cap."

"How could I have known that," Zalyzin said, with a wary shrug.

"I came here for the first time, still a young kid, to visit the capital with my pals—pompadours down to our eyebrows, bell-bottom pants as wide as the great outdoors in the Urals. And we saw a poster advertising a soccer game with your team, with the great Lyza, whom we had only heard about on the radio. We already had TVs in the Urals by then, but we couldn't afford one. We spent the night in line at Dynamo Stadium, but they ran out of tickets just ahead of us. The scalpers wanted triple price. The only valuable thing I had was my deerskin cap. I sold it at the flea market and we used the money for tickets. I didn't regret my hat at all. You played like a god. Nowadays, soccer's gone downhill—it's disgusting to watch."

"It has to be privatized, that's all," the Ice-Hole Democrat rattled off like a machine gun.

Office workers, much perkier than last night, ran in one after another bearing vinyl-covered folders marked "For signature" on outstretched arms. But the President, failing to notice them, continued in his lyrical soccer mode. "It's not a question of privatization. If you privatize a dying nag, it's not going to turn into a winning trotter. It's a question of people. Why don't we get an all-stars Russian team, instead of the USSR team? And have Zalyzin as the coach?"

"Wonderful. As usual, wonderful and simple," exclaimed the Ice-Hole Democrat.

"I don't need an all-stars team of grownups. They're all spoiled," Zalyzin said, taking the proposal seriously. "I'd like a team of boys. They'd get bigger, and they could become teenage all-stars, and then, only then, adults. It would be a different kind of soccer . . . the way Bobrov and Streltsov played it . . . the kind we've lost."

"I'm for it," said the President and then, turning to the Ice-Hole Democrat, "I'm designating you to take care of it. You're our soccer specialist."

The President sighed deeply and, almost without looking, starting signing the papers that were handed to him.

"It will be done," the Ice-Hole Democrat said with a happy nod. "Perhaps Zalyzin should speak at the rally now? We have to use every famous name we've got."

The President, not usually known for fastidious care in his own choice of words, this time made a face. "It would be very good if you were to speak, Zalyzin. But that's a bad word, 'use.' It's usually followed by the word 'discard.' You don't mean that someone could use me and then discard me, do you? Eh?"

"Of course not. The people love you so much," said the Ice-Hole Democrat.

"The people loved the tsar, too. And after he was killed, they loved Lenin. They loved Trotsky, Bukharin and Kirov. And after they were killed, they loved Stalin. So did I," the President noted grimly.

The people crowding his office looked around in bewilderment. But there was only an empty kefir bottle on his desk.

"Why are you so gloomy on such a victorious day?" the Ice-Hole Democrat tried, with a smile.

The President was still thirsty, but there was no more kefir in the bottle or the glass. And he didn't want to ask anyone for anything. He thought angrily that if he asked for a glass of tea, someone might ask for permission to privatize the Kremlin in return!

In the meantime, someone's hands had Zalyzin by the elbows and led him to the microphone out on the balcony. From a distance, he heard a voice say, "Our next speaker is the pride of our sports, the legendary Russian soccer player, member of the USSR All-Stars, comrade of Bobrov and Streltsov, a personal friend of Pele, and now a staunch fighter for freedom and democracy—Prokhor Zalyzin."

Either a lot of the crowd did remember his once-renowned name or they were all in an elevated and festive mood, but people welcomed Zalyzin with applause and kind, reminiscing smiles.

It was the first speech in his entire life. He was afraid, the way he had been during his first All-Stars game.

A photographer got close to the mike, pointing his Nikon at Zalyzin, and when the camera came away from his face, Zalyzin saw Alexei Petrovich, Tiger, who still wouldn't accept that he was dead.

From far away there came a ringing sound. It was a soccer ball. And from below there came a clanging response to the ringing. Van Gogh broke open the lock of the metal crate and the watermelons danced over the barricades, moving from hand to hand among the defenders of the White House.

The watermelon brigade waved crimson half-moons up at Zalyzin.

Zalyzin gathered his thoughts. And he spoke: "History is not round like a soccer ball, but it can roll in any direction—and crush you. Good coaches used to look for talent in the empty lots, brought them up. And nations have be brought up that way, too. From kindergarten. Instead of that, our nation has been turned into a soccer team with leg irons.

"The best coach in the world, Boris Arkayev, used to say, 'You have to start thinking about the next game before this one is over.' We seem to have won this game. But you can lose a won game at the next game. Let's win the next one, too, how about it? Let our life be good and our soccer, too."

As soon as Zalyzin left the mike, a young TV reporter almost knocked noses with him.

Would you like to be chairman of the sports committee?" he asked.

Zalyzin grinned joylessly at such a proposal. "I don't play soccer with politicians."

The Snipers

AS THE SPEECHES ON THE BALCONY continued, Zalyzin left the White House.

People recognized him, open palms reached out to him from all sides, to shake his hand. The hands belonged to laborers, with calluses; to "intellectuals," soft but with a hard ridge on the middle finger, caused by a pen; to retirees, wrinkled with darkened life lines; and to students, fresh as apple skin. . . .

"Watch out you don't end up a People's Deputy," joked Van Gogh. "Our plumber, he was also in Afghanistan, his wife and two kids left him when he was elected a deputy. I tried to help them make up, but she wouldn't have it. 'If at least he'd cheat on me with a woman — but with politics!' she said. 'That's like cheating on your wife with the sewers.'"

Boat handed him a slice of watermelon. "I never heard you over loudspeakers before. . . . You know, I had the feeling that they were taking you away from me again," she said sadly. "It wasn't your voice at all. When we were apart, we spoke in my dreams frequently. But in my dreams you didn't use a microphone."

Just then someone covered Zalyzin's eyes from behind. The hands weren't callused, but not a pampered intellectual's either — they were rough and chapped, not from work, but naturally. The palms were broad and cold and slippery, like two flat fish.

The palms smelled of nonsocialist cigarettes and Russian rifle oil.

Zalyzin would bet anything that the man who had covered his eyes so play-fully had cleaned his rifle just today.

"Well," Zalyzin grumbled, trying to remove the tight-laced and unpleas-antly damp fingers from his eyes. "Who is it? This is no time for jokes."

"It's always a good time for jokes, Lyza," came a rather hurt chuckle. "Don't tell me you can't recognize my voice? You're forgetting your old soccer pal, you're neglecting your old friendship."

The voice was as unpleasant as the fingers, and the breath stank of vodka. Zalyzin recognized the voice and tore away the fingers. He turned sharply and avoided giving his hand to one of those hands.

It was none other than Numero, with his unique, indecent sincerity, glistening as if it had been smeared with rifle oil.

"You've got a strange idea of friendship," Zalyzin snorted. "A written one. You write denunciations of your friends."

Numero was sincerely astonished. "What are you on about? That old business in Chile? I saved you from a greater blow with my letter to the KGB. I softened and balanced things. You should be thanking me and your fans at the KGB — they're great guys! You got off with a scare. They could have gotten you for being mixed up in a political thing. There's lots of good people in the world, as they say. We worked out the wording of your dis-missal together. My brainchild, actually. It's in there: "for undervigilance." I'm proud — I introduced that word into the language. I'm following in the footsteps of our great lexicographer Dal. That letter may have been the most humane act of my life, and you've been keeping a grudge against me all these years. Boy, it's true what they say: no good deed goes unpunished."

Numero lowered his voice and added, almost in a whisper, "And I'm going to do you another favor."

He looked around and, seeing Boat, said, "Lady, can you leave us alone? We have man talk here."

"She's my wife," Zalyzin said sharply. "I have no secrets from her."

"Let's get acquainted," said Numero and then, taking a closer look, exclaimed with exaggerated pleasure, "Why, we're old friends already — back from the Moldavian tour. But you were . . . how can I put it . . . not more beautiful . . . you're still very . . . uh . . . but you were uh . . ."

"Younger," Boat helped him.

"I didn't say that, not me," Numero laughed and wagged his finger at her. "Well, congratulations on making it legal."

"Get to the point," Zalyzin insisted. "You told me that it was something good."

"I'm a good guy, just not many people see that," Numero said with an injured air. "I'm a—whatchacallit?—an altarist. Everything on the altar of friendship. . . . Remember how we used to yell 'Atanda'—scatter?"

"Yeah," Zalyzin said reluctantly.

Numero continued, but not in a low voice, not even in a whisper, but in a wheezing breath, half-vodka, half-tobacco. "Do you know where I am now?"

"How am I supposed to know?" Zalyzin was filled with disgust.

"There," Numero said significantly, and Zalyzin caught a whiff of rotten teeth, too. "There, you know what I mean, get it? I'm a coach. General physical training, soccer and shooting. I have a rank. I have entree. . . . So listen, Lyza. I'm telling you—Atanda, chickee! Get out of here. Last night the Alphas blew it . . . got scared of a little blood. Like they're virgins or something. . . . But there's another group, really top secret. They cut fear out with your tongue. But I know one or two things. They're already on the case, understand? There's going to be blood. Go home, Lyza, with your Siberian babe—her fists won't help here. There's going to be major blood-letting and your White House is going to drown in it like a paper boat. . . . They're just waiting for the signal."

"I don't believe you, Numero. I think you're just bullshitting," Zalyzin pretended.

"Me? Bullshitting?" Numero got angry. "The snipers are on the roof already."

"Sure. What roof?" Boat asked, almost indifferently.

"That one there . . . see?" Numero pointed it out, infuriated by their disbelief.

"I don't see anything," Boat said, peering up at the building.

"Well, do you think they're stupid? They're there, ready. They'll start shooting soon."

"At the President?"

"Him first. But not only him. If he's not available, they'll shoot anyway. They need blood, Lyza, blood. On both sides. Then things will get moving.

And later, go figure out who started it. And the Alpha troops will get involved, too. So get out of here while you can, Lyza, you and your—" he coughed sarcastically "—spouse. My congratulations again. I told you this, even though I wasn't supposed to. I've got my trusty Makarov with me. But do you think I'm stupid enough to die in somebody else's battle? I'm off...."

And Numero, re-establishing his reputation as that rare bird, a Sincere Bastard, vanished in the crowd that did not know it was a target.

Boat looked again at the roof Numero had pointed out. No one was visible, and then suddenly, something glinted for an instant in the triangular opening of an attic window. Two glimmers, almost as one. A sparkle and it was gone.

"Looks like binoculars," Boat said.

Then a single glimmer appeared. It swayed slightly. Then it too vanished.

"A sight?" thought Zalyzin aloud. "Are they taking aim already?"

Boat gave Zalyzin a pleading look.

He didn't need an explanation.

Before, he sometimes was awed despite himself by her overwhelming freedom; most of the time he was annoyed with her climbing mania, and almost died of embarrassment over her behavior. But he had never been afraid for her.

He knew that she could bring him an icicle from a Kremlin tower, a fluffy branch of pussy willow from a ruined onion dome of an abandoned village church, a still-warm feather from an eagle's nest.

But today, for the first time, he was afraid for her.

Palchikov And The President Of Russia

"YOU CAN'T KEEP YOUR EYES OPEN. You should take a nap, for a half hour," Palchikov said to the President, escorting him to his office.

The President, stifling a yawn, like an enormous baby who was being tugged in all directions by a bevy of unasked and mutually negating advice-giving nannies, sighed hopelessly. "Where am I supposed to find a half hour? I have to make a speech on the balcony, and I don't even have an outline. Without an outline, I can't do it. I'm no Diogenes. And I have to decide who's going to fly Gorbachev down to Foros. The French Ambassador informed me that Mitterand is going to call . . ."

"When he calls, I'll wake you. You have half an hour," Palchikov said, leading the President by the elbow into the little room beyond his office. Palchikov knew that the President meant Demosthenes, not Diogenes, but pretended not to notice.

"The only thing," the President said, "well, no one should know, I mean, don't tell them I'm . . . just sleeping. They'll misunderstand."

"Everybody will misunderstand everything anyway," Palchikov offered as a strange consolation.

The President lay down on the couch with his shoes on and fell asleep instantly.

He looked even more like a baby in his sleep, a willful, pouting baby. He wheezed through his nose. His fingers, damaged by a grenade when he was a boy, seemed to be holding something—a cricket he caught in his dream or the scepter of power he had grabbed in real life.

Leaving him, Palchikov went back through the office and opened the door, pushing back the Labyrinth Lover who stood outside, his hand on the doorknob. With every word flattening his boxer's nose even more, he said, "The President is working on his speech. For the next half hour, don't let anyone in and hold all calls. Except for Mitterand."

It seemed to Palchikov that the Labyrinth Lover seemed to like him a little bit more over the last twenty-four hours.

Palchikov went back into the office and, satisfied by the sounds of snoring coming from the back room, sat down at the President's desk. He didn't feel like the President of Russia, nor was he trying to feel like him. But he was trying to find some missing links in the chain of events.

He's not such a child, thought Palchikov. But how did he manage to get to the White House on the first morning of the putsch, safe and sound from his own dacha, surrounded by the KGB? Why did they let him through? Even though they are Soviet people, they can't be that stupid. That means they had been given orders not to touch him. Who? Only one man could do that. Cherubino, KGB chief. But why? Maybe they had talked on the phone before he headed out for the White House? Maybe the President promised to support the coup when he got to the White House and then tricked them? If that's the way it was—well, what else could he had have done, anyway? He had no choice. Someone will get to the bottom of it someday. Or maybe not . . . oh, almost forgot.

Palchikov dialed a number, without having to look it up, on the special government phone with the USSR emblem.

Fang's voice came on the line. He was still lisping, his gold crowns still not replaced by porcelain ones.

"Well, how's your boss?" Palchikov asked.

"Thuffering. He went to thee a prietht. I didn't know he wath religiouth," Fang lisped in some confusion.

"Depends on the priest," Palchikov said, avoiding a direct answer. "We're having a big rally. Lots of young people. It looks quite proper. No hippies. Saw some around yesterday, but today they're gone. Must have been ashamed of their shaggy hair. . . ."

"You're not looking hard enough," Fang said. "Do you have your raincoat? They're exthpecting a thtorm tonight."

"I have a request," Palchikov said. "I owe a guy a favor—his file. Remember the one who was blackmailing Razgulai Restaurant, over on Rozhdestvenka, and then retired? Got a job with Alex . . . yeah, that's the one. You have a good memory for names. Can you check in the computer?"

"I am right now. He'th no angel, of courthe. But no killingth on his sheet. Blackmail, but mothtly it'th all talk. Mothtly thmall buthiness. Need a dry cleaning?"

"Yes, a rush job."

"Done. The man never blackmailed in hith life. File number B 7690049."

Mitterand's phone call interrupted, and he had to wake up the President before the half hour was up.

Then they brought the President the outline for his speech.

Palchikov had to check the balcony and other places. He kept thinking about Fang's words. "You're not looking hard enough. Do you have your raincoat? They're expecting a storm tonight."

Palchikov went out on the balcony.

It was filled with people and seemed to be listing, like the deck of a ship with a large, but not very insouciant, party in full swing. The eloquent liberals, who hadn't been around yesterday morning, were now taking turns waltzing with the same lady, democracy, taking cheap feels of her waist and back.

Many had come only to sign in the guest book of history.

The clever sculptors of their own faces had—belated—chiseled themselves features of modest heroism and ascetic readiness for sacrifice.

In all of history, there have never been so many heroes in the struggle for democracy as there are on this balcony today. Palchikov chuckled to himself as he zigzagged through the crowd, taking stock of the danger surrounding the President's coming appearance.

Palchikov was particularly annoyed by a showbiz-handsome hunk who bustled up and down the balcony in a helmet, and with an automatic rifle on his chest, its barrel bumping into people. Finally satisfied that the cameras of the world were clicking around his mustache and gun, the hunk tried to push his way to the head of the line for the microphone, using his innate charm, rather negative but still potent.

"The gun," Palchikov said quietly but firmly, putting out his hand.

The hunk understood by the imperial curtness of the gesture that Palchikov had the right to make the demand.

"It's not loaded," he whispered to Palchikov so that no one else could hear.

"All the more reason," Palchikov replied.

The automatic leaped into his hands with relief.

Palchikov hung it over his shoulder, pointing downwards, just in case. He went to the edge of the balcony and peered carefully into the crowd.

He had not seen so many good people at once in a long time.

In general, he liked the people below more than the people on the balcony.

The people below were more open-hearted and free.

On the balcony, if anyone embraced, it was purely for political reasons. Men kissed only other men and only like comrades-in-arms.

Below, men and women kissed, particularly the tank soldiers and the working girls, which had very little to do with the struggle for democracy, thank goodness.

Palchikov suddenly recalled the first time he kissed, or almost kissed, Alevtina. It was the first day he ever saw her. They were students at Moscow State, celebrating the October Revolution at a small café.

Eighteen-year-old Palchikov, a first-year law student, was untwisting the wire cage on a bottle of cider — the student champagne — and the cork flew on a foamy stream into the portrait of Khrushchev hanging on the wall.

The students burst out laughing, but they were called to order by the Komsomol Leader, who was also about eighteen, and who had seemed to be modestly elegant ever since kindergarten, his hair parted neatly on all occasions.

"I see nothing funny about that. I want to tell you laughers, by the way, that you are laughing thanks to our Party, which gave us the freedom to laugh at anything we want. I'd like to see you laugh if that had happened to a portrait of Stalin in his day."

And a girl Palchikov had never seen, with two black currants for eyes beneath her glasses and two coal-black braids that stuck out like an imp's horns, laughed even louder.

"And who are you?" the Komsomol Leader demanded, trying to stop her laughter.

"I'm not you, that's who I am," she gasped, laughing harder. "I'm a biologist." She was practically on the floor laughing. "Study animals . . . invertebrates . . ."

She had tears in her eyes and took off her glasses to wipe them. Her black eyes seemed even bigger and now sparkled with anger. "I can't stand politics! None of it! I refuse to think that I have to be grateful to someone for not being arrested."

Palchikov walked her home. He knew that her name was Alevtina. A frost had covered puddles with a thin sheet of ice, and the future lawyer and biologist fell together, slipping on the silvery asphalt, beautiful but treacherous.

The front door to her peeling building on Neopalimovsky Alley was loose, creaking on one hinge.

Palchikov went into the hall with Alevtina and decided to kiss her when they went up the stairs.

But she lived on the first floor.

The street was cold and moonlit, and the entry was dark, warm and smelled of cats.

Alevtina's dark, moist, black-currant eyes blended with the hall's darkness, and he could tell where her eyes were only when the headlights of passing cars splashed light on her glasses, lighting up the lenses. Palchikov put his arms around her carefully, and she did not pull away.

She was afraid of him, but she was even more afraid of scaring him off. "It's too late," she whispered. "I'm afraid we'll wake my parents."

He brought his face to hers. Sensing that he wanted to kiss her eyes, Alevtina reached for her glasses. She was about to take them off when she saw something on the street over Palchikov's shoulder.

Reeling and waving his arms in a conversation with himself, a black figure moved in the middle of the street. Cars, slipping and fishtailing on the ice, steered around him. Alevtina did not let Palchikov kiss her. She ran out of his arms and into the street. She grabbed the elderly workman, who had lost his hat and all sense of where he was and was muttering about the wife who had walked out on him.

Palchikov came to help and they dragged him to the sidewalk, before a car hit him. A lot of people were drinking and driving that holiday night.

The drunkard put his face on the ice and started snoring.

"He'll freeze out here," Alevtina said. "I'll have to take him home."

"Home? But you don't know him."

"We'll get acquainted when he wakes up," Alevtina said with a laugh.

"What will your parents say when they see him?"

"They're blind," Alevtina replied.

"That's not funny," Palchikov said and thought, What kind of a person is she to make jokes like that?

"They really are blind," Alevtina said. "And very old. I'm their only child, a late baby. I'm afraid they'll die soon. Listen, could you spend the night, too? It's a little scary with this fellow. And he's kind of heavy."

And that was how Alevtina and Palchikov spent their first night together, in her tiny six-by-nine room. She slept on the couch, he slept on four chairs pushed together, and between them on the floor, like the sword between Tristan and Isolde, blissfully snored Vasil Vasilyich, master tiler, as he introduced himself the next morning. They had breakfast with Alevtina's parents, who left early in the morning to work at the society for the blind, where they reupholstered car seats. Alevtina's mother ran her fingers over Palchikov's face. Her sensitive, seeing fingers moved over his features slowly, either hoping to find something, or afraid of finding it.

"He has a good face," she said. "I wouldn't say a handsome face, but a human one."

And that's what Palchikov recalled as he stood on the balcony of the White House, looking down at the soldiers kissing girls.

And then he noticed a doubled glint on a building roof not very far away. It didn't resemble Alevtina's eyeglasses.

Palchikov noted the spot. A triangular attic window. The doubled glint vanished. But then came a single, moving glimmer that swayed and moved up, then moved down, then floated a bit to the left, then a bit to the right. Fang had been correct.

Palchikov rushed inside, elbowing people aside in the hallways as he ran to the Labyrinth Lover's office.

"Palchikov, my old comrade from the alma mater! It's been a long time! Glad to see you in our ranks, especially on a day like today!" It was none other than the former Komsomol Leader. He was in a rush, his whole attitude suggesting that his modest elegance itself was democracy's invincible weapon against the brute military force of the coup makers.

The Labyrinth Lover stared at Palchikov. His gray brush mustache bristled. The nostrils on his boxer's nose flared.

"Snipers," Palchikov said, breathing hard from his run. "Four of them on the roof opposite. We have to take them. Give me some men—but pros."

"How many?" the Labyrinth Lover asked, his unblinking eyes steady on Palchikov.

"Five."

"That's all? Where am I going to get five men? Professionals are as rare as counterfeit coins. You'll have to do with one. You told me that there were four snipers, right? Well, isn't one democrat worth two coup plotters?" the Labyrinth Lover asked with a cold chuckle. "Go to the service entrance. A man will be waiting for you there. The password is 'Spark.'"

Alevtina, I might be killed, and we'll never make up, Palchikov said almost out loud, hurrying down the labyrinths of power. And I'll never learn who wrote "Where it doesn't get better, there it will be worse, but it is not far back again from bad to good."

At the service door, someone spoke softly, imported beer on his breath. "'Spark.'"

Palchikov turned around.

The Former Racketeer smiled at him.

Boat And The
Last Cliff

LAKE BAIKAL HAD TAKEN BOAT'S father when she was very small. But she remembered Father well, or maybe she just thought she did. His eyes were like two big drops of the Baikal, lying in deep granite pools.

The scales of the omul, which lived only in the Baikal, glittered in his young beard. His hands smelled of campfire smoke, fish and the boat engine. He was tall and he liked picking her up high.

When she was a child, Boat thought sometimes that he had not died, but just gone up somewhere, as high as the smoke of his campfire.

When she climbed cliffs, she thought that he was waiting for her at the top.

But she never found him.

Once, quite recently, she had seen her father again, in her dreams.

He was sitting on a peak and repairing his nets. He was the age at which he had died. And she was now a bit older.

"Who are you?" Father asked.

"Your daughter," she replied.

"I don't seem to recognize you," he said suspiciously.

She showed him the scars above her left wrist, made by the bear cub he had given her. Only then did he recognize her.

"You've changed a lot," Father said with a sigh. "Your hair used to be white. Now it's gray. Well, where are your grandchildren?"

She lowered her head. "I don't even have any children, Father."

"Didn't you fall in love?"

"I did."

"And did he love you?"

"Yes."

"Well, where are the children then?"

"Don't ask, Father."

Her father embraced her, running his young tanned fingers through his daughter's gray hair. "Do you want me to make you a young girl again so you can start life over?"

"I don't know."

"There's only one condition," Father continued. "You will lose all memory of your former life."

"Does that mean I will forget him?" she asked in fear.

"Who?"

"The one I loved all through my former life?"

"You will. What do you need to remember him for? He didn't make you happy."

"He did."

"I don't understand. Where's your happiness?"

"I can't explain it. Father, I don't want to trade my memory for youth."

Father vanished, and Boat saw that she was all alone on a bare mountain peak. She did not dream of him after that.

But now, Boat, who was almost sixty-five years old, was climbing another cliff, this time the rusty fire escape of a gray, grim building opposite the White House. Zalyzin and Van Gogh had a plan — Boat would scare the snipers out of the attic, and the two men would deal with them on the ground. Van Gogh had given her a couple of smoke bombs, all he had managed to get on short notice from a paratrooper friend. The bombs were heavy in the canvas bag over her shoulder.

Boat had never been out of breath like this. She had never felt dizzy from heights before, either. She wanted to forget about her age, but it would not let her.

"Now will you trade memory for youth?" came her father's voice.

"No," she whispered. "I want to be young, but I will not give up my memory."

"That is impossible," Father said. "You always have to lose something to gain something else."

"But isn't memory of youth the same as youth?"

"I wish it were so, but then I would be alive," he replied sadly.

Her father was not at the top of that lifeless cliff, nor could he have been. He was higher.

At the top of this cliff were men who had been trained to shoot at other people.

Zalyzin and Van Gogh were downstairs, trying to break down the door leading to the stairwell. But the metal door was reinforced, and would not budge.

Palchikov and the Former Racketeer saw the small figure climbing to the top of the fire escape and hurried towards her.

Then they saw two men, one with gray hair, in a yellow T-shirt with BRAZIL on the chest, and another with hair like a red sunflower. They were banging at the door, with their shoulders and with chunks of metal pipe. Palchikov and the Former Racketeer exchanged a quick look and hurried to help then.

"And where's my file, chief?" the Former Racketeer suddenly asked, angrily, his automatic rifle banging against his belly as they ran. "Forgot your promise, right?"

"I keep my word. File 7690049 has been dry-cleaned. The grease spots are gone," said Palchikov, also running. The Former Racketeer's automatic bounced on his chest.

"I'm impressed, chief," the Former Racketeer gasped.

"Damn it, I forgot that this weapon isn't loaded," Palchikov said, furious with himself. Suddenly it occurred to him: Now that his file is cleaned up, he could kill me.

"Use my spare magazine," the Former Racketeer said, suddenly generous.

"What are you waiting for? Shoot the damn lock off, you mothers!" Van Gogh shouted at them.

"No," Palchikov said. "No shooting. Unless it's an emergency."

The little figure on the fire escape tossed something at the attic window. It was hard to tell from below whether it got in or not. No, it missed—the smoke bomb was on the edge of the roof. But the smoke poured out, covering the attic window. Now, they could only shoot blind.

The Former Racketeer nodded his head towards a pile of panels, covered in bird droppings, lying in a courtyard beside the building. The four men heaved the top panel up onto its edge, in the process sweeping away someone's crushed cigarette butts and an empty bottle of rotgut.

The Former Racketeer slipped a board, that had been lying in a puddle, under the panel. The four men pushed hard and the panel slid down the wet board like a crushing battering ram. The door gave way and the men rushed up the stairs.

Meanwhile Boat, her hands orange with rust and bloody with metal splinters, realized that the fire escape did not reach the roof. The final section was gone, probably because it had rusted through.

The attic window was close. Boat could see the blurred contours of the hippie-like heads passing in front of the window and could hear snatches of curses. The snipers knew they had been found out.

She had only one smoke bomb left and she wanted to get it right into the window, to smoke them out for sure.

She got as high as she could, so that her knees rested against the last metal step of the broken stairs, and her body above the knees, buffeted by the wind, had no support. Boat took out the smoke bomb, lit it, burning her fingers as she did, and tossed it into the attic window, right into someone's curse.

But she lost her balance and her center of gravity was gone. And a gust of wind mixed with smoke pushed her in the chest. And the last rusted step that she did manage to grab cracked, and Boat fell to the earth, which had not forgiven her for always trying to rise above it.

In the meantime, Zalyzin ran up the last few flights of stairs, gasping, carrying a length of pipe in his hand. As he neared the top, he could see a sniper's legs dangling down from the attic trapdoor in a cloud of smoke, but then they disappeared back up into the attic. Apparently, the snipers had decided to take the roof.

When Zalyzin reached the roof, the first thing he did was look for Boat, not the snipers. He ran to the roof's edge and peered down at the fire escape.

The rusty stairs, not quite reaching the roof, were empty, and the top step was broken. Slowly, Zalyzin's eyes followed the stairs, step by step, landing by landing. Finally, at the bottom, he saw a crowd, like a flower that had grown in the asphalt, at the heart of which was a tiny, still figure.

When Zalyzin reached Boat there, on the ground, her eyes were open — no one had thought to close them. They were still the blue lanterns, but now viewing such heights as she had never scaled in her lifetime.

Do you want me to be the Boat that will always be there, waiting for you? Zalyzin heard the voice and realized that she would be waiting for him once more, but now in a place other than earth.

Forgive me, Boat, Zalyzin's inner voice replied. Forgive me because we did not live long and happily together and did not die on the same day.

"You were the one who was supposed to die, chief," the Former Racketeer said to Palchikov. "She took your death. And maybe, not only yours."

"Why didn't you kill me?" Palchikov asked. "You had your orders."

"Because you were the first man I ever met who did not trick me, chief," the Former Racketeer replied. "Put the safety on your machine gun."

That Night:
The Bullets

THIS TROLLEY MIGHT HAVE BEEN the one of song — the last trolley, not going anywhere now, except into other songs that were still to be written about it.

It formed part of the barricade, at the exit from the tunnel to the Ring Road. Its wheel-topped antennae that had jumped from the catenary wires swayed above the Moscow night, wet and anxious, the second night of the coup.

Inside, on the torn seats, slept the people who had not slept the night before.

And one of the weary sleepers was the Poet of the Twenty-First Century.

That night he had dreamed of a verse. The line walked through his dream like an unknown girl in the street who turned around and smiled. It had been searching for him on the streets of Moscow ever since the Parisian Russian Lady had said, gently and anxiously, "Be careful about making predictions about yourself and others! Why don't you change the poem, eh?"

After their conversation, he had repeated the lines to himself:

> You will die when the dawn trembles
> Blinded by a pistol shot.

And suddenly, he felt an eerie chill, as if he could hear the creak of that strangely slow and hard-to-pull trigger. Of course, being doomed in a beautiful way has its attractions. Beautiful doom is applauded even by cowards who think other people's courage is their own—and girls like beautiful doom—sometimes their own, but more often, someone else's.

He wanted girls to like him. He wanted to overcome his shyness, which the Parisian Russian Lady had seen through his literary all-knowingness, as she once had seen it in Vladislav Khodasevich, as he waited for her, a young girl then, with a nosegay of violets from Antibes in his uncertain fingers, stained the same violet by the ink with which he had written: "I, I, I . . . What a crazy word!"

But Khodasevich had been a poet of the nineteenth century who was thrust into the twentieth, while that sweet, vain boy, so desperate to seem beautifully doomed, was a Poet of the Twenty-First Century in the twentieth, instead.

Actually, he wasn't the gloomy romantic he tried to appear, and what he loved most in the world was the book about the brave soldier Schweick and homemade dumplings with fresh cherries.

But the verse calling for his own death was already written, and the line reversing his incantation had just come to him in a dream, and in the trolley that had come out of song. The dreamed verse wanted to save him.

The dreamed verse took a step toward him, and he took a step toward it. The dreamed verse reached out to him and he reached out to it.

But just then a horrible blow struck the trolley. It was an armored personnel carrier, a BMP 536 of the Taman Division, striking head-on to get through the barricade. It had tossed aside a correspondent who had tried to stop the military column, his arms outflung as though he were a living crucifix, and with a fragile plastic pen in his hand.

The Poet of the Twenty-First Century leapt up, rubbed his eyes and jumped out of the trolley car into the crowd that was showering the personnel carrier with stones and curses.

As he ran he tried to remember the verse he had just dreamed, but it vanished from memory.

Ahead he saw an Afghan vet running toward the personnel carrier with a piece of canvas.

The Poet of the Twenty-First Century had read his poems to the vet around the campfire by the White House. The vet hadn't said anything about the poetry but he did give him some bouillon, made with army beef cubes and boiling water. The vet was a few years younger, but looked older, like all the vets from the war in Afghanistan.

Now the vet jumped on top of the carrier, trying to cover the viewing slit with the canvas. "Stop, or I'll piss on your heads!" he shouted, as the people who were there later recounted. Others, who claimed to have been there too, didn't hear anything like that.

History is full of moments with many more people claiming to have been there than could possibly be believed.

The gunner turned the turret, trying to knock the vet off the roof. The vet barely avoided the slamming gun. Then the driver jerked the carrier to throw him off, braking and starting, then hitting the tunnel wall. But the blow knocked open the hold, and the vet got up and jumped down inside. Shots rang out, and the driver jerked his BMP 536 so hard that the vet was thrown out of the hold, where his clothing got caught on the hold cover, and the carrier drunkenly veered around the tunnel, dragging his body along the ground.

The Poet of the Twenty-First Century rushed to help him, to unhook him, but another man from the crowd beat him to it, and he was mowed down by a bullet. There were so many shots that it was impossible to tell where they were coming from — the carrier, or from somewhere else as well.

The asphalt in the tunnel turned crimson under the crazed caterpillar treads of the carriers. One had a torn sleeve dangling from it. Perhaps just yesterday a mother had darned a tear in it.

"Murderers!" the crowd shouted. "What are you doing, fascists?"

Molotov cocktails flew into the carrier and it burst into flames.

From its flaming bowels came very young soldiers, confused by History, not understanding what was happening; certainly not resembling fascists, shooting into the air and all around them meaninglessly, with guns that trembled in their hands.

But the Poet of the Twenty-First Century saw them only as fascists, who had shot a stranger, who had died instead of him only by chance. That was unfair, because that death had been predicted in his poem for himself. The Poet of the Twenty-First Century was scared, because he remembered the Parisian Russian Lady's warning and he couldn't remember the line that had come to him in his dream. But he was still very young and he was ashamed of his fear, even though sometimes, fear is simply the necessary instinct for self-preservation.

And so, suppressing his fear, he stepped forward and shouted, putting himself in the path of the death he had predicted, "Murderers, shoot at me, too!"

Some of the people who "were there" said that that was what he shouted. Others who "were there" said he shouted nothing at all, but merely threw a stone at another carrier, a BMP 521, where the first soldiers — crying, miserable, accidental and perhaps only alleged killers — had fled to hide from the mob.

The bullet that killed him was not found in the autopsy. Perhaps it will be found someday.

And when the Poet of the Twenty-First Century fell in the blood of those who took death in his place, the dreamed verse came up quietly and wept that it had not been in time to save him.

THE THIRD DAY

The Tanks
Are Leaving

NASTENKA LOVED BOOKS AND SHE had learned to read when she was very little, when her first mother was still alive, before the polar bear at the zoo had killed her. But her second mother, Alevtina, had special books that had belonged to her late, blind parents.

When no one was home, Nastenka opened those heavy, clumsy books with Braille writing, and moved her fingertips over the letters. Nastenka did not know Braille, so she could imagine that it meant whatever she wanted it to mean.

She spoke with two people through those books, people she loved very much and who were gone: her first mother and her second father, the only father she knew.

"Don't listen to Mama when she chases you away. Because afterwards, she sits and cries. Mama loves you very much, Papa, but she doesn't tell you about it. She tells Pitey. I overheard them recently," Nastenka told Palchikov, who was hiding somewhere among the raised Braille letters. "But Mama really hates the two ladies you're always with, Auntie Urgent Work and Auntie Politics. Spend more time with Mama, not with them."

Nastenka felt for the answer, reading her father's imagined response with her fingertips. "I'll be back soon, Nastenka. I'm to blame, but I won't do it anymore. You can make me stand in the corner and don't give me any candy. But I love Mama and you and Pitey and I miss you terribly. And give my love to your moonwalker. Be careful with him, because he can run away very far."

Nastenka usually listened to her father. But on this sunny August morning, wearing her white straw hat against the sun, Nastenka went outside and let her moonwalker go for a walk.

Nastenka paid no attention to the noise on the street. She was getting used to it over the last three days. It was the tanks.

The moonwalker trundled along the path in the little park, while Nastenka stopped to play for just a little with the neighbor's marmalade kitten. But when she looked up, the moonwalker was gone. She could make out its tracks in the sandy path, and Nastenka followed out into the street. Here's what she saw.

The moonwalker had successfully negotiated the curb and was crossing the street, slowly but confidently, with its rolling gait. And around the corner a column of tanks came rolling towards the tiny, peaceful, defenseless creature. The tanks were leaving Moscow.

Nastenka rushed out into the street to save her moonwalker. The first tank missed it, but now the next was barreling down upon it. The Marshal in the bouclé cap and old-fashioned raincoat with the "Friendship Factory. Made in China" label was watching the tanks leave. He ran out to help the girl and was almost knocked down by a tank himself. He was lucky. When he got up, he — a man who had seen three wars, the Finnish, the World War and the Afghan war — shuddered.

Right where the girl and the moonwalker had been, the column of unobservant tanks was passing, their treads smearing and grinding into the asphalt everything that was left — the white straw hat and the plastic and plexiglass crumbs. After the last tank had passed, there was nothing left of the hat but a few white threads, like someone's gray hairs, pressed into the road.

The Marshal had already had a report about the three young men killed in the tunnel the night before.

He made up his mind.

That Night:
Outside KGB
Headquarters

SITTING ON THE SHOULDERS OF the statue of Dzerzhinsky, which was covered with graffiti of damnation and curses, was a tipsy fellow in a jean jacket, savoring the pleasure of tying a noose of metal wire around the green bronze neck of that romanticized inquisitor.

They were just about to haul him up.

The cranes were ready.

Once upon a time a young Polish revolutionary named Dzerzhinsky, tossed behind bars by the tsarist secret police, swore in his prison diary to do everything to make a world without prisons.

It was a sincere but misguided thought.

It was this man, who came to be called Iron Felix, who founded the most powerful police-spy-prison organization in the world, which changed names and bosses several times: VChK, OGPU, NKVD, MVD, MGB and finally KGB.

If he had not died of a sudden heart attack after a fiery revolutionary speech, he would have ended up tortured in the cellars of Lubyanka like so many of the *Chekists*, the secret police who had themselves tortured so many people to death in those same cellars.

He had a temporary reprieve only because he had turned into a monument. But now it was dangerous to be a monument.

I had no pity at all for Iron Felix, but the momentum of destruction that drove the crowd frightened me. This destructiveness could unleash itself in any direction. I remembered how the frenzied crowd had pushed through people's apartments to get to Stalin's coffin on the day of his funeral and how a child crawling on the floor in one of them was crushed.

That night on Dzerzhinsky Square I did not see the beautiful faces of the people who had formed a living ring around the White House (for those people, having done their work, were catching up on the three nights of sleep they had missed), but only the angry, snarling faces of vandals who had gotten lots of rest during the coup. These vandals probably sat out the coup, cravenly waiting to see who would win, and then appeared after its ignominious end, at night, like jackals on the battlefield.

They came from all over, with nostrils flaring vengefully and eyes gleaming with an unhealthy triumph, pupils dilated with the drug of destruction. Voices demanded that the monument be blown up with dynamite instead of simply taken apart. Others called for storming the KGB building across the street from the statue, where behind closed curtains terrified majors and generals peeked out nervously.

In various parts of the square, with intoxicating impunity orators spewed out everything that had collected over the years of censorship, mental institutions and dissident trials. However, their protest against ugliness and intolerance was ugly and intolerant.

This was turning into the Mother of Monsters from de Maupassant's story, pregnant with the evil intent to sell her children to be jesters. A cynical Monster Mother, who wore tight bands around her belly to squeeze the fetus, or who put her newborns in special forms that would change the shape of their bones. The mutual moral deformity of the oppressors and the oppressed was to shape the tragedy of the anti-Communist revolution.

The former oppressors were unable to stifle freedom, but the formerly oppressed could not manage to preserve freedom's purity, dirtying it with vengefulness and a lack of culture and elementary good taste.

A furious man, contorted by hatred, choking on his rage against anyone who was famous, which oozed like pus from his mouth, ears and nose, shouted, "It's time to knock everyone down from his pedestal, not just the political toadies, but the literary ones, the Chekists, the stoolies! And we should start with Pushkin! Yes, Pushkin! Time to stop idealizing our monuments. Pushkin ran to Beckendorff, chief of the gendarmes, to get him to intercede on his behalf with the tsar! And Gorky, who sang the praises of the Belomorkanal, which was built on the bones of prisoners! And Mayakovsky needs no introduction, he was a Chekist himself!"

A gray-haired, stoop-shouldered man with a row of stainless steel teeth replied, quietly but clearly, "That's not true. Pushkin went to the gendarmes chief only to get the censors to pass his *Boris Godunov*. And Gorky saved many people during the revolution. I was an inmate at Solovki Prison Camp when Gorky visited. We were washed and barbered, dressed up and even given fresh newspapers. As a protest, we turned the newspapers upside down. Gorky understood what we were trying to say. He came over to me and turned the paper. His eyes were filled with tears. I am certain that Gorky came to Belomorkanal only so that Stalin would let him abroad, where he planned to tell the world the truth about the camps. But Stalin knew his plans and had him killed. And Mayakovsky was a victim, not an executioner. Shame on you!"

But just then the contorted little man recognized me and groaned with the sweet pleasure of publicly insulting someone living, rather than just the dead. "Look, it's Yevtushenko! Look, it's him in the flesh. Must be just back from his beloved America. And so accessible, without his numerous wives and girlfriends, on foot and not in his black Mercedes! How lucky we are. Now answer us a question, dear future monument, if you're such an honest man, why weren't you ever arrested? What have you done for them that the Soviet powers have treated you so well? Didn't you frequent this hospitable building, as your literary colleagues tell it?"

I don't think I felt anything except deadly weariness. I wasn't even hurt. I had heard it all before. I simply turned and left.

Without knowing what freedom was, we had fought for it, the imagined beloved of our intelligentsia. Without ever having seen its face except in our social dreams, we had imagined that it would be beautiful. But freedom has many faces, many mugs, and some of them are unbearably repulsive. One of the mugs of freedom is the freedom to insult.

Back in Brezhnev's day, one of the Cerberuses of television and radio, who had a vast collection at home of the very literature that he ruthlessly suppressed in public, was practically hysterical after a lecture on poetry that I gave on TV. "Why are you so thrilled by the word 'freedom,' repeating it like a woodcock warbling away as the hunter creeps up on him? You're calling for your own destruction. If you give the low-lifes freedom, sooner or later they'll trample the very people who gave it to them. And that includes you, pal. . . . I hate the very word 'freedom.' Your sweet 'freedom' smells of blood."

The man was no fool, even though he was a reactionary.

Then what do you do when you see violence? Do you not struggle against it, because rebellion against violence is also violence? Do you avoid revolution, because every triumphant revolution is a future reactionary regime? Does St. George eventually turn into the dragon, no better than the one his spear had killed? What does that mean — should people not be given freedom because they will turn it into excess and libertinism, into the freedom of theft, crookedness and murder? Do you wait for things to shape up by themselves? But it is shameful to stand by with folded hands and watch history. . . .

These were the contradictory thoughts that filled my mind on Dzerzhinsky Square, in front of the statue of the inquisitor with a metal noose around its neck, placed there by perhaps potential future inquisitors, or by those who give rise to inquisitors through their thirst for destruction that outstrips the desire for creation, and by a spiteful rancor that cannot turn into a noble revenge of generosity.

The terrible house where both my grandfathers were interrogated, where the Man With Eyes Like Drills had tried to recruit me, was before me like a gigantic monument, with roots that went very deep, back to the Oprichnina, Ivan the Terrible's secret police, to torture chambers, serfdom and the Tatar-Mongol invasion.

For a Soviet writer and the KGB not to cross paths at least once was physically impossible, because the KGB was everywhere.

In 1960 I was a member of the Soviet delegation to the World Youth Festival in Helsinki. They were charming and wild days, deliciously infected by the microbes of a naive faith in the revolutionary universal brotherhood, when a young and little-known Jacques Brel, who later became a friend, sang on a Soviet ship; when Muslim Magomayev on his first trip abroad, I think, with teenage acne and in a borrowed tuxedo with too-short sleeves sang my new song, "Do the Russians Want War?" in a Finnish school that had been turned into the French dormitory; when Arabs and Israelis walked around with their arms around each other; when Cubans and Americans shouted together: "Cuba si y Yanqui si!" and I had an affair with a young and very left-wing Californian, who had just come back from Cuba, as had I, loving it madly.

We were in love, not only with each other, but also with Fidel Castro, and we could converse only in a third language, Spanish. This didn't keep us from making love one night in the grass of some unfamiliar Helsinki park, only to wake up in the morning and burst out laughing to realize that we had spent the night right across from a very important palace where two soldiers stood frozen at attention. I was fascinated by the ordinary hole in the stocking of my leftwing California girl, which revealed the merry eye of her heel, just as if she were a girl from Moscow.

But the festival had another life, where the main protagonists were not us, but the intelligence services of hostile countries and systems. Here I saw once again the Man With Eyes Like Drills, several years after his unsuccessful attempt to recruit me. That failure must have been small potatoes in his work and did not have a negative effect on his career. I heard that he had been made a general even before the festival, even though he naturally did not wear his uniform in Helsinki. He was responsible for the safety of the Soviet delegation.

There was need for it, because in the middle of town, at the sculpture of the Three Blacksmiths, right-wing extremists were holding rallies. A Moscow ballerina's knee was broken by a Coca-Cola bottle thrown onto the open-air stage in a park, and the night before the festival had opened, hooligans burned down the Russian Club. Soviet cars filled with athletes and KGB agents raced from the harbor where our ship, the *Gruzia*, was docked, into town, which smelled of fire. Afterwards there was a furious fight between them and the festival protesters.

We were strictly forbidden to leave the ship before the festival opened, but I managed to sneak away. My California girl was waiting for me, this time with the hole in her stocking darned, and this also amazed me, because I had been sure that Americans didn't darn stockings, but threw them away. Hand-in-hand we walked through the vicious anti-festival shouts as if on the thin, dangerous ice of the cold war, whose children we were. But even when we fell through that ice, we were breaking it up and clearing it away.

That night the Ruddy Communist Youth League Leader and the Man

That Night: Outside KGB Headquarters

With Eyes Like Drills burst into my cabin, reeking of smoke and cognac.

"Everyone's in a lousy mood," said the Ruddy Communist Youth League Leader. "Could you write something to cheer up the kids?"

"I already have," I replied and read my poem, "Snotty Fascism," which I had just finished.

The blindingly blue eyes of the Ruddy Communist Youth League Leader, always wavering between sentimentality and ruthlessness, stopped and grew moist. "Now you're talking. If you wrote only poems like this you would be worth your weight in gold. We'd make you the national poet. Why do you have to write other poems, ones that — that — lead the wrong way. Why waste your cannons on sparrows, all those bureaucrats . . . or the ones you call Stalinists and anti-Semites. That's what *Krokodil* magazine is for. I'm not defending them, but at least they're our own. We have outside enemies, and they're more serious. They're enemies of our country — just what you called them, fascists. And they're not always snotty and young."

"They're all fascists as far as I'm concerned," I replied. "And if I didn't write poems about our own fascists, I wouldn't have the right to write about foreign ones."

The Ruddy Communist Youth League Leader wasn't in the mood to discuss this. He would betray me in just a few months. But for now he was in administrative ecstasy, and ran out on deck, shouting, "Sound the horn to bring everyone on deck! Yevtushenko is going to read his new poem!"

The Man With Eyes Like Drills took out a bottle of cognac from his pocket, drank from the bottle, and said, "Hmm . . . The poets who come to us with denunciations of you won't ever write a poem like that. But you should be more careful with your friends and acquaintances. And I suggest you be more careful in your poetry, too. You denounce yourself. But you know, ever since that time. . . . I've started reading you . . . and not just for the job. What I want to say is, if I can ever be of use to you . . . you never know . . . here's my phone."

And in fact he did help out, not always, but a few times, when I called on behalf of dissidents and refuseniks. He never called me and he never asked for anything.

But whatever his personal attitude toward me, I was kept under constant surveillance.

Some people gave me the reputation of a hero, which I never was. It's just that sometimes, I managed to overcome my fear—a dangerous thing, in the eyes of a system built on fear, because it incited others to do the same.

And then the professional disinformation specialists decided to start de-heroizing stories about me. The ideology section of the house on Lubyanka played its Machiavellian music like a highly qualified orchestra on the strings of inferiority complexes and envy. The art of pitting the intelligentsia against one another was one of the finest arts of the KGB. Alas, people of our writers' profession were pathologically predisposed to think ill of their colleagues, because that created a false but flattering sense of one's own moral and literary superiority.

In 1968 I was the only member of the Writers' Union to send a telegram to Brezhnev to protest our invasion of Czechoslovakia. Another member of the Writers' Union, a poet of the older generation who had taught me many things, exploded one day. "You've insulted all of us. And me too!"

"How?" I was sincerely astonished.

"Because I feel the same way about it as you do. But if I had written such a telegram, they would have ground me to dust. But it's like water off a duck's back with you. You're our 'people's favorite.' And you can get away with anything."

The poet had exaggerated. I wasn't forgiven for many things. The censors stopped my book. My appearances were banned. My trip to England, to receive an honorary degree at Oxford, was canceled.

And then the British press began publishing some articles, expressing doubts about whether I had ever sent a telegram or whether it had been invented by the KGB to build my reputation in the west, so that I could get the Oxford degree. This disinformation was spread by the KGB through "well-informed sources."

It was then that I wrote these four lines:

> Much in this life is given to me,
> But what I don't have in it
> Is the right to freely choose
> Between crap and shit.

I had an invitation from the United States to repeat Mark Twain's voyage down the Mississippi. But a professional well-wisher from the Writers' Union, lowering his voice significantly, told me that he had heard that the KGB chief Andropov was against my trip and suggested that I ask to see him, especially since the chief also writes poetry, sonnets to be precise.

The Maker of Sonnets and Spy-Nets, an inscrutable man with a hooked nose and unhealthy blotches of color, buttoned up in his clothes like a sonnet in its rhymes, behaved very warily and told me right off the bat and rather harshly that they were lying to me at the Writers' Union, that the KGB had never stopped any of my trips, and he'd never heard of such a thing.

And suddenly I saw a flash of something human in his inexpressive eyes, something like longing. "The Mississippi, you say? It must be a beautiful river." And then he allowed himself some frankness. "The first time I saw you, you were defending abstract art so emotionally from Khrushchev. Do you know what made me wary about you? Your eyes—they had the glitter of fanaticism that I saw in the boys in the Petofi Club in Budapest, when they called for hanging all Communists."

Those words sent chills up my spine. He had been ambassador to Budapest then, and in charge of the bloody suppression of the 1956 rebellion.

"I've never called for hanging anyone," I said, my mouth suddenly dry.

"I was just mentioning it. First impressions are sometimes mistaken," he said, rising and letting me know that the audience was over. "So you should settle this question of the Mississippi in your own dear Writers' Union."

The voyage on the Mississippi never did take place. But had he been telling the truth that the KGB had nothing to do with it?

In 1991 I was burned in effigy in my homeland by some chauvinistic writers; the Romantic of the Coup poured kerosene onto the dummy in front of the statue of Leo Tolstoy; then I was flung by the whirlwind of events into space, like my ashes, onto which no fewer than fifteen professional humanists spat in a collective letter, to keep the ashes from smoking.

I ended up with my family in the beautiful, hospitable city of Tulsa, Oklahoma. Here on the infamous Trail of Tears that the Indians once followed to flee with their families from extinction, I felt like a gob of sixties' romanticism which no one needed, coughed up across the ocean by the chaos of the nineties. Sometimes I gasped in homesickness, especially when they burned leaves and pinecones in the local park, and the Oklahoma air began to smell like the samovars of Peredelkino. And I would catch myself wanting to go to the local zoo, which nostalgically reminded me of our zoo in Moscow because it was so neglected and shabby, in a constant dreary state of disrepair, and the animals looked sad and half-forgotten by the administration. In this zoo I felt that I was in my own Motherland—Russia.

And trying not to despair because I had been burned, I started breathing gently on my own still-warm ashes, and saw the glowing ember eyes of a slow-catching fire of a novel.

On a March night in 1993, just before dawn, my fax machine released a slithering paper snake with these words in black and white on its head:

THE KGB, under the COUNCIL OF MINISTERS OF THE USSR

Dawn's false light shimmered in the window, the draft of my novel was done, and I was surrounded by the ghosts of my characters. I myself was a ghost of the era we shared, which was aging like us but was unlikely to die with us. I thought that I was losing my mind and that I had dreamed that paper snake. But the snake went on crawling, and turned out to be thirty pages long.

On the first page it said:

7 July 1969 Secret 22332

Subject to [illegible]

To the Central Committee of the Communist Party Soviet Union

The letter was signed by the Maker of Sonnets and Spy-Nets himself. But why was I getting it by fax? Over twenty years later? In Oklahoma? Was it from another world?

There was, as it turned out, a simple explanation. The newspaper *Trud* [Labor] had gathered these documents from the now-open secret archives, and was sending them to me for commentary.

As I looked through them, I realized with a shock that, during the years when Martin Luther King, Robert Kennedy and Che Guevarra were killed;

in the years when Vietnamese mothers used bone needles to remove shrapnel from the bodies of their children; when Czech students threw cobblestones at Soviet tanks, and the Great Camp Inmate was preparing his explosive book at the dacha of the Human Cello—during those years the all-powerful KGB chairman, in his moments of free time, was reviewing my poetry and, like a petty stoolie, denouncing me and my work to the Central Committee.

Here is how that All-Mighty Maker of Spy-Nets, the Buyer of Communist Parties, the Wizard of Plastic Surgery and Artist of False Passports snitched on me, with such detail, such ardor, such pettiness:

"In September 1968 in conversation with participants in the anniversary celebration of Nikoloz Baratashvili in Tbilisi, Yevtushenko criticized the domestic and foreign policies of the USSR, saying that bringing in Union troops was an act of violence against an independent state and our actions in Czechoslovakia were 'unworthy.' Under cover of 'civic duty,' Yevtushenko sought support for his position among representatives of the Georgian intelligentsia, and a bit later in Moscow defended it before the leaders of the dramatic theater on Malaya Bronnaya, announcing, 'They can't gag Yevgeny Yevtushenko! I will shout about the way they are treating little, lovely Czechoslovakia!' . . . In Tashkent at a meeting with students, Yevtushenko introduced the American writer Styron and with a blatant subtext announced that Styron like all writers does not like his government."

He had read my new book with a maniacal thirst to find hints about himself and his ilk: ". . . reprinted in it are individual works of a tendentious sort, for instance, 'Honey,' 'Ballad about the Versifier Lermontov,' 'On the Death of a Poet,' and especially about the chief of the gendarmes. Historical examples are used as a warning to all contemporary 'scoundrels, gendarmes, and court flatterers' of the retribution awaiting them."

So this was the Top Secret Yevtushenkologist!

His conclusion was rather scary. "Yevtushenko's actions, to a certain degree, are inspired by our ideological foes, who given his 'position' on a number of issues, try to raise him onto the shield in certain situations and turn him into an example of political opposition in our country."

The last time I spoke with him was on the day that the Great Camp Inmate had been taken again. I called from a telephone booth, and was told he was in a meeting. I could guess what the agenda was. First they had arrested the Great Camp Inmate and now they were thinking about what to do with him. I insisted that he come to the phone.

At last I heard the dry, creaky voice. "Yes?"

"Is it true that he's been arrested?" I asked, gasping.

"It's true." He spoke as if he were merely stating the name of the newspaper, *Pravda*, which means "truth."

Choking on my indignation, I shouted that if they put the Great Camp Inmate away again, I would be prepared to die on the barricades.

The creaky voice on the end of the telephone wire had a brief response to my revolutionary, romantic blackmail. "Sleep it off."

Once a fearless woman journalist showed me notes of a fearlessly hypocritical trial, as a result of which a young poet was sent into exile in the country for being a vagrant. I liked his poems very much. It was his own independent voice, unlike any other in our generation.

The Empress of Russian poetry, Anna Akhmatova, deigned to approve of his poems. Shostakovich, Chukovsky and Marshak defended him, but nothing had helped.

I decided to try to help Akhmatova's Favorite in a different way, from Italy.

During my trip there in 1964, I was asked about him several times. I wrote a letter to the Central Committee, colorfully describing how literally the entire Italian intelligentsia had stopped eating its fiori de zucchini and stopped drinking its Barolo because it was suffering so over the talented poet, Akhmatova's Favorite, stuck in a collective farm up north, shoveling manure.

I asked our ambassador to Italy, Kozyrev, a friend of the sculptor Manzu and the artist Guttuzo and an admirer of my poetry, to send my letter as a coded telegram from Rome. I knew that the Center paid special attention to coded messages.

Kozyrev knew very well that my letter was bull, but worthwhile bull. He sent my telegram as asked, and added the opinion of the Italian Communist Party leadership that the release of that young poet would knock a big ideological ace out of the hands of the enemies of socialism.

This clever Italian operation plus the help of the regional Party secretary, who published the exiled poet's verses in a tiny northern newspaper as evidence that he had improved, led to the return from exile of Akhmatova's Favorite.

We met at the Aragvi, the Georgian restaurant in Moscow. Akhmatova's Favorite was dressed too lightly, shivering from the cold, and I instinctively took off my jacket and offered it to him. He blushed furiously. "I have no need of jackets from other people's backs."

In 1972 I was returning home by plane after a two-month trip in the US. When the young men with judo muscles opened my suitcases, their eyes lit up as if they had won the Olympic gold in combat — ideological, in this case.

They had a good catch. According to their list, I had brought in 124 illegal books. The most precious were the seventy-two volumes of the best émigré journal, *Sovremennye zapiski* (*Contemporary Notes*), once published in Paris.

The first time I ever saw those yellowed, battered volumes breaking down into pages was on the book shelves of the young Princeton professor James Billington, who read the mute appeal in my eyes and acted like a Georgian. He took them down and gave them to me.

I was also bringing in books by Trotsky, Bukharin, Berdyaev, Shestov, Nabokov, Aldanov, Gumilev, Mandelstam, Bunin's *Cursed Days*, and the first book confiscated after the revolution by the Bolsheviks, *Untimely Thoughts* by Gorky, Stalin's "toady" according to the "deformed little men," those self-appointed judges of history today. But the court is as twisted as the judges.

They held me at the airport for about four hours while they compiled the list. And they confiscated not only the books but photographs, including an official White House photo of my meeting with President Nixon and Henry Kissinger, and all my notebooks, letters, drafts, everything written by hand or set in print or typed.

The whole procedure stank of operetta prison; a border guard accompanied me to the bathroom and even kept the door open at my most private moment.

When I signed off on the scrupulously recorded list, I acted like a clever Mowgli of the Soviet jungle and added something like:

During my trips abroad to propagandize the ideas of our Homeland,
I sometimes feel ideologically unarmed in the struggle with our enemies,
because I am not familiar with the original sources on which they base
their fervent hatred. Most of these original sources are impossible to get in
the USSR even in the special departments of the Lenin Library. That is
why I brought these books—not for distribution but to increase my ideological vigilance. I demand that all the confiscated books that I need for
my work for the good of peace in the world and in our Homeland be
returned to me immediately.

The next day I put in an indignant call to the Man With Eyes Like
Drills. He received me, this time not in the main building but in the reception offices of the KGB on Kuznetsky Most. I played out my deep insult over
the obnoxious behavior of the customs officers, who with their political
myopia did not understand that I had filled my suitcases with anti-Soviet literature only out of Soviet patriotism. He listened to me with ennui. I pulled
out all the stops: "And anyway, what right did they have to search me?"

He smirked condescendingly at the word "right," and tried to halt my
fiery monologue of injured innocence. "I once warned you to be more
careful in your friends. There must have been a signal to our people from
wherever you came from. The world is full of helpful people."

He was obviously talking out of school—or was this some refined
game? "Even if there had been a 'signal' why did they have to humiliate me,
hold the toilet door open? Did they think I'd hide all seventy-two volumes
of *Sovremennye zapiski* in my pants? Do you really suppose that this will make
me love my homeland any more?"

"Procedural problems," he said with a shrug. "A lack of culture,'" as
you yourself put it so fairly in your prologue to the poem *Bratsk Station*."

I went on working myself up into a lather with only one goal in
mind—get the confiscated books out of the claws of the KGB, especially
Billington's precious gift.

"The KGB is turning writers into your enemies. For instance, why did
the KGB forbid the publication of Akhmatova's Favorite's book in Leningrad?
He was charged with vagrancy. Where's the logic? Why don't you allow him
to make a living with his labor?"

"Who told you that?" he demanded furiously.

"Oleg Shestinsky, secretary of the Leningrad Writers' Organization."

"Lies!" The Man With Eyes Like Drills banged his fist on the table so hard that the cork of the decanter bounced. "We told Shestinsky that it was a decision for the Writers' Union. Then the coward asked for our written recommendation that the book be published. But if I write a recommendation like that and then your Akhmatova's Favorite pulls another trick—like trying to skyjack a plane—I'll lose my job. . . . But enough of that. He's been wanting to leave for a long time and he's put in another application. We've made a positive decision on that. He can leave if he wants to so badly."

"What do you mean? Forever?" I was stunned. "But that's a terrible tragedy for a poet—to be without his language. Will he be able to return?"

"That's up to him," the Man With Eyes Like Drills replied evasively.

"Do you expect him to shout, 'Long live the Soviet regime!' from every rooftop?"

"You really are making us sound much too primitive," he said with a grimace.

"Well, at least don't torment him with humiliations as a going-away present, with accusations of lack of patriotism, as is so often done with those who leave," I said in a fallen voice.

"I cannot be responsible for all our workers, just as you cannot be responsible for all writers," he said irritably and then added reluctantly, "But I'll try to keep an eye on it."

"Say, can I tell him about our conversation?" I asked.

"It's up to you," he said. "Although"—and he paused—"I don't recommend it."

Unfortunately, I didn't follow this recommendation.

(The books were returned to me, including the ones Billington gave me—but not right away, about three months later. I guess they read them first, and perhaps with pleasure. The only books that were not returned were some contemporary works by dissidents written in the USSR and published in the West. And also a collection of jokes, *This Is Radio Yerevan*. They must have read it to pieces.)

Akhmatova's Favorite came to see me and I told him in the greatest detail how and why I was at the KGB and how the conversation went. Even though Akhmatova's Favorite had been trying to get permission to leave for a long time, he was stunned and depressed. That day he displayed no signs of superciliousness. I saw him to the elevator.

"Zhenya, please, whatever may happen, never think badly of me," he said, switching to the formal "you" even though we had been on more informal terms.

The elevator door opened. He went in and seemed to plunge down.

I tried not to think badly of him and I'm still trying now. But he could never forgive me for the jacket I offered out of simple kindness.

Rumors began reaching me from abroad that, semi-directly, semi-obliquely, he was saying very bad things about me, hinting that I had taken part in casting him out of the Soviet Union.

I was shocked. When I got to New York I called him and he came to see me at my hotel.

He was back inside his supercilious chiton shell.

I asked, "You must hate the people who wrote false denunciations against others in 1937? In essence what you've done is a false denunciation against me."

He interrupted me arrogantly. "I've yet to meet a man worthy of my hatred."

"How could you say I had a part in getting you forced out of your homeland?"

He bristled. "But you yourself so eloquently described how you were practically a consultant to the KGB on my case."

"What do you mean?"

"You admitted that you suggested they not torment me as a farewell."

I burst out, "If I see a drunken cop across the street kicking a pregnant woman in the belly and I cross the street and say, 'Don't you dare kick her, she's pregnant!' does that make me a police consultant?"

He said nothing, his head down.

"I will read your poetry," I said. "But I will never shake your hand again. Go."

He put on his coat and raised the collar as if it were raining, but he stood there without leaving.

Suddenly he spoke simply, humanly, the way he had at the elevator then. "You've never been an émigré. You don't know how terrifying it is. Maybe especially for a poet. You start looking for someone to blame for why you are not at home. Forgive me."

"You say that when we are alone," I replied. "But you've told so many people something very different."

"What can I do?" he asked.

"I'm off to have dinner with some American friends. Will you be able to apologize in front of them?"

"Yes," he said.

The formulation of his apology, which he barely managed to squeeze out, sounded like this: "I know that you are all friends of Zhenya's. I want . . . I must . . . in your presence ask him to forgive me for . . . for . . . saying things about him that he did not deserve."

"Sorry, but I don't quite get what you're talking about. Could you clarify a bit?" one of my American friends started in on him, knowing perfectly well what was going on.

I stopped him, because it could have turned into an interrogation and torture.

Akhmatova's Favorite and I embraced as a sign of our reconciliation. But six months later he was saying the same things again.

O our era, O Mother of Monsters, you have deformed your most talented children — what can we expect of those less fortunate?

The son of the Man With Eyes Like Drills was still a child when his father tried to recruit me. As if to punish the father, he became a poet, but one without talent. He wanted to be me, and Voznesensky, and Eliot and a Patriot all at the same time. But he was not Yevtushenko, Voznesensky or Eliot. That left only being a Patriot. Not long before the putsch his father had wisely retired. But it was his son — with his nose held high like the beak of the ugly duckling and wearing the dark glasses of a Tonton Macoute and a Parisian silk scarf knotted like Voznesensky's — who came to the Writers' Union as a representative of the junta. He was offered hospitable but cautious tea, with orange wafers which crumbled cravenly in the trembling fingers of the engineers of human souls. It was only their cowardice that kept them from signing a letter in support of the coup. Later, when the coup misfired, the Failed Eliot and Failed Patriot called me, piteously justifying himself, because he expected to be treated the way he would have treated us if they had gained power.

O our era, O Mother of Monsters. What have you done to us all? Perhaps Akhmatova's Favorite and I could have been brothers, but you made us feud, tossed us apart, even though we needed each other as no one else. Will we never again talk like human beings, and will we die separately? Yes, we are all dwarf birches. And I am a monster, distorted, twisted, broken. And yet I want to be happy. What if I don't deserve it, like the rest of us? What then?

Masha, I love you, and you love me, right? We're only alive if we love. To stop loving means dying before your death.

Masha, we must not let the children of our love for each other not deserve our love for them.

Masha, Russia will be the way our children will be.

God, save our children from our monstrosities! Scrape out all the monster genes from them and leave the genes of hope! Don't make them monsters in reverse!

These were my prayers on Dzerzhinsky Square in front of the empty pedestal, while the tumbled monument lay on the ground and the mob danced its savage, meaningless dance with triumphant cries.

Empty pedestals are frightening.

They are frightening because the people who will be placed on them may turn out to be worse than their predecessors.

Not long ago I had chaired a ceremony at this very square, for the unveiling of the memorial stone dedicated to the victims of the war against our own people. The boulder had been brought from the Solovki Islands, the territory of the first concentration camp in the history of Europe, opened on Lenin's personal initiative—a fact that was carefully hidden for many years by the Institute of Political Cosmetics under its pseudonym of Institute of Marxism-Leninism. Who knows, maybe Father Florensky or the future Academician Likhachev had sat on that very stone?

The morning of the unveiling I got a phone call, the first one ever from the new chairman of the KGB, whom everyone called Cherubino behind his back, and who was to be a main protagonist of the coup.

"We know that you are chairing the rally today across the street from our building," he said a bit nervously, though he tried to hide it. "Our colleagues would like to lay wreaths from the KGB in memory of the Chekists who died in the purges of those years, too. Do you have any objections?"

"No," I replied.

"But there might be excesses," he added. "I hope that this will not be a hate rally. After all, we did not object to having the memorial stone so close to us."

"The unveiling is planned as a requiem and not as a hate rally," I replied.

However, things happened differently, despite the church choirs and the blessing of the stone. Next to the icon there were totally unsuitable, vulgar political caricatures and cheap slogans. The requiem did not work. No one even mentioned the names of dead dissidents, or Sakharov and Solzhenitsyn, without whom this monument would not exist. Almost all the speeches were turned into an angry dialogue with the KGB, into threatening fist-waving at the curtained windows, not a dangerous gesture in that situation. Who knows, maybe the idea for the coup originated that day, as those behind the curtained windows stared out at the endless threats? I was horrified at the indignity of it, especially in the presence of the Solovki stone — unscheduled speakers pushing their way onto the podium, shouldering aside the people from Memorial who had made this event a reality. These "progressive" operators had nothing to impart except self-asserting hatred.

Was humanity in a vicious circle from which there was no escape?

I walked over to the silent boulder brought from Solovki Islands.

Everyone was busy with joy or hatred.

There was no one near the stone.

AFTERWARD

The Marshal's Uniform

PALCHIKOV WALKED ALONG THE Izmailovo Park flea market.

The Soviet Union was still in existence, but it was already being sold as souvenirs. Vendors were selling the banners of army divisions, factories, collective farms. They were even selling the printed slogan "Communism Is Inevitable." They were selling portraits and busts of people still remembered and people now forgotten.

The most popular items were military: belts with large stars on the buckles, caps with small stars, helmets, straps, field glasses, epaulets, planchets, army shirts and officers' and generals' uniforms.

"Do you have a marshal's uniform?" Palchikov would inquire idly.

The Marshal had committed suicide and his grave had been defiled. The coffin was opened and the Marshal's parade uniform had been removed from his body.

No one had assigned this case to Palchikov. He took it on his own, without really knowing why.

You could count the number of marshals in the country, and it was unlikely he would find the rare uniform.

It was strange that the Marshal had hanged himself, succeeding only on the second try, instead of shooting himself. Had he turned in his gun? Palchikov couldn't believe that a professional soldier would remain without a gun, especially in times like these. Was there a suicide note? Yes, he had left one. But similar notes had been left by two others, who had known the secrets of Party money and who, officially, had jumped from windows.

However, an experienced handwriting expert could compose such notes in the correct handwriting.

Palchikov knew one such expert, an old bachelor, a collector of autographs, manuscripts and letters. He called him. There was no answer. Palchikov went to the graphologist's house and found the apartment sealed. The neighbors said that he had been killed by a truck in a hit-and-run. Of course, there were lots of drunken drivers. But this seemed one coincidence too many of late.

Palchikov was assigned to be present during the arrest of the Crystal-Clear Communist. Palchikov refused, but he was asked again, and very firmly. Palchikov was amazed to see the Young But Famous Economist in the group going to the apartment. Never in Palchikov's many years of work had there been a case where an expert of that sort was invited to be present at an arrest. After a long time ringing the bell, the door's chain was removed by the Crystal-Clear Communist's father-in-law, a decrepit old man with the aimless eyes of a gray-haired infant. He seemed to be dead even as he went on living and he did not understand the most simple question. Maybe he's not such an infant? Palchikov wondered professionally.

The Young But Famous Economist and Palchikov looked at each other in shock as they saw the Crystal-Clear Communist lying in a pool of his own blood on the bed. His Walther was on the bedside table.

"How did he manage to shoot himself and then put the revolver on the table?" whispered the Young But Famous Economist to Palchikov. Palchikov didn't have the answer.

The Crystal-Clear Communist's wife was sitting on the floor in a puddle of blood near the other bed, her face covered with purple bruises. She was trying to say something.

What had happened to her face? Which of them had shot the other? Or hadn't either one done the shooting? Who did, then?

"Maybe she'll be able to tell us something. Let me take her to the hospital," Palchikov proposed.

"There are other people for that," he was told and stopped.

According to the official version, the Crystal-Clear Communist's wife died right after surgery. She had said nothing.

Curiously, Palchikov was not asked to participate in any other assignments after that. Nor was he reinstated in his old job.

But why had the Young But Famous Economist been there? There was no professional reason for it. Maybe at the moment of the Crystal-Clear Communist's death, a witness was needed, one with an unbesmirched, crystal-clear reputation?

Palchikov, grimly thinking about all this, was about to leave the flea market when his casual question, "Would you have a marshal's uniform?" got a response, from a young bodybuilder with pale eyebrows, an admiral's cap and about fifty medals and ribbons on a cavalry cape as big as a black cloud that still remembered General Dovator's legendary raids.

"Got greenbacks?" the bodybuilder asked, without lowering his voice in posing this not quite legal question, which as far as he was concerned was the major achievement of democracy and proof of his personal courage.

"Depends how much," Palchikov said with a shrug.

"Five hundred. The goods are in fine shape. Fresh."

"Can I feel the cloth?" Palchikov asked.

The bodybuilder looked around. "Not here," he said. "Go down this path, make a right, then a left, then another right. You'll see a shashlyk stand. Ask for Kyra. From Gray."

Following these directions, Palchikov came to another bodybuilder, this one wearing a paratrooper's uniform and turning shashlyk spits over coals. Pieces of meat alternated with slices of onion and whole tomatoes.

Palchikov took one, it smelled so good. But he burned his tongue, it was so spicy.

"I see you like pepper," Palchikov said. "Is it true that pepper is good for impotence?"

"Not my problem," the bodybuilder guffawed. "But I'm ready to serve humanity."

"Are you Kyra? Gray sent me. The goods here?"

"There," Kyra said. "In that donut van. I'll show it to you in there. Do you have the greenbacks?"

"Do I look crazy, carrying around my own death, and green at that, like a drowning victim?" Palchikov laughed. "End up dead in a donut van? That wasn't my dream when I was kid and wanted to be an Indian pathfinder.

If the cloth isn't filled with moths and all the buttons are in place, I'll bring the greenbacks in a flash."

Kyra looked him up and down. "Let's go."

He opened the van from the back and let Palchikov in. Then he followed.

It was crowded with that living pyramid of muscle. He twisted Palchikov's arm behind his back, pushed him down on the floor of the van and went through his pockets. He found no money. Palchikov did not resist.

"You weren't lying," Kyra said with a disappointed sigh, and Palchikov realized that if he had been carrying dollars, he would probably not have lived to give Alevtina the pass to the Human Cello's concert, autographed by him.

"All right, I'll show you the goods," Kyra said reluctantly, and then carefully unwound a cape raincoat that lay on the floor.

In the dim light the gold threads of the marshal's uniform glimmered hypnotically.

"Not enough light. Maybe it's falling apart at the seams," grumbled Palchikov. "Open the back door a bit."

Kyra did, and suddenly in the ray of light an earthworm crept out of the marshal's pocket.

A second later Kyra was on the floor of the van with his arms twisted behind his back. "Where did you get this uniform, you scum? Who brought it to you?" Palchikov pressed his knee ruthlessly into the twisted arm.

Kyra howled and spoke a few words that came out like lumps of vomit. "One guy's called Vovchik, the other Levchik. They used to work at the cemetery, now they're at the zoo."

So that's what can come after our death — the Vovchiks and Levchiks, thought Palchikov sadly.

Farewell To The
Red Flag

THREE MEN, GATHERED IN BELOVEZHSKAYA Forest, decided to remove from the map the four letters "USSR" that covered one-sixth of the globe and were painted red.

The three men in Belovezhskaya Forest were thinking of things much too insignificant for such a significant step. The first wanted to be rid of his rival, whom he had reason to distrust. The second was thinking about the Ukranian nationalists who would not be able to overthrow him once he became the first president of a now independent country. The third was afraid not to join such powerful partners as the other two, because if he were left alone, he would be eaten alive by his well-wishers.

Once again they lacked the time and the culture in which to think.

The children of Bolshevik improvisation were back to improvising again. Of course, they wanted to do what was best. None of them had bad intentions. Their imprudence seemed to them like historic courage. But they did not have the courage of caution, to foresee the gigantic consequences of that gigantic decision.

Once again, history was not allowed to change naturally. Once again, history was being rushed.

But three other men, part of a small crowd on Red Square on a December night, when the red flag was being lowered without any fanfare from the Kremlin dome, did not feel as triumphant as the three in Belovezhskaya Forest.

Semyon Palych, the coatroom attendant, recalled how he had hoisted that flag under fire from the Hitlerjugend on a roof of the Reichstag in Berlin and how later, the big chiefs from the Red Army public relations and SMERSH pushed him and the other soldiers with unchecked biographies away from the flag.

Zalyzin, the soccer player, recalled how that flag would be raised to the anthem of a great country that no longer existed, when they played and did not always lose in the stadiums of the world, in the red shirts with the four letters that were now erased from the maps.

Palchikov, the investigator, recalled how he was doing his college practical work in a rehabilitation commission under Khrushchev. A man came to them, just out of the camps, where he had spent twelve years simply because he had been captured by Germans when wounded. He had escaped from the POW camp. He was known as the famous partisan Vanya in Italy, where his name was etched in gold on Carrara marble.

"The flag," he said curtly. "Give me my flag."

"What flag is this?" Palchikov had asked.

"The partisan flag made from the red skirt of an Italian girl who made it for us. It was taken away when I was searched upon my return."

When Palchikov managed by some miracle to find the flag, where you could see the skirt's seam in one place and the patched bullet holes in another, the partisan Vanya, famous in Italy, cried.

And now on Red Square, when the flag of their Atlantis, shamed by the Gulag and glorified by victories, was lowered, and the December snowflakes touched the fluttering red fabric in a sad farewell, these three men wept.

Faraway So Close

WHEN FILM DIRECTOR WIM WENDERS was told that the former
president was willing to play himself in the film *Faraway So Close*, he didn't
believe it.

The fairy-tale movie, already overstuffed with his fantasies, was
moving into a realm of surrealism. It was as if the director making *Waterloo*
were to call Napoleon and say, "You know, Rod Steiger is playing you in my
film. He's a good actor. But why shouldn't you, dear Mister Napoleon, play
the part of Napoleon yourself?"

The director had tried out the idea, not taking it too seriously himself,
on the mystery man who could get whatever he wanted in Russia—even
one of the Kremlin towers for the weekend.

The mystery man had the slightly mad eyes of a miserable, Russian-
German culture maven, and he almost lost his mind once, when some wino
laborers in Moscow took apart a huge sculpture made of nails by Jucker, his
countryman, when the exhibit was over, and sold the nails by the pound to
an enterprising construction cooperative. Nevertheless, the mystery man
was always ready to be the victim of friendship between two former enemies,
devoting to the cause his heart and soul and even his body, exhausted by a
physically requited and yet spiritually unrequited love for a Russian woman,
who like Russia herself had decided to become a capitalist instead of a sentimental Turgenev heroine.

"What would the former president have to do in your film?" the
mystery man asked and then, being much more like a Turgenev heroine than

like a modern Russian woman, added sentimentally, "I hope that his honor and dignity will not be impugned."

"Of course not. . . . He'll simply talk with an angel," the director improvised, with great aplomb. He had two angels in his screenplay, and he hadn't quite decided what to do with them. But, why shouldn't one of them meet up with the former general secretary of the atheists. They should have plenty to discuss.

He himself didn't know why his film was based on the adventures of angels. What was an angel? . . . The image of repentance? A white cloud of charity? The only judge who has the right to accuse us? A winged know-it-all sick and tired of other people's secrets? A symbol of morality so bored that a crime seems interesting? There was something cheap and kitschy about it. You had to make sure the angels didn't come out sugary and marzipany. But that depended on the actor and the director.

The director forgot about his strange whim, as if it had been an over-confident joke, when the mystery man called and announced that the former president of the USSR would be in Munich in March and was prepared to be filmed.

The director managed to speak after a pause. "Are you serious?"

"I'm serious," the mystery man replied.

"How much?" the director asked even more quietly, expecting an astronomical sum.

"Nothing. He even made a joke— 'What, am I supposed to take money from an angel?'"

The director did not believe the filming would actually take place.

But the former president came to the Four Seasons Hotel in Munich at the appointed time.

The director was in shock, face to face with a man known by the whole world, which used a friendly, albeit vulgarly shortened nickname for him: "Gorby."

As a professional, the director noted that when the former president wanted to make an impression, he turned on his eyes as if they were charm bulbs, but he couldn't keep it up for long—it wasn't easy anymore and he turned them off to conserve their energy.

Charm bulbs apparently burn out, too.

But while they were still turned on, the former president said, "A lot of people ask me now, what am I: liberal, conservative or communist? . . . Do you know who I am now? For the first time in my life I'm simply Mikhail Sergeyevich Gorbachev. I'm trying to invent my whole life. And I'm doing things that I never did before: for instance, being an actor in your movie."

The former president, to the director's surprise, was not only obedient but professional as an actor.

According to the script, he sat and worked in the hotel room on an upcoming speech. He did not speak on camera — his inner voice would be added as a voice-over. A white-winged angel came up from behind and, watching the pen fly and sometimes stumble over the paper, read the thoughts written and not yet written on the page.

The former president's lips did not move, but this is what his inner voice said: The meaning of life. . . . A brief instant compared to eternity. . . . Why does man come into his life? I don't know whether it's better or worse that man does not know his fate. I think it's better. It's better because then man spends his life seeking the meaning of life.

Otto Sander, the actor playing the angel, was amazed that when he placed his hand on the former president's shoulder, the president's shoulder muscles let him know that he knew that the angel was behind him — like an experienced film actor.

When the shoot was over, Sander asked, "If I'm ever in Russia, may I visit you at home?"

"Of course," replied the former president and gave him his business card in English.

"No one will ever believe that I got this from you personally," the actor exclaimed.

Gorbachev smiled and autographed it.

The mystery man leaned over Sander's shoulder to see what was written on the card. "President of the Foundation." But the actor didn't get past the word "President" and said, "It says you're President. But there is no more Soviet Union, and you're no longer Presi — "

The mystery man stepped on Sander's foot, even if that were blasphemy, since he had not yet removed his white angel's wings.

Fortunately, the interpreter had the tact not to translate.

The President Of Russia,
Where The Tracks End

THIS WAS THE FIRST TIME THE President of Russia was playing tennis with this partner.

The man was a former Communist Youth League activist, but tried to hide it. He had a neat English part in his hair, which magically did not get mussed from playing, as opposed to the President's shock of hair, which had to be kept back with a band to keep it from flopping around as if he were dancing in a village square open to all the winds of the Urals.

The partner had wheedled him into the game. Not directly, but cleverly, subtly, as if by accident. He worked at it quietly. He had the boyish face of an overgrown Lilliputian, whose governmental concerns had been ironed out along with the Komsomol wrinkles, so that it looked fresh from the dry cleaners, like his suits. They were usually businesslike grays, but he wore a bright, not too startling tie. He came to meetings not only with his files, but sometimes with his tennis racket, as if he couldn't leave it in his office.

The President noticed that the racket was always on the side that faced the President, always teasingly in view.

The President pretended not to be aware of the offer. But one day he got trapped.

No sooner had he sent one of his steady partners to work abroad, than the fellow with the magical part in his hair showed up, agilely balanced on the poorly strung wire of politics, with his tennis racket in his hand.

The President did not know him very well—he was one of the "third wave advisors."

There were more and more of them around the President, because the advisors of the first wave, who had survived all the storms and squalls with him, were gradually being shunted aside by the very people they had recommended to him. But that was only half the problem, because the advisors of the second wave were bringing the third wave with them, and they the next, and the President was horrified to see that he didn't know the people who surrounded him like an advising and slurping swamp.

He fell asleep with a headache each night from the constant whispering in his ears, and he felt his Gulliverlike body as a separate burden on which his Lilliputian advisors leapt and hopped, fencing with one another using straightened paper clips, hating one another and probably him, too.

And he began playing tennis more clumsily, feeling dozens of advisors hanging on to the laces of his tennis shoes, scrambling around in his shorts, climbing up his back, sitting on his neck, crawling into his armpits and the hair on his head.

The partner with the magical part was neatly pressed even on the courts. The crease in the white shorts with a green alligator on the side was as flawless as his part. There was an alligator on his T-shirt and on his socks too, a foreign consistency of style. "Wants to look like a Kennedy," muttered his foes, who did not have the ability to wear either suits or state ideas elegantly, as if they were tailor-made. His restrained, loyal eyes did not distract from the seriousness of his face, which resembled a small exhibit of honesty. His image as enlightened democrat, combining intellect with a willingness to do the dirty work, radiated a modest readiness to take on any responsible post—speaker of the house, minister of foreign affairs or any other ministry, even an ambassadorship in some hard-currency state, and in the future . . . in the future . . . perhaps, successor to the President. The last he carefully hid for now, as well as the fact that he had learned to play tennis quite recently, coached by a pro at night, right after he had learned that the way to the President's heart lay in a tennis racket.

He learned everything quickly. He already played better than the President in both politics and tennis, but he held back, neither stooping to tennis toadying nor humiliating his partner with superiority. His main tactic was to help the President hit well and take pleasure from his own game, which might turn into pleasure in spending time with such a sparring partner off the courts. Thus, by tactfully losing, he could win the battle for influence over the President — to create a need for an advisor and pleasure in his company.

However, the President was not as simple-minded as he chose to appear. When the man with the magical part gave him easy shots, doing it with maximal tact, the President saw through him. With a heavy heart he thought, I know you're going to ask for something today or tomorrow. You'll slip me a paper you need me to sign. Permission for a dubious pop concert on Red Square . . . or a transfer of a sweet building to somebody . . . or a cozy spot for a pal. Look how you're giving me that shot — ready for my right. And now you seem to be slamming, but delicately, inviting me to reach the net in time and win. Now you're going to pretend to be nervous, hit hard a few times, so that I won't feel that you're letting me win. What a phony game. . . . I can see you, I can see right through you, as the inventor of X-rays, Ivan the Terrible, used to say in the joke.

And in fact, the man with the magical part didn't even wait for morning. In the showers after the game, he used Stanislavsky's method to act exhausted. "You really made me work up a sweat," he said, even though his part was dry.

And then, as if by the way, he felt out the President. "Would you have about fifteen minutes before the session tomorrow? I've got a few trifles piled up, but of a highly confidential nature."

The President tried to mumble something vague. Mumbling had turned from a liability into a form of self-defense, because now people did not dare to make him repeat himself. But he knew that the man with the magical part would show up in his office, armed with files and prepared resolutions, exactly fifteen minutes before the session and slip in his small but necessary papers — necessary for him.

Outside, an armored limousine that had practically driven through the doorway was waiting for the President, along with two security men helpfully holding open umbrellas with rain banging wildly on them in the night. And through the lashing wall of water a man without an umbrella, soaked to the skin and definitely unarmed, bolted towards the door. The security men held onto him, twisting his arms behind his back.

"Let him go," the President said, recognizing Stepan Palchikov, Special

Affairs Investigator, who had acted as a Presidential bodyguard during the putsch, holding a bulletproof shield in front of his chest.

"Hi," said the President and held out his hand with sincere friendliness and just a grain of caution—was he going to ask for something, too?

Palchikov's eyes rolled significantly towards the security men.

The President understood and literally tore the umbrellas out of their unwilling hands. He offered one to Palchikov and kept the other.

"We're going for a little walk," the President said to the head of security, suddenly realizing with revulsion that he was practically sucking up to them.

"It's not allowed," the head of security replied with an unwavering voice left over from the days of stagnation.

"Your job is to protect me," the President said sharply. "Mine is to be myself. Do you get it?" And then he added amiably, "We won't go far—you'll be able to see us. We'll stay under the streetlights."

They walked about ten paces, still under the eyes of the security men, which cut through the rain like lasers to the nonstandard capricious uneasy object with which they were entrusted. The edges of the two wet umbrellas confidentially bumped into each other.

"Well, what happened?" the President asked. "Are they stealing?"

"It's more like taking than stealing," Palchikov said. "But the point isn't in the stealing, but in who's doing it."

"Who is it?"

Palchikov named two people. These were people for whom the nation—even such professionally untrusting people as Palchikov—had voted, had trusted; people who were not despised even by Alevtina, who despised almost all politicians; people who quite recently, in August, had stood on the balcony of the Russian Parliament, heroes of victorious democracy.

The President shuddered with loneliness. He felt a horrible icy cold that went to the bone, as it had when he was a child, living in a drafty barracks, when it got to forty below and all the corners were covered with ice crystals. But his whole family—father, mother, his younger sister and brother and their nanny goat—all slept under a pile of rags on the floor, huddling together, and their collective breath kept them from freezing. But with whom could he huddle up now? Who would not betray him?

"Take that! And that! And that!" From his childhood he heard Father's gasping, unjustly furious voice, his belt whistling over his head, beating his innocent son, taking out his frustrations over his life, and over the authorities who had beaten him with their equally cruel belts.

But now, with his father long gone, why was the belt of punishment still whipping him? Was it because when he was a Party secretary, he had used his belt on people? Was it because he had obeyed the coded orders from the Politburo and leveled the Ipatyev House, where the tsar's family, including the children, tutors and doctor, were shot—a house that should have remained standing as a museum of our shame? But he had done it only because he was afraid of another, even heavier belt—Moscow's. What was this country of belts, where everything depended on punishment by greasy belts with military buckles?

"Do you have proof?" The Barracks Boy, blue with cold, longing for the warm, shaggy side of the nanny goat, asked with the President's voice.

"Incontrovertible," Palchikov replied grimly.

"A trial of corrupt democrats," said the President no less grimly and squirmed. "Do you realize what a gift that will be for all those who want to chase us back into the Gulag?"

"I do," Palchikov replied. "But if we keep quiet, then what kind of democracy will it be? Then what will make us any different from the people we got rid of? What the hell were all our barricades for then? What should I do?"

"Why are you asking me?" the President rebuked him, still feeling the sharp needles of chill on his skin. "Do you think that I'm all-powerful and all-knowing? It was a lot easier when I was in Party disgrace. Russians like the underdog. Do you know what power is? The itch from your advisors. So don't try to turn me into an advisor. You decide and you answer for your decision. But"—and the President's voice softened—"don't get into trouble. . . . And keep the umbrella. . . . It is the only protection I can give you." And then, hopefully, he asked, "You don't happen to play tennis, do you?"

"No," replied Palchikov. "I grew up in a place where we didn't have a single tennis court."

The Barracks Boy, hidden inside the well-fed President's body, wondered, Why did I start playing tennis? Maybe because the barracks and tennis courts are unimaginable together? Maybe I followed a tennis ball like a sunspot, hoping it would lead me out of the barracks forever?

Aloud, the President said, "Yes, it's time for Russia to become a tennis country. It's time." He spoke stiffly, pompously, as if there were a reporter's microphone in his face, nonetheless hating that manner in himself, the way he tried to hide his hand, which he thought everyone noticed immediately, which was damaged from the time he had tried to take apart a grenade he had stolen from an army warehouse.

Palchikov dove into the rain and suddenly felt the Presidential umbrella filling with wind, pulling him upward, but Palchikov had never wanted to be at the top. He wanted to go home, to Alevtina. She didn't like politics, but she loved him, and it would have been much worse if it were the other way around.

The President threw himself into the limousine and said to the head of security, "I've really got bad chills. I wonder if I'm coming down with something. Do you have anything to warm me up?"

The security chief shrugged, half in disapproval and half in guilt.

"Afraid that I'm an alcoholic?" the President laughed. Don't worry. My health permits me to drink."

"Mine, too," the man replied with understanding.

"Where can we get some?" the President continued this human communication.

"I guess only in comstore at this hour," the security chief said after glancing at his watch, even more guiltily but not so disapprovingly.

"Where?" asked the leader of a market economy.

"In a commercial store. They stay open after the state stores close." The security chief barely hid his smile.

"Let's go."

The armored limousine passed the bastions of state trade, their lights long extinguished, and drove up on the sidewalk right beside a brightly lit foxhole of home-grown capitalism, with the old "kvas" sign still on top.

"Some kvas would make a good chaser," said the President.

The security man regarded him with quiet sympathy, this last romantic of democracy, who didn't know that kvas, the Russian fermented soft drink, had practically disappeared after democracy had won.

The armored limousine elicited first a dumbfounded reaction from the vendor, and then businesslike activity. The man, who obviously came from one of the Caucasus Mountain nations, was wearing a Harvard sweatshirt, and his leechlike mustache swallowed rain as he leaned out welcomingly from the kiosk.

The President rolled down his window and studied the wares.

He knew Pepsi-Cola and Fanta, especially since the names were written in Russian. The other bottles presented a problem.

"Bit-ter le-mon . . . Schwepps to-nic . . . pine-ap-ple jui-ce," he sounded out the Latin letters. "That's not our *kvas*. . . . Do you have anything to drink?"

"Of course, dear heart," said the man with a light accent. "Dutch gin . . . Italian cinzano . . . Apricot brandy from Austria . . . Japanese beer . . . Napoleon, put in a Hungarian version . . . Liqueur made from kiwi fruit, but in Poland . . . I didn't hear before that Poland is kiwi-country . . . Free trade. Exchange! Wan-dollar-wan-hundred-thirty-sefen-roobs! Yeltsin-Bush very good!"

"Well, and where is *it*?" The President grimaced, searching the shop window in bewilderment. "I say, where is *it*?"

"I have lots of it!" cried the kiosk owner, instantly understanding what "it" was. "Here's by Smirnoff, here's some Finnish, some German—it's called schnapps—and this is Korean—with a dead snake inside. With eyes!"

And for proof he shoved the bottle through the rain towards the President. The dead snake stirred hostilely, its apolitical, unrecognizing stare slipping over the President.

"And where's ours?" the President asked, growing angry. "Our plain old honest Russian vodka? I am a nationalist in drinks. . . . Don't you sell any?"

Sensing the growing threat in the President's voice, the man clutched his breast. "Sell it? Of course I sell it. And more than that, I drink it! Only it—I swear! With pleasure! That's why I don't have any. . . ." Then he smacked himself on the forehead. "I have something! Just for you, honored one." He ducked under the counter and came up with a bottle of Stolichnaya, usually with a metal cap that did not screw on well, which one had to open with a pocket knife or sometimes with one's teeth. But this bottle was already opened, and half empty.

"How much?" asked the President.

"What how much? It is just a half bottle. . . . And how can I take money from such a great man!" And he reached out with the bottle towards the Presidential limo from his heart.

"Oh, no! I've got investigators swirling around me as it is," the President said and wagged his finger at him. "I don't want to be charged with corruption. . . . How much? And no discounts. Give me the regular price!"

"Well, then, because the bottle is half-empty, just half-price . . ." the man said, hurt.

The President reached into his pocket, and then remembered that he had stopped carrying money a long time ago.

"Do you have any?" he asked the security chief in embarrassment, lowering his voice.

The security chief rummaged in his pockets and came up with three crumpled tens and a couple of disintegrating rubles.

Between them, the two bodyguards came up with a twenty-five ruble bill and ten threes.

"I don't have a kopek," said the driver. "They couldn't pay us yesterday, the bank didn't deliver any cash."

"No matter, we'll get by," said the President, whose chills were now racking his body. Trying to be polite, the President turned to the vendor. "Sorry, capitalist. Let's just say we took stock and managed to morally withstand your temptations."

And then the President shuddered. The kiosk with the "kvas" sign and the vendor, and all the Fantas, Pepsis, Schweppses, Cinzanos, schnapps and kiwi liqueurs vanished like a bad-weather mirage, as though swallowed up by the Russian soil that would not put up with it.

In its place appeared that granite stoop from the Ipatyev House, miraculously intact despite orders to wipe that house from the face of the earth, turn its memory into an empty lot and pave it into oblivion. The stoop stood like an eternal anti-Leninist mausoleum, reminding people that what begins in blood ends in blood, and reminding the President of his unshriven sin.

The belts of crazed rain lashed the limousine: Take that! And that! And that!

"Home!" the President said, thinking he had shouted, but in fact the command had come out in a hoarse whisper.

The limo took off into the stormy Russian weather, like a wounded black elephant charging with its yellow tusk headlights into the rain.

The great city swayed like a rudderless ship. A few years earlier, when the future President had first moved to Moscow and no one knew his face, he could walk around incognito, like a Haroun al Rashid from the Urals, ride trolleys and the metro, listen to people talk, drop by a store and modestly ask for some veal and if they lied and said there was none, burst into the director's office and morally whip him with a belt till the man saw stars. Straps again? Would they ever do without them in Russia?

His fame among the people as an unexpected Party Robin Hood, rising in rebellion against the boyars of the Politburo and the tsar of USSR — Gorbachev — saved the future President. It invented him. The people remembered only his stormy insubordination and forgivingly forgot his weakness, his mumbled repentance, the wet or foggy storms in which he kept getting caught.

In America, a man with holes like that in his background would be a political corpse. But in Russia people puff up their cheeks and blow air as hard as they can into the holes to keep him afloat.

They wrote his name in huge letters on trucks, bulldozers and street sweepers, and they tattooed it on their bodies. The people wanted a man of the people in power — big, direct, not sly, capable of banging his fist on the table and using earthy Russian, of laughing out loud at a joke and drinking like the people, wiping his mouth on his sleeve.

National television gloatingly ran an American videotape that made him look like a Russian merchant on a spree. And the people were incensed, not by him, but by the authorities who, it was rumored, had doctored the tape to make the people's favorite look bad.

He was humiliated in parliament, forced to explain why he had been found in the country on a dry summer night soaked to the skin and half-conscious. The people's favorite told a fairy tale about being attacked by robbers who tried to stuff him in a sack and throw him in a pond. The fairy tale was a Russian one. And which tales do the Russian people love best? They love their own, Russian fairy tales. And so our first Russian President became our Russian fairy tale.

Fame took away his former asset — being unrecognizable. Now he could not wander around unknown like Haroun al Rashid from the Urals.

But even from the window of his armored limousine he saw lines, which were not decreasing, outside stores, and the outstretched hands of beggars, which were increasing, and the pathetic flea markets, where there was nothing Russian sold except rubbish and the wooden monsters of glasnost — politicized matryoshka dolls with the faces of himself and the former President. The Russia of the barracks still had far to go to be the Russia of tennis courts.

"Take that, and that, and—" History yelled and hit.

The horror was that his advisors all tried very hard to please him with their advice and tried to guess what advice he was expecting. And what he needed was unexpected advice. Perhaps that advice was scratched by a rusty nail on that stoop that had stood for a long time on the deserted lot in Sverdlovsk, and even though he had driven past it every day in his official car, he had never stopped and gone over to it, whispering penitent words.

The rain was so heavy that the President could not see beyond the wet, fluttering, tricolored flag on the hood. And suddenly that damned stoop, seemingly entwined by streams of rain, came down upon the gleaming hood, as if it were a black marble pedestal lowered by an invisible crane. The stoop trembled along with the hood as they drove, and there did seem to be something scratched on its side — perhaps by the murdered tsarevich using an old nail, but it was impossible to make it out in the water that had turned into thick fog.

The security chief took off his jacket and put it on the shoulders of the shuddering President, but it did not help. His teeth were chattering and now he was feeling alternately hot and cold.

He recalled working on a tower crane when he was young. One night he was awakened by a similar squally storm that had broken the glass of an open window and sent shards flying onto the cot where he slept, his love-tamed shock of hair resting on the quietly rising breast of his beloved, pale blue in the moonlight. Suddenly he remembered that he had been lazy last night and had not attached the crane to its tracks.

Barefoot, cutting his feet on the glass, he rushed to the window and was stunned by what he saw. The crane near the barracks was moving quietly. It looked like a large man, stooped by the blows of fate, planning to commit suicide. A little farther, and the crane would be where the tracks ended, and the huge hulk would fall onto the temporary plywood housing for the workers, crushing them.

The Barracks Boy did not waste time. In nothing but his underpants, he ran out into the storm that was lashing the earth with fiery belts of lightning, seeming to say, Take that . . . and that.

He found the switch in the dark, turned on the electricity and, heels bleeding, feverishly began the climb up the rusty steps of the narrow metal ladder leading to the crane's cab. It all depended on who was faster: the crane, slowly crawling to the end of the tracks, or the man, desperately trying to stop his own mistake, which could be fatal to others and to himself.

It was dark in the cab, and the Barracks Boy barely found the level that released the boom. The boom turned into the wind and stopped floundering. Then he reversed the crane. It groaned and squealed and stopped almost at the very point where the tracks ended.

"Would you like to drop by my house? . . . I have some vodka," said the security chief, understanding full well that he could be demoted for such hospitality.

"All right. Just for a short time," the President said. "Your wife won't scold us, will she?"

The armored limousine slipped off the highway and buckled along the side streets, belly-deep in puddles.

The President had the feeling that the hulk of Russia was crawling towards the end of the tracks. The hulk could fall—and that would be forever. And it could crush people—forever, too.

He had to get there first.

The President remembered Palchikov setting off into the black night, under the Presidential umbrella that didn't protect him all that much.

"I wish he'd learn to play tennis," thought the President of Russia.

The Tadjik,
Once Again In A Tank

THE TADJIK TANK DRIVER NEVER, ever wanted to be in a tank again. He did not want people to be afraid of him. He did not want to be afraid of people. He missed his old friend with the long gray beard, Waterfall, and the girl to whom the old beard had whispered so tenderly.

Sometimes, during the long Russian nights in the barracks, where the frost hid like a thief in the corners, the Tadjik banged his cold lonely knees against the wall and dreamed of the granite grotto in the cliff where, he hoped, the peach with the bite from his beloved's teeth still waited for him.

The Tadjik couldn't take it. He didn't run, he deserted, in military parlance. But he didn't reach his native village.

In Dushanbe, the capital of Tadjikistan, he was taken by a military patrol and shoved back into a tank.

Things were more unsettled in his homeland than in Russia, and all the Tadjiks who hated other Tadjiks needed tanks and tank drivers.

He couldn't understand who was fighting against whom or why.

There were tents in the central square and there were endless rallies, and he and his tank were on alert.

He ran again, and this time he reached his native village, or rather, what was left of it.

The border with Afghanistan was open once more, but the miserable ghost of his grandmother who had howled from the minaret had not returned. However, arms and hashish flowed across the border freely.

His parent's house had been razed by a tank, in which sat his beloved's brother. The foul-smelling corpse, pecked by birds, had been left intentionally unburied.

The Tadjik dared to bury the body, because he knew that his beloved's brother had been forced, under threat of death, to do this to their house.

For this shameful pity, his relatives tied him up, tore off his shirt, and bloodied his back with whips. It was forbidden to forgive blood enemies or to bury them.

But they did not whip him to death. They needed him, beaten but alive.

He, a deserter who hated every tank in the world, was the only person in the village who could drive one.

All he wanted to do with a tank was to roll his fingers into a flute and whistle a melody that would charm the dangerous metal animal.

But his relatives held a gun to his temple and said that he had to avenge the destruction of his house by destroying the house of his beloved.

Seeing that there was no way out, he agreed. But at the last moment he turned the tank off the mountain road and drove it into the river, and sank with it to the bottom, where his grandmother, who never did get home, was waiting for him.

Lyza, The Laborer
And The Kolkhoz Woman

On the banks of the Seine two young Soviet giants raise the hammer
and sickle in an unyielding upsurge, and we hear a heroic hymn pour
from their chests, which calls people to freedom and unity and will
lead to victory.

— *Roman Rolland (about V. Mukhina's*
sculpture on the roof of the
Soviet Pavilion) Paris, 1937

ZALYZIN WAS DRINKING ALONE AT the Agricultural Exhibit, in the
Ocean Restaurant, where the director used to be Rosa, a Tatar as huge and
kind as a Mama Whale, who was once hopelessly in love with the King of
the Heel Pass and therefore treated anyone who had played soccer with him
as a higher being.

Young sharks had pushed Rosa out of the restaurant a long time ago,
creating capitalism for themselves within communism and now communism — also just for themselves — within capitalism.

Before she left, Rosa had approached Zalyzin one day. "Come on, I
want to show you a secret." He hoped she was taking him to where they
kept the red and black caviar and the Kamchatka crabs. Instead she pushed
him inside the toilet of the men's room on the first floor.

Zalyzin feared that she might try raping him, and he couldn't really
say no, for old times' sake. But Rosa showed him a cellophane package, then

got up on the toilet, which almost cracked beneath her, and hid the package behind the water tank.

"There's money in there, Lyza. They're getting rid of me and I may even have to do time. If things get rough for you, take the money. Think of it as money in the bank."

After Boat died, things had gotten rough for Zalyzin, and so tonight he came here. But what used to be a big sum was nothing much now, what with inflation, and he spent it all on booze, ordering champagne for strange "ladies," and giving generous tips to the waiters and musicians, just like an adolescent.

He left the Ocean drunk and empty. The night was damp and chilly, and Zalyzin didn't want to go all the way across Moscow to an empty apartment where not even a Chunya was waiting for him.

He decided to spend the night in the shelter of the post-perestroika homeless, the shared belly of the steel monster, that is, the laborer and the kolkhoz woman in "unyielding upsurge," as the romantic French writer put it. The powerful figures were first erected on the roof of the Soviet pavilion at the World's Fair in Paris in 1937, the most horrible year in the Soviet Union for arrests and executions. Perhaps the Chief Architect of the Camps had had an ulterior motive, to use the monumental figures to dwarf the "zeks," the inmates, behind barbed wire, in the eyes of Europe and the rest of the world.

The steel deceivers did their job. However, they did not settle in Paris and came back home dismantled. They were put together and set up at the entrance to the Agricultural Exhibit, planned to be a city of the future. But years passed and the city of the future began to fall apart. Even the record-breaking cows at the fair mooed piteously and sadly, because people were trying to get too much milk out of them.

The steel symbol of socialism was empty inside, and its belly gradually turned into a den for petty thieves and a lair for tramps — just as the miserable huddled, if Victor Hugo is to be believed, in the hospitable belly of the ornamental Parisian elephant during the French Revolution.

There was no entrance in the trousers of the steel laborer. The entrance was down a ladder and through a hatch concealed in the steel skirt of the steel kolkhoz woman.

This was the belly of socialist realism.

The belly was warm and fetid with the breath of many people sleeping in there. The ordinary Moscow bums were joined by refugees from the republics.

Zalyzin followed his bachelor habit of smoking before sleep. It was a mistake here, because hands reached out from all around for a cigarette.

A lit match came close to Zalyzin's face, illuminating him with a fragile petal of fire.

"Lyza?" The voice was accented. "Where is your girl, Boat?"

"Who is it?" Zalyzin asked warily.

Another match flared up, revealing an unshaven face with sunken cheeks, a big nose and a torch of still unruly, but now gray curls.

"They call me Little Karabakh. You don't know me, but I know you, Number 10. I'm a friend of Boat. I met her in Baku, at the soccer game when you played and she watched you and cried. I took her to you at the hotel and she called but you wouldn't see her. Why didn't you? She loves you very much. How could you not want to see a girl like her? Did you marry her? Do you have children?"

Zalyzin said nothing and Little Karabakh understood that he shouldn't be asking questions. He did ask, "Where is she now?"

"She's far away," Zalyzin whispered.

"How far?" Little Karabakh persisted.

"Very far."

"Will you see her?"

"I will."

"And you'll be together then?"

"Then we will."

"Tell her that Little Karabakh remembers her and that Little Karabakh respects her."

"All right, I will. But why are you here?"

"Because my whole life is like Big Karabakh. I'm half-Armenian and half-Azeri. The Azeris started hating me for being Armenian, and the Armenians for being Azeri. But I love both, because I am both. My wife and children and I fled from Baku. First we went to Sukhumi, in Abkhazia, to be with my wife's parents. But my wife—here she is. Look, isn't she a pretty girl?—is half-Georgian and half-Abkhazian. Sukhumi is also a Karabakh. Georgians are killing Abkhazians and Abkhazians are killing Georgians. It's a Karabakh all over the place. Karabakh is chasing us. We had to flee from Sukhumi too. Look at my children."

Another match and three black unruly heads lay on the floor.

"Listen, I have an apartment, it's just one room, but I live there alone. You can have the room, I'll sleep in the kitchen. You'll catch your breath and then you can see what you want to do," Zalyzin whispered feverishly. "Let's go to my place, all right?"

"*Shnora golyutsyun*, Number 10. *Chokhsagol*, Number 10," Little Karabakh thanked him in Armenian and Azeri. "Your Boat is right to love you so much."

"*Didi madloba. Itabu*," whispered his wife in Georgian and Abkhazian. She had just woken up and her face was exhausted but truly beautiful, as if it had come from a fresco.

And suddenly the hatch opened and well-fed young men in black shirts, creaking bandoliers and shiny boots burst into the statue's belly, twirling whips and moving their flashlights over the bodies.

"Where are those lousy Chechens?" shouted one of them.

"There aren't any Chechens here," Zalyzin replied glumly. "Let us sleep."

"What do you mean there aren't any Chechens? Here they are, I found them!" The men set upon Little Karabakh, his wife and children and started dragging them to the hatch. "Get the hell out of Moscow, you damned crooks!"

Little Karabakh's three children didn't even cry. They must have gotten used to this treatment. They merely looked around in a hunted way.

"They're not Chechens. But even if they were, does that make them not human?" Zalyzin shouted.

"What do we care? They're all black-assed, anyway!" the brave men replied, hauling Little Karabakh's family from the steel symbol of socialism. "Get the hell out of Russia!"

"Wait . . ." Zalyzin rushed after them. "They're refugees. They have no place to go. I'll give them my apartment."

But one of the men lashed him criss-cross with the whip. "A fine defender you are. You wouldn't happen to wear a yarmulke, would you?"

Zalyzin had been beaten many times. His parents beat him when he was little, with whatever came to hand, even an iron once. Other kids hit him with chunks of lead in their fists, with pickets torn from fences and with pieces of pipe, bicycle chains and bricks. On the soccer field he had been kicked, and when the referee wasn't looking, he had been punched.

But no one had ever whipped him. He had only seen that done, and only in the old movies about prerevolutionary times; when Cossacks rode in on horseback to break up a workers' demonstration. It turned out not only to hurt, but to be monstrously humiliating. The whip made the person being beaten feel that he was not human, but cattle.

Another boy in a black shirt kicked Zalyzin in the back and Zalyzin, trying to hold onto the ladder, fell out of the hatch and down onto the asphalt while the so-called Russian patriots guffawed. Grimacing in pain, Zalyzin saw—perhaps for the last time—the eyes of Little Karabakh, shining sadly and gratefully and perhaps even guiltily. He and his family were being pushed into the back of a muddy dump truck.

"Where are they taking them? They wouldn't . . ." he thought with horror and shame. He saw something on the ground, something that looked like a burgundy icicle, perhaps formed by frozen blood. It was a candy from the Caucasus, *churchkhela*, made of thickened grape juice enveloping hazelnuts on a string. One of Little Karabakh's children must have dropped it. Zalyzin remembered buying *churchkhela* at the market when they were playing the Soviet finals in Tbilisi, one of the most beautiful cities in the world, shot in the heart by its own inhabitants.

The *churchkhela* on the ground was broken, and the eye of a nut peeked out with the sadness of Little Karabakh's eye. The crude peasant string that formed the candy's tail moved on the asphalt as if it were alive.

Zalyzin pulled himself up and wandered off, feeling the goal made in his back with the whip, and feeling terribly insignificant. But he was a master of his work, and the feeling of dignity that all masters have prevailed. The response to the other side's goal is one of your own. He had to gather his strength and go for it.

But where were the opponents' goalposts? And who were the opponents? What colors were they wearing?

The goalposts were nowhere and everywhere. The opponents played in various T-shirts, cleverly changing the colors. Everything was so confused that it was impossible to tell in the name of what they were playing anymore.

In the morning Zalyzin tried to get to see the man he couldn't stand, the Ice-Hole Democrat, his only connection with the authorities. Zalyzin wanted to tell them what was going on, about the injustices. He wanted to remind the Ice-Hole Democrat that the President wanted Zalyzin to create a Russian soccer team.

But the Ice-Hole Democrat had a lot of meetings and banquets. Zalyzin almost caught him by his walrus tail at some business reception. He was so elusive, you'd think the whole world had turned into his ice hole. He managed to get away, muttering, "Tomorrow, tomorrow . . ."

Young business types were circulating, exchanging business cards. Many were near one man, looking like small fry around a big fish. He looked like a weightlifter who had squeezed his muscles into a shimmering Armani silk suit. He had a name tag on his lapel. Zalyzin could make out only "General Director." Then came a fancy name for a joint enterprise. Zalyzin recognized him as one of the two men who had come to help him and Boat, automatic rifles in hand, but were too late. The Former Racketeer was generously handing out business cards and feeling on top of the world, draining can after can of imported beer stacked within his reach.

Nodding patronizingly and yet somehow entreatingly, a man with a seemingly noble gray brush of a mustache and a boxer's broken nose made his way through the crowd, like a fox. It was the Labyrinth Lover. As the available products and hopes in the country diminished, the number of labyrinths and their twists and turns increased.

He looked around and saw amidst the table groaning with food and drink, a huge iced cake shaped like the White House, with toy tanks in the chocolate asphalt around it. They vulgarly transformed even the struggle for freedom into their dessert.

Zalyzin decided to swallow his pride and go directly to the White House to tell the President about it all. There he was politely given a number and told that the line was very long.

He left the White House and suddenly heard the familiar roar of tanks and motors.

The White House was surrounded once more — not by toy tanks in chocolate, but by real tanks. People were erecting barricades.

His life took on meaning once more. He rushed to the barricades, wildly dragging sand bags, garbage cans, boards and metal.

But then came a foreign voice over the loudspeaker: "Cut! Many thanks! All the extras will be paid money. Fifty in rubles, and one dollar."

Zalyzin walked down the embankment, not knowing where, and the cold wind that blew the no-longer-needed Xerox copies of the August decrees made the green dollar bill flutter in his hand.

Zalyzin thanked God that Chunya was out in the woods.

Palchikov And
The One Happy End

═══════════

THE MARSHAL HAD BEEN MISTAKEN, when he thought that Nastenka had been killed by the tanks. When he himself slipped, he did not see the girl escape at the last moment, losing her white straw hat in the street.

The death that could have come to the girl came instead to the moonwalker.

"Mama, don't go to work right now. Papa told me in the book that he would come back this morning," Nastenka said. "Papa will be hurt if you're not home. I'll settle things with Pitey."

Alevtina, who had stopped smiling a long time ago, broke into a smile and said, "All right. I believe you. But what will we make for Papa?"

"He likes eggplant with tomatoes best of all," Nastenka said, raising her finger.

"But where will I get any in the winter! The Georgians have stopped almost all deliveries," Alevtina said with a sigh.

"Why buy them?" Nastenka replied. "You have a whole jar that you made up last year. You just have to heat it up."

"Where is it? I was sure that you and I ate it."

"We didn't eat it, because I hid it away for Papa."

A key turned in the lock. Alevtina picked up a broom and started cleaning the floor, as if she weren't waiting for anyone.

Palchikov came in. He was holding a hedgehog.

"So—joined the Young Naturalists' Club?" Alevtina said, not very friendly and still sweeping the floor. "You think my zoo's not enough for me?"

"You see, I was walking in the park," Palchikov explained. "And suddenly I see this hedgehog on the path. He sees me but doesn't run away. I keep walking and I hear him pattering behind me. I turn, and it really is him. He's very unusual, this hedgehog. So I decided not to leave him all alone."

"He'll catch mice," Nastenka said. "Right, Mama?"

Alevtina said nothing.

"And I have a pass . . . for a cello concert. Look who signed it." Palchikov beseechingly stuck the autograph under Alevtina's nose, but she wouldn't look.

"Palchikov, as long as you're here, why don't you stay home a bit without Auntie Urgent Work and Auntie Politics. We have eggplant for you. . . ."

"Auntie Urgent Work fired me," Palchikov said. "And I left Auntie Politics on my own."

"Do you want them cold or heated up?" Alevtina asked, at last.

The day passed in peaceful but cool coexistence. In the evening Palchikov got on the folding cot and Alevtina on the bed. Nastenka put out the lights.

Palchikov started to fall asleep. He woke up because he felt someone looking at him. Alevtina in a short white nightie stood over him.

Her eyes looked like two black currants on a dewy morning. They always looked bigger when she took off her glasses.

"I remembered where those lines come from, the ones you kept asking about like a paranoid crazy, Palchikov. 'Where it won't be better, there it will be worse, but it isn't far back again from bad to good.' It's from Lermontov's short story, *Taman*. And you can get in bed with me."

"About time," Nastenka said in the dark.

Palchikov moved over to Alevtina's bed.

"I won't do it anymore," he said.

In the dark he felt her smile against his cheek.

Goodbye
Our Red Flag

Goodbye our Red Flag.
You slipped down from the Kremlin roof
                not so proudly
                  not so adroitly
as you climbed many years ago
                on the destroyed Reichstag
smoking like Hitler's last fag.

Goodbye our Red Flag.
You were our brother and our enemy.
You were a soldier's comrade in trenches,
                you were the hope of all captive Europe,
But like a Red curtain you concealed behind you
                        the Gulag
              stuffed with frozen dead bodies.
Why did you do it,
              our Red Flag?

Goodbye our Red Flag.
    Lie down.
    Take a rest.
We will remember all the victims
deceived by your Red sweet murmur
that lured millions like sheep
              to the slaughterhouse.

But we will remember you
                    because you too
                        were no less deceived.
Goodbye our Red Flag.
                    Were you just a romantic rag?

You are bloodied
                    and with our blood we strip you
                                from our souls.
That's why we can't scratch out
                    the tears from our red eyes,
because you so wildly
                    slapped them
                        with your heavy golden tassels.

Goodbye our Red Flag.
    Our first step to freedom
we stupidly took
                    over your wounded silk,
and over ourselves,
                    divided by envy and hatred.
Hey crowd,
                do not trample again in the mud
the already cracked glasses
                        of Doctor Zhivago.

Goodbye our Red Flag.
                    Pry open the fist
that imprisoned you
                    trying to wave something red over Civil War,
when scoundrels try to grab
                    your standard again,
or just desperate people,
                    lining up for hope.
Goodbye our Red Flag.
    You float into our dreams.

Goodbye Our Red Flag

Now you are just
                          a narrow red stripe
                                    in our Russian Tricoleur.
In the innocent hands of whiteness,
        in the innocent hands of blue
maybe even your red color
                          can be washed free of blood.

Goodbye our Red Flag.
                          Be careful, our Tricoleur.
Watch out for the card sharks of flags
                          lest they twist you around their greasy fingers.
Could it be that you too,
                          will have the same death sentence
                          as your red brother,
to be shot by our own bullets,
devouring like lead moths
                          your silk?

Goodbye our Red Flag.
In our naive childhood
                          we played Red Army — White Army.
We were born in a country
                          that no longer exists.
But in that Atlantis we were alive,
                          we were loved.
You, our Red Flag, lay in a puddle
                          in a flea market.
Some hustlers sell you
                          for hard currency.
        Dollars, Francs, Yen.
I didn't take the Tsar's Winter Palace.
        I didn't storm Hitler's Reichstag.
I am not what you call a "Commie."
But I caress the Red Flag
                          and cry.

Postcript

THE RUSSIAN POET SERGEI ESENIN wrote about history: "Face to face you can't see faces. You can see more at a distance." This novel was written face to face with history, and probably therein lies its flaw, as well as its value — I hope. The incomparable Tolstoy wrote *War and Peace* when the gravestones of Napoleon and Kutuzov were covered by the moss of oblivion, and his heroes could not sue him for attributing actions, words and thoughts to them. The heroes of this novel are still alive, and even though they have not sued the author, many of them have been taken to court by history itself. The final verdict is still unknown. But I did predict a thing or two:

"And [the President] began playing tennis more clumsily, feeling dozens of advisors hanging on the laces of his tennis shoes, scrambling around in his shorts, climbing up his back, sitting on his neck, crawling into his armpits and the hair of his head . . ." "History helped him, but history doesn't offer its help for free. He would still have to pay."

It is no accident that even during the liberals' euphoria of the barricades, my heroine quotes Thomas Carlyle: "Revolutions are thought up by Utopians, realized by fanatics, and exploited by scoundrels." Sometimes this trinity can be combined in a single personality. Could I have imagined that Yeltsin, with whom I had stood shoulder to shoulder on the balcony of the Russian White House, surrounded by tanks during the August, 1991 coup attempt, would order those same tanks to fire on that same White House in October 1993? Could I have imagined that in December 1994, after the bloodshed in Chechnya, I would have to refuse his invitation to the Kremlin to receive the Order of Friendship Between Peoples and write the following bitter lines:

> Well then, two-headed eagle,
> Where have we flown
> With ignominious new glory
> In the Chechen blizzard?
>
> Shame and fear
> Up in the peaks
> Will not let the two eagle heads
> Look each other in the eye.
>
> Your feathers have been blown away
> By a hail of rockets over the ashes.
> This is no choice for an eagle —
> Between shame and fear.

However, there are two transitional states between shame and fear. One is the fear of shame, and the other is the shame of fear. And if the human heart is always filled with one or the other, then people will never have to face that humiliating choice between them.

I still have hope that we did not take to the barricades in vain. After all, those 250,000 handcuffs ordered before the coup were meant for our hands. Now Russia is nowhere — between the past and the future. Nevertheless that is better than ending up behind the barbed wire of the past. Maturity is measured by the number of lost illusions.

The secret is not to lose hope along with the illusions.

A year and a half has passed since I put the period on the last page of this novel. That period turned out to be a comma. History has not stopped, and, just as unpredictably, my novel continues. I have only to observe and write.

Yevgeny Yevtushenko
January 20, 1995

Glossary

adzhap-sandal eggplants with tomatoes and herbs.

bandura Ukrainian stringed musical instrument.

Belovezhskaya Puscha one of the largest remaining areas of primeval mixed forest in Europe, encompassing part of the west of Belorus and part of Poland. Both nations have established flora and fauna reserves in the forest, a habitat of the European bison. In December 1991, a meeting between Yeltsin, Kravchuk and Shushkevich took place in this forest; the consequences of the meeting led to the disintegration of the USSR.

Beriozka stores shops that sold scarce goods for hard currency in the former Soviet Union.

bogatyri heroes of Russian folk songs, *byliny*. These songs relate heroic deeds, often loosely connected with some historical event.

burzhuiki iron stoves.

chacha Georgian vodka made from grapes.

Chechens natives of Chechnya, a North Caucasian republic; Sunni Muslims. Living in tribal groups, the Chechen (and other Caucasian tribes) resisted Russian attempts to conquer them in the nineteenth century. Upon the capture of their leader Shaykh Shamil in 1859, one-fifth of them emigrated to Turkey. The Chechens fought both the Cossacks and Bolsheviks, and continued to oppose Communism by guerrilla warfare. Deported in 1943 for anti-Communist uprising, they were rehabilitated in 1957. In Moscow and other parts of contemporary Russia, they are perceived as racketeers and gangsters, the Russian version of the Mafia.

dacha country holiday house, used mainly in summer.

dardi samshebloze (Georgian) nostalgia for the Motherland.

genatsvale (Georgian) beloved friend.

fleighlekhs Jewish folkdance.

karutsa type of bullock cart, equipped with a wicker basket; used to carry charcoal.

kefir cultured milk drink, similar in flavor to yoghurt.

kharcho (Georgian) lamb soup with rice.

kolkhoz abbreviation for *Kollektivnoye Khozyaistvo*, collective farm. These were cooperative agricultural enterprises operated on state-owned land by peasants from a number of households. Conceived as a voluntary union of peasant workers, the kolkhoz became the only form of agriculture in the former USSR as a result of the state's program of expropriation of private holdings.

magarych colloquial expression for a treat sealing a successful transaction.

matryoshka doll doll dressed as a peasant girl; often hollow wooden doll containing a set of similar, smaller dolls.

mishka bear; used as the symbol for the 1980 Moscow Olympic Games.

muzhik literally tough peasant, macho.

nash-arabi a sauce made from pomegranates.

No pasaran (Spanish) 'They shall not pass'. A slogan used by republican anti-Franco forces during the Spanish Civil War (1936–39).

oblepikha berry fruit of the sea buckthorn, also called sallow thorn, a willow-like shrub common in Europe and Asia. Orange-yellow in color, the berries are often made into jams and fruit liqueurs.

omul white fish found in Lake Baikal and regions bordering the Arctic Ocean.

Pavlik Morozov Soviet schoolboy who, during the Collectivization, took active part in the requisition of grain from rich peasants (the so-called "kulaks"). He and his younger brother were killed by the kulaks.

pelmeni Siberian boiled dumplings, made from unleavened dough and meat fillings.

pirozhki small savories eaten as hors d'oeuvres or with soup, consisting of meat, fish, cheese or vegetables encased in pastry. The savories are shaped like small boats and may be baked or fried.

pkhali (Georgian) green beans with herbs.

plov Caucasian dish of meat, fish or other ingredients, served with warm rice and sometimes wrapped in unleavened bread.

Radio Liberty one of the network of radio stations sponsored by the USA that beamed their broadcasts into the USSR from headquarters in Germany.

samizdat from the Russian *sam*, self, and *Izdatel 'stvo*, publishing, the term is a parody of the official acronym *Gos izdat* (State Publishing House). It describes the system of preparing, copying and circulating writings usually critical of the government of the former Soviet Union. Samizdat writings began to appear in 1953 as a revolt against restrictions on the freedom of expression after Stalin's death. Samizdat expanded its focus to include critiques of various aspects of Soviet life, including ideology, law, economic policy, culture, etc. Authors and distributors of samizdat literature often operated under difficult conditions and risked arrest and imprisonment.

satsivi (Georgian) turkey with nut sauce.

sharashka top-secret research and development institute, where high-level political prisoners (scientists and technicians) continued their research in various spheres. Solzhenitsyn's *The First Circle* depicts such an institute.

shestidesiatniki the generation of the early 1960s in Russia, children — and, in a sense, fathers — of the so-called thaw.

streltsy musketeers, literally shooters; a standing army of infantry formed in 1550, stationed in Moscow and various border towns. After several mutinies, Peter I disbanded the streltsy in 1698, and raised a regular army.

taiga open coniferous forest on swampy ground that is commonly covered with lichen. It is the characteristic type of vegetation of the subpolar region spanning northern Eurasia, between the colder tundra zone and the warmer temperate zone.

tamada master of a Georgian feast.

tsitsinatella (Georgian) for fire-fly or glow-worm.

tsitsmati Georgian herb.

tkhili nuts type of nuts used in Georgian cuisine.

zhok Moldavian dance.